INCOMPETNCE

'A tequila-sniffing, lemon-in-the-eye kind of affair – all wrong but so right' MAXIM

'It's a tequila-sniffing, lemon-in-the-eye kind of affair – all wrong but so right' *Maxim*

'A revolutionary black comedy. The scenes build until laughter is unavoidable. Very funny. Spookily similar to that other science-fiction writer, Douglas Adams' *Daily Express*

'Crime fantasy Fawlty Towers-style' *Daily Mirror*

'Not that different to most holidays in France' *Front Magazine*

'Hilarious. Extremely competent' *Edge Magazine*

'An hilarious vision of the near-future. Surreal, refreshingly different and genuinely funny' *East Anglian Daily Times*

'Who needs Red Dwarf? Rob Grant doesn't any more' *SFX*

'The perfect, page-turning laughathon' *Daily Echo*

'Fabulously funny – his best offering yet' *Birmingham Post*

'Rob Grant is clearly quite a competent man' *Manchester Evening News*

'Rob Grant writes like a dream. A surreal Monty Python-esque (or should that be Red Dwarf-esque?) detective novel, peppered with laugh-out-loud gags and elaborately conceived, vastly silly set-pieces' *Dreamwatch*

'Worth staying in for' *The Portsmouth News*

'Satire abounds in this consistently amusing comedy of errors'
Starburst

'Undemanding'
Leicester Mercury

'Teeth-gratingly funny thriller'
Warwickshire Evening Telegraph

'Red Dwarf and Colony fans will gleefully recognise it as Grant's work'
City Life

'A comic novel which is funny, witty and, although secondary to the brilliant writing, has a great plot. A rare thing indeed'
Ottakars

'Would have had me rolling about on the floor in hysterical laughter if it wasn't for all the dog hair'
Vikki From Durham

'Incompetence by Rob Grant is published by Gollancz'
Swindon Evening Advertiser

Also by Rob Grant

Backwards

Colony

INCOMPETENCE

A novel of the far too near future

Rob Grant

First published in Great Britain in 2003 by
Gollancz
An imprint of the Orion Publishing Group
Orion House, 5 Upper St Martin's Lane, London WC2H 9EA

This mass-market edition first published in 2004
by Gollancz

A CIP catalogue record for this book is
available from the British Library

ISBN 0 575 07449 3

Typeset by Deltatype Ltd,
Birkenhead, Merseyside

Printed in Great Britain by
Clays Ltd, St Ives plc

www.orionbooks.co.uk

Article 13199 of the Pan-European Constitution:
'No person shall be prejudiced from employment in any capacity, at any level, by reason of age, race, creed or incompitence.'

This book is for Joe

ONE

The flight was uneventful enough, except the pilot accidentally touched down at a slightly wrong airport and forgot to lower the landing gear, so we left the plane by way of the emergency chute, and I lost my shoes.

I was fairly pooped by the time I'd hobbled through Customs, filled in the usual lost luggage forms with the assistance of a stone-deaf baggage complaints officer and taken a three-hour taxi ride to the country where I'd intended to land. The ride would have cost about a month's salary, if the cabby had remembered to charge me. All I wanted to do, once the hotel receptionist had finished denying all knowledge of my reservation, was to flop down on the bed and sleep for a millennium or two.

Only there was no bed.

I punched a small hole in the bathroom wall and dialled Reception.

A woman picked up the phone and said: 'Restaurant. How may I help you?'

'I dialled Reception.'

'Well, this is the restaurant.'

'Right. Could you possibly patch me through to Reception?'

'That won't be a problem, sir. One moment.'

There was a silent pause, then the ringing tone again, and the click of the receiver being lifted. The same chirpy voice said: 'Restaurant. How may I help you?'

I dragged on an imaginary cigarette and exhaled slowly. 'It's me again.'

'I'm sorry. Who did you want to speak to?'

'I wanted to speak to Reception.'

'Well, this is the restaurant.'

'I know. You accidentally patched me from the restaurant back to the restaurant again.'

'It sounds to me like there's a problem with the internal phones.'

'Yes, indeedy.'

'I'll put you through to House Services.'

'I'd be very grateful.'

Again, the silence, the ringing, the click and the voice. 'Restaurant. How may I help you?'

I told her how she might help me, and she threatened to report me to Security for verbal violence. I wished her good luck getting through and slammed down the phone. I reckoned she'd probably spend the rest of the afternoon phoning herself.

There was no message from Klingferm, though, let's be realistic, the chances of the hotel staff receiving the message and actually delivering it to me in the correct room on the right day were less than promising.

I spent twenty minutes trying to assume a vaguely comfortable position on a sofa perfectly designed to deny humans rest or comfort, then decided I'd be better off sorting out some clothes and other essentials. My luggage was probably having a good time scooting round a baggage carousel in Rio de Janeiro, and my shoes no doubt graced the feet of some scavenging bastard ground staff at Verona airport.

I didn't expect to find a local Yellow Pages, so when I did, I kissed it passionately. Sadly it was the local Yellow Pages for the Los Angeles area, and I was in Rome. I enlarged the hole in the bathroom wall and steeled myself to scour the streets of the Eternal City for shoe shops in my stockinged feet.

I opened the hotel room door. A security guard was standing just outside, looking puzzledly at a clipboard. He looked up, grinned, and said, 'English?'

I tried to look German and shook my head.

'This is room 407, yes?'

I looked at the room number on the door. 407. I tried shaking my head again, Germanically.

'Mr Vascular?'

That was indeed the name I was travelling under. I tried to make an expression like it was the first time I'd ever heard it. Pulled it off, too, I think.

'I have a complaint against you. Very serious. A proposition of a sexual nature to the restaurant manager.'

Again, I tried to shake my head in a foreign language.

'You requested her to masturbate over the phone for you.'

Not exactly. I suppose I had, in a way, suggested that the woman should have sex with herself, though not for my titillation. I put on my best Teutonically perplexed expression.

'I don't need to tell you that this sort of thing cannot be tolerated. I must ask you to accompany me to the holding cells, where we will await the arrival of the vice squad.'

I tried not to notice the polished black leather gun holster strapped to his belt, but failed, I think. It's astonishing how naked you can feel in stockinged feet. Especially in the presence of a uniformed man bearing firearms. Verbal sexual violence invoked a mandatory jail term, even in Italy, where it used to be a valid career choice. Even if the charge didn't stick, I'd spend a sorry few days in a damp cell, with only some bored, sadistic guards carrying sturdy lengths of rubber hose for occasional company.

'I think you've got the wrong party,' I said, wisely abandoning the dismal German tourist ploy.

'Are you suggesting a bribe?'

Nonplussed at the non sequitur, I hesitated, then reached into my jacket pocket. 'Certainly not, officer. Though I was thinking it would be a nice gesture to make a small contribution to the Security Guards' Widows and Orphans Fund.' I tugged out a deck of notes – a big denomination on the top, singles underneath. That's how I keep them. Believe me, it comes in handy. Tips, beggars, muggers, MEPs. You name it.

He pulled a neat disappearing trick with the money and consulted his clipboard again. 'I am now thinking perhaps Mr Vascular is in room 507.'

'I wouldn't be at all surprised.'

He snapped a polite salute and turned right down the corridor. I gave him a couple of minutes, then stepped out of the room, turned left and headed for the elevator. It arrived almost immediately, which I should have seen as a warning.

Two hours and a small suffocation scare later, the elevator car finally decided it'd had enough of me and spewed me out into the lobby. I padded over to the Reception desk and tried to complain about the bedlessness of my room, the uselessness of the internal telephone system and the sheer cussedness of the lift, but the shifts had changed and the new receptionist was a ninety-year-old man who could only communicate in what appeared to be Polish with a Cuban accent. I took up a pen and a notepad, and tried drawing a bed, but he seemed to think it was some kind of amorous initiative. Frighteningly, he appeared to be excited by the prospect. I gave up.

I was about to squeeze into the street through the tiny gap offered by the hotel's jammed doors when I spotted a piece of paper in 407's cubbyhole. Briefly, I contemplated engendering another fruitless exchange with the superannuated clerk, then leapt over the counter and scrambled for the message. It was addressed to a Mr Faro in room 333. While the ancient receptionist clubbed me about the back of the neck with a rolled-up city centre map, I checked the other boxes and found a fax with my name on it in 207's cubbyhole.

It was from Klingferm all right.

He'd set up a meet less than a mile away, in just under an hour. Which meant I was facing an uncomfortably long walk in my flimsy socks or a terrifying cab journey with a Roman taxi driver. I had to pick up my Italian ID. I wondered if I could also afford the time to stop off and buy a pair of shoes.

As it turned out, I could afford that time. If I hadn't stopped to buy those shoes, I'd probably have been as dead as Klingferm turned out to be.

TWO

Rome was buzzing. Quite literally. Absolutely everyone had a mobile phone, and absolutely everybody was calling absolutely everybody else absolutely all the time. I wondered if there were some law making them compulsory. Frighteningly, it's possible, these days. I swear I saw a street beggar stop and take a call on his cellular. I even heard a trill from a baby carriage, but it turned out to be a toy mobile phone. They start dickhead training early in Italy.

All the Romans were grumpy, it struck me. This was only a couple of months after the cigarette riots, so everyone was probably in tobacco cold turkey. Italians are genetically programmed to smoke in your face almost as incessantly as they use mobile phones, so the legislation banning public smoking didn't sit too well with the good citizens of the capital. As ever, the *carbonari* enforced the law with their usual insane rigour, and lighting up a sly one would like as not draw you a severe truncheoning. Several people were actually beaten to death for endangering their health. That's how things work in the United States of Europe.

I picked up my ID and found a shoe shop easily enough. Finding a shoe shop assistant who wasn't on a cellphone or out in the back risking a pistol-whipping for a quick draw of nicotine proved harder. My feet had swollen from walking around shoeless, but I squeezed them into my regular size, so at least they'd fit in the morning. Nice shoes, too. Genuine vegetable leather and reclaimed materials. Carrot hide and cardboard. With any kind of luck, they'd probably last right through to the afternoon.

I was supposed to meet Klingferm on the thirty-third floor

of an office block in the Via Torino, but I smelled trouble before I even reached the Piazza della Republica. Police cars kept whizzing by, sirens and lights flashing. You ever get that feeling they're heading in the same direction you are?

A big crowd was gathered at the intersection of Torino and the Via Nazionale.

Something big had happened, and everyone was on their cellphone, waving their arms and telling everyone else about it. I was probably the last person in Italy to find out.

I shoved my way through the mobile mayhem and ducked under the yellow and black striped tape that was cordoning off the street. A police officer who'd rather have been doing more interesting things tried to shoo me away like I was some kind of cheeky puppy. I flashed my gold Europol detective badge at him, and he suddenly found some manners.

I nodded down the street where the blue lights were flashing and a milling mob of Rome's finest were busily obliterating anything that might be forensically useful at the crime scene. 'Quite a circus,' I said.

'Seven dead.' He nodded. 'Elevator accident.'

Elevator accident? I waved an offhanded salute, and the cop snapped a neat one back. I wandered towards the circus.

I suppose I knew Klingferm would be one of the bodies. The closer I got to the mêlée, the more certain I became. Whatever had happened, had happened at the Casa Martini, the building where we were supposed to meet.

The elevator, or what was left of it, was actually in the street. It had been smashed up plenty. I had to do some serious visio-spatial mental juggling to rearrange the pieces in my head and work out what it must have looked like intact. One of those neo-Nouveau external elevators, I guessed. Mostly glass. The kind that glide up and down outside the building, and you either go gaga at the view or goo-goo with vertigo. I checked the exterior of the Casa Martini. It had three identical elevators, all frozen now, ranked high along its façade. Beside them, there was an empty track which the crashed elevator had probably once thought of as home.

The bodies had been banged up pretty good. There were seven gurneys with stuffed body bags on them, but the body bags weren't body shaped. There were still some extraneous portions of human detritus that hadn't yet been allocated a bag. There were bizarre chalk outlines everywhere: blobs of indefinable God knows what. Even while I watched, I saw some idiot chalking around what looked like an eyeball that had flung itself clear of the impact. Good plan. That was going to help the investigation no end.

In the thick of the activity, I spotted an officer who looked like he might be in charge of things. He looked the hysterical type, yelling instructions and chewing people off. I wasn't in the mood for that, so I checked around and found an officer who looked like he knew what he was doing, and how to do it without making a fuss. He was sifting through what I guessed would be the personal artefacts of the victims.

I flashed my shield again. The officer looked up from what he was doing and scrutinised it a little too closely for my comfort. I don't like being too well remembered. I started wondering if the badge was still current. I hadn't checked in a few years. That could have been embarrassing. 'Europol?' he said, surprised. 'You boys got here pretty fast.'

Good. I was 'you boys'. I shrugged. 'Coincidence.' I put the badge away.

'You believe in coincidence.' He smiled. 'That's nice.'

I don't, of course. I shrugged again. 'I had a meeting at the Martini building.'

'You're not here officially, then?'

As a federal officer, I could technically pull rank on a local flatfoot. I decided to play nice. 'I'm not here at all, if you don't want me to be.'

He smiled and offered me his hand. 'Salieri,' he said. 'Detective Sergeant Salieri.'

I took the hand. 'So, what happened here, Sergeant?'

'The elevator took leave of the building, is what happened here. Eyewitnesses say it shot to the top and just kept on going. Straight up in the air, like a rocket.'

'And then it came down.'

'And then it came down. Big time.'

'Got any ID on the victims?'

He clicked his fingers and grabbed a clipboard from a passing sergeant. 'We've got their names, we've got their effects. We just haven't got all the bits of them together yet.'

He showed me the list. I already knew Dick Klingferm's name would be on it. It still knocked the wind out of me to see it in black and white.

Salieri was watching my face. 'Somebody you know?'

'No,' I lied. 'Seven people, though.' I handed the clipboard back. 'Such a stupid way to go.'

He turned back to the list. 'I'm having a problem with the personal effects.'

I had an idea what that might be. 'Really?'

'Yeah, I've got seven stiffs with eight IDs.'

Naturally. Klingferm would be carrying a spare. 'Maybe you nabbed a pickpocket.'

'Maybe,' he said. But I don't think he bought it. Not a problem. They'd run a trace and it would lead back to nowhere.

'So, you're looking at an accident here, or what?'

'Accident, negligence, take your pick. There's going to be some engineers and some building planners who won't be sleeping too good tonight.'

I nodded towards the wreckage. 'You mind?'

'How could I mind? You're not even here.'

I nodded to thank him.

He leaned in and spoke softly. 'I wouldn't attract the attention of Captain Zuccho, though, if I could help it.' He flicked his head back towards the officer in charge, who appeared to be beating an underling with a rolled-up newspaper.

'Trouble?'

'Let's just say he has anger containment problems.'

Anger containment problems, heh? I let out a long whistle. It's nice to meet a smart cop once in a while. I don't know how Salieri managed to slip his way through the system, but it was a pretty sure thing he'd never rise above the rank of sergeant. He had talent.

I circled around the elevator debris. Not to avoid disturbing the evidence, but there was a whole lot of gore over everything and I doubted that my carrot and cardboard shoes were guaranteed blood proof. I didn't want to be walking the streets with my footwear haemorrhaging.

I didn't really know what I was looking for until I found it. The brass housing that contained the lift buttons. Very interesting. I bent down to pick it up, and all hell broke loose.

I felt the force of a human storm sweeping in from behind me. Captain Zuccho was on the rampage.

'Who the hell do you think you are, you syphilitic son of a bitch?'

Well, hell-oo to you, and top o' the morning. I turned, still in my crouch. The purple-faced captain was flanked by a pack of scared subordinates. I got the feeling that if he ordered them to leap on me and tear me to pieces with their teeth, they'd probably do it just to keep out of his bad books.

I stood and held up my shield. Zuccho didn't look like he was in the mood for reading, so I reinforced it with: 'Europol.'

'I don't give a rolling, flying fuck if you're the living incarnation of the holy arsehole of Jesus, Son of God. You're tampering with my evidence!'

I smiled. 'Can we calm down, here?' Out of the corner of my eye, I saw Salieri wince. Wrong tack to take. Whoops.

'Calm down? Did you tell me to calm down!?'

I held up my hand. 'I didn't mean to imply any –'

'Don't tell *me* to calm down! Don't *you* tell *me* to calm down, you whore peddling spastic. Here! I'll fucking calm down!' He unholstered his gun. 'I'll calm down! I'll calm the fuck down!' He pointed the weapon at the pavement to his left and fired. 'There!' He shot again. 'And there!' He emptied the clip into the ground. Five more shots. 'And there! And there! And there! And there! And there! Is that calm enough for you? Am I calm now? Is that calmed down sufficiently?'

The entire crime scene fell silent. Zuccho just stood there, breathing heavily, his weapon smoking, everybody watching him. Slowly, his rage subsided. He looked around. 'What is this? Fucking happy hour? Get to work, people!'

The circus started up again. Zuccho holstered his weapon and lowered his voice. 'I'm going to make an apology to you about that. You have to understand: things get a little . . . fraught for me sometimes. I have anger management issues, and sometimes . . . well, sometimes I get just a little too frisky.'

Just a little too frisky? I felt he was being too hard on himself. All he'd done was empty an entire clip of live ammunition into the ground less than a metre away from what he thought was a federal officer at a hot crime scene.

'I'm OK now,' he said.

'You're sure?'

'Sure. That's how it is. It passes. You say you're a fed?'

'I'm not here to take over your investigation, Captain. I just happened by, is all.'

'OK, that's good. I'm still in charge?'

'I'm not even here, really. Just passing by, thought I might help.'

'And that little contretemps – that won't be appearing on any reports, or anything?'

'I didn't see any contretemps, Captain.'

'OK. Good. No harm done, then. What have you got there, Detective?'

'This is the contraption that housed the lift buttons. Notice anything odd?'

I handed him the housing. He turned it over a couple of times. 'It's bent,' he deduced cleverly. Sherlock Holmes, or what? 'But then, it would be, wouldn't it?' He flung it back among the debris. I winced.

I turned and looked at the Martini building. 'Mind if I take a look at one of the other elevators?'

Zuccho didn't answer me. I glanced back. He was biting his lip, hard, and the knuckles on his tensed fists were bone white. Clearly, for some reason, he *did* mind my taking a look at one of the other elevators, and he was struggling to choke back the fury.

'No,' he said, finally, but the concession didn't come easily to him. 'No, you go take a look at one of the other elevators, Detective.' And he added, very quietly, like he didn't want to say it, but he couldn't help himself: 'I'm only the officer in charge of the scene, after all. I'll just stand here with my thumb up my arse and wait for you to tell me what to do next.' His voice started rising. 'Or maybe I should go away on vacation and leave the entire investigation up to you.' Now he was back at full volume again. 'Or wait, wait – better still: maybe I should retire from the whole God-damned police force and you can have my fucking job. Be my guest. You can go home and nail my wife while you're at it.'

'I meant we should take a look together, naturally. If you thought it was a good idea.'

This seemed to appease him, marginally. He took some deep breaths and managed to lower his blood pressure down to just plain bursting point. 'Great,' he choked. 'Thank you. Let's do that.' I didn't really want him with me, but then I didn't particularly want a gun-happy idiot with a hair-trigger temper lurking around where I couldn't see him, bearing murderous grudges against me, either.

I allowed him to lead the way. He took time out en route to chew out and piss off any subordinate who hadn't the good sense to be somewhere else. Zuccho made Captain Bligh look like a man-management genius.

The elevators travelled up the face of the building, but they were accessed from inside. Zuccho blustered up the entrance steps and stood at the top, arms folded, foot tapping, building up a head of ire while I looked up the building's façade again, just to confirm my calculations.

I'd only hesitated for about ninety seconds, but he reacted like I'd left him standing at the altar for the third time running without phoning ahead to let him know I was calling off the wedding.

'So nice of you to join us, Detective. I was thinking of renting out one of the offices here so I could catch a few nights' sleep while you finished your sightseeing tour of the whole of Italy, and deigned to favour us with your sainted presence. But, no, you're here already. Doesn't time fly when you're waiting for someone special? Would you like to see the elevators now, or shall we stand here atop these steps another few months or so, drinking in the glory that is Rome?' There was actually spittle beginning to foam in the corner of his mouth. I wondered how he could exist at this level of consistent fury without his brain literally exploding.

'Now would be dandy.'

'Thank you so very, very much, only I do have an entire police department to run, and I'd like to think I might actually get back to my office at some point during my lifetime, if that doesn't inconvenience you overly.'

'Like I said, right now would be a very good time to inspect the elevators.'

'Excellent.' He swept into the building. I followed, fast enough not to piss him off any more than I had to.

THREE

Incidentally, here's a little-known fact about Captain Bligh: the *Bounty* wasn't the first or the last vessel that the magnificent seafarer lost through mutiny. In his glittering naval career, his crews mutinied on him seven times. *Seven* times. Not two or three times. Not four or five. Seven. Why the hell did they keep giving him a boat? I wonder how the masterminds who put him in charge of that seventh voyage felt when the salty old dog turned up yet again in a rowing boat at Portsmouth harbour with three midshipmen in filthy long johns and an empty canteen smelling of urine?

Zuccho strode right across the marble hall towards the emergency stairs.

'Whoa, whoa!' I called. 'Captain Zuccho? Where are you going?'

He stopped and turned. 'Where am I going? Well, I thought I might try a quick camel trek across the Andes, Detective. Where do you think I'm going? I'm going up these stairs to inspect the elevators. I thought that was the plan. Only if the plan's changed, it would be nice if you could let me know.'

'Wouldn't it be quicker to bring one of the elevators down?'

His eyes widened and he took a staggering step forward, waving his arms in front of him, as if suddenly stricken blind. 'Oh, merciful Father!' He fell to his knees. 'I cannot bear to look upon thy countenance. For thine is the true blinding face of pure genius! Don't go *up* to the elevator, bring the elevator down to *us*.' He started crawling towards me. 'The scales have fallen from mine eyes. I seeth it now, so clearly.'

He reached my feet and started kissing them. 'Oh what misery it must be for thee, to be compelled to worketh with mere mortals.'

I looked down at him. 'Is there something wrong with bringing one of the elevators down?'

He looked up at me, his tongue hanging out of his mouth. 'Are your shoes made of vegetable matter?'

'Carrot leather and cardboard.'

'They taste disgusting.'

'I hadn't planned on serving them up.'

'Is there something wrong with bringing one of the elevators down?' he repeated, clambering to his feet. 'Oh, yes, there may possibly be something wrong with bringing one of the elevators down, don't you think? Given that the last time someone tried to operate one of the elevators, it launched into fricking *deep* space. *That* might be a problem. To send another elevator to the fricking *moon*. Do you think we should risk it? We may have to clear it with the European Space Agency first.'

'Captain Zuccho, I don't want to piss you off here, any more than I do by just being alive and breathing, but have you been given any strategies to deal with your anger containment problem?'

'Yes, I have. And I'm fucking using them. You should have seen me *before* therapy. I was a fucking nightmare to live with, believe me.'

'Personally, I think we can risk summoning an elevator. I'm guessing the elevator was going up when the accident happened.'

'OK, you fricking carrot-shoed moron. Let's say we go with your genius plan. Let's say we go ahead and call the elevator, it blasts off into the stratosphere and comes crashing down on the crowds outside like an intercontinental ballistic missile, crushing everyone within fifty kilometres? How'm I going to explain that little faux pas? I say, "Whoops, sorry:

the federal agent wearing vegetables on his feet thought it would be a good idea"?'

'What floor is the nearest elevator on?'

'Fourteen.'

'You'd rather climb fourteen flights of stairs?'

'Good point. I'll press the button.'

Zuccho leaned over and made a big pantomime point of pressing the lift button with his extended forefinger, and, of course, nothing happened. 'Oh wait, it's not working. Duh, let me see: why could that be? Could that be because the power to the elevators has been cut? Could it be that I, myself, *ordered* the power to the elevators to be cut? Why would I do such a crazily random thing? What possible motive could I have? Could some tiny part of my minuscule little mind have been worried that some innocent party might come along and try to *use* the elevator, thereby inadvertently becoming an unwitting volunteer astronaut on an unofficial and ill-fated mission to Mars?'

I'd known the power would have been cut. I'd intended Zuccho to get the building engineers to isolate one of the elevator cars on the central computer, and lower it remotely, which they must have been able to do. I was thinking about trying to explain that to him, but, suddenly, it seemed like considerably less effort to climb fourteen storeys' worth of staircase.

I made for the emergency stairs. Victory did not dim Zuccho's appetite for sarcasm. 'Oh, *now* the stairs are a *good* idea, Mr Cabbage Boots! Let me see, who thought of that one . . .'

I let the door slam shut behind me and started up to the fourteenth floor. Hopefully, a couple of hundred stairs might knock the wind out of Zuccho's sails.

It certainly left me in the doldrums. Climbing stairs is about the most demanding exercise you can subject your body to, and I'm not exactly at the absolute peak of physical fitness. I was ready to lie down and die by the time the door with '14' on it hazed into view. I could hear Zuccho below me, though, still giving some serious wellington boot to my stupidity. Fortunately, I'd reached the elevator car and found out all I needed to know before he caught up with me.

He spilled through the emergency door and onto the polished corridor floor. Even though he was breathless and fairly close to collapse, the good Captain couldn't still his savage tongue. 'There you go,' he rasped. 'Whaddaya know? It's an elevator car! It looks exactly the same from here as it does from the ground floor, only bigger. A-fricking-mazing. How do they do that? Thank God you dragged me all the way up the stairs to admire it, you son of a bitch. If I had the energy, I'd take out my pistol and shoot you where you stand.'

'See here?' I tapped on the car's glass with my knuckles.

He hoisted himself upright and started staggering towards me. 'Don't do that! Do not do that! Do not touch the elevator car. That car is a weapon of mass destruction. We're going to have to declare that car to the United Nations. Do not touch it.'

I rapped on the glass again. 'How many buttons do you see?'

Zuccho took out a large handkerchief and started mopping his brow. 'How many buttons do I see? What is this? A magic trick? That's why you dragged me up here, Mr David Blaine? To show me a little abraca-fricking-dabra?'

'How many lift buttons? How many floors?'

He peered in gingerly. 'Including the zero and the basement?'

'It goes all the way to floor number thirty-three, right?'

He dabbed again. 'Thirty-three, Einstein. You counted all the way up there all on your own. I bet you could reach forty if you used an abacus.'

'How many floors in the building?'

'A wild guess? Let me try thirty-three.'

'Seventeen.'

'Seventeen?'

'There are seventeen storeys to this building.'

'How do you know there are seventeen storeys to this building, you wiseacre? What are you, the architect? You built the building with your bare hands or something?'

'I counted them from outside.'

'Well, maybe you counted wrong.'

'You saw the elevators from outside. They were all pretty close to the top of the building. You want to climb three more flights of stairs and check it out?'

'OK. Maybe you counted right. So what?'

'So what?'

'What if you're right, so what?'

'Why would you have thirty-three lift buttons on a building with seventeen floors?'

Zuccho shrugged. 'I'm going out on a limb here: maybe the button panels were designed for another building. Or maybe all of these type of elevators have the same panels. Is that too incredible to contemplate? What would that be, the fricking Twilight Zone?'

'I checked the back of the panel on the wrecked lift. Buttons eighteen through thirty-two weren't wired. Button thirty-three was.'

'What are you suggesting? Are you suggesting someone screwed up? An electrician screwed up some wiring? Because *that* would be mysterious and unusual. *That* would be para-fricking-normal. Oo-ee-oo! No wonder we needed the feds in here to bust this case open. It's a fucking X-file.'

'How long has this building been open?'

'I don't know. Six months?'

'So here's the scenario: the building open for six months, people using these elevators all that time, and from the opening ceremony until this very morning, nobody ever tried to press the button for the thirty-third floor. Does that sound likely to you? That not a single soul would even try to press that button?'

'Here's a long shot, Miss Marple: nobody pressed the button because nobody ever wanted to go to the thirty-third floor. And the reason nobody ever wanted to go to the thirty-third floor is because the thirty-third floor *does not exist*! No one ever had an appointment to visit that particular floor because it *isn't even there*.'

'Until today.'

'It's possible. Are you saying that's impossible? Because it's not.'

'The wiring on the panel outside: it was fresh. Someone rigged that wiring very recently. I'm guessing some time this morning. I'm also guessing each of these elevators had the same wiring job done on it. All those things, you can check them out. An elevator repairman: someone will have booked him in and out. There'll be video footage on the security cameras. The wiring, you can check that, too.'

'Pardon me, but what will that prove? All that proves is an elevator repairman came along and screwed up the wiring. Like I said, that's not going to make me pick up the phone book and dial Rod Serling's number. It happens every day. Because, what are you suggesting is the alternative? Someone deliberately wired up those buttons, knowing someone was going to come along and press them? That it was some kind of elaborate, premeditated murder plot? That maybe the killer rigged the wiring, then arranged to meet his victim on the thirty-third floor that doesn't exist? The victim presses the button and wham! Suddenly he's looking out of the window at Sputnik 3 and wondering if he remembered to keep up his life insurance payments? Is that the wacky scenario you're suggesting here?'

Zuccho was right: it was incredible, and no one would ever believe it.

But that's exactly what happened.

Exactly.

And that's the essence of the perfect murder. It doesn't even look like a crime.

The killer arranged to meet Klingferm on the thirty-third floor of a seventeen-storey building, and rigged the lifts to take him there.

And those other six passengers who just happened to be in the elevator car with the wrong person at the wrong time?

So what?

Too bad for them.

Whoever killed Klingferm was a cold-hearted bastard.

It was a pretty sure thing he'd killed before. And unless I could stop him, he'd kill again.

FOUR

It filled me with an uncommon sadness, going through Klingferm's rooms. And not just for the predictable reasons. Of course, you'd have to have the heart of a kidney salesman not to feel a tad melancholic sifting through the bric-a-brac of a life now spent; the favourite mug that will never be drunk from again; the forlorn mundanity of an underwear drawer, with its neatly rolled socks all ready for nothing in particular; the taunt of the desk calendar with so many unnecessary sheets all full of false promises of tomorrows. Hundreds of little details like these peck away at you, deflate you at every turn. It makes for slow going, and you do a lot of unconscious sighing.

But the thing about Klingferm's stuff, the real heart of the sadness, wasn't what was there, it was what wasn't there. No photographs of friends or loved ones. No ornaments, no souvenirs, no unwanted gifts.

And the lonely oneness of everything. Soaking in the sudless scummy water of the kitchen sink: one plate, one knife, one fork. One chair at the kitchen table. And in the bathroom: one toothbrush, one towel, one dressing gown. No perfume. No feminine hygiene products. Nothing that gives a place life.

It could have been my rooms I was looking through.

It could have been my life.

The rooms were all untidy. I assumed professionally so. It was impossible to tell if anyone had been through his things before me.

There was no correspondence in his desk, as I'd expected; just a few utility bills, all marked 'paid' with the payment date duly noted in Klingferm's own neat hand, a dry-cleaning receipt and some pizza delivery flyers. Nobody was going to make a literary splash by publishing Klingferm's letters posthumously. His sad little library consisted mostly of manuals for household appliances and various electronic devices.

There was a computer printer on the desk, but no sign of any computer. Klingferm would definitely have had a computer. I checked, and there was a manual for a fairly recent model. Which meant that somebody almost certainly had been here before me. The printer was a big break, though. I liberated the memory chips from inside it. Most people are criminally unaware of the fact that printer memories don't just store fonts and stuff, they also keep a record of the documents they've printed. Good. There was an excellent chance the chips would give me enough to start up some kind of a lead, but I'd still have to check Klingferm's trash, just in case.

The kitchen bin held no great revelations, except for the telltale Englishness of old, used tea bags in various stages of desiccation. And, skilfully, I managed to impregnate my hands with the powerful odour of overripe bananas in such a way that it would last for many, many months.

I checked in the kitchen cupboards. Big mistake for this old heart of mine. There was a half-empty bottle of tequila staring down at me. I'd been trying to avoid making this personal, but seeing the bottle put paid to that.

The last time we'd been together, me and Klingferm, we'd killed a bottle of tequila between us, and then some. It was the end of my training, and I was going out into the big bad world, all on my lonesome. We did that tequila thing. You know: with the salt and the limes. You put some salt between the crook of your thumb and your forefinger, suck up the salt, take a slug of tequila and squeeze the lime into your mouth. We did that. We did a lot of that. We got all emotional, the first and last time we ever did. Klingferm said, in honour of the occasion, I should call myself Harry Salt. I said, not only would I call myself Harry Salt, I would also call myself Harry Tequila. Klingferm nodded sombrely and said that was fine so long as I didn't call myself Harry Lime, then he literally fell to the floor, laughing. I couldn't work out why. I wanted to get the gag and join him down there on the floor, but my booze-furred brain couldn't work it out. Then Klingferm, between guffaws, had a bash at singing the zither theme, and I remembered. *The Third Man.* Right. Hilarious. So I fell down laughing, too. It doesn't sound like sterling comedy now, in the cold light of death, but you try it after a quart of tequila. It's a show-stopper.

Apart from the small stab of heartache, the kitchen cabinets didn't turn up anything useful. Nothing for it, then: it looked like I'd have to undertake the unpleasant business of trawling through the main bins that serviced the entire building, though it was deeply unlikely that Klingferm would have dumped anything in the way of valuable information there. My last, best hope was his wardrobe.

It was fairly spartan as clothes collections go: three lounge suits, one still in the dry cleaner's polythene; six shirts, two pairs of jeans and a dozen black T-shirts which probably performed the classic hopelessly single man's triple function of vests in winter, casual wear in summer and pyjama tops all the sad year round.

A thorough pocket search revealed absolutely nothing, which meant they'd already been gone through. Definitely. There isn't a man in the world who has absolutely nothing in any of the pockets of his wardrobed clothes, even if he thinks he's being fastidious. You ask any divorce lawyer.

I began to despair about the printer chips. Surely anyone this scrupulous about erasing evidence couldn't have made such a classic mistake.

The communal garbage search, then, was unavoidable. Pointlessly, since my fingers already stank of banana and probably would until the height of summer, I took a pair of Klingferm's gloves and steeled myself for the job.

The refuse zone was outside, round the back of the apartment block, mercifully locked away from sight so I wouldn't have to endure the pitying glare of passers-by as I plied my filthy trade. It was accessed by a standard utilities key – all the services carry one: the refuse collectors, the various meter readers, the police, the fire brigade. And me.

The bins were those big wheelie affairs, ranged round a slippery, uncovered cobblestone yard, slimy with mildew. Behind them was a small stretch of wasteland which clearly served as an unserviced public convenience for the local feral animal population. Your average wild city fox tends not to be too choosy about his diet, and his output has a unique and biting stink. All of which contributed tremendously to the exciting allure of the job in hand.

I'd done garbage searches before. A lot of them. They're not exactly pure jet fuel to the engine of your self-esteem, but you can't get away from the fact that they get results.

People are a little loopy about their rubbish. It's a curious thing: if they have to destroy an old credit card, they make damned sure it's destroyed. They fold it, bend it, break it, cut it up into thirty thousand pieces and scatter every individual fragment in different locations around the globe, with one eye over their shoulder to make sure no one's following them, collecting up the snippets with a view to joining them back together again and somehow passing them off as an undamaged card. But compromising material? People will happily put compromising material in a black plastic bag, tie it up and heft it into a flimsy container, put on the lid, and, they think, hey presto; it's vanished! They think by some miraculous yet undocumented physical law it's been utterly wiped out of existence, as if the bin itself contains some kind of tiny singularity that swallows up matter and obliterates it from all known universes for ever and a day.

Truly. I've found material in waste bags that was so

compromising, you'd still feel nervous about it if you'd shredded it, burnt the shreds, and then eaten the ashes in sweet and sour sauce. And even then you'd want to check your stools for the next three weeks to make sure it hasn't by a terrible twist of irony reconstituted itself into some kind of readable form.

So, times aplenty I've searched garbage, and the results have been fruitful, if rottenly fruitful. The straight fact is: there is no pleasant way of pulling it off. You can tip the stuff out into sanitised groundsheets, you can wear gloves and toxic fume masks and disposable plastic clothing, you can use forceps or tongs or remote-controlled robotic arms, but it all comes down to the same thing. Sooner or later you're going to find yourself up to your humerus in indefinable rancid gunk, peeling putrid mackerel flesh and rotting chicken viscera off a promising-looking document that turns out to be a junk mail flyer someone probably used as an emergency toilet wipe.

Glamorous it is not.

The only way to do the dirty deed is to plunge straight in. And that I did, knowing full well that, within the hour, I'd be reflecting back with warm fondness on the time when the worst lingering smell on my digits was rotten banana.

Garbage disposal is not straightforward. Used to be; you had some stuff you didn't want, you put it in a bag, took the bag out of the house and once a week some men would come along and take it away in their truck. Not any more. The disposal of household effluence is now a highly complex operation. The garbage first has to be divided into recyclable and non-recyclable or landfill waste. And woe betide you if you try to dump more than one bag of each in the same week, or try passing off landfill garbage in a recycling bag. You can do hard time for that kind of evil, my friend. But that's not the end of it. The recyclable stuff then has to be further subdivided into organic, glass and metal waste. But the glass can't be brown glass, and the metal can't be a defunct machine part. And you can't put batteries in there, or circuit boards or electrical appliances. I kid ye not, taking out the trash is now a full-time job in the good ol' US of E.

In a way, the subdivision was helpful – I doubted Klingferm's bottle or beer-can count would have been useful either as a lead or a morale booster, and it did mean that all his paper would be in just one bag. But it also meant he had to share his organic bin with four other apartments. Which in turn meant I'd have to conduct a detailed and doubtless stinky search through some very unpleasant glop before I even found out which bag was his.

It being, for some unknowable reason, my turn in this particular lifetime to experience every frustration the natural world can possibly hurl my way, Klingferm's bag was, inevitably, the last one I came across, at the bottom of the pile. On the upside, by the time I got to it, I felt I'd gained some valuable insights into the private life of the modern Italian household.

There was one sack that appeared to be entirely filled with nothing but faecal matter. Really. And, believe me, that wasn't the worst one by a long way. I won't dredge up the more gruesome of my discoveries, but I'll give you a handy tip: if you're ever in dire need of a total appetite suppressant, try taking a trawl through some Roman rubbish. Trust me, they'll have to force-feed you before your digestive system can even begin to think about operating again.

Maybe the fumes of putrefaction were beginning to scramble my mind, or maybe it was the bizarre foreignness of what I'd just subjected myself to, but going through Klingferm's garbage, I actually began to feel homesick. Stupid, I know. I'd only been away from home a few short hours. It was such homely rubbish, though, so familiar, so . . . unhysterical.

It wasn't homesickness, of course. It was grief. I didn't expect it, and I didn't want it, but it just sort of snuck up on me and wrapped its cold fingers round my windpipe. There was a whole pile of squeezed lime husks in Klingferm's garbage, and I suppose they set me off again on a maudlin trip back in time, because I didn't hear the key click in the lock, and I didn't hear the bin area door open, and I didn't even hear the footsteps coming over the cobbles towards me, but all of these things must have happened, because what I *did* hear was the unmistakable snap of a shotgun breech closing, and I certainly felt the cold barrel of a more than amply calibred shotgun press into the vulnerable bone of the crevice behind my ear.

PROLOGUE

On the last day of my life as I knew it, I woke up with a gulp of air that was far too fresh to qualify as breathable. I blew it out immediately, and it just hung there in front of my face like a lazy smoke signal. I blinked in the direction of my window, just to check I was actually in my bedroom and hadn't somehow contrived to fall asleep in a tent on the summit of K2, or drunkenly booked into some kind of igloo hotel on an Alaskan glacier.

No, this was home. This was my cruddy London apartment.

Nature had carved an astonishing set of icy geometric fractals on the lower half of the panes, and the sills were packed with thick white bricks of snow. That told me two things: getting around London today was going to be the bitch of all bitches, and my landlord had almost certainly sabotaged my central heating again.

I really didn't want to get up, but I had to get up, plain and simple. I was between investigations, and mostly pretty fancy-free, but today was contact day, just about the only day I was truly compelled to leave the building. But it was awfully warm underneath the duvet and awfully cold everywhere else, and I had had a very pleasant, very erotic dream I could probably slip back into without too much effort. On top of which, my latest rigorously observed wheat-free, dairy-free, sugar-free, pleasure-free diet meant that breakfast promised no joy whatsoever, and even less sustenance and comfort. So it was only with the greatest effort of will power and self-discipline, the likes of which are hardly encountered even in the saintliest of martyrs and the holiest of yogi mystics, that I was able to pupa myself out of the cocoon of my bed into the cruel reality of the walk-in freezer that was my apartment.

It was cold all right. Cold enough to burst your nipples. I shucked myself into the chilly towelling of a dressing gown I'd left on a radiator in a moment of freakish optimism and padded to the cupboard that harboured the central heating system. I made the major mistake of feeling the tank with my bare hand. It was, at a conservative estimate, just below the temperature of liquid oxygen, as if it had been stored overnight in a frozen ocean on the planet Pluto. My hand actually stuck to the metal, and I ripped off ninety-three per cent of my fingerprints tugging it clear. It hurt plenty, but at least I was now in a position to commit the perfect crime, should the need arise.

I knew from bitter experience that the central heating system control panel was no more or less complicated than the interface of the average intercontinental missile defence shield. It took me fifteen minutes just to remember how to open the casing that housed it. As usual, I studied the baffling array of buttons, dials and switches, hoping some part of their function might be intuitively obvious. As usual, I got no joy. Clearly it would require at least three highly trained and motivated personnel working in perfect synchronicity just to turn the damned thing on. Isolating and activating the radiator in my bedroom could easily be accomplished by a small consortium of theoretical physicists, so long as they were on their sabbatical year and didn't plan on going out much.

No two ways about it, I was going to have to try the final desperate option of a hopeless man. I was going to have to read the manual.

Naturally, the manual turned out to have been translated from Japanese into English by a Kalahari bushman whose closest contact with either language had been a chance encounter with a German explorer trying to ascertain the going barter rate for a second-hand camel in terms of petroleum and shiny beads. I tried a number of the proposed solutions 'In the eventuals of notworkingness', but having attempted to 'glide the initiation of the Captain illuminator' (fig.8.a) and 'rotate the combustion circle device (also fig.8.a) with repeated vigour until click-clickety sound produces whoosh of small explosion thump' (also, bizarrely, fig.8.a), I gave up, and tried to feed the manual to my recycling unit. The recycling unit wasn't working either. I was about to feed that to the street below when I realised the two things might be related.

I checked the fuse box. The trip switch had been flipped. Impossible to say if that was down to landlordly sabotage or the marvellously inept wiring that tripped the system in the event of the major electrical surge produced by, say, turning on a light bulb, or even just thinking about turning on a light bulb. I decided to carry on hating the landlord anyway.

The landlord's trying to get rid of me, see, because my rent is fixed. It's fixed high, of course, orbitally high, but it's steady, and he could certainly get even more for the hovel if he could persuade me to leave. The apartment's in central London, prime location, big demand. The fact that it could barely qualify as adequate living space for a cot-bound baby munchkin doesn't seem to affect its desirability. So my landlord plays these little games to try and wear me down. His favourite is rigging the thermostat on my water heater to such a stupidly high temperature that if I make the foolhardy mistake of actually using it, the water in the tank boils over, spills into the ceiling cavity and eventually starts to drizzle through, so I come home to a room slowly filling with rusty, warm rain. It's one of the reasons I never bring a date home for coffee. Making romantic small talk on my soggy sofa under umbrellas doesn't seem too likely to impress even someone with such a low expectation threshold she'd be prepared to date me.

The other reason I don't bring a date home for coffee is that I never actually have a date.

I finally did it. I finally got the heating on. I actually managed to successfully effect the rotaration of the combustion circle device with repeated vigour until the telltale click-clickety sound produced the promised whoosh of small explosion thump. The pipes started creaking and banging like the sun-parched decks of a ghost galleon. With luck, in six or seven days the apartment would be warm enough to accommodate a couple of exceptionally hardy and daring polar bears, so long as they huddled together, dressed warm and hibernated until July.

A shower was out of the question. I would have died of shock or exposure or both. A bath was also out of the question because, naturally, the apartment didn't have one, the apartment being many, many times smaller than the average bath. So I boiled up a kettle and performed my ablutions in the sink.

I tried to dress without actually taking my towelling robe off, but the shirt proved too much of a problem, and I had to endure another few frightening sub-arctic moments of upper body nakedness. I dressed warm like Momma always said and walked from my luxury kitchen area, through my superiorly appointed lounge slash dining zone and into my bright and airy reception hall area in only two steps. Just one thing to do before I left: take a photo of the rooms. Not because I was going to miss them awfully for the few minutes I planned to be away; this was a professional thing.

If you came to my apartment, you would definitely file me under 'messy housekeeper'. Clothes and bric-a-brac are strewn over the floor and the few sticks of furniture are arranged in apparent chaos. Exactly the opposite is true, though. Every single item is carefully positioned. That's why I take a couple of digital photos of the rooms before I leave, just to make sure everything's exactly where it should be. Here's the thing: any idiot can enter and toss a tidy room, and leave everything in its place so you'd never even know you'd been searched. A messy room, it's difficult even for a talented professional to avoid leaving traces. I don't go the whole hog and leave a layer of cornflakes under key areas of the carpet, or any of that weird stuff, but that's because I don't keep anything compromising in my apartment. I just need to know if anyone's been going through my things.

I tucked the camera into my pocket, double-locked my front door and went downstairs. I didn't bother checking my mailbox. I never get any mail I want to read. As usual, I read the sign one of my fellow tenants had kindly taped to the wall to fill us all with inspiration for the day ahead. It read, 'Please make sure the front door is fully closed, as heroin addicts use the hallway for shooting up.' Suitably inspired, I stepped out into Bing Crosbyland.

Snow is more than beautiful. Snow is Nature's Tippex: it covers up mistakes and ugliness. You put a carpet of snow over Nagasaki, it probably looks like the Ice Queen's castle. Even the stinkiest, most crap-strewn streets of London's grimmest thoroughfares take on a fairy-tale, virgin beauty under the thinnest skein of snow.

If you can actually get to them.

Because, in London, of course, we always have the wrong kind of snow. All public transport is rendered instantly static and useless by the merest hint of a flurry of white. Moscow, on the other hand, always seems to get exactly the right kind of snow, somehow, and gets it with humiliating frequency, too. In Moscow snow, poorly built and ancient trains, trams and buses plough on about their business through twenty-foot drifts and swirling blizzards without missing a beat on the timetable. Here, as soon as the first flake falls, train points are frozen, engines seize up and tyres spin ineffectually on roads that instantly become giant ice-dance venues for buses to demonstrate their pirouetting virtuosity. We should try importing some of that good stuff, some of that Moscow snow. Then, maybe, we wouldn't get caught by surprise every God-damned year, when, unpredictably, it snows exactly the same kind of surprisingly wrong snow it did last year, and the entire Thames Valley might not be thrown back to the Mesozoic era for the duration of the winter.

The first suck of air froze the tooth-rinsing water still lingering on my gums, turning my mouth into a deadly cavern of stalactites and stalagmites. I probably had a smile like Nosferatu. But I felt good. Like I was suddenly living somewhere clean and unsullied. It was peaceful, too. Almost silent. So silent, in fact, that I wondered, for a moment, if the bomb had finally fallen and this was the start of the nuclear winter. This was pretty much how I'd expected it to happen most of my life: the bomb would be dropped, eliminating all human life except for me and a small group of ludicrously beautiful and unfeasibly large-breasted women, desperate to avail themselves of a procreating male. In my mind's eye, though, it hadn't been this cold. In my mind's eye the temperature had warranted much bikini wearing and body oiling. But sadly, no. No bomb at all. It was only the fallen snow muffling the bedlamic clamour of London traffic, human and otherwise, that's all. Still, bomb or no, it would have ranked as one of my life's few perfect moments if only I'd had the smallest amount of feeling in just a single one of my toes.

The reason I had to get out, like I said, was this was contact day. I had to check a number of publications' personal columns for messages. I could have had them delivered, I suppose, but that would mean paying for them. Not that I'm mean, or I have any problems with money – I have a virtually bottomless expense account which I hardly ever touch. It's just more fun to consult them in my local newsagent's, where a suspicious Asian staff member drops all his other duties to stand watching me relentlessly from embarrassingly close range with his arms crossed, daring me to carry on reading and not buying. I dare. I dare.

Usually, there's nothing, or at least nothing I have to do anything about. Today was different. Very different.

Here's how it works, my organisation. It's a fairly standard cell structure. There's me, and there's one operative either side of me. I only know the two of them, that's all. There are obvious advantages to the set-up. If I get uncovered and interrogated, I can only give up the names of the two people I know. And that's pretty much all I do know: two names. I don't know their addresses, I don't even know which country they're operating in. And even the names I know aren't real. We all have several identities, none that are really our own, all fully authenticable, no matter how you try to check. Me, I mostly go by the name of Salt. Harry Salt. That's what we call my core ID. But I have dozens of alternatives. I can be Cardew Vascular, or Simon Simons, or Harry Tequila. If you get even a sniff that an ID's been compromised, you dump it, quick as a Chinaman's orgasm. Me, I don't even wait for that sniff. I trash an ID as soon as I've used it in an investigation. I go through identities faster than a supermodel goes through international football squads.

So, you could torture me for years, and that's all I could give you: two names that aren't even real. Nice to know, eh? Something for me to hang onto when they're warming up the old gonad electrodes.

The three of us keep in contact through the personal columns of three different publications, in case one or two of them suddenly go bust, or get withdrawn or just plain old go on strike. That hardly ever happens. What does happen, and happens frequently, is that the copy desk gets the message more or less completely wrong, or forgets to print it at all. Even in this climate, it's unlikely that all three publications will screw the messages up. It's unlikely, but they do manage it, on occasion.

Of course, all three of us use different publications, which means on contact day I have to scour twelve different personal columns, to check both of my neighbours' messages, and to make sure my own haven't been royally screwed up. That's why the hawk in the newsagent's loves me so fine. That's why he makes a noisy and laboured point of smoothing out and refolding every single newspaper and magazine once I'm through with it, even though I handle them with the same tender respect I'd handle the Dead Sea Scrolls.

A standard message will be something like: 'Harry Salt – All old ketchup. K.' or 'Harry Salt – Ask overt Kenyans. K.' You don't have to be an international master spy to work out that's someone called K telling me everything's AOK.

K is a fellow I know as Dick Klingferm. He's the guy who briefed me up on procedure way back when I was a raw greenhorn, so I spent quite a few weeks with him before I went operational. And although I'd never actually met him in the flesh since then, he was the only living person who actually knew some things about me that were essentially true, and that made him the closest thing I had to a friend.

This time, though, the message was different. This time the message from Klingferm was: 'Harry Salt – Rip Van Winkle. K.'

This was a big one. This was Klingferm setting up a meeting. In the flesh. An actual meeting. Two operatives face to face? In the same place at the same time? Bad, bad and very bad. Klingferm wouldn't even *think* of arranging something so exposed unless he was facing trouble only just short of a nuclear threat.

I checked, and it was the same message in all three of Klingferm's periodicals. Even more worrying. Dick Klingferm liked playing games, and normally he would vary the messages. One of them would have been 'Rampant Vole Warts' or 'Rub Vulvas Willingly', or some such, you get the idea. The 'R' and the 'V' meant rendezvous and the 'W' was the location. It had been a while, so I had to dredge my memory deep for the mnemonic I'd used to retain the rendezvous sites – it's not the kind of thing you commit to paper.

W, as I finally recalled, was Rome. A fairly small, fairly central hotel there.

I shocked the hell out of the newsagent by actually buying all three publications. He looked like he was going to have to spend the rest of the day lying down with a cold compress on his head in a darkened room to recuperate.

I hate having to hurry. Having to hurry makes me cranky. I double hate having to hurry in snow. The only way to hurry safely in snow is to waddle like a giant penguin.

But a message like that required an urgent response. Klingferm was onto something very big and very dangerous. He was probably in some serious personal danger himself. I had to get me to Rome as quickly as humanly possible.

So I did the waddle thing back to my apartment block.

I tried not to notice the heroin addict on my stairs jacking up in full view. There was a state-sanctioned 'shooting gallery' less than four hundred metres away, but the trip was clearly too demanding at this time of the morning for a junkie with nothing but blood pumping through his system. I tried to step over him while still maintaining the illusion I hadn't spotted him. I didn't want him thinking I'd noticed him, in case he asked me to help him, or something. In case he asked me to hold the belt round his arm just a little tighter to help him seek out a vein in there that was still capable of protruding. Incredibly, I actually managed to accidentally stand on his head without his seeming to notice *me*, either.

You have to strike a balance when you're packing for any kind of journey where you're going to be separated from your luggage. It's an art form. You need to travel as light as possible, because the chances are you'll be spending an inordinate amount of time carrying your own baggage over distances you wouldn't normally contemplate without a good supply of camels or elephants. So you pack only essentials. But these essentials can't be so essential that you can't live without them, because, somewhere along the line, there's a reasonable chance they're going to get lost. You carry what you can on your person, bearing in mind that you're going to have to take everything out of your pockets at every one of a dozen or so security checks, and put it all back again. You wear spare socks and underpants, or carry them in an overcoat pocket, and you cram what you can into your hand baggage, once you've triple-checked it's the correct regulation size for hand baggage on your chosen airline, which, as a general guide, is likely to be approximately the same cubic capacity as a stingily filled beef sandwich with the crusts cut off.

And you take a spare pair of shoes. Leather shoes. Leather shoes are not exactly illegal absolutely everywhere in Europe, but they're pretty hard to come by. In those states where they're not just plain outlawed, the manufacturers and retailers – and therefore, the consumers – are hit with a savage Environmentally Unfriendly Tax, which makes leather shoes close to commercially unviable.

The final tip: never lock the suitcase. It just pisses off thieves and customs officers, who are usually one and the same thing, and forces them to brutalise your luggage to get at what they want.

So I packed quickly and, I think, wisely, and set about the epic task of finding a way to actually get to Rome this side of the fourth millennium. I booked a flight easily enough, but getting to the airport and actually catching it was going to be something else entirely.

I managed to book the flight from City airport. This has the unique advantage amongst London airports of actually being in London, which ought to have minimised my transport problem. Trains and buses were unlikely to be running anything like a normal service, which is, let's face it, useless anyway. The Tube wasn't much of an option either. You'd have thought that an underground train line would be relatively unaffected by a few centimetres of snow forty metres above it, but you'd be wrong, and the prospect of being stalled in a packed, airless carriage with a herd of commuters, of whom a good seventy per cent have failed to grasp the basic rudiments of personal hygiene, was not a pretty one.

Taxi it was, then.

I locked my door, stepped as best I could over the junkie lying on the stairs in his extremely temporary happy torpor, and left my apartment building.

I didn't know it then, but I was leaving it for the last time in my life.

FIVE

Having a loaded gun pressed to the back of your head is not very nice. You may think that sounds a little obvious and trite, but then it probably hasn't ever happened to you, and if you're only even slightly lucky, it probably never will.

It's happened to me five times, and I can remember every single millisecond of every single one of those times with such a stark and vivid sensory clarity, it's hard to imagine how my memory has any room left for anything else.

It certainly focuses the mind. Everything gets amplified. You can hear flowers budding. You can hear injured insects limping. You suddenly realise that the air you breathe actually has a taste. You can feel your hair growing and your gums receding. Your skull suddenly feels like it's nothing more than an oversized eggshell, and you're excruciatingly aware that this ludicrously fragile crust of flimsy bone, no thicker than a pastry case on an apple tart, is the only thing that's keeping your brain inside your head. This brittle dome of ultra-thin blackboard chalk is all that's stopping your brain from glooping out of your ears onto the pavement and splattering there like a tossed blancmange in raspberry coulis. Your brain, your beautiful brain, with all its complexity, all its memories, all its thoughts, everything that's actually *you* is protected by a casing you wouldn't consider sturdy enough to use as a child's fucking piggy bank. What kind of design genius thought *that* was a good idea? Your skull should be made of steel, at the very least. Reinforced steel. It should be made of reinforced steel that's been reinforced with even more reinforced steel. Hell, it's protecting your brain, the second most important part of you; why spare the expense?

It should be made of reinforced hardened platinum and at least five centimetres thick. You have to be talking about reinforced, hardened platinum, reinforced with reinforced steel as an absolute minimum requirement for skull construction. Bottom line, it should be bullet proof.

A man's voice gruffed in heavily accented Italian that I shouldn't move. It was an unnecessary injunction. I had no plans to move for the next century or two without ample permission – written, signed and in triplicate if need be. If they ever turn the kiddie party game of Statues into an Olympic event, I would breeze the gold, my friends.

Even so, still as I stayed, the gun bearer saw fit to deliver an unnecessarily cruel jab to the back of my starkly unprotected head with his shotgun muzzle. 'What you doing here, Mister?'

Now, this was a tricky one to gauge. What would the right answer to that question be? No pressure, Harry, but if you get it wrong, your frontal lobes wind up decorating the cobblestones, and a wild fox gets to take your hypothalamus home as a tasty treat for tea.

What was this idiot worried I might be doing amongst the garbage? Why was he patrolling the garbage with a loaded shotgun in the first place? Just what threat was he supposed to be protecting the garbage from? Surely, garbage, by its very nature, is something you don't want. Is that not, in fact, a stunningly accurate definition of garbage? You no longer want something, you throw it away. That's how it becomes garbage. It wasn't born garbage, you made it garbage by the very act of throwing it away. If you cared about some part of the garbage, why throw it away in the first place? Why put *valuable* garbage out here with the garbage nobody could give a hootenanny about, so you have to patrol the garbage with a shotgun of sufficient calibre to blow a blimp-sized hole through an adult sperm whale? It just didn't make sense.

So: was producing a police badge the right thing to do

here? Was that the tack to take? Would that keep my mind where it mattered?

I was just about to reach, very, very gently for my inside pocket, when another alternative struck me.

I was in Rome, right? In Italy? What if this was a wiseguy? What if this was some giant mob garbage racket I'd inadvertently stumbled on? It didn't seem likely: how could anyone hope to derive any kind of substantial income from bags full of faecal matter? But if it was some sort of Mafia scam, producing the detective shield was probably not my best move.

I suddenly realised I had my hands up in the air and I hadn't even noticed, because I felt something gooey trickling down my right shirt cuff. I glanced up at my hand, half expecting that the shotgun had somehow gone off and blown it away without my noticing. Mercifully, my hand was still there, and glued to its palm by some unknowable and unpleasant sticky green gloop there was a chunk of what looked like some very rancid cheese.

And out of the blue, a life-saving plan came to me.

It occurred to me that I probably didn't look like a man of any moment, on my knees, there, sifting among the bilge. My carrot-hide shoes were already separating at the soles, my suit was crumpled and caked in mildew and slime, and God knows what else. Plus, I had nameless gunk drooling down my hands from the garbage I'd been rooting through. My whole look was saying 'vagabond'. I thought I could pull it off.

I tried half turning my head. I wanted to show how unthreatening I was, but the attempt was rewarded with another savage jab of the barrel.

'I'm looking for food,' I said. My mouth was dry with fear, and I'm pretty sure I sounded suitably weak and vagabond-ish. I held up my right hand and showed him the slime-soaked cheese.

'Food?' he growled. 'You hungry?'

'Yes.' I nodded. '*Si, si.* Hungry.'

'You hungry?' he snarled. 'You eat.'

Did he mean the cheese?

Did he mean I should eat the filthy putrid cheese in my hand?

The rancid, stale chunk of mould caked in green sludge that was at this very moment dribbling down my arm?

You bet your boots he did.

So I did something disgusting.

I ate the cheese.

I closed my eyes, and like I was savouring the most delicate morsel that ever graced an emperor's banquet table, I popped it in my mouth.

And I ate it.

Slime and all.

To this day, I can still taste that cheese.

And I'm pretty sure I always will.

Not even death could wipe that taste away.

The gunman swore behind me. Then he started laughing.

I chewed, he laughed. I was silently praying for him to go away, but he kept watching and laughing, the bastard retard, and I kept chewing, but eventually there was no choice: I had to swallow.

I had to swallow and make it look like that piece of cheese really hit the spot. So, God help me, I swallowed it. It didn't want to stay down, but stay down it had to. And stay down it did.

The gunman swore again, and cracked me behind the ear with the wooden butt of his shotgun.

I hit the garbage with my face and blacked out.

I was unconscious, but I could still taste that cheese.

SIX

Something was nibbling my right ear.

Not nice nibbling, neither. Nibbling like they meant to take a chunk out of my lobe.

Something nasty was nibbling my ear, and there was a very, very bad smell. Way beyond funky.

I sat bolt upright and slapped at the side of my face, but whatever had been doing the nibbling was long gone.

The stink remained.

My left cheek was sticky. I looked back where I'd been lying. I don't want to tell you which particular bag I'd chosen to take my little nap upon. It's enough to say that the bag had split open on impact, and that's why my cheek was sticky.

My wallet was lying open on the floor. The cash had gone, but all the ID was still there. So, amazingly, was the credit card.

I dragged myself to my feet. Something didn't feel right. I looked down at my stockinged feet.

The evil bastard had stolen my carrot shoes.

What kind of sick mind would do a thing like that?

But, hey. I was alive, right? That definitely qualified as a result.

Now, my experience of near-death situations – that experience being, as you know, more than copious – is that once your adrenaline settles, and you realise you've actually lived through it, you undergo the most incredible high. You're in love with the world, with life itself. All malice flies from your spirit. You want to write, personally, to everyone who was ever even slightly mean to you and forgive them.

You want to swim with dolphins. You want to run naked on beaches. You want to frolic naked in heather. You want to throw back your head and laugh for forty minutes out of every hour. You want to make love through the night, every night, and you don't care who or what with. You want to be reckless. You want to parachute in blizzards, naked. Fly unpowered gliders, blindfold and naked. You want to ski down sheer glaciers, blindfold and naked and without skis. You want to ride untamed horses, possibly blindfold though probably not naked, and definitely without skis. You're high, but you're not insane. You want to get together all the world leaders, possibly naked, and bang their silly old heads together till they agree that war is a stupid thing and they're definitely going to stop doing it. You're so giddy, you actually think you might pull it off, too.

I'm guessing everyone's experience is reasonably similar, though I'll accept maybe my reaction is overly focused on excessive nakedness. I've no idea why that is.

This time, though, it was different. I certainly had a strange feeling in my stomach that was kind of on the giddy-ish side of things, but all I really felt like doing was puking for the next decade.

I had to get out of that yard.

I found a relatively clean scrap of material and wiped myself down as best I could. I mustered all the dignity that was prepared to report for duty, and walked out into the street.

I was getting all kinds of looks. Women were whisking toddlers over to the opposite side of the road, without worrying too hard about the traffic, or even whether the toddlers were theirs to whisk. I could probably have breezed an audition as a circus freak-show attraction. I badly needed a shower. I badly needed seven or eight showers, as a matter of fact, back to back, followed by a leisurely soak in a pit of lime. Though the truth was I would probably never be truly clean again. Not in this lifetime.

I badly needed a change of clothes, too. But what I needed worst of all was a change of luck. Klingferm's garbage had yielded no great insights, and all I had for those hours of painstaking search was a lump on the back of my head, a couple of printer memory chips which may or may not have been wiped, and a lingering cacophony of smells and tastes I could quite frankly have lived my whole life without.

I made a rudimentary stab at washing my hands in a beautifully ornate street drinking fountain. It had probably been there since the Renaissance, and now nobody would be able to drink from it ever again.

I wanted to go back to my hotel room, lie on my bed and cry myself to sleep. But, of course, my hotel room didn't have a bed, and for all I knew there was an entire team of armed security guards in full riot gear waiting to arrest me on any number of counts, ranging from verbal sexual violence to stealing my own mail.

I caught an aroma that caused a strange lolloping panicky reaction in my stomach. I looked around to find myself outside a cheese shop. I had to do something to get this taste out of my mouth. I knew that nothing was ever going to completely eradicate it, but I had to mask it at least, if only for a little while.

I checked my trouser pockets, and found about €3.70 in change. I ducked into the dingiest, dirtiest café I could find, and ordered the thickest, blackest espresso they could offer. Sure, people moved away from me at the bar. I didn't hold it against them. *I* would have moved away from me if I could.

The coffee was vile, but it offered a pleasant respite for my taste buds, and freed my mind to face up to the investigation. And it did not look good. I was pretty close to drawing a blank here. I had to do some serious thinking.

Now, Klingferm had been onto something. Something he knew was pretty big and pretty dangerous. So big and so dangerous, he'd gone to the extraordinary lengths of requesting a real-world visit from me. He must have known there was a possibility he might not be around for that meeting. He would have made provision for that. He would have left some kind of sign. A sign that most people, even a good professional, would miss. I felt pretty sure I'd missed it. Certainly, he wouldn't have relied on the printer chip.

I went over his apartment in my mind's eye again. If it had been me leaving this hint, I wouldn't have hidden it somewhere obscure, somewhere nobody could find it. It would have to be fairly easy to come across, but innocuous, so most prying eyes would slip over it without noticing. A business card, maybe, of a contact who didn't know enough to be in danger, just enough to push you off in the right direction. A key to some kind of locker?

And it hit me. It hit me like love's own arrow.

Klingferm *had* left something like that. Maybe all of those things and more.

I drained the coffee and slammed a big and noisy tip on the counter. I didn't even wait to use the washroom facilities, though, let's be honest, I was in dire need of them all.

I headed back to Klingferm's place at quite a lick for me. I wasn't running, but I was definitely walking briskly. Of course, there was a risk I'd run into the armed garbage patrolman again, but I was feeling good enough to consider taking him on, armed or not. Klingferm was a genius and so was I for spotting it.

Because what Klingferm had left me, was his dry-cleaning ticket.

SEVEN

I got back to Klingferm's apartment building without even stopping to buy some more shoes, but the garbage patrolman was nowhere to be seen. Shame. I had complicated plans for him involving a rusty metal crowbar and his backside

I grabbed the dry-cleaning ticket, and checked the address. The shop was on the way back to the hotel. Good.

I picked up Klingferm's bathrobe, and hurried out onto the street again.

This time, I did stop off at a shoe shop. Again, they were out of leather models, and fresh out of carrot wear, too, so I picked up a lovely pair made of dehydrated courgettes and cardboard. Zucchini hide: comfort you can rely on.

Maybe my luck was changing: the dry cleaners claimed to offer a one-hour express service. I handed over Klingferm's receipt, and got back a polythene-wrapped suit and a small brown envelope they'd put the contents of his pockets in. It was a shame Klingferm hadn't been my size. It was a pretty natty suit he'd left me, and I was in fairly desperate need of decent apparel.

Riding my luck, I stripped down to my underwear, right there and then in front of the shop assistant, slipped on Klingferm's robe and handed over my shirt and my suit for the one-hour express deal. I could see the girl would have liked to refuse to even handle the filthy rags I'd landed her with, but I guess I didn't look like a guy anyone ought to be messing with right now.

There was no chair, but I'm not an idiot, and I wasn't about to let my only remaining suit of clothes too far out of my sight, thank you, mister, so I rested my handsome derrière against the window sill and checked out the contents of the envelope.

Klingferm had left me three things: a newspaper clipping about a highfalutin dinner party in Paris where all the guests had died of food poisoning; some kind of locker key; and a business card from the Plaything Club in Vienna, with a signature on the back that looked like Twinkle or Twonkle with a big, smoochy X underneath it and a lipstick kiss print, and beside that, in Klingferm's own, neat hand, the word 'Thursday'.

Well, it wasn't much, yet. But at least it was something.

Which did I go for first? The key was a mystery. It had a seven-digit number etched into it, which told me exactly nothing, and it appeared to be made by Ingersoll. Trying to hunt down the lock it opened didn't sound like a thrillingly quick and easy job, and I had to get moving on something fast. I slipped the key back into the envelope.

Paris, then, or Vienna?

I'd heard about the dinner party deaths. They'd happened a couple of weeks ago, and the whole business had sounded pretty peculiar to me. In fact, I'd been toying with the notion of looking into the incident myself just before I'd got Klingferm's summons.

Vienna, the Plaything club, Twinkle? That could be anything. And Thursday? Today was Tuesday, so either I'd missed it, or I had two days to get there. I made my decision. Next stop Paris.

My clothes came back in world record time – less than forty minutes. Wonder if the speed of the service was in any way related to the powerful aroma I was slowly impregnating the entire shop with?

I decided to walk back to the hotel in the towelling robe, carrying my suit and shirt over my arm. I didn't want to put them on until I'd had a shower or nine.

On the way, I found a decent-looking computer shop, and

dropped off the printer chips. They promised to print off anything they found on them within the hour. Yeah, right.

The hotel's doors were still jammed, but I managed to squeeze through without causing myself too much damage. The geriatric receptionist actually ducked below his desk and tried to hide when he saw me, but his old knee joints couldn't quite cut the mustard and his quivering pate was clearly visible above the countertop.

Avoiding the elevator, naturally, I walked up the stairs to my room.

The room still had no bed, but that didn't bother me. All I wanted was to book a flight to Paris and take a long, relaxing, soapy bath. I tried to hang my clothes in the wardrobe, but the wardrobe didn't appear to be equipped with a pole for hanging clothes on, which, for my money, is a minimum requirement for a wardrobe to warrant its job description.

That was fine. That was not a problem. I'd made a decision not to let these petty annoyances niggle me any more. I hung the clothes on the wardrobe door, removed my courgette shoes and my abominable socks and glided into the bathroom.

There was no bath in the bathroom.

Not only was there no bath in the bathroom, there were no bathroom facilities of any kind.

I was pretty sure there had been a bath in the bathroom when I'd originally arrived. I knew for certain there'd been a working toilet in there. And a sink. Now there were just a series of pipes jutting up through the floor and out of the tile work.

I punched a second hole in the wall and dialled House Services.

A woman picked up the phone and said: 'Restaurant. How may I help you?'

'There is no bath in my bathroom.'

'Well, I'm sorry, sir, but this is the restaurant.'

'I know. Every number in this hotel seems to be the restaurant.'

'I'll put you through to House Services.'

'No . . .'

But she'd gone. I waited for the ringing and the click of the receiver being lifted. I waited once again for her to say: 'Restaurant. How may I help you?'

'Yeah, see, lady, what you've done there, you've put yourself back through to yourself.'

'Oh. Really?'

'Don't worry, it's an easy mistake to make. It must be. You do it all the fucking time.'

There was a long silence. 'It's you again, isn't it?'

'Well, how could it not be? How could it not be me? Yours is the only phone I can get through to from this room.'

'I'm warning you not to call me again.'

'I don't *want* to call you again. I never wanted to call you in the first place. I can't *help* but fucking call you every fucking time I pick up the fucking phone.'

The line went dead.

Well, fine. Let her send up Security again. Let them arrest me. Even the worst jail in Italy would surely have a shower, or at the very least a crapper I could wash my face in.

I went over to the minibar. I needed something to calm my ragged nerves.

Predictably, there was nothing of a nerve-calming nature in there. I didn't think a Toblerone or a tube of overpriced nuts would do the job.

There was a firm, officious knock at the door. I began to regret losing my rag with the restaurant manager. I couldn't afford to waste time getting myself all arrested, and that swine of a garbage patrolman had stolen my bribe wad.

I opened the door. A tall, well suited man with grey hair and a trim moustache was looking at me. 'Mr Vascular?'

He wasn't going to get me that easily. 'Who wants to know?'

'My name is Farelli, Mr Vascular. I'm the hotel manager. I understand there have been certain complaints.'

'Complaints? Yes, there've been certain complaints. I've got certain complaints aplenty. Take a look.'

I opened the door, and swept my arm back for him to enter. He strode in with regal leisure, his hands clasped behind his back. He looked around the room slowly, nodding his head as it panned, like a general inspecting a regimental parade. 'I see,' he said, finally, and turned to face me. 'Mr Vascular,' he said, 'there is no bed in this room.'

'Exactly.'

He nodded again. 'What have you done with it?'

'I sneaked it out in my jacket pocket.'

'This is a serious matter, Mr Vascular. I'll thank you to treat it as such.'

'Come here.' I walked to the bathroom door. 'Take a look in here.'

He ambled into the bathroom, still keeping up his regal gait, still nodding genteelly.

I waited a while.

I waited a while longer.

He ambled out again. 'Mr Vascular,' he said.

'I know.'

'There is no bath in the bathroom.'

'Mr Farelli, I know.'

'Nor is there a lavatory.'

'I know.'

'Nor a sink.'

'I know.'

'Are you suggesting all these things were missing when you checked in?'

'No, no. Just the bed. The bathroom left town while I was out.'

'You should have reported this, Mr Vascular.'

'I did. I reported it to the restaurant manager.'

'You should have reported this to House Services.'

'I tried. Believe me.'

'If you'll excuse me one moment.' He ambled to the phone, pulled out an enormous monogrammed silk handkerchief from his jacket pocket, made a big brouhaha about wiping down the receiver like it had just been used by a plague-carrying rat and dialled.

I watched and I waited.

'House Services? This is Mr Farelli. I'd like someone up in 407 immediately.'

He smiled at me thinly. I smiled back at him, only thinner.

His brow furrowed. 'Well, I *dialled* House Services ... Very well, then, could you kindly transfer me to House Services? Thank you.'

I waited and I watched.

'House Services? No, no, this is Farelli again. You've put me back through to yourself ... Well, I'm *trying* to get through to House Services ... Yes, could you do that for me? Thank you.'

Farelli turned away from me and found something interesting to look at on the picture rail while he waited to be reconnected. 'Hello? No, no. No. I'm trying *not* to phone the restaurant ... No. No, that's all right. I'll dial again myself.'

He put the phone down, picked it up again and dialled. He still had his back to me. 'Hello? No, it can't be you again ... No, I dialled Reception this time ... No, I definitely dialled zero ... No, thank you.'

He put the phone down once more, then he picked it up and dialled again. He didn't give up easy, old Mr Farelli. He had a stronger appetite for frustration than most. He waited. He listened. He didn't even bother talking this time, he just slowly replaced the receiver, put his handkerchief back in his pocket and turned.

'I think, perhaps, we should find you another room, Mr Vascular.'

'That would be nice.'

'This one appears to have a strange smell in it.'

'Indeed it does.'

'I'll organise that for you, right away.'

I thanked him, he nodded a polite bow, and ambled out of the room.

I was relocated to room 409, which didn't have a bed, either, but it did have a deep bath, and for that I was grateful. And so, for that matter, was the rest of Rome.

I stopped off at the computer store to pick up what they'd recovered from Klingferm's printer chips.

There was just one sheet, which didn't bode well.

That meant someone had been smart enough to wipe the chips and leave me a message.

It was a page downloaded from some website. A page about an American folk hero called Johnny Appleseed. Apparently old Johnny had travelled across America, barefoot, in shabby clothes, wearing a tin pot as a hat, planting apple seeds he'd collected from cider presses in Pennsylvania all the way from Ohio to Illinois, then spent the rest of his life tending the vast nurseries of apple seedlings his labours had produced.

I didn't much like the sound of this. Either it was Klingferm leaving me another, unnecessarily obscure clue, which seemed elaborate and unlikely. Or it was Klingferm's killer himself, leaving me a very clever taunt.

A clever, cold-blooded perpetrator of multiple homicides had taken time out to fuck with my head.

Now I was beginning to worry.

EIGHT

There was no queue at the Air Europa ticket desk; a pleasant surprise. The clerk was a charming-looking kid with a gold tooth in his smile. He asked if he could help me.

'Can I book a seat on the next flight to Paris?'

He looked down at his computer screen and tapped away. He tapped away for quite a while. Finally, he looked up and glinted another smile. 'No. I'm afraid not, sir.'

'It's full?'

'I don't know.'

'You don't know if it's full?'

'No.'

'Well, can you check for me?'

He sighed, looked back down at his screen and tapped away again. He shook his head. 'No.'

'No, it's not full?'

'No, I can't check for you whether it's full or not.'

'Is the computer down?'

'I don't think so.'

'Then why can't you check?'

His eyes flitted from side to side, then back in my direction. 'I don't know how to do that, sir.'

'You don't know how to do that?'

He shook his head sadly. 'I haven't got a clue.'

'Didn't they train you how to do that?'

'They tried, sir, but I didn't listen too good.'

'You didn't listen?'

'It was pretty boring. And I have attention-deficit issues.'

Attention-deficit issues. Super. 'Well, can you book me a seat, anyway?'

'No. I don't know how to do that, either.' He looked forlorn. I got the feeling he really wanted to help me.

'Look, try typing in the flight number.'

He brightened. 'OK. Yeah. That might work.' He tapped away at the keypad enthusiastically. He tapped away for an awfully long time. Then he stared at the screen. 'No. This is getting us nowhere.'

I gave him a genuine smile. 'You don't know the flight number, do you?'

'Not really, no.'

I tried not to sigh. Exasperation wasn't going to help here. 'Try EA 599.'

He tried EA 599. His eyes widened in childlike glee. 'Ye-es! Will you look at that? It's, like, a picture of the inside of a plane, with all the little seats and everything. That's amazing. How do they do that?'

'So, there are seats available?'

'I have no idea.'

'Do any of the seats have little Xs on them?'

'No.'

'Any mark at all?'

'Some of them have little red circles. Is that any use?'

'I'm guessing the ones with little red circles are booked.'

'That would make sense, yes.'

'So, are there any seats that *don't* have little red circles?'

'Yes. There's a whole bunch of them.'

'OK. Can I book one of those, then?'

'Ha! I don't see why not. I'm on a streak, here.'

'That's terrific, son.' I reached for my wallet. 'How much will that be?'

'That'll be twenty-five euros.'

'Twenty-five euros? That's all?'

'You think that sounds too cheap?'

'Way too cheap.'

'All righty. Let's say . . . two hundred and fifty.'

'Wait a minute. What are you doing? You're just making the price up?'

'Is that bad?'

'Look, just click on a seat on the screen and see what happens.'

The kid fiddled with his stylus. He looked up from the screen with real admiration. 'Have you ever worked at Air Europa?'

'No. I can't say I have.'

'Another airline then?'

I shook my head. 'Never worked for any kind of airline.'

'Then you are some kind of fucking *genius*, mister. Lookee here. Price: one hundred and twenty euros. Just one little click, and thar she blows.'

I held out a credit card. 'I'll take it.'

The kid was still transfixed on his screen, head nodding, his tongue pressed into his cheek, like he'd just found the elixir of youth, the philosopher's stone and an infallible method of turning base metal into gold all in the same moment. I looked up at the departures monitor. Flight AE 599 was flashing 'GO TO GATE'. I leaned further over the desk. 'We'd better get a move on, son. They're practically boarding.'

'Right, right.' He looked at the card in my hand. 'What's that?'

'It's . . . it's a credit card.'

'Right, right.' He took the card and examined it. 'This is great. Look, it's got like a little hologram here. See?' He held the card up for me to see.

I tried to sound equally enthused. 'It's amazing, isn't it?'

'Amazing. You said it.' He twisted the card around twice and gleamed his winningest grin. 'What's it for?'

'The hologram? I don't know. Prevent fraud, I guess.'

'No, I mean the card. What's it do?'

'Like I said, it's a credit card.'

'Oh, right. I see.' He didn't see, of course. He just stood

there swivelling the card over and over, as if the speed of the twist might somehow reveal its arcane secret. 'It doesn't have any, like, instructions or anything.'

I resisted a very strong urge to invert the kid, debag him and run my MasterCard up and down his rectal chasm till his backside got magnetic. My chances of catching flight AE 599 were starting to look skimpier than a Chinese pudding menu. 'It's like money, sonny.'

Suspicious: 'Yeah?'

'You keep the card, I get the plane seat. Understand?'

'I knew that,' he glimmered. 'What am I? An idiot?'

He popped the card in his cash drawer, and sparkled: 'Have a nice flight.'

'The ticket?'

'The ticket! Of course.' He remained immobile, his mouth set in a 'Go away' twinkle.

'I need a plane ticket.'

'A plane ticket. Sure.' Still glimmering. Still no attempt to move.

'To get on the plane?'

'Absolutely. I've seen one of those. Let me just dig it out for you.'

He retired through a doorway at the back of the booth, and, for reasons unclear to me right now, I let him. He was gone for five full minutes before I realised he'd probably found something else to engage his fickle attention. I walked around the counter and ducked my head through the door. There was just an empty office. It was certainly bereft of teenagers with metallic dental work.

I turned back to the counter with the intent of recovering my credit card and maybe trying to run off a ticket for myself, but a strangely pretty, small woman in a stiff Air Bali uniform and an unreasonably sturdy hair sculpture with a pillbox hat somehow balanced atop it skittered over from her desk and started pounding my back with small, yet painfully bony fists, all the while badgering me in a ribald mixture of squeaky English and some unpleasant, unknowable tongue to kindly leave the ticket enclosure without delay, so I had to forget the notion of running off my own ticket, though the machine looked simple enough for a lotopomised chimp to operate.

The departures monitor was flashing 'NOW BOARDING' for AE 599, and I had no option but to hightail it down to the gate and pray, beyond reasonable expectation, that I might bluff or even charm my way onto the plane. Abandoning, with equal regret, both my credit card and the tiny, bellicose stewardess, I started towards Departures.

You know how I feel about having to hurry, but I had to get this plane to stand any chance of getting some kind of a jump on Klingferm's killer. But I wasn't going to run. I don't do running. Let's just say I walked energetically and with vigour.

NINE

Even though the clock was against me, I was forced to spend a few minutes lurking around outside Departures check-in, waiting for a suitably large party to mingle with. It was worth it. I managed to breeze through the ticket check amidst an alpine snowboarding team with just my passport, an empty discarded boarding-card holder, and a swagger that suggested I was some kind of bodyguard.

Getting through Security and Passport Control were simple enough. Just a small delay when my cotton shoelaces managed to set off the metal detector, prompting an all-over body search no more humiliating than undergoing haemorrhoid surgery in public. Though, thankfully, it stopped short of my cavities.

Actually getting to Gate 15 was more of a challenge.

Gate 15 was a long way away. I was working up quite a glow by the time I hit the fifth moving walkway, which, like precisely seventy-five per cent of the ones that preceded it, was in fact a static walkway. Misleadingly optimistic signs regularly indicated that I actually was on my way to Gate 15, and not, say, some hitherto uncharted region of Tibet or the dark side of the planet Mercury.

En route, I passed the lad from the Air Europa ticket desk playing a video game and chomping a sandwich. He caught my eye and looked as if I were someone he kind of half remembered, maybe from some long-ago childhood dream or something. Then a sound from the game machine caught his attention, and he bent back to wreaking his electronic mayhem.

The tannoy announced the final call for AE 599 to Paris. I

seriously considered breaking into a waddle. I began to worry that Gate 15 wasn't in Roma airport after all, but somewhere around the perimeter of Naples airport. Or Verona. Or even Heathrow Terminal Nine.

I was gravely close to a pulmonary embolism by the time the gates hove into view. For mysterious reasons, Gate 15 was the furthest away from civilisation. Gates 24 to 40 were much, much closer. The relentless pattern on the airport carpets was starting to induce some kind of hallucinogenic episode by the time I was able to stop and catch my breath. Amazing. What sort of planning genius thought it would be a neat idea to make the journey from the check-in to the plane longer than the actual flight? Still, it hadn't worked against me: a lot of passengers were still queuing, most of them wiping away tears of exhaustion.

I had been so convinced of the non-existence of Gate 15, I arrived without a ticket or a coherent plan to acquire one. No big deal: I'm good at thinking on my feet. I scoped out the two stewardesses checking people through the gate. The senior one had *Obergruppenführer* written all over her. Impeccable uniform. Starch in her collar and starch in her spine. My guess? She'd rather give a Mexican agave cactus deep throat than allow me to buy a ticket from her desk. The other one was the better bet: a slightly frazzled-looking redhead with a plastic smile that looked close to its use-by date. She wasn't the type to sell me a ticket either, but she might succumb to a little mental torture.

I needed some props. I'd spotted a print-your-own-business-card machine just by the coffee counter round the last corner. I put in my money and typed out a message:

THIS MAN HAS NO SHORT-TERM MEMORY.
PLEASE TRY NOT TO CONFUSE HIM.

I added a spurious doctor's name, with some convincingly medical letters after it, and finished with 'BRITISH MEDICAL COUNCIL' in brackets.

The machine churned out a dozen cards. I signed them all illegibly and stuffed them into my wallet. I adopted a suitably vacant expression and strolled up to the gate.

Frazzled redhead asked for my ticket and cranked up the plastic smile. I handed her my empty boarding-card packet, and smiled right back.

'There's no ticket in here, sir.'

'I'm sorry?'

'This is empty, sir. There's no ticket in it.'

'Didn't I just *give* you my ticket?'

'No. You just gave me an empty boarding-card holder.'

'Wait a minute.' I slapped all my pockets, dug out my wallet and handed her one of the cards. 'I think this will help.'

She read the card slowly. 'You have no short-term memory,' she repeated, quietly. 'Well, that must be . . . That must be very trying for you, sir.' She handed the card back to me. 'But I'm afraid I can't let you on the plane without a ticket or a boarding card.'

I studied the card and looked up sympathetically. 'You have no short-term memory? That must get very confusing.' I handed the card back to her. 'Especially in your line of work.'

'No, no.' She pushed the card gently into my jacket pocket. '*You're* the one with no short-term memory, sir.'

'I am?'

'If you can just retrace your steps, sir, I'm sure you'll find your ticket.'

'Didn't I just give you my ticket?'

'No, just an empty boarding card. If you can just stand aside while I –'

'Here it is!' I smiled broadly and handed her the empty boarding-card holder again.

'No. Look: you've lost your ticket. It's fallen out of here, see? You're going to have to try and find it, or you can't get on the plane.'

'Wait. Wait.' I hunted through my pockets again and handed her another of the business cards. 'I'm sure this will clear things up.'

The plastic smile was wearing thinner than the elbows of a geography teacher's jacket. She took a deep breath and tried again. 'I know about your problem, sir. Unfortunately, I still can't let you on the plane. Look . . .' She placed her hands gently on my shoulders and steered me away from the gate. 'If you just retrace your steps, you'll find where you dropped your ticket.'

'Retrace my steps?' I looked appropriately bewildered. 'Which way did I come from?'

'You must have come in this direction. Did you buy anything from the duty-free shops?'

'I have no idea.'

'That's probably where you lost your ticket.'

'Thank you.' I gave her my most genuine smile. 'You've been very helpful.'

'You're welcome, sir.'

'Especially considering your mental problem, and all.'

She smiled and wiggled back to her desk, her eyes doubtless cast up to the ceiling. She really thought she'd seen the last of me, the poor fool. I gave her a minute or two, then rejoined the queue. Commendably, her smile hardly quivered at all when she spotted me. 'So, you found your ticket, then?'

'Sorry?'

'You managed to find the ticket you lost?'

'I lost a ticket?'

Her smile was shrinking in on itself. 'Can I see your ticket, sir?'

'Right here.' I handed over the empty boarding-card holder.

'No.' Strangled dramatic sigh. 'This is still empty.'

'I'm sorry, I'm confused.' I started patting my pockets again and took out another business card.

'No, no. I know about your memory problem.' Her smile had now shrivelled into a very tight, puckered circle.

'What memory problem?'

She was a patient gal, I'll give her that. It took three more trips up the airport concourse and back to her queue before the smile finally collapsed in on itself like a neutron star, she lost the will to live and decided her life would be infinitely more enjoyable if she let me on the plane.

Now, you know my general feelings about air travel. Business class is just about almost nearly tolerable, so long as you don't weaken and try reading the in-flight magazine, or succumb to watching a movie with the interesting bits excised and the expletives dubbed, so hardened terrorists who are quite prepared to blow up entire nations suddenly get sheepish about swearing and wind up yelling things like: 'Get down, you melon farmer!' So long as you don't give into the temptation of actually trying the food, get morbid thinking about sudden death from deep vein thrombosis or hijackers, and you can get through the trip without the humiliation of having to squeeze into the toddlers' shoebox they call a toilet, the experience is survivable. Just.

Economy class?

Forget about it.

The original slave ships to America had kinder living conditions below decks. Better service, too.

Of course, I didn't have a business class ticket. I didn't have any kind of ticket, so I snapped into my guaranteed upgrade ploy. I took two steps down the aisle past the unconvincing welcome grin of the steward, and fainted.

Now, the aisle was pretty narrow anyway, and I don't like to fall too hard, so it was a fairly slow-motion, theatrical kind of a faint, and I hit the sticky carpet without causing myself too much damage.

Here's how it works: the stewards want to get everybody in their seats, so they don't lose the plane's take-off slot. They can't have you blocking the way, but you're big, you're a dead weight, and they can't carry you too far without risking a hernia. So they lift you into the nearest seat, which happens to be business class. You tell them you'll be all right in a minute, but act all woozy. They don't want to risk giving you a heart attack by trying to force you back into the cattle truck. Shazam! You've got yourself a free upgrade.

Well, that's the plan, at least.

In the beginning, it seemed to be working like a charm. There were two stewards, one blond, one with a flat-top. They immediately snapped into headless chicken mode, shrieking at everyone to stay calm, barking orders at each other and running up and down the plane like the Keystone Kops with firecrackers in their underpants, looking for the non-existent medical kit which is, of course, a compulsory requirement for airworthiness, before blond mop, the slightly more together of the two, mustered the wherewithal to raise my head and check whether or not I was still actually alive. He opened my right eye with his fingers. I rolled it back so only the white was visible and moaned softly.

Flat-top asked: 'Is he alive?'

'I think so.'

'Because I'm trained to administer CPU.'

'I think we should loosen his clothes.'

'If it's a heart attack, I can resuscitate him.'

'We should loosen his clothes and keep him warm.'

'How can we loosen his clothes *and* keep him warm, you silly tart?'

'Well, loosen his tie at least. That's not going to bring on a terminal chill, is it? Unbutton his collar.'

'Why? Isn't he breathing? If he isn't breathing, I should try cardiac massage.'

This flat-top guy sounded all too keen to start pounding my chest, which I was in no mood for, let me tell you. Time to stage my recuperation. 'I'm OK,' I croaked weakly. 'I just need to sit . . .'

But Blondie the clothes-loosener had grabbed my tie, and

in a panicky attempt to unfasten it he'd tugged it tighter than a pygmy's noose. I started choking. I flailed at my neck, trying to slap his hands away.

'He's going!' he screamed. 'We're losing him!'

I felt a crushing weight on my chest, followed by a massive bolt of pain in the middle of my ribs. For a terrible second, I really did think I was having a coronary. I strained to raise my head and saw, with bulging eyes, the CPU genius kneeling on me, his hands clenched and raised above his head, poised to administer another dreadful blow.

'Look at him,' the tie-tightener screamed. 'He's gone all purple.'

'I'm fine,' I rasped, sounding anything but, through my tightened, mashed windpipe. 'It's not a heart att –'

Bam! The flat-topped bastard brought down his fists, missing my ribs completely, but hitting my solar plexus dead centre. Simultaneously, I lost three things: all the air in my body, the ability to breathe, and the will to live. My head rolled back involuntarily.

Somewhere, a long way away, I heard Blondie squealing: 'He's going, Freddie. You're losing him.'

I began to believe him. I had visions of being CPU-ed to death. A hail of inept blows shattering my ribcage, puncturing my lungs. Breathing my last on a terribly designed Air Europa nylon carpet. My accidental murderer congratulated for trying his best to save me. Maybe even receiving some kind of award or something. And the worst of it was, I couldn't work up the enthusiasm to care.

Bam! He hammered me again, this time a bullseye in the middle of my ribs. By sheer dumb luck, the blow actually did have the effect of forcing air into my lungs. I grabbed at my tie and tugged the knot loose with demented strength.

I sucked in the sweet, sweet air.

'You've done it!' the blond one trilled. 'You've gone and saved his bloody life, you bloody genius.'

I propped myself up on my elbows and looked around.

The entire plane applauded. Passengers started congratulating Freddie Flat-Top, the life-saving genius, shaking his hand, patting him on his back. If there'd been room enough, they'd have raised him on their shoulders and given him a ticker-tape parade.

'Please, please.' He was grinning. 'It's all part of the training.' He bent over me. 'And how's the patient?'

I nodded, and grunted: 'I'll live.' I wasn't going to thank the son of a bitch.

'That's a relief. For one terrible moment there, I thought I'd have to give you mouth-to-mouth,' he grinned again, 'and I've forgotten me lipstick.'

The entire plane laughed. All except for one of us.

I moaned, and rubbed my throbbing chest gingerly, wondering just how many wonderful shades of purple and yellow my ribs would be when I eventually worked up the courage to actually look at them, and mumbled weakly: 'Just get me to a chair.'

Blondie and Freddie hoisted me up and dumped me in the nearest available seat, which, joy of joys, turned out to be business class accommodation.

So, I got my upgrade, for what it was worth. It seemed like an awful lot of pain and effort for ten centimetres more legroom and a different-coloured seat.

I put on the Lone Ranger sleeping mask the airline provided and jammed the yellow earplugs home, though I harboured no illusions that I might actually get any sleep.

I spent the entire flight worrying away at just how far I was behind Klingferm's killer.

I really would have been better employed worrying just how far Klingferm's killer was behind me.

TEN

I began to suspect something was horribly wrong as soon as I reached the hotel door: it opened with a single swipe of the keycard. I stood there for a few moments, a little dazed, examining the card and the lock. I even contemplated closing the door and trying the card again, just in case it had opened accidentally, or the door hadn't been properly shut in the first place, but I decided not to push my luck. I stepped inside, and braced myself for the worst.

The suite was fine. More than fine: it had actually been cleaned in very recent history, and it smelled, well, nice. There were fresh flowers in a vase on the table, and a welcome basket with fresh fruit in it. I peeked cautiously inside the TV cabinet. Bizarrely, there was a TV in there. I flicked it on and hunted through the channels. The reception was superb. Some of the programmes were even in English. Underneath the TV, there was a refrigerated minibar. With a barely credible flourish of luxury, there were actually drinks inside it.

I popped out a malt whisky – my nerves needed steadying – and found, to my horror, the ice tray contained cubes of ice. Really. Ice that was actually frozen. I dropped three into the worryingly clean glass and sucked a generous draught, steeling myself for the bedroom.

Cautiously, I pushed open the bedroom door and sneaked a quick peek around it. It looked like there was actually a bed in there. I craned around the door again. Yes. Indeed a bed. A big bed, too, with clean linen on it.

I took another slug and strolled over to the lounge

window. There was a breathtaking view of the city. I scanned the whole area, and could not see a single construction site.

Whatever was wrong with the room – and something surely *had* to be wrong with the room – it wasn't immediately obvious to the naked eye. Perhaps it was located directly over some all-night thrash garage rave party venue. Perhaps the river flooded it regularly at high tide. Perhaps it was directly on an air-force flight path, and fighter jets would come screaming through the bedroom window, break the sound barrier over the bed, then carom out through the bathroom all night long.

I went back to the entrance and checked the number on my keycard holder against the numbers on the door again. They still matched.

I took off my jacket and gingerly opened the cupboard by the front door. Surely it wouldn't be a functional wardrobe. Surely there wouldn't be clothes hangers in there. In fact, wouldn't there be a body in the cupboard, at least one, all nice and stabbed and ready to slump into my unsuspecting arms, so I could inadvertently clasp the dagger that was buried in its back, just in time for the homicide detective who was doubtless lurking outside to burst in and catch me in flagrante?

I braced myself and tugged.

But no. No bodies at all. Nary a one. And coat hangers aplenty. There was even a generous bathrobe that looked like it might actually accommodate my entire body comfortably. Worst of all, and you'd better sit down for this one, people: there, at the bottom of the wardrobe, was a suitcase.

My suitcase.

My long-lost suitcase. With my long-lost clothes in it.

With trembling hands, I lifted it up, carried it to the bedroom, and set it on the bed.

The locks had been removed, naturally, by some customs officer with all the artful skill and grace of one of the clumsier lower primates, but my clothes were there. Almost all of them. A pair of shoes, too. My shoes, that fit me. Leather shoes. With the soles attached. And there were socks. Clean socks. I don't want to talk about what was left of the socks I was standing up in. That's Stephen King country.

By now, my nerves were set completely on edge. I drained the whisky and headed for the bathroom. As my hand reached down for the handle, I froze. I could hear running water. I put my ear to the door. Yes. The shower was running. And somebody was humming, very softly.

I stepped my senses down from Def Com Three. That's what was wrong with the room: it was double booked. All was right with the world again.

The shower stopped. I strolled over to the minibar and took out another whisky miniature. I settled back into the unfeasibly comfortable armchair and waited.

I didn't have to wait long. The bathroom door opened and a woman stepped through.

I say 'woman', but that hardly does justice to the apotheosis of femininity that padded into my room wearing only a man's shirt – completely unbuttoned, mind – and a pair of ghostly underpants that redefined the word 'skimpy'. You could have had a long philosophical debate about whether or not they actually existed at all. They seemed to be hovering in some barely visible reality, halfway between this world and the next.

Now, a man reaches a certain age, and pretty much all women start to look beautiful. Whether that's because your standards get lower, or because the scales actually do fall from your eyes is a moot point. But this woman was a heart-stopper by any measure. You could have employed her in an abattoir as a humane method of stunning animals before slaughter, and, trust me, they'd have died happy. You could have stood this woman in a queue at a bank, then robbed the vaults, picked all the tellers' pockets and staged an impromptu performance of Wagner's Ring Trilogy without even the closed-circuit cameras noticing you.

She had long copper hair that cascaded over the right side of her face like a waterfall of molten bronze and danced on her shoulder in laughing ringlets of pure silk. The shirt – my shirt! – fell teasingly open, to show just enough of the gentle swell of the underside of a perfect breast to make me want to run away immediately and join the Foreign Legion. I wanted to measure that breast. I wanted to weigh it. I wanted to paint a face on it and make it my new best friend. I wanted it with me everywhere. I wanted us to grow old together, me and that breast. And then I wanted it to be buried with me. It was perfection, pure and simple.

And yet, compared to her stomach, it was nothing. Now, it's been a goodly while since I had anything remotely resembling a six-pack of my own and a tightly packed female stomach has long been an object of insane desirability for me, but this belly was ludicrously beautiful. Tight skin stretched over racks of abdominal muscles so firm, you could have taken a thimble and played them like a washboard in a skiffle band. Sammy Davis Junior could have tap danced on that stomach. You could have fitted wheels to her back and used her as a skateboard.

Not that I looked too hard, you understand. As soon as I realised I was staring, I looked away immediately. How long my gaze had lingered was anybody's guess. It could have been a matter of seconds, or it could have been hours or even days, for all I knew.

Certainly, it had been long enough for drool to dry in the corner of my mouth. I took a thick slug of whisky to wash it away.

She spoke. Yes, she could speak, too. What a gal. 'I hope you don't mind my using your shower.'

Ye gods. She used a gerund. If there's anything in God's good heaven more erotic than a beautiful woman who can parse a sentence correctly, then whisk me up there, angelic host; take me now. Myself, I didn't reckon I'd be quite capable of speech, just for a year or so. I gave her a cool smile and the tiniest shake of my head. I was trying to remember which was my better side, so I could somehow point myself towards her at my least unattractive angle. Don't misunderstand me, I had no illusions that this . . . this vision, this Helen, this Venus would entertain for a nanosecond the remotest prospect of anything mildly resembling a kind of romantic entanglement with a piece of flabby filth like myself, but I was keen, schoolboy keen, to have her think as well of me as possible.

She smiled with a set of teeth that really belonged under bullet-proof glass right in the centre of the Louvre, with their own set of lights permanently trained on them. 'You're terribly sweet. I wonder if I could beg another favour of you?'

Could she beg a favour of me? Seriously? I would have sawn my mother's arms off without anaesthetic and mailed them to her first class if she'd asked for a back scratcher.

She turned her back to me and hitched up her shirt – my shirt! Did it look that good on me? – so that the rear of her ephemeral thong was in full view, guarded either side by hummocks of flesh so completely round and taut that just the tiniest amount of dedicated buffing would have turned them into perfect pink crystal balls. I would have gladly signed away my own soul, and the soul of everybody I'd ever met to Mephistopheles himself, just to be able to squeeze them together for fifteen seconds. From now on, that's all I would ever want in life.

My head was thrumming. She looked over her shoulder and with a little flick of her hair, she said: 'My thong seems to have got caught up my bottom. I wonder if you could . . . ease it out for me?'

Well, it would have been ungentlemanly of me to refuse, don't you think? The poor girl was obviously in discomfort. She'd turned her head back to face the wall, and was standing on her tiptoes, shifting her weight from side to side. I grunted, not a grunt of acquiescence, you understand, just an involuntary animal grunt, drawn up from the depths of my oldest ancestral memories.

The problem was, I wasn't sure if I could stand up. I had a swelling in my trousers you could use to roll pizza dough. I took a final swirl of whisky and started to edge myself out of the chair. I put my glass down where I thought the table was. It thudded to the ground and rolled under the minibar. I stood, as best I could, and slouched slowly over to her. I had to slouch, so my penis didn't reach her an hour or two before the rest of me. I really was dizzy. I ran my finger around my shirt collar, partly to release the heat that had built up inside there, and partly to check the digit was still working correctly, and wouldn't fail me in what would surely be its finest hour.

When I was just an arm's length away from those perfect orbs, reaching out slowly, oh so slowly, for the thin strip of ghostly material buried in that divine canyon of pert flesh, she turned her head again suddenly, so a curled whip of copper flails fell over her cheek. Her sweet breath caressed my face as she said, in a throaty groan so thick and liquid, it might have been made out of maple syrup: 'With your tongue, big boy.'

I think I must have grunted again. Certainly, there was some sound from somewhere around my throat that might have come from a hibernating bear. My entire body seemed to be engorged with blood. Thick, sticky blood, too. It was no longer running through my veins; it just sat there, pulsing wetly, thudding in my temples, in long, globular queues, unable to pass through the melted lump that used to be my brain.

Alarm bells should have been going off, but I couldn't hear them. Frankly, I'd have ignored them anyway. If there was a price to pay for this, so what? I lowered myself slowly to my knees, not only to stretch the moment and savour the anticipation, but I was half afraid if I went down too quickly,

I'd get the bends and faint dead away on the brink of this, my greatest sexual triumph.

I was eye to eye, now, with the twin moons, and close enough to feel their heat flowing over my cheeks. I swallowed as best I could, then reached out my tongue and hooked it under the vee at the nape of her wraithy thong. My eyes glutted themselves on the curve of the silken band that dug into the flesh of her waist and disappeared over the top of her sculpted hip bone. I dragged my tongue down slowly, excavating the flimsy material from its heavenly channel, unable to differentiate between the smoothness of the silk and the satin softness of her supple skin.

And down I went.

And down.

And round.

And just as the scent of her was intoxicating what was left of my mind, just before my train pulled in at Paradise Central, she gave a little shimmy and stepped to one side, so the thong snapped back into place, leaving me on my knees with my tongue hanging out and drool dribbling down my chin like the miserable, wretched dog I truly was.

'Thanks for that. You're awfully sweet.'

You know, the human tongue must be made of erectile material. Certainly, mine seemed massively engorged, and I couldn't quite work out how it was supposed to fit back in my mouth. Strange, there'd always seemed to be room for it in there before. I tried to say that the lady was welcome, but I'm guessing I sounded like Charles Laughton after the whipping in *Hunchback*. I really found myself hoping her name wasn't Esmeralda.

'Mind if I fix myself a drink?'

I shook my head, mumbled something like 'Esthbuthe be' and without looking back, staggered into the bathroom as quick as I could, trying not to look like a gut shot cowboy, but doubtless coming up short.

I shut the door behind me, and tried to remember how to

breathe. In and out, wasn't it? Or was it out and out? Or in and in? I finally worked out something close to the correct combination, sucked and blew a few big ones, then ran a sink full of cold water and dunked my head in.

I stayed under a long time. Long enough for my brain to stop glowing like a plutonium fuel rod in a drained coolant tank. When I was finally happy I no longer constituted a major nuclear threat to the city of Paris and its environs, I emerged and stuffed my face into a thick, fluffy and, yes, warm towel.

What was that woman doing here?

She *was* here, wasn't she? This wasn't one of my crueller, more tormentory erotic dreams was it?

I clicked open the bathroom door and peeked. She was there all right, bent over the minibar in a primally provocative L shape, her long, straight legs doing their long, straight magic thing. I clicked the door closed.

OK.

She had to be real. I wasn't this good at dreaming.

There were several possibilities that ran through my fevered mind, none of which seemed good. She could have been a hooker – a very high-class hooker, granted – who'd somehow got the wrong room. That would have been disappointing, but not the end of the world, so long as she didn't discover her mistake and try to correct it anytime soon. She might be some kind of undercover assassin who liked to toy with her victims before offing them. Again, not great, but I could live with that, even if only for a short while. Let's face it, there are many, many worse ways to go, and I've almost tried them all. She was a crazed, man-hating serial killer who'd escaped from some kind of high-security mental institution, and was about to dismember me bloodily and brutally with the hotel fire axe. Likewise, fine with me, so long as I got to squeeze her buttock cheeks really firmly while she was swinging away with her chopper. Or, and this, to my shame, seemed the most likely and desirable alternative of all:

she was a plant, sent by Johnny Appleseed himself, no less, to divert me while he wreaked more of his mayhem. Possibly while he even sneaked up behind me and did away with me himself. If so, good plan, Mr Appleseed. Excellent plan. I'll bet it works.

I freshened up with the entire contents of the astonishingly well stocked bathroom cabinet and, smelling like a perfume fight in a whorehouse, went into the lounge to discover my fate.

She was curled on the sofa, sipping at a highball. I checked as discreetly as possible, but I couldn't see a fire axe anywhere within her reach.

I decided to drag up the armchair and sit opposite her. The view was better.

She smiled and ran her finger round the rim of the highball glass. 'Well, Mr Salt, how do you like your room?'

Mr Salt, eh? Well, that narrowed things down. It definitely eliminated the mistaken identity option, and cast serious doubts on the psychopathic escapee alternative. So: undercover assassin or honey trap?

'I like the room plenty. I'm practically in love with the room, truth be told. I'm seriously considering buying the hotel just so I can be in this room whenever I want. I hope, one day, to retire to this room and serve out my dotage in it. That's how much I like the room.'

'So that would be . . .' She raised her buttocks and reached under. What was coming up? The old ice pick? A serrated hunting knife? No. She produced a clipboard. 'A plus?' She raised her eyebrows and shot me right between the eyes with that Louvre smile.

'A plus?'

'You'd rate the room "A plus"?'

'Certainly, I'd rate the room "A plus". I'd rate the room "A double plus", lady. "A triple plus", if that's an option. How many plusses are we legally allowed, here?'

She made a tick. Somehow, she made it erotically. 'And the . . .' lick of the lips '. . . facilities?'

'The facilities? Are you included in the facilities?'

That smile again. ''Fraid not, sirrah.'

'Then that's just a straight triple A. Were you included, we'd have to put our heads together and come up with an entire new classification scale, you and I, because they haven't yet created enough As to come close to conveying that rating.'

'Oh – I borrowed your shirt.'

'Really? I'd hardly noticed.'

'I hope you don't mind?'

'Mind? No. The shirt needed it. It's having the time of its life. However, if you'd care to return it once you're through, I would like to spend the rest of eternity pressing it to my face.'

'Cleanliness?'

'Isn't that next to Godliness? I've never been to either.'

'The cleanliness of the room?'

'Look, I'm happy with this hotel. I'm happy with this hotel like I'm seven years old and it's Christmas Day, and somebody gave me this hotel as a stocking filler. Why don't you just put down a whole bunch of As and plusses, then we can get this paperwork out of the way, and try and find an even more interesting way of whittling away at the afternoon.'

'Just one last question?'

'Shoot.'

'How do you rate your welcome?'

'My welcome? Is this the part that includes you?'

She nodded. 'That's my job: I'm guest liaison. I do the welcoming.'

This was a genuine questionnaire? I still thought we were flirting elaborately. 'You do it good. What can I say? You're a world-class liaiser. You welcome to Olympic standard and beyond.'

'Right. You don't think I'm . . . a little over the top?'

'Over the top?'

'Perhaps a little bit too . . . I don't know . . . flirtatious?'

'Flirtatious? What on earth can you be meaning?'

'Well, the whole getting naked and flashing my body and wearing your shirt and asking you to adjust my netherwear with your tongue kind of thing?'

'I *enjoyed* adjusting your netherwear with my tongue. And the shirt and the nakedness? I wouldn't call it flirtatious, no.'

'Well, let me tell you, Mr Salt. Some people do. Some people make complaints about it.'

'They do?'

'They do.'

'You welcome everyone this way . . . I'm sorry, I don't know your name. I know what your buttocks taste like, but I don't know your name.'

'Gina. Gina Pallister.'

'You welcome everyone so warmly, Gina?'

'No, of course not. Not couples. Not women.'

'Of course not.'

'Not unless they specifically register as lesbians.'

'But single men?'

She nodded.

'And lesbians?'

She nodded again. 'Do you think that's wrong?'

'For me, Gina, you could never do anything wrong.'

'I can never judge, you see. I have this Sexually Inappropriate Response thing. There's a little bit of my silly little brain that doesn't kick in when I'm being overfamiliar.'

She was SIR. That's one my mental bookmaker didn't give me odds on.

'You know and I know there's nothing small or silly about your brain, Coppertop.'

'Did they grow you in bunches, Mr Salt? Only I could use a whole bouquet of you and that silver tongue of yours.'

'Well, you won't be getting any complaints from me, Ms Pallister.'

'Honestly?'

'Nuh-huh. I'm going to write a personal letter to the hotel manager with a glowing report on the welcome you gave me. Believe me, it will glow like it's made of uranium.'

'Great. Great. But you won't mention the nakedness?'

'I won't mention the nakedness. I won't mention the nakedness and I won't mention the netherwear licking.'

'Thanks Mr Salt. You're a straight shooter. 'Cause, truth be told, the nasty old managerooni's about a gnat's foreskin away from firing me.'

'He'd have to be crazy.'

She rose. She rose like Venus on the half shell. My shirt fell away from where it had dreamed of being since it was born and lay there on the sofa in a limp kind of post-coital ecstasy. 'I'd better get me gorn, pardner. Can I get my clothes from your bathroom?'

I nodded. I doubted I was capable of any other form of communication.

She clicked my bathroom door closed.

Eventually, I clicked my mouth closed.

By the time she emerged from my bathroom in her business suit, my voice was almost fully operational again. I have to tell you: she looked pretty damned fine. She looked almost as good in her own clothes as she did in mine. She smoothed down her skirt and held out her hand. 'It's been a pleasure, Mr Salt.'

I took her hand and shook it. 'All mine, Ms Pallister.'

'If there's anything I can help you with during your stay . . .'

'There are two things you can help me with, Coppertop: one, you can call me Harry.'

That smile. 'And the second?'

'You could see me for dinner tonight.'

'I'm sorry, Harry.' Hey – it wasn't a slap in the face, which

I'd been braced for, and it wasn't a final, out and out rejection, neither: she didn't look away from me, she kept her eyes steady on mine, which meant I had manoeuvring room. 'I can't say I haven't taken to you; you're sharp, and you don't like yourself so much you've got no like left over for someone else. That's a rare thing in the male of the species where I've been finding 'em. But the fact is, I like my job, and nasty old manager man comes down distinctly unambiguous about the consequences of carousing with the guests.'

'I'll move hotels.'

'There's a bar across the street. Eight thirty?'

'I couldn't possibly wait that long. Eight twenty-nine?'

'I'll be there, you impetuous fool.'

ELEVEN

I know what you're thinking. You're thinking all I cared about was the inappropriate sexual response thing. You're thinking I was planning to take advantage of that beautiful girl's over-friendly nature, but that's not true. That's not even part of it. I was smitten. Old Harry Salt finally got the thunderbolt.

See, I have my own rule about carousing; just the one: don't do it. No, not and never. Not under any circumstances. That's Salt's First Law. No exceptions. No by-laws, no loopholes, no excuses. There are a million reasons why, and you can probably imagine most of them. I have a hell of a business just looking after myself, as you may have spotted. But I just couldn't not, this time. I couldn't even think that she'd walk out of that hotel room, and I'd never in my life see her again. That was the very definition of unthinkable.

And did I feel bad? Did I feel bad that I was about to break my one, inviolable law, as I lay there bubbling away in the ridiculously superb comfort of the jacuzzi hot tub?

Yeah, I felt bad. I felt awful, with my cheeks aching from the insanely wide idiot grin that had encamped itself on my face with the relentless determination of Agamemnon's boys outside Troy. I was singing opera, for crying out loud. I don't even *like* opera. I didn't even know I *knew* any opera.

I had a date. I might as well have been fourteen years old. In fact, mentally, I would probably have rated less than half that. And I still had business to attend to 'ere nightfall. I still had a killer to catch.

I scrubbed away until I was fairly sure my hands no longer

smelled of Roman bananas, doused my vocal cords with a gallon of brutal mouthwash and got dressed for business.

I can't tell you how good it was to slip my feet into clean, fresh socks and comfortable shoes. It was like wading in the river Jordan, my friend. It was like walking on a carpet made of angel wings.

I bundled up my old clothes and stuffed them into a hotel laundry bag. Here's a tip: if you ever go to the Hotel Ambassadeur in Paris, don't use the tongs from the ice bucket in room 777. I used them to handle my discarded socks – I didn't want to undo all the good I'd done myself in the jacuzzi by actually touching the toxic sons of bitches. I had it in mind to do all of Paris a favour by dumping the bag in the hotel's incinerator.

I scrubbed up pretty good, all things considered. As far as I could tell, I hardly smelled at all of rotten fruit or cheese, and there was only the faintest aroma of faecal material about me. In any case, I figured I'd have time for another couple of baths before the evening.

I was wrong.

I didn't wear the shirt that had adorned Gina. I didn't plan to ever wear it anymore. I planned to treat it like a favoured child. I planned to save up so I could put it through college.

I wrapped it up and laid it safe in the wardrobe.

I would never see that shirt again.

TWELVE

I have an apartment in Paris. Well, it's just a shell of a place, really. It's a bed with a room round it. I keep a couple of things there, including a key to a sports locker in a mid-town health spa.

I picked up the key and headed off to the spa.

You may think a health club locker is a fairly flimsy, pretty public spot to be storing anything of importance, but in my experience you're less likely to get anyone poking around a place like that looking for valuables. I've never had any problems with it.

Where I was going, a straightforward Europol detective shield probably wouldn't cut too much ice. The Fabrizi dinner party deaths had got a lot of press exposure. A lot of the victims were fairly high profile, from several different states, too, and chances were there might well be federal agents on the case already. So I picked out a PCID badge, which ought to do the trick.

Food crime takes up a lot of police resources in the United States of Europe. Food kills, my friend. Food crime is apparently the fifth biggest killer in the Union. The FC department handles not only the thousands of food poisoning and catering malpractice cases that occur every day, it's also responsible for enforcing all the food production and sale regulations, of which there are literally millions, and dozens more pour out of Brussels every day.

So, in most jurisdictions, the Food Crime department is big and well resourced, if not exactly garlanded with respect by other branches of law enforcement. It lacks the grit and glamour of Narcotics or Vice. Let's face it: few food criminals are likely to try blasting their way out of a catering bust with an AK-47 and a bandolier stuffed with grenades. The most exhilarating danger you're likely to face is a desperate greengrocer wielding an oversized leek with a disproportionate percentage of green in a threatening manner. Which tends to mean that senior FC officers feel undervalued, are permanently grumpy, and have a deserved reputation for throwing their weight around unnecessarily.

Which is why I decided to wear my PCID detective badge in plain view, dangling from my jacket pocket. Police Corruption Investigation Department. It's like a snowplough for bullshit when you're dealing with the rank and file. Nobody likes you, but you get their attention.

The departmental office was large, and thrumming. I reckoned there must have been about a hundred desks, most of them manned by report-typing, phone-call-making, suspect-interviewing food detectives. Two long ranks of glum-faced kitchen staff were seated morosely in the waiting area, identically dressed in their white smocks and caps, blue and white checked catering trousers and standard-issue cooking clogs, waiting their turn for interrogation. I picked a desk whose tenant seemed unoccupied by work. He was a young, plain-clothes officer: feet on the desk, gigantic sandwich in one hand, folded newspaper in the other.

'Hey, friend. Eating the evidence?' I made an ill-judged stab at humour.

'Say what?' he mumbled through half-chewed cheese and ham.

I should have let it drop, but I didn't. I grinned and nodded at his sandwich. 'Eating the evidence, I see.'

He tore his attention away from the newspaper, looked up and swallowed. 'What evidence?'

'The sandwich.' I smiled.

He looked at the sandwich in his hand. 'The sandwich is evidence?'

'I was making a dumb joke.' I shrugged. 'Listen, do you know where I can find—?'

He slid his feet off the desk. 'Are you saying this sandwich was involved in the commission of a crime?' Gingerly, he put the sandwich down on the greaseproof wrap on his desk as if he'd suddenly discovered it was spread with nitroglycerine.

'No, no. It was just a wisecrack.'

'Because, listen, I swear, I just bought this baguette from Henrie's. Round the corner. He makes a straight sandwich. All the cops use him.'

'No, look, seriously, I was kidding. Really.'

'So it's not an illegal sandwich?'

'No. As far as I can tell, that is an upstanding, law-abiding sandwich.'

'You were just joking about its legal status?'

'Can we forget about the sandwich now?

'What kind of a joke is that, buddy? To imply I'm eating a criminal sandwich?'

'It's a bad joke, I agree. I apologise.'

'Because you come here, I look up, you're PCI and for all I know, you're looking to bust me for felonious snacking, or some such.'

'We got off on the wrong foot here. Can we start again?'

'I mean, for Christ's sake: it's a cheese and ham baguette, is all.'

'One last time, son: there is nothing wrong with your sandwich.'

'Are you saying there's too much ham, or what? It's really a ham and cheese sandwich, not the other way around? Is that what you're saying?'

I wasn't getting through, now was I? 'Let me ask you a question.'

'A question? Am I going to need my union rep?'

'I don't think so. It's a very simple question.'

'Well, go ahead. But I reserve the right, and all that.'

'You ready for the question?'

'Fire away.'

'Are you stupid?'

'Yes, I am.' He hooked his finger in his shirt collar, tugged out an ID card dangling from a short, plastic chain around his neck, and thrust it towards me with what I could have sworn was pride. 'I'm registered NSS.'

I craned forward. He meant it, too. NSS. Non-Specific Stupidity. It was a fairly new catch-all categorisation for people who weren't classifiable under any of the acknowledged learning disorders or mentally diminishing diseases.

'NSS.' I nodded. 'I see. You're actually officially stupid.'

'Non-Specifically Stupid,' he corrected me. 'Wait a minute!' He held the card up to his face and studied it intently. 'That's wrong. It says SSN. What the fuck is SSN?'

'No.' I coughed quietly. 'The card is upside down from your point of view.'

He twisted the card, tightening the chain around his neck. He studied the inscription intensely. His face began to turn red, and veins started bulging on his temples. 'Right you are,' he concurred throatily, and released himself from his own choke hold. 'For a moment then,' he swallowed dryly, 'I thought I'd been reclassified. *That* could've screwed up my promotion prospects.'

'I wouldn't worry about that, kid. You'll probably make captain before the week's out.'

'Really?' The kid grinned. 'You've heard something?'

'I'm looking for the officer who headed up the Fabrizi investigation.'

'DSI Debary?'

'Him, yeah.'

'He in trouble?'

'Not yet, he isn't.'

'He should be in the squad room. They're tooling up for some big bust or some such. Captain, you say? You really think?'

'Trust me; it's in the bag.'

I patted the kid on the shoulder, thanked him and turned to go. He called me back.

'Hey! What should I do with the sandwich?'

I had some seriously interesting suggestions, but I kept them to myself. 'What do you think you should do with the sandwich?'

He inspected the sandwich at arm's length. 'I'm guessing I should send it down to the evidence lock-up.'

'Good plan.' I nodded tightly. 'Bag it and tag it, and lock it away.'

He opened his drawer and slammed a thick wad of paper and an evidence bag on the desk. 'Fucking paperwork,' he mumbled grimly. 'For a cheese and ham bag-fucking-uette.'

I left him filling out the forms.

Amazingly, the kid had got it right. Debary was in the squad room, briefing his team on the bust. The room was fairly packed, but my PCID badge bought me a seat at the back and a whole lifetime's worth of filthy looks. Thankfully, the briefing was almost over.

Clearly, news travelled fast. Debary dismissed the squad and strode straight up to me. 'I hear you're looking for me, cop fucker.' He swept past me, forcing me to follow in his wake at a fairly fierce stride. 'If this is about those Pascal girls, you're wasting your time.'

'I am?'

'Because my arse is covered, bud. They all three of them consented to have sex with me, one at a time and all together. Of their own free will. In writing. I still have the papers.'

'I'm sure you do, but that's not –'

'And their father's restaurant? That would have got a clean bill of health whether or not they slept with me. You can take that to the bank.'

'It's not about that. It's about the Fabrizi dinner party . . .'

'Fabrizi? What the hell's that got to do with PCI?'

'I'm afraid I can't go into that at this time.'

'Of course you can't. You people, you've got to sneak around. Like a carrion feeder.'

We swept into the gun dispensary. Debary ordered an armoured vest and a semi-automatic Glock, with five clips.

I couldn't help asking: 'You always go on restaurant raids armed?'

'We do now.' He checked out a magazine and chocked it into the gun. 'Ever since my sergeant lost a big chunk of his marrying meat to an overly excitable Chinese chef with a king-sized cleaver.' He snapped the magazine back into place. 'Wouldn't you?'

'Me? I wouldn't leave mine dangling.'

'You? You probably don't have much to dangle.' He holstered the weapon. 'OK. The Fabrizi thing: what about it?'

'I just want copies of the files, is all.'

'Again? What is it with this case? That guy from Homicide took the files less than a week ago.'

Less than a week? That was good news. I probably wasn't as far behind Klingferm's investigation as I'd feared. I smiled. 'Well, now *we* want the files. No rush. Absolutely immediately will be fine.'

'Hey, why would I care?' He took out a pad and started scribbling. 'Only, like I told Mr Homicide, you're wasting your time. The whole thing was just a gigantic screw-up. But I guess a couple of high-profile corpses in the headlines stirred up a big stink downtown.'

'You could say that.'

Debary tore off a sheet and handed it to me. 'They'll give you everything you want in Records.' He nodded down the corridor. 'Now, if you'll excuse me, I actually have some police work to do. You remember what that's like, don't you? You must have done some yourself way back when.' He smiled, all nasty like, and patted my shoulder just hard enough to hurt.

I smiled right back at him and returned the pat with interest. 'Thanks, Debary. Watch how you dangle, now; those

Pascal girls are going to need you fully equipped if it comes to an identity parade.'

I picked up the files from Records. I don't want to make that sound like an easy accomplishment, because the clerk in charge of the photocopier had lost both his hands, and his metal hooks shredded several of the files several times before I managed to secure a complete record. But, eventually, I picked up the files from Records, and headed for home.

On the way out, I passed Mr Non-Specifically Stupid at his desk, raking through his drawer. He had a bad-tempered guy in an apron sitting opposite him. I assumed this was poor old Henrie the sandwich maker. I called over: 'Nailed the bastard, eh?'

The kid looked up. 'Damn right.' He nodded. 'Only . . .' He held up his hands. They were manacled. 'I accidentally went and cuffed myself. You don't know where I keep the key, do you?'

Captain? The kid would probably make chief commissioner before sunset.

THIRTEEN

I flashed my gold detective badge at Path Lab Reception, and asked for Dr Rutter. He'd been in charge of the Fabrizi dinner party autopsies. A pretty nurse at Reception with a very bad stutter told me where I could find him. In less than ten minutes, too.

The main cutting rooms were three floors down, deep in the basement. I chose to take the stairs. I was developing a thing about elevators.

The lab was bright and large: there must have been fifty operating slabs spread out over the chamber, and most of them were occupied. It looked like the unexplained-death business was flourishing.

There was a sick-looking intern on a chair by the door. From the greenness of his pallor, I surmised that he'd just finished enjoying his first autopsy. He pointed out Dr Rutter, who was at a slab in the corner of the room, busy working away on some corpse or other. I approached him from behind, so we didn't have to conduct a conversation over some half dissected dead person with his entrails dangling out. Call me squeamish.

'Dr Rutter?'

He turned.

I flashed my badge again. 'Harry Tequila.'

'Nice to meet you, Detective Tequila.' He wiped his gloved hands ineffectually on his blood-smeared smock and offered me the right one to shake.

I satisfied myself with a simple nod of greeting. 'I'm just following up some leads on the Fabrizi case. I was wondering if I could pick your brains.'

'That's what I'm here for.' He smiled. He crossed to the sink and started to wash his hands without taking off his gloves.

'Listen, I don't want to interrupt your work . . .'

'Work?' He glanced over at the slab. 'No, that's not work. That's just a little project I'm working on, on the side. Hobby, really.'

I could see the little project in the corner of my eye. I didn't want to look too hard, but the little project was definitely a dead person who was having gory things done to his backside with a scalpel. Some hobby.

'Fabrizi . . .' Rutter mused. 'That was the poisoning thing, right?'

'That's right.'

'Awful business. Twenty-six corpses. What a nightmare. That was not pretty, let me tell you. They came here, they were covered in dried puke and cacka. I'm not kidding, *covered* in it. We couldn't even wash it off them – it was evidence, see?' He dried his hands on a paper towel and dropped it in a basket. 'This place stank to high heaven. We stank. Didn't matter how much we showered. My wife made me sleep on the sofa for a week. You want to see the bodies?'

I shook my head. 'Just wanted to look over the reports with you.'

He seemed disappointed. 'Sure, no problem. I keep the reports in my office. This way.'

He led me off across the room. An entire wall was divided into square compartments with handles on. Body booths. I was hoping we were going to go straight past them, but I didn't think it was a very realistic hope.

Predictably, Rutter stopped about halfway along. 'Listen, Detective: before we get to the reports, there's something here I want you to take a look at.' He walked along the bank, and started ducking and diving to read the labels.

I was busy steeling myself. I'd been here before. They always pull some stunt like this, forensic pathologists. Dig out the worst, most mutilated, stinking decomposed corpse they can lay their rubber gloves on and present it to you, dah dahhh! to see if you can keep your breakfast down. I've never been beaten yet, but it's not a game I enjoy.

'Here we go!' He found the drawer and laid his hand on the handle. 'This one came in a couple of days ago. I think you might find it interesting.'

He tugged at the drawer. It slid out easily on its smooth castors. He put his hand on the sheet that was draped over the body. 'It's a little out of the ordinary, so be prepared.'

I was as prepared as I was ever going to be. It was not prepared enough. He tugged the sheet right down, exposing the naked corpse all the way to its knees. 'Male, Caucasian, approximately eighty-three years of age, two seventy-two cm, a little under seventy kilos, cause of death: cardiac infarct.'

I couldn't believe what I was looking at.

He caught my expression and smiled. 'Never seen anything like that, huh?'

I shook my head, but my eyes never left the cadaver. 'Never.'

'You've spotted the anomaly then?'

'Yes.'

'Pretty easy to spot, I guess.'

'Yes. He's got a very large pair of female breasts.'

'They are large, aren't they?'

'Very.'

'Firm, too.' He leaned over and squeezed the left one. 'Try them.'

'I don't think so.'

'Go on.' He grasped the right breast. 'Grab a handful.'

'Another time, perhaps.'

'You're missing a treat. These beauties came from a twenty-three-year-old pole dancer. One-hundred-per-cent natural.' He really was enjoying his work. 'Sure you don't want a little squeezerooni?'

'I'll pass, if it's all the same to you.'

'It's your funeral.' He shrugged, and reluctantly tugged the sheet back over the body.

'That's your work, is it?'

'My work?' He slid the drawer back home.

'You sewed those breasts on the old geezer's body?'

'I did indeed.'

'After he was dead?'

'Certainly after he was dead. I don't think he'd've liked me doing that when he was alive, no sir. I think he'd've had plenty to say about that, don't you?'

'I imagine so.'

'Neat work, don't you think?'

In actual fact, it was surprisingly neat work. Most autopsy stitching is exceedingly crude; I've seen superior needlework on prison mail bags. But Rutter's handicraft, you could barely see the joins. However, I wasn't in a frame of mind to discuss the stitching.

'I'm just trying to wrap my head around this: you removed the mammaries from a dead pole dancer and stitched them onto that old man's corpse?'

'That's right.' He was scanning the bank of drawers again.

'Is that . . . Are you allowed to do that kind of thing?'

'Allowed?' He shrugged. 'Well, who knows? Nobody's told me *not* to do it. I mean, it would probably be frowned upon, if anybody found out about it. Here!' he found the label he was looking for. 'This one's a bobby-dazzler.' He slid out the drawer. 'You are going to cream your pants over this one, my friend.'

It was clear, even with the sheet over it, that this particular cadaver had been laid face down. Most of me didn't want to look at what I was about to be shown, but there was a small, not very likeable part of me that was undeniably curious.

He started to tug down the sheet, slowly at first. 'Female, Caucasian, fifty-six approx. Two sixty-five cm, fifty-six kilos. She's been here a fortnight, so she may be a little ripe.' As the sheet reached the small of her back, he suddenly whipped it off with a magician's flourish. 'Tah-rahhh!'

I think I actually staggered slightly. It surely was a sight to behold.

He was looking at me with a big, expectant grin on his stupid face. 'Whaddaya think?'

'It's . . . I don't know *what* to think, to be honest.'

'Well, do you like it or not?'

'I don't think "like" really covers any part of my reaction.'

'So you don't like it?'

'I wouldn't say I don't like it. I just think it's a little fucking bizarre, that's all.'

'Bizarre?' He mulled it over. He wasn't displeased. 'Bizarre.' He nodded thoughtfully. 'I'll go with bizarre.'

'Where did you get the faces from?'

'Some car wreck.'

'And how long did it take you to sew the faces onto her buttocks?'

'It was slow work, I can tell you. There's a lot of stitching in there. A lot of stitching. A lot of intricate needlework to keep the shape of the face.'

'I'm guessing you're not very busy down here, then?'

'Busy?'

'I mean, you seem to have an inordinate amount of time on your hands.'

'We're plenty busy. We are swamped, Detective. Take a look around. This? I do this in my spare time. This is my art.'

'What about the relatives?'

'What about them?'

'Well, don't they ever complain? Don't you ever get any comebacks?'

'Comebacks?'

'Like, someone comes in, says kind of: "Hey, one of you bastards has transplanted dead people's faces onto my sainted mother's buttocks, and I'm feeling fairly truculent about it"? That type of thing?'

'No, I'm pretty careful who I choose to work with. I mean, you wouldn't want this sort of thing on display in an open-coffin ceremony.'

'No. That would definitely work against the solemnity of the occasion.'

'Sure.'

'Seeing a stranger's face sewn onto your loved one's arse.'

He nodded, all serious. 'For sure. Absolutely. No, I only ever pick loners and losers. Plus, I always specify "closed coffin". Trust me, *nobody* wants to peek in when the pathologist writes "closed coffin".' He gazed down admiringly at his handiwork. 'This one – it's going to be a shame to bury this one. Look at those faces. Look at their expressions. Don't they look like: "Duh, what am I doing here on this woman's backside?" Aren't they a scream?'

'Yeah, they're a regular laugh riot. Can we move on now?'

He took one last, lingering look, then replaced the sheet and slid the drawer away. 'You've got time for one more?'

'No, really. I've got a lot of ground to cover.'

'One more. Just one.' He scoured the body banks animatedly.

'No. Thanks, but no. OK?'

'One. Just one last . . .'

'Really, no.'

'This one is truly worth waiting for . . . Yes.' He found the drawer and tugged it out. 'Trust me: this really is fantastic.' He drew back the sheet.

Reluctantly, I turned and looked at the cadaver.

'Female, Afro-Caribbean, mid twenties. Two eighty-five cm, fifty-two kilos.'

I looked, but I couldn't see any anomalies. She had one of everything she was supposed to have one of, all her fingers and toes and two of everything else, and it all seemed to be in the right place.

'You spotted it?'

I shook my head. 'She looks normal to me.'

'It's very subtle. Take a closer look.'

I didn't want to; I'd had more than enough of this. But I decided to humour him. I leaned in and scrutinised the body. 'I don't get it, no. I can see there's been some stitching around the areolas –'

'Bingo!'

'Bingo what?'

'You found it.'

'I don't understand.'

'I swapped her nipples round.'

'You swapped her nipples round?'

'The left on the right, the right on the left.'

'You swapped her nipples round?'

'Subtle, isn't it?'

'Excuse me, because this isn't going in for me: you took this dead woman, you cut off her nipples, and you switched them over?'

'My next project, I'm going to do the same thing, only with buttocks.'

'You're planning a buttock-swap operation?'

He nodded. 'The left on the right, the right on the left.'

'Dr Rutter, you're insane.'

'I know, I know. That's what my wife said. Swapping the buttocks over, that's a real technical nightmare, she says. But like I told her: once you've performed a successful face to buttock transplant or two, you've really got the basic principles nailed.'

'Can we see the reports now?'

'For sure,' he said, and reluctantly tugged the sheet back over the body. He slid the drawer back into the wall. 'You know, Detective? It's nice to find someone who appreciates the work I do here. I don't mind telling you, a lot of people think it's screwy.'

'That's people for you, Doc. People are weird.'

'Tell me about it.'

I picked up the autopsy reports, and it will not surprise you to hear I did not linger.

FOURTEEN

Here, as far as I can piece it together, is the time line for the fatal dinner party.

Bear in mind, this is constructed from pooling together witness statements and the official police reports. There are four official police reports, each from a different officer, and they fail to align on several key points, including, but not limited to, the actual date of the offence. Believe me, if these idiots had written the Gospels, the whole of Christendom would now be worshipping Arthur Wilbert Christoburger, a one-armed albino from Latvia. The few witnesses who survived the incident have almost random recall, and it's hard to believe they're describing the same event. That's understandable enough: two of them were interviewed in oxygen bubbles in an Intensive Care Unit, while the others were brutally grilled in police interrogation rooms, facing attempted murder charges, and would naturally have been bending their memories every which way, looking to save their own sad, sorry arses.

Still, I think I have managed to wade through most of the blather and eliminate most of the blatant lies and mistakes. I'm pretty sure this is how things went:

2.15 p.m. The catering team arrives.
One chef, one sous-chef and a commis.

This might seem like overkill for an informal dinner party with twenty-four guests, but this is a very swank affair. The guests include a couple of B-list celebrities, some stock market high-flyers and one or two up-and-coming movers and shakers on the Europolitical scene. The caterers bring most of the food with them, but the fish is arriving later, because the chef feels the refrigeration capacity of the apartment is inadequate to accommodate seafood safely. Diligent man, the chef, but then, in this day and age, he has to be. He doesn't want Superintendent Debary and his boys abseiling in and shooting up his kitchen for incorrect temperature control.

3.25 p.m. The party planner arrives.
Like I said, it's a Swanky Dan dinner party. In this rarefied social stratosphere, you can't even invite your next-door neighbour round for a toasted sandwich and a glass of milk without going through a party planner. She's responsible for organising the whole thing, from the invitations to the clean-up operation. She books the caterers, selects the menu, the decor 'theme', the florists, the launderers: the whole shebang, soup to nuts. She, of course, would be our primary suspect. If she'd managed to survive the fish course. Unfortunately, she will be the first to croak.

3.45–6.25 p.m. Various arrivals and departures.
This is the black hole in the investigation. Nobody was taking too much notice of the comings and goings, but during this period the following events almost certainly happen: the flower arrangements arrive, as does the flower 'sculptist', whose task, as far as I can make out, is to make sure the vases with the arrangements in them all point in the right direction.

The table linen arrives.

The interior designer arrives, but the decorations he's ordered don't, so he flumps out in a strop.

The hired tableware arrives.

The hired glassware arrives.

The interior decorations arrive.

The waiters (four: two male, two female) arrive, and are coerced by the party planner into putting up the decorations, though not without low, mutinous grumblings. It transpires that one of the female waiters is blessed with Tourette's syndrome: given to uncontrollable and sudden violent twitches, accompanied by equally uncontrollable bursts of filthy expletives and invective. This will make the soup course very interesting. Also, one of the male waiters is a registered sexoholic.

The seafood arrives. Fresh eels and a crate of razor clams. The razor clams, as bottom-feeding shellfish, will head the list of suspected murder weapons, but after exhaustive forensic attention, they will turn out to be innocent bivalves.

The interior designer arrives again, sees what the waiting staff have done to his decorations and flounces out again in another fit of pique. The party planner chases after him.

6.25 p.m. The host arrives.

He's a young gun in Eurobank. By all accounts, he's a sharp operator, and his career is on an upward trajectory so fast it would induce enough G force to crush a lesser man's spine. He's also forgotten he is hosting a dinner party tonight. He retires to his en suite bathroom with a cocktail shaker full of very dry gin martini and soaks in his jacuzzi.

The party planner returns with a mollified interior designer, who immediately starts tearing the decorations off the walls and out of the hands of the waiting staff and demonstrates his astonishing people-management skills by shrieking abuse at them, then attempting to recruit them to help him put all the decorations back up again along the lines of his original design. The waiters offer to help redecorate his back passage with sharpened pine cones, but that's as far as they're prepared to co-operate. In my humble opinion, the most tragic element of this entire tragic evening is that the interior designer is one of the few survivors.

7.15 p.m. More food arrives.

The pre-party nibbles. Miniature savoury pastries and so on. The chef has been on the phone all afternoon, chivvying these along. Apparently, it's common practice to contract out these delicate little bite-sized canapés to another supplier – in fact, that's where the phrase 'hors d'oeuvres' comes from – they're time-consuming and, quite frankly, beneath the chef's attention.

The Tourette's waitress takes the delivery. As luck would have it, the delivery man also turns out to be a Tourette's sufferer. The delivery is late because he twitched at the wrong moment and flung his original consignment into the apartment building's fountain, shouting, 'Fuck piss wank testicle bitch cunt.' The handover goes relatively smoothly.

The invitations stated '8.00 p.m. for 8.30 p.m.' so there's a serious possibility that some of the more gauche guests might actually turn up in an hour, or even less.

The party planner, by all accounts, is everywhere now. Helping the interior designer hang wall coverings, placating mutinous serving staff, chasing up the well overdue drinks delivery, while simultaneously trying to avoid the unwelcome attentions of the sexoholic waiter who keeps hitting on her, and generally having a ball.

The hostess has still not arrived.

7.32 p.m. The first guests appear.

This is precisely timed in a number of accounts, presumably because it's such a squirmy event. A Mr and Mrs Lungher turn up, thinking they are being Prussianly punctual, but it turns out they've just flown in from England a couple of hours earlier, and have forgotten to reset their watches.

The party planner has no option but to invite them in for a drink. Politely, they are forced to accept. They step into a human maelstrom of panic, haste and despair. They order schnapps, and, despite being vitally required in at least seven other places concurrently, the party planner, without a host or a hostess to call on, is compelled to remain with them making the smallest of small talk and smiling bravely.

The Lunghers down the schnapps as quickly as good manners will allow, then suddenly remember an urgent engagement elsewhere, make their excuses and leave.

7.45 p.m. The hostess finally shows up.

She has been delayed at several salons and the odd boutique or twenty. She races round the room, clutching an astonishing consignment of shopping bags and boxes, blowing air kisses and screeching with theatrical delight at the hired helps' professional prowess and artistic achievements.

She disappears into the bedroom. There, she has what she claims is a small marital dispute with her martini-enriched husband. There is yelling, there are threats of lethal action, there is some projectile activity, no more percussive or sustained than an all-out American gunship assault on a Vietnamese village. But all this comes under the heading of normal familial interplay, it would seem, and is irrelevant to subsequent events, since it is followed by a noisy bout of make-up sex, which, to the waiters' ears at least, sounds even more violent and dangerous than the original argument.

8.05 p.m. The interior designer leaves.

The party planner asks the chef if he has any aspirin, though she denies she has a headache. The chef tries to persuade her to sit and gather her energies for a few minutes, but she's far too busy to rest.

Even though she has an exceptionally unhealthy-looking grey pallor and is quite blatantly ill, the waiter hits on her again.

8.32 p.m. The first guests arrive again.

Shamelessly, the Lunghers are now the first to arrive, twice.

Most people would have had second thoughts about returning at all after their original faux pas. But then, the Lunghers are German, and therefore impervious to embarrassment.

8.32–8.55 p.m. The rest of the guests arrive.
That is to say, twenty-three of the twenty-four invitees show up. The twenty-fourth, the hostess's brother, is unable to attend. Ironically, he is bedridden with food poisoning.

Cocktails are served.

As are the canapés.

There is no definitively comprehensive list of the components of the canapés, but they are typical of the current fashion for unusual foodstuffs to tempt the chicly jaded middle-class palate. Certainly, they memorably include mini blinis with sour cream and frog 'caviar', tiny tartlets of emu foie gras foam, liquorice bark 'canoes' stuffed with dry-roasted Granny Smith pips, nasturtium crisps, and some rather brutal-sounding, but evidently popular *ennemis mortels*: bruschetta spread with cat liver pâté and dog butter. Conversation is lively, laughter abounds. Sophisticated fun is had.

8.55 p.m. The host emerges from the bedroom.
Though the lighting is fashionably low, he is wearing sunglasses. He meets and greets.

The party planner takes the host to one side and explains that the chef is ready to serve dinner, and enquires politely as to the approximate ETA of the hostess. The host assures her that his wife will emerge in exceptionally short order.

10.17 p.m. The hostess finally does emerge.
The canapés have long since run out, even the frogspawn blinis, the guests are all rather too drunk, and the chef is very close to a murderous rage. The hostess appears oblivious to this. She swoops round the room like a Stuka in strafe mode, machine-gunning air kisses and compliments.

10.18 p.m. The party planner announces that dinner is served.

10.30 p.m. The guests are all seated at the table, and the starters are served.
Now, who ate what, how much of it and when is of critical importance here, so bear with this.

Of the twenty-five remaining diners, six are vegetarian, two are full-on vegan, three are piscatorians – vegetarians who eat fish, and five are a bizarre kind of quasi vegetarian who eat fish and chicken. This is quite an unusual haul of pernickety eaters for a French table, and no doubt reflects the pan-European nature of the event, by which I mean there are many English people present. It does very little, though, for the chef's patience.

Fortunately, the first three light courses are mostly unsullied by meat, and it would appear that most of the guests ate most of them. A Gascon bean and slow-roasted tomato soup is rejected by only one of the guests, largely because the waitress describes the dish to him as 'Gascon fuck piss shit bean soup wank', which largely dims his appetite. And only the vegans feel compelled to turn down a much acclaimed melting red pepper jelly tartlet, because the pastry contains animal fat. Of course, the jelly is made from veal bones, but the chef neglects to bring attention to the fact, and the vegetarian contingent don't appear to suffer any ill effects.

At least, not yet.

Finally, in the trilogy of relatively uncontroversial starters, there is a small pasta dish: tagliolini with fresh cep mushrooms. Wild mushrooms are obviously high on the suspicious substances list – there are some wild mushrooms which are so poisonous, you could die from just handling them – but these ceps are unlikely candidates: they came from a very reputable supplier, and many other clients enjoyed mushrooms from the same batch without adverse reactions. Surprisingly, the ceps are the most expensive single ingredient in the entire repast. The plates, reportedly, come back clean.

So, most people ate most of the three first courses.

The party planner does not eat, officially, though by all accounts she appears to have availed herself of the canapés, more out of nervous energy than hunger, and the kitchen staff thoughtfully prepare small versions of the dishes for her to sample, once the meal is underway.

The razor clams are less of a hit. They are long, yellowy orange molluscs in thin grey pearlescent tubular shells. Like oysters, they are served live, on their shells, but, unlike oysters, they actually move. They squirm. They twitch. They wriggle away from your touch if you prod them. Now, it's probably programmed deep into human genetic make-up to avoid food that is still fidgeting, and though they are greeted with 'oohs' and 'ahhs' of admiration, and excite much conversation, all but five of them are returned uninjured, having been poked around warily on their shells without managing to excite the appetites even of many of the supposed omnivores. Still, as far as the hostess is concerned, they have done their job. The party will be talked about.

Boy, will the party be talked about.

By now a number of the guests have asked for aspirin, and one or two of them appear to suffer some kind of sporadic stabbing pains in their chests.

The hostess begins to worry that the evening which started so well is beginning to flounder. It is when the eel is served that things start to go rather badly awry.

10.55 p.m. The vomiting begins.

The party planner is the first to suffer. The chef recalls that she had been looking greener and queasier for the past hour, and was growing more and more unsteady on her feet, but he'd assumed that was because of the stress and tensions of the day. He tries to cheer her up by showing her, with a flourish, his pièce de résistance: the Electric Eel *à l'Italien*, which is decorated with cleverly crafted sugar-worked light bulbs that actually glow.

She puts a rather unconvincing, brave, green face on things, attempts to make suitably impressed noises, then throws up, violently and uncontrollably, over the chef's hands, three of the plated meals and most of a waiter. This occurs in the kitchen, out of sight of the dinner party, and though one of the female waiters claims the vomiting was blatantly audible at the table, none of the guests acknowledges it.

By now, almost everyone seems to be struggling to conceal a headache. A couple of guests are clearly experiencing breathing problems. Conversation around the table is growing more and more subdued and stilted.

In the staff washroom, behind the kitchen, the party planner is still throwing up, while the waiter she decorated with her stomach contents is optimistically trying to sponge down his uniform. He is amazed at the amount of vomit the young woman is able to disgorge, while at the same time making curiously tuneful groans of distress at operatic volume. Brilliantly realising her powers of resistance will be at their lowest ebb at this moment, he takes the opportunity to proposition her again.

The chef, meanwhile, has managed to sanitise the kitchen again, re-portion the eel, and the fish course is served.

11.10 p.m. (approximately) The vomiting stops.

As the final plate is delivered, the chef notices that the party planner is no longer making sick noises. He makes a final check on the horse ragout, before popping into the washroom.

The party planner is on her knees with her face in the toilet bowl. He asks if he can help.

She does not reply.

She does not move.

Gently, he puts his hands on her shoulders and lifts her

head out of the bowl. Her eyes are open, but there is no life in them. She doesn't appear to be breathing.

The chef puts two fingers to her neck. There is a pulse, but it seems unusually faint. He puts his hands under her armpits and drags her out into the kitchen.

He tries to sit her in a chair, but she keeps sliding off. In the end, he lays her on the floor, puts a cushion under her head and covers her with a rug.

He takes out his mobile phone and calls an ambulance.

Unfortunately, he is far, far too late.

11.22 p.m. The vomiting begins again.

The hostess is really beginning to worry now. Conversation has all but ceased around the table, and nobody is touching the eel. She tries desperately to get things going again, but it's all she can do to elicit a polite nod in response to her prompts. A few people can't help groaning. Someone expels a long, unearthly fart that seems to last for many, many minutes, varying impressively in timbre and tone, like an alpine horn player being thrown off a rather big . . . alp. The perpetrator does not even apologise, but no one seems to care.

Mr and Mrs Lungher are the first to go. Naturally. They are seated at opposite corners of the table, and they launch their first plumes almost simultaneously, each looking painfully in the other's direction, so their discharged loads arc towards the stunning floral centrepiece in the middle of the table, giving almost total coverage of the tablecloth.

This is too much for the many guests who've been struggling against the inevitable. A concerto of vomiting begins. There is a decidedly unchivalric rush for the lavatory, in which two of the smaller women who have probably fainted are quite badly trampled.

The toilet facilities are, of course, wretchedly inadequate to cope with even a small proportion of the guests' sudden irresistible requirements, even though the bath, the sink, the bidet and the shower tray are all amply put to use. The afflicted who are excluded fight, literally, for space at the windows in the dining room and the bedroom, and the long streaks of multicoloured vomit they produce down the face of the white-stuccoed apartment block are clearly visible many kilometres away, and probably will remain so for the foreseeable future.

11.35 p.m. The ambulance arrives.
Nineteen minutes after the chef's phone call. Quite an impressive response time for a Saturday night in Paris. Unfortunately, as he leaps from the decelerating vehicle, one of the team slips on a slick pool of puke and twists his ankle badly.

Crouching to attend to him, his partner is hit on the head by an impressive plume of projectile vomit which has been accelerating at thirty-two feet per second for thirty-nine floors. His collar-bone is snapped and he is rendered unconscious, so the third team member is forced to devote his attention to reviving the other two, and a second ambulance is summoned.

The chef, who by now has abandoned all hope that his main course or any of his clever puddings will be able to tease the guests' appetites back to normal, and realising that he may never be allowed near a balloon whisk ever in his life again, returns to the kitchen to escape the chundering mêlée. He catches the waiter unbuttoning the party planner's blouse and slipping his hand inside her bra.

She is comatose.

The waiter's claim that he was loosening her clothing in accordance with his first aid training fails to impress the chef, who attacks the waiter violently with a ladle.

11.42 p.m. (probably) The party planner dies.
Having assuaged a good part of his rage on the sex addict waiter, the chef checks the party planner's pulse again, and

finds none. He gives her mouth-to-mouth and heart massage for several minutes, but the cause is clearly lost.

The hostess appears to be the only one of the diners unaffected by sickness. She races around the room in a panic, cooing useless words of comfort and asking people who are quite clearly nanoseconds away from terminal corpsehood if they're feeling all right.

She comes across one of the B-list celebrities, who famously plays a surgeon in a popular Eurowide TV hospital show, and asks if he can use any of his medical expertise to help the others. Bizarrely, he agrees, and starts examining an unconscious woman, before his stomach cramps get the better of him again, and he collapses, groaning, to the floor.

11.52 p.m. More medical assistance arrives.
This time it's a paramedic on an ambulance motorbike. He fails to hear the urgent warnings of the first ambulance team, brakes far too hard on a slippery bilious slick and skids sideways into the metal railings around the apartment building. Fortunately, he appears to be relatively unscathed. He gets up immediately and dashes into the building.

Unfortunately, he is almost certainly suffering from shock, and possibly even a minor concussion, because he eschews the obvious benefits of the elevator and elects to race up the emergency stairs to the thirty-ninth floor. Between floors twenty-two and twenty-three, he decides to lie down for a little rest, and he sleeps, undiscovered, for thirty-six hours.

11.55 p.m. A third emergency team arrives.
This time in a fire engine.

This is standard practice. Should the primary emergency service prove unable to respond to a call out, the fire service is the de facto back-up. The firemen are trained to give rudimentary medical assistance, and that training is fairly broad.

Sadly, it does not cover lethal poisoning.

Still, the firemen are at least able to assist the first, injury-ridden medical team up to the apartment, and they are capable of finding the elevator and staying awake till they get there.

12.02 p.m. The medical team actually arrives at the disaster scene.

Forty-six minutes after the chef's first desperate phone call.

Things are not pretty.

Every square centimetre of every conceivable surface is dripping with vomit, including the ceiling and the frighteningly expensive Venetian crystal chandelier.

Most of the guests are draped, immobile, around the room. A few of them are still sufficiently fit to manage a spot of aimless crawling. Only one or two are still retching. The hostess is sitting in the corner of the room, sobbing gently.

The stink is close to unendurable, and the firefighters put on their smoke masks.

The chef, the sous-chef and two of the waiters are doing what they can to bring comfort to the few who are still capable of caring.

In the kitchen, a fireman finds another waiter, with a bruised face and a bloody nose, who appears to be attempting to strip the knickers off a woman's corpse. He gives the waiter a savage kicking.

Most of the victims are comatose by the time they're stretchered down to the ambulance, and only two of them survive as far as the hospital.

On the night, Twenty-five are dead, including all of the guests, the host, and the party planner. The commis chef and one of the waiters survive as far as the hospital's ICU. The commis pulls through, but two days later the waiter expires.

The only survivors unaffected by the poison are the hostess, the chef, the sous-chef and the three remaining waiters.

Now, here's a shortlist of the investigating officer's problems. As far as he can tell, there doesn't seem to be any kind of sensible link between who ate what, and who died and who survived. Autopsy results, even if they were accurate, would be scant use in this regard, in that none of the victims had any stomach contents to report on. The hostess, who, of course, originally approved the menu, claims to have eaten everything, up to and including the eel. She didn't eat all the food exhaustively, it being her habit, as is apparently the fashion in her circle, always to leave half of what she's served. The chef insists he tasted everything, quite frequently at various stages in the cooking process, in order to adjust the seasoning correctly. The party planner had little nibbles of a few of the dishes, but probably no more than the chef. And yet she was the first to succumb to the poison, and the first to die.

It's obvious to you, of course, when the poison was administered, and it's obvious to me. But then we have the benefit of a clean and probably accurate report.

The forensic reports, as you might expect, are ambiguous: four separate pathologists conducted the autopsies, including Dr Rutter, and, naturally, they disagree over just about everything, including the cause of death. The majority verdict, though, is cyanide poisoning.

Superintendent Debary's conclusion is that it's manslaughter by catering carelessness, and arrests the chef. But Superintendent Debary is wrong.

It's murder of course.

In fact it's another perfect murder.

FIFTEEN

It's a perfect murder, because even when you know how it was done, there's no way to prove it.

I put the report together in the Paris apartment, rather than the hotel room, because I had my computer there, and I figured I'd be undisturbed.

I needed to consult with a toxicologist who actually knew what he was talking about. Such people still do exist, but they're never going to climb the career ladder, and they're a dying breed.

I called up a guy I've used before. He's a research assistant in London University's poison and toxicology department; one Jonhan Linder. He's been a research assistant there for forty-two years, and he's unlikely to make professor for the next forty-two. He's possibly the world's leading authority on toxins, and if I told you what his take-home pay was, you'd be weeping from now till Christmas.

He came on screen almost immediately, and smiled when he saw my face. I was a guy who gave him interesting problems, and he liked that.

I laid out the Fabrizi story for him, and he listened intently.

'Frogspawn?' he asked.

'No, I checked that out. Seems it wasn't really frogspawn, it was clarified fish stock, heavily reduced and set into pearls of jelly with a single beluga caviar egg suspended in the middle. Looks like frogspawn, tastes divine. A whole lot of fuss to create even a single pearl. Only a truly dedicated idiot would even think of trying to make it.'

'Right. And only a truly rich idiot would even think of paying for it.'

'So? Have you got me a murder weapon?'

'Absolutely. It's the canapés all right.'

'I figured.'

'Thing about seeds, most seeds are indigestible. That's how they work, see? Tomatoes can't run around planting themselves, so they just hang around getting all ripe and delicious-looking till some animal comes along, gets himself all tempted and eats them. The seeds survive the trip through the digestive system mostly intact. The animal dumps his load. *Voilà*! He's not only planted the seeds, he's provided them with natural fertiliser to boot. You check it out next time you see a sewage outlet: you'll find tomato plants growing wild. In fact, that's how they assess the level of human sewage in the sea: measure the percentage of tomato seeds in a given volume.'

'Checking the levels of human sewage? Now there's a job from hell's own situations vacant column.'

Jonhan laughed. 'What did you do at the office today, darling?'

'Sheese. You'd never get your hands clean. So, the murder weapon?'

'The liquorice bark "canoes" are the killers.'

'The liquorice bark "canoes"?'

'Not the liquorice bark, though; the stuffing.'

'Dry-roasted Granny Smith pips? Are you serious?'

'Lethal at twenty paces. Chock full of cyanide. A bucket of those, you could take out a battalion.'

'You're sure?'

'Never surer.'

'Apple seeds?'

'Three or four of them, no problem. A few dozen, you're an ex-parrot.'

I made a little more small talk, out of respect for Jonhan, but I wasn't feeling in a small-talk frame of mind.

Apple seeds.

Well, well, well.

Now I knew for certain I was on the case Klingferm had got himself all dead about. On the same road in that case, too. I'd better be careful where I put my feet: Klingferm stepped on the wrong set of toes somewhere along this line, and I'd do well to avoid them.

I'm a lone wolf. That's the nature of my business. I don't have the time or the resources for truly dogged detective work. So I have to play the probabilities. Maybe some things slip past me that way. Maybe a lot of things. But, most times, probabilities will get you there.

My best guess, here, was that the killer would turn out to be the canapé delivery guy who faked having Tourette's. He was late arriving because he took time out to add a little something extra to the menu. Chances were a couple like the Fabrizis would have a video security camera on their front door, and Mr Tourette's would be on tape. Chances were Superintendent Debary probably had a copy of that tape down at Food Crime HQ. Chances also were the tape would probably be useless. Mr Tourette's would have been aware of the camera, and would have steered clear of it as much as possible. He would certainly have been heavily disguised. Making mistakes was not Mr Tourette's favourite hobby.

I had his modus, but that's all I knew. I had no idea which of the guests was his intended target, or why. Or how he could have guaranteed nailing his victim. Was he killing indiscriminately, just for the fun of it, or was there just one, specific target? Did twenty-six people die needlessly so Johnny Appleseed could get his man? He was probably capable of that.

He was probably capable of anything.

Someone had to stop him. And now I was the only someone who even knew he existed.

Like I say, I have to play my hunches, and my hunch here was that I'd got as far as I was going to get in Paris. I decided

I'd head for Vienna tomorrow, and track down Twinkle or Twonkle.

And tonight? Well, tonight I had a date so damned hot you could brand cattle with it.

I kidded myself I wasn't being even slightly irresponsible by not hotfooting it to Vienna right away. I'd been through three cities in one day, had I not? I deserved a little R & R, *n'est ce pas*? But the truth was, I'd have been in that bar all washed and powdered at eight twenty-eight if there'd been a nuclear bomb to diffuse and I was the only man in the civilised world who could do it. I hadn't spent an evening with a woman in, what? Thirteen years? Who was going to begrudge me?

I checked my watch. I had a little over forty-five minutes. Time to get back to the hotel and get another couple of baths in.

I went out onto the street. The traffic was in nightmare mode, even for Paris. There had been talk of a public transport strike, and it looked like it was just happening. I decided to walk. I could make it back and still have time for at least a shower.

Halfway there, I realised I'd left my IDs at the apartment. I didn't have time to retrieve them and still get back to the hotel for a scrub up. Well, I needed to be squeaky clean tonight, my friend. Who knew what long-lost parts of me were going to have to put in a convincing appearance? I decided the IDs would be safe till morning.

Good decision, Harry.

I was just strolling up the Ambassadeur's front steps when a big guy in a serious suit stepped out in front of me. He held up a gold shield. Europol. Federal. It looked genuine enough. But then, so do mine. He said: 'I think you should turn around, my friend.'

I didn't much like the sound of that, but he didn't make it sound as if the subject were open to conversation.

I turned, slowly. The lump behind my ear I'd earned this

very morning began to throb, anticipating that it might soon acquire a companion and become part of a matching pair.

But I didn't get cold-cocked. I got something much, much worse.

I turned to find Captain Zuccho standing at the foot of the steps, his temples throbbing, his eyes bulging and his gun unholstered and aimed at my three favourite things.

The fed behind me called out, 'This him, Zuccho?'

'This is him, all right. This is him. Gotcha! You dirty whore's pussy canker!' His bulbous eyes widened with glee. 'You're under arrest, you son of a bitch.'

SIXTEEN

REVISED CAUTION CODE AAZ PARA. 10.4
You do not have to say anything, but it may harm your defence if anything you do not say is later relied upon in court by you. Anything you do say which is later contradicted by something else you say, may be counted against you. Things you do say which are not true may later be considered lies, and will also be counted against you. If you do *not* say something at the time of your arrest, which you at some later time claim to be true, your credibility may be impinged upon. You have the right to request legal advice, though if you do request legal advice, this may be considered an admission of wrongdoing. If you do not request legal counsel, and later require it, this may count against you. If you waive your right to legal advice, and are later found guilty, you may regret it. If English is not your primary language, you may ask the arresting officer for a transcript of this warning in any official European language, not including Basque or Catalan. Do you understand?

If you do not understand, or fail to acknowledge understanding, this may count against you down the line. If you do understand, you must acknowledge in one of the following ways: 1) you may say 'Yes' or the alternative affirmative in any official European tongue; 2) you may grunt in an affirmative manner; 3) you may sign the word 'Yes' or the letters 'Y-E-S' in any official sign language; 4) you may nod your head briskly; 5) if you are mute, illiterate in sign language and wearing a neck brace for bona fide reasons and cannot therefore nod your head, you may write the word 'Yes' or an acceptable alternative on the notepad with the unsharpened wax crayon provided by the arresting officer; 6) if you are a deaf mute who cannot sign and are suffering severe neck injury, and are a registered dyslexic, you may indicate comprehension by simply smiling.

The following alternative words and phrases may be substituted for 'Yes': 'Yup,' 'Yep,' 'Yeah,' 'Yo,' or any colloquial variation of 'Yes'; 'OK,' 'Aye,' 'Sure,' 'Why not?' 'Agreed,' 'If you say so,' 'I do,' 'No problem,' 'Fine,' 'Okey dokey,' 'Of course,' 'Roger,' 'Ten-four,' or 'Uh-huh.' Non-committal responses such as 'Whatever,' 'Blah blah,' 'Yak-yak,' and 'Who cares?' will be taken to indicate a positive understanding, as will expletives, curses and profanities, though these, in themselves, may lead to further charges including, but not limited to, verbal violence and blasphemy.

If you do *not* understand, you must indicate with the word 'No' or any official European linguistic or acceptable colloquial substitute, or sign language, or written alternative, or grunt in a negative manner, or shake your head briskly from side to side, or any combination of these techniques. If you are a dyslexic deaf mute with neck trauma, you may indicate incomprehension by pulling a very sad face.

If you do not understand, and have indicated that lack of understanding by employing one of the officially acceptable methods described, you will be read this caution one further time. If, after this second reading you still do not understand, the arresting officer will read you an alternative, simplified warning. If you do not understand that, you may be compelled to undergo a battery of IQ tests in custody, which may be counted against you in a court of law.

This caution is also available in Braille and Morse code.

ALTERNATIVE, SIMPLIFIED CAUTION

You do not have to say anything, but if you do not say anything, bad things will probably happen to you. You can ask for a lawyer, but some people might get mad at you if you do. Do you accept this simplified caution, or would you like me to read out the full version again?

SEVENTEEN

Zuccho seemed pleased to see me, but in all the wrong ways. I was none too delighted having him point his weapon at tonight's star prize, the mood he was clearly in. I put my hands up, all polite and everything, and smiled warmly to try and reduce the tension.

'Captain Zuccho. Good to see you again.'

'Yeah, I'll bet it is. I'll bet it's good to see me. I'll bet you'd like to come on over here and give me a warm embrace. I'll bet you'd like to kiss me. I'll bet you'd like to drop my trousers on the spot and dry-hump my butt hole with glee, you prick.'

Good, he was getting calmer. 'You're arresting me?'

'No. I flew over here all the way from Rome to bring you a Christmas card and a message of world peace from the blessed Father, His Holiness the Pope, you whore-sucking scumball.'

'What's the charge?'

'What *isn't* the charge? That would be quicker. What *didn't* you do, you filthy piece of dried dog crap? Let me see, let me see. You didn't try stealing the British Crown Jewels lately, as far as we know. But that's about it. That's about all you didn't do. I'm not going to throw the book at you, though. I'm going to take the book and force-feed you with it. I'm going to shove the book so far down your throat, you'll be getting newsprint on your toilet paper.'

The fed behind me said: 'We can start with impersonating a federal officer.'

What? Not possible. My credentials should have checked

out better than bona fide. 'Obviously, there's been some mistake, here . . .'

'Yes, there's been a mistake.' Zuccho's trigger finger was looking awfully trembly. 'Certainly there's been a mistake. Your first mistake was being born, you dumb punk. Your first mistake was crawling out of the abortion clinic trash can, where your hooker momma left you. Your second mistake was trying to play me for a cocksucker and thinking you could get away with it.'

Zuccho was close to foaming. He was pretty het up, even by his own dismal standards. Still, he *had* just caught the plane from Rome to Paris, and we know what that can do, even to a normal, even-tempered, completely non cranky person. Such as me. Right?

'Captain Zuccho,' the fed behind was sounding nervous, 'can we calm things down here?'

Whoops. Whoops a doody.

'You want me to calm down?' Zuccho was rumbling now.

'It's not like the guy raped your cattle and stole your children.'

'You think I should *calm down*?' He was about to erupt. I started edging backwards, subtly.

'Just take it down a notch or two, that's all.'

'Here!' Zuccho was almost screaming now. 'I'll calm things down! This should be calming for us all. How's this for *calmmmmmmmm*!?'

He dropped into firing stance, drew a bead on my crotch and pulled the trigger.

He pulled the trigger fifteen times.

I know, I counted every last one of them.

And though I jerked back at every pull, all that came out of the gun were fifteen empty clicking sounds.

Zuccho just stayed there, motionless in his shooting crouch, breathing deep and heavy, his chest heaving, his forehead purple and throbbing.

I didn't move, either, except to tilt my head slightly to check my valuables were still safely in my netherwear.

The fed said, 'Shit.'

Zuccho looked at his gun and chunked out the clip. 'You are one lucky son of a bitch, you son of a bitch. I must've forgotten to reload after this morning.'

The fed stepped in front of me. Brave man. 'Captain Zuccho, maybe it would be a good idea if you waited in the car for us?'

Zuccho stared. Slowly the red mist of ire began to fade from his eyes. He lowered his head and nodded. 'Yeah. Yeah, maybe that would be best.' He holstered his weapon. 'Yeah. Yeah, I'll do that. I'll go wait in the car.' He turned, took a step, then stopped and turned back to face the fed. 'I'm going to offer you an apology for what just happened. You, not him.' He jerked a venomous little nod in my direction. 'Guess I got a little overly frisky, back there.'

He nodded again, to himself, then turned back and slouched off towards the waiting cop car.

We both watched him go, the fed and I, just in case he decided to reload and get a little overly frisky again.

The fed shook his head. 'What is with that guy?'

'He has anger management issues.'

'He has shit for brains.'

'That too.' I nodded. 'That too.'

'He sure hates the crap out of you.'

'Zuccho? No. Zuccho just hates the crap out of everybody.'

The fed took out the laminated card, unfolded it, and read me my rights. I was looking over at the bar where I was supposed to meet Gina. It was just a little after eight, so she probably wouldn't be there, yet. I'd have been disappointed if she had. She was my perfect woman, right? And my perfect woman would never be ahead of time. My perfect woman would always keep me waiting, just a little. Just long enough to let me know she knew her value. And I'd always be waiting there patiently, with nary a cross word, to show her I knew it, too.

I made the fed read me my rights again, then asked for the simplified version, and then asked for the whole thing all over again. I wasn't trying to cheese him off, I just wanted to make sure Zuccho had plenty of time to calm down.

Even with the sirens on and Zuccho driving with a total disregard for the sanctity of human life, his or anyone else's, the trip downtown took a good forty minutes, which gave me a chance to wheedle a couple of things out of the fed in the back.

'This is a big mistake, you know,' I told him.

The fed nodded. 'So you said.'

'You tried calling my superiors?'

He nodded again. 'We made all the calls. Nobody ever heard of you, friend. Nobody ever heard of a Detective Harry Pepper. You're the original man who wasn't there.'

That was bad. All my IDs are supported – they have to be. Someone makes an enquiry on one of them, the enquiry gets rerouted, I get verified: I'm a valuable member of department whatever. Long-serving, diligent, all that. Somehow, my Harry Pepper identity had been deactivated without my knowledge. I didn't see how that could have happened.

I thought I might try pulling myself out of this mess by claiming I'd been operating undercover in Rome, but I'd have a hard time corroborating the claim. I'd left my French IDs in the apartment. Ultimately, that was probably a good thing. Getting arrested with another couple of identities in my pockets could have made things very complicated.

'Somebody tip you off?' I tried.

The fed just kept his lips tight.

Zuccho bought it though. He turned his head round and grinned. 'Yeah. A little bird sang us a sweet song. You're such a nice guy, Pepper. All your friends love you. They love you like a rat loves poison.' A horn blared and Zuccho had to turn back to yank the wheel round and thereby handily avoid ploughing through a bus stop crammed with screaming teenagers.

Well, I had a pretty good idea who'd set me up. But how? How did he get hold of my ID? I never let it out of my sight.

Then it hit me.

The ID *had* been out of my sight for a few minutes in Rome.

The garbage patrolman.

He wasn't looking after the garbage yard. He wasn't interested in my money. He'd just wanted to cold-cock me to get his hands on the details of my ID. But why? It didn't make sense. If that had *been* Klingferm's killer, he could have done away with me easy. He could have blasted my brains all over the trash bags there and then, and buried me under the fox poop. No one would have even come looking. He could have slit my throat, quiet like, while I was out cold, dreaming of cheese. He could have bundled me into a landfill bin bag and topped it up with faecal matter, ready for collection on Wednesday.

But he didn't.

He didn't do any of those things.

And you have to wonder why.

I was formally charged under the name of Harry Pepper: impersonating a federal officer, and stealing evidence from the scene of a crime – the security tapes from the Martini building, it turns out. I didn't even bother denying it. My address was a problem. I didn't want to give away my Paris apartment – those IDs were my lifeline, and I needed to keep them free from search warrant scrutiny. And I had to assume they didn't know I'd booked into the Ambassador as Harry Salt, so I couldn't give them the hotel, either. So I wound up having to give my address as 'no fixed abode', which is a real magistrate-pleaser. They took my prints, for all the good that would do them, and had me pose for some snapshots, which would be a problem down the line, if I ever got out of this mess.

I asked for my phone call. Zuccho flipped me a coin gleefully and wished me luck finding a friend who'd be prepared to talk to me.

I wasn't going to call a lawyer. What good would that do me? I could call Home, and leave a message, but that would get me nowhere in a big fat hurry. My cover was blown, and the policy is official denial.

No. I was going to put Zuccho's coin to better use. I was going to call Gina, or at least someone at the hotel who could get a message to Gina. I dug the hotel number out of my pocket and dialled.

A woman picked up the phone and said in a voice that had become far too familiar to me: 'Restaurant. How may I help you?'

In-be-credi-lievable. I'd called the wrong hotel. I'd called that cesspit of a flea dive in Rome. There was no way Zuccho was going to flip me another coin. He couldn't wait to clap me in irons and melt the key. I decided to try a long shot.

'Listen. This is a very big favour I'm going to ask you. I'm trying to get through to the Hotel Ambassadeur in Paris.'

'Well, this is the Belize Hotel in Rome.'

'I know, I know. I dialled the wrong number, and I don't have any more change. Do you think you could put me through to the Ambassadeur?'

'You want *me* to transfer *you* to the Hotel Ambassadeur in Paris?'

'I know it's a lot to ask.'

'You want the restaurant manager of a hotel in Rome to put your call through to a hotel in Paris?'

'Like I say: I know it's a big favour.'

There was a pause. I wondered if she'd recognised my voice. Probably not, because finally, she agreed. 'OK, I'll try.'

I was beginning to revise my opinion of the restaurant manager. I made a personal, sacred vow never to subject the poor woman to verbal violence again, of a sexual or any other kind of nature. I dug out the Ambassadeur's number, the right one this time, and gave it to her. She asked me to hold. I listened to the ringing. I heard the click of the receiver being lifted, and then I heard her voice again. 'Restaurant,' she said. 'How may I help you?'

I gave her verbal violence all right. I gave her a whole pent-up tankload of extremely sexually explicit verbal violence, then I thought up some more and gave her that, too. Then I hung up. I thought of some more verbal violence I would have liked to have given her after I'd hung up, but by then it was too late. I'd use it next time, though. I'd definitely use it next time. Because there surely would be a next time.

Zuccho was waiting for me with a big, fat grin on his big, fat face. I wished Dr Rutter would work on that face. I'd like to see how it looked sewn onto my backside.

He led me by the elbow through processing. He didn't want to miss a minute of my misery. On the positive side, I have to say he was more relaxed than I'd ever seen him before. He hardly threatened anybody with lethal violence.

They made me hand over the contents of my pockets, my watch, and my trouser belt. I bent down to remove the laces from my shoes, but the desk sergeant didn't want them. Oh no. He wanted the entire shoes.

I straightened. 'You want my shoes?'

'I do.'

'Both of them?'

'Just the left and the right.'

Deeply troubled, I made a big business out of removing my shoes and placing them tenderly on the desk, like they were no more precious than newborn twins.

'You're going to look after them, right?'

The desk sergeant smiled. 'Of course I'll look after them; I'll treat them like royalty.' Then he grabbed the shoes roughly, stapled a label on them, and hurled them brutally into a box with a whole bunch of other shoes. 'Oh look, there's been a revolution. Liberty, equality, fraternity. The Shoes Royale are mingling with the common citizen shoes.

How about that? Let's hope they don't meet Madame Guillotine.'

I stared forlornly at the shoes I'd probably never see again. To me, they *did* look regal, lying there among the courgette- and beetroot-hide trash that passed for footwear, if only just. That desk sergeant had plans for those shoes, and I knew it. 'Don't you usually just take the laces?'

'Used to. Not any more. You'd be surprised how many detainees beat themselves to death with the heels of their shoes.'

'People beat themselves to death with their own shoes?'

'Regularly.'

'That does surprise me.'

'Right.' He grinned. 'But then, you haven't been down to the holding cells, yet, have you?'

EIGHTEEN

We descended some very steep, dimly lit steps, me with one hand on my waistband, struggling to prevent my trousers from crumpling to my ankles, and the other firmly clasping the rail, desperate to keep my footing in my slippery cotton socks, all the time giddied along by legally 'harmless', yet astonishingly painful shocks to the small of my back, administered willy-nilly by a cop who was overly fond of his electrified truncheon.

We stepped out into the fluorescent light of the holding cells.

There were a lot of holding cells.

A lot of holding cells.

Perspex pens, maybe thirty metres square, stretched away as far as the eye could see, separated by a network of thin corridors. The room must have taken up the entire city block. Maybe more.

And yet every square centimetre of legitimate seating space was taken up with unbelted trouser buttock, and every footstep's worth of floor room was occupied by shoeless feet. Each pen must have been accommodating at least fifty men, and there had to be more than twenty pens, ranked around the vast room. Maybe double that.

And this was just for people waiting to be *arraigned* for an offence.

Already, I felt like clubbing myself to death with a shoe.

The cop gave me another painful shot in the back. I explained to him that, like many human beings, I was capable of responding to language, especially simple, polite commands, such as 'Would you care to go this way, please,' and 'Hurry along there, old chap, if you wouldn't mind,' so he zapped me again.

I turned to see he was prodding me down towards a further set of stairs. There was more of this?

There was more of this all right.

We descended to the next level, me trying to strike a reasonable balance between not going so fast my socks might slip on the concrete steps and not going so slow as to risk yet another sizzling from Terry Truncheon behind me and his frazzling friend.

The next level was identical to the first. Identically over-populated, too.

So we went down yet another set of steps.

And then another.

I was 'assisted' down at least twenty-three flights of steep stairs before I gave up counting in favour of fighting for breath and staving off claustrophobia.

And still, we kept going down.

It was at this precise moment, I think, that I conquered my recently acquired fear of elevators. I decided I'd rather risk being trapped in a lift for all eternity or being blasted out of the solar system in an elevator car than set foot on another staircase ever again.

I began to fancy I caught the odd whiff of sulphur and brimstone curling up from the floors below, and the distant moaning of souls in eternal torment.

Down, down we went. You may not know this, but all big men have a very rational fear of falling and never getting up again. That fear was exponentially multiplied here by the reasonable dread that any sudden stumble might send me crashing down the endless, steep concrete steps, with my trousers around my ankles, as far as I knew all the way to the molten core of the planet Earth.

Just as I was on the very brink of grabbing the guard's truncheon off him and assessing its effectiveness as a rectal thermometer, we reached what appeared to be the bottom level.

It seemed no less crowded than any of the others we'd passed.

It turned out, though, that this particular level of the Inferno had its own unique attractions. A construction team was noisily busy building yet another floor below. After which, presumably, they'd start on the floor below that, then the floor below that.

It's a very simple equation: the more laws you pass, the more laws there are to break, and the more lawbreakers you'll have to deal with and accommodate.

So the construction team worked around the clock, in shifts, to provide all the detainees with that most demonic of cacophonies to the poor soul in search of sleep: intermittent and unpredictable bursts of industrial-strength power tools in unbearably close proximity. Hell's own orchestra.

I shuffled along the corridor between the pens. Sad wretches in tieless shirts pressed their hope-drained faces against the bullet-proof perspex that stood between them and the sweet air of freedom.

I was herded into the last of the pens with a final electronic flourish, and the perspex door slid shut behind me. I took a moment to watch him leave, trying to hate him well enough to vow blood vengeance, but failing, then turned to face my fellow internees.

Bizarrely, my pen seemed, if anything, more crowded than any of the others I'd passed. It was crammed so far beyond its capacity, the world's most agoraphobic sardine would have been sweating with fear and pleading to be crammed back inside its tin so it could get a little breathing room.

I felt a strong wave of communal loathing towards me. Space was already at a premium, and another big, sweaty body was the last thing anyone hoped to be entertaining. I brazened it out and squeezed my way slowly through the muttering, grumbling throng, towards the wall, and, eventually towards a tiny section of the corner of a bed onto which I sank perhaps one tenth of one buttock cheek and breathed the world's longest and most grateful sigh.

There were maybe a hundred and twenty men in an enclosure built for thirty. A hundred and twenty men. And, as luck would have it, I managed to squeeze myself next to Hinton Wheeler.

Quite possibly Hinton Wheeler was the unluckiest man in the world. He was almost certainly one of the smelliest.

He was a short, skinny, mouse-like man, with a shock of unkempt hair and a scraggly Ben Gunn of a beard. His shirt and trousers were ragged and threadbare, and his socks seemed like they'd all but worn away.

He was smiling at me. I tried not to notice – rule number one for staying healthy during incarceration: never catch another inmate's eye – but the smile was so earnest and needy, I found myself inexplicably drawn to return it.

He introduced himself, and I grunted, trying to inflect the grunt so it sounded sufficiently like 'Fuck off'. But he wouldn't. He had no intention of fucking off. Instead, he came right out and asked me what it was I was in for.

Now, that question used to be another big prison taboo, but these days, it's considered legit: the real criminals, your professional thieves and hard men, don't like to hang around the kind of Eurotrash idiots who are doing time for displaying their raw meat products next to the roast ham, or quoting prices for pounds and ounces rather than kilos. I mumbled some deliberately ambiguous response, just in case Hinton turned out to be a serial killer, unlikely as that seemed.

I wasn't looking to carry the conversation on any further, but Hinton clearly hoped I would ask him the reciprocal question. I stonewalled him, and tried not to notice, out of the corner of my eye, his expectant, puppy-like anticipation slowly collapse into a hangdog, crestfallen slump. I tried not to imagine that he'd already tried to initiate some kind of communication with each and every one of the hundred and eighteen other internees and failed. I tried not to feel the palpable waves of desperation and loneliness he gave off. I tried, but I can only take so much.

'What about you?' I caved in.

'Me?' He grinned with astonished delight. 'What am *I* in for? Me – I'm in for nothing. Nothing at all. Fact is: I'm not even here, officially. I'm officially free. What happened, see, I was working for this law firm, nothing fancy, legal cleric, and I comes here to take a client's statement, but in the middle of it, turns out my firm's decided to downsize me, and my access privileges get automatically revoked. So, when I tries to leave, my pass is invalid, see? And since I don't have a valid pass, I can't have gotten in here in the first place, so the fact is: I can't be here at all. And if I'm not here, they can't let me out, is the way it goes.'

All this came out in a kind of strange, boring, Zen monotone, so that by the time he'd hit the fourth word of any sentence, you'd already managed to forget the first three. Hinton would have made a perfect government spokesman for dispensing unpalatable news. But, of course, he'd never get past the job interview without driving the interviewer to blow out his own brains rather than ask a second question.

My eyebrows were striking all the right Bezier curves, but I got the feeling old Hinton wasn't too interested in my actual response. He just needed to talk it out. He just needed to vent. I couldn't have stopped him if I wanted to, so I just kept up the eyebrow aerobics and let him blow off his steam.

'See, I haven't been accused of a crime, or anything, so there's nothing for them to process. I'm not even allowed to make a phone call – that's only for people who've been *accused* of stuff. I don't even have the right to a lawyer, because I'm not *charged* with anything, so, technically, there's nothing for me to defend myself against. So they tell me. When they bother to tell me anything, which is basically never. So that's it: I'm stuck here. A free man with an unblemished record, and I can't even habeas my own corpus. Get that beat, will you?'

Like I said, Hinton's voice had this quality, and even though this was possibly the most pathetic tale of dismal luck I'd ever heard, I still found myself fighting to stave off sleep. I thought if I chipped into his monologue, it might help keep me awake. 'So: how long have you been here?'

'Here? In the processing pens? A little over three and a half years.'

'Three and a half *years*?'

'You heard it right. And get this: I'm still wearing the same pair of underpants. Can you imagine that?' I desperately tried not to imagine that. 'They can't issue me with new clothes, see, because, as per like I said: I'm not here. I don't want to tell you what happens to underpants, even sturdy underpants, after forty solid months of constant wear, but it's not pretty. Believe me, it's not pretty.'

I believed him. There wasn't enough room for me to put any kind of desirable distance between me and Hinton's veteran underwear, given my already precarious perch on the bed's edge, but I shifted my weight as best I could.

Three and a half years in the holding pens.

The worst-case scenario ought to be an overnight stay. Maybe two. But by then you'd be crawling up walls and praying for a shoe to beat your brains out with.

There were no provisions for long-term internment: no exercise yard, no canteen, nothing in the way of entertainment, and only the most rudimentary and humiliatingly public toilet facilities.

Three and a half years was inhuman.

'But isn't there anybody . . . ?' I flailed at the question, already suspecting the answer. 'Haven't you been . . . missed?'

Hinton's eyes fired up with ironic delight. '*Me?* Missed *me*? Who's going to miss *me*? I got fired from my job, remember? You think I have a wife or something? The little lady waiting patiently at home? A guy like me? I haven't had a girlfriend since I was six years old, and *she* dumped me after one kiss, the little bitch. So what, then? You think I have *friends*? You imagine there's someone in the world somewhere who can stand my company for more than thirteen seconds without hurling themselves off of a roof? Someone who'd like to go to the ball game with good old Hinton Wheeler? Who'd like to chew the crap with me in some neighbourhood bar and throw back a few cold ones? This is the longest conversation I've ever had with a living person, not counting a few unfortunate telephone salespersons who cold-called me and lived to regret it. You think *you'd* still be here listening to me if you weren't trapped in a holding pen and pinned back by a wall of human flesh? No, sir. You'd be on a plane to Alaska by now. Anywhere that was at least a hemisphere away from me. There's something about me, see? I bore people. I don't know why, but I know it's true. I don't want to bore people; I want to be interesting. You think I don't want to be interesting? This tale of mine, my current predicament, you'd have thought it was of some kind of interest, at least, wouldn't you? But every time I buttonhole someone and start to tell them, I can see their eyes glaze over. I can see the will to live literally draining out of them. Like with you, now. Why is that? Is it some kind of chemical thing, do you think? I'm giving off, like, bore-omones?'

I'm admitting to you, here and now, that I've reconstructed Hinton's speeches more from imagination than from memory. Certainly, that's the style in which he spoke, and more or less the gist of his message, but in reality, it washed over me like a grey, sucking fog.

I had to help him out. I had to help him out even if it was only to stop him talking to me. 'Listen . . .' I tried not to look like I was trying to remember his name.

'My name is Hinton,' he offered, wearily.

'Right, Hinton . . .'

'Hinton Wheeler. Though, why I'm telling you, I have no idea. You'll forget it in less than thirty seconds.'

'I won't.'

'You will, see . . .'

'Now, will you shut up for a second? I'm trying to help you here.'

'Help *me*?' This was new ground for Hinton. 'In what way "help me"?'

'In the way where we get you out of here, for a start.'

'Right.' Hinton nodded and smiled like a pinched balloon. 'Which is mightily reassuring, my friend, you being a forlorn and hopeless prisoner incarcerated deep within the most forgotten intestine of the most forgotten bowels of the entire judicial digestive system. Whoopee. If only there were room, I'd do a little whirligig of joy.'

I swivelled round, grabbed his tieless shirt collar, and hauled his face within bristle distance of my own. 'Let's just try it this way for a few seconds: I talk, you listen. OK?'

Hinton nodded as best he could, without actually throttling himself.

'You can't get out of here, because you're not officially in here, right?' Hinton opened his mouth and I tightened my grip. 'Don't answer that; it's rhetorical. So what you have to do before you can get out, is somehow to get in. To get in, all you have to do is commit a crime. Just a small crime, a little misdemeanour, just big enough for you to get caught, get charged, get tried, get processed. To get out of the machine, first you have to get in it.' I relaxed my grip, but Hinton stayed where he was, in a kind of tortured crouch, halfway between sitting and standing.

He waited as long as he could bear, and then he croaked: 'May I speak now?'

'It's your turn.' I nodded. 'What do you think?'

'What do I think? Two things: first, you lost me my space on the bed when you lifted me off it. Second, you ripped my shirt, which is more than a little frustrating, because I may have to wear the damned thing for the rest of my natural life.'

'Didn't you hear me? None of that matters. With the worst luck in the world, you'll be out of here in twenty-four hours.'

'It took me seven months to get that space on the bed.'

He hadn't heard me. He was in denial. Understandable enough. His entire life for the past three and a half years had been focused on the injustice of the bungling that trapped him here; it had become the only thing that kept him going. He'd given up long ago entertaining any serious hope of release, because it was the only way for him to hold on to some kind of sanity.

'Winton, you're going to walk out of here. Don't you understand?'

'Don't *you* understand? I can't commit a *crime.* I'm not a *criminal.* It's not in my *nature.*'

'Are you kidding me? You can't *avoid* committing a crime in Europe, now. You can't walk across the road without breaking forty-seven city ordinances, two federal laws and a pan-European international edict. That's the Union's greatest achievement: it's made criminals of us all.'

I was starting to get through to him. 'What? What crime? What crime could I do?'

'What's it matter? Buy a bootleg cigarette and smoke it in the toilet. Make a disparaging remark about Hinduism. Pick your nose and don't put your pickings in a bag. Ask a female guard for a *date,* for chrissakes. They'll have you in official lock-up quicker than a reincarnation of Jack the Ripper for sexual intimidation.'

Hinton's face was locked in the half-smile, half-grimace expression, but his eyes were sparkling strangely. 'Just one little crime . . .' he was beginning to believe '. . . and I'll be out of here?'

'Easy as that. Course, you'll probably have to stump up a fine, or even serve a short custodial sentence, depending on the particular offence you commit. But you'll get a proper meal, at least. And a whole bed to yourself. And you won't have to spend one more day wearing underpants that are old enough to be attending pre-school.'

'A whole bed?' He cast his eyes upwards. 'All to myself? Is it possible it could be that simple?'

A low, throaty grumble spread towards us from the pen door, and feet began to shuffle. Another internee was being herded in to join our happy band. Before I could stop him, Hinton was fighting his way through the crowd towards the door. I had a good idea what he had in mind, and it wasn't pretty. I tried to get through to him before he caused himself unnecessary pain. But Hinton was skinny, not to mention extremely well practised at moving through a static crowd of incarcerated flesh. By the time I was in sight of the door, he'd already assaulted the guard. I caught a last glimpse of his face as it disappeared under a storm of electronic truncheons. Even as the shocks were juddering through his body, he tipped me a jagged smile, clicked me a spasming wink and yelled a heartfelt, if painful 'Thaaaaaaaaaanks.' Then he disappeared beneath a flurry of unnecessary blows.

NINETEEN

With Hinton gone, I struggled my way back to the bed and made enough space on it for an entire buttock. Bliss.

What now?

I didn't have my watch, but I figured it must be around ten, ten thirty. I wondered if Gina would still be in the bar, those long, heavenly pins wrapped magnificently round the legs of some lucky bar stool, playing boredly with the maraschino cherry that garnished her fourth highball, and dreaming up wonderful new ways of hating men in general and me in particular.

Who was I kidding? She was probably showing her appreciation of the bar steward's cocktail mixing skills by forcing him to remove a martini olive from inside her netherwear with his bare teeth, while the band struck up 'La Vida Loca'.

If I was lucky – and why wouldn't I be? – I'd be arraigned before a magistrate some time tomorrow, and, if there were sufficient evidence to warrant the charges – and why wouldn't there be? – I'd be handed a trial date and sent to grown-up prison. Wow. There's a handsome schedule to titillate you with a tremble of anticipation. By Friday night, if I was lucky – and why wouldn't I be? – I could be the unwilling bride to a dozen or so homicidal lifers with an over-abundance of Y chromosomes and facial tattoos reading: 'Death To Mother'. By the weekend, I could be gainfully employed as a full-time human toilet. What treats I had in store.

What were the chances of my making Vienna by Thursday?

A number so far below zero, it existed only in the fifth dimension.

Plus, I had to place my contact ads tomorrow, if they were going to hit next week's deadline. Those messages didn't appear, alarm bells would start ringing. I missed that deadline twice, my cell would be closed down, permanent, and I would cease to exist. I'd drop off the map. No identity, no history, no background. I'd become the Cartesian antithesis:

I would think, yet I would not be.

Well, there was nothing I could do about any of it, right now. Maybe there'd be a window of opportunity to stage some kind of escape en route to the magistrate's court. That would probably be the point where security would be at its weakest. I mean, who would be expecting some idiot on an impersonation charge to be reckless enough to make a bolt for freedom from a van-load of armed cops?

On top of which, I might get lucky – and, hey, why not? – I might even get a police escort who suffered from Non-Specific Stupidity or some such. Or a quadriplegic courtroom guard.

It could happen.

Right now, I needed sleep. It had been a very long and strenuous day, and my engine was running on fumes.

Ever tried catching a few Zs with one cheek perched on the corner of a bed, surrounded by one hundred and twenty noisy, smelly men in a room built for thirty?

I'd have told you it couldn't be done.

But I'd have been wrong.

It took a while, and I didn't think I was going to pull it off at all. But I must have, because I was awakened the following morning by some kind of kerfuffle in the pen. A guard was approaching the cell.

I tried to straighten up, but I couldn't. I realised I'd dropped off at some point in the night, and started using my neighbour's shoulder as a pillow. He, in turn, had used my head as a pillow, and someone else above us both had used his. I was trapped under a human pyramid of snoring flesh.

The guard tapped on our perspex with his truncheon and called out, 'Harry Pepper?'

I shouted, 'Here!' and struggled free of my sleepover buddies. Without me to prop them up, they collapsed into a painful heap, and a few curses and some friendly blows were exchanged.

I squeezed my way through the reluctant, grumbling swamp of flesh towards the door.

The guard said, 'Harry Pepper?' again.

I told him, yes, I was Harry Pepper.

He consulted his clipboard, then looked up again and said, 'You're coming with me.'

He unlocked the pen door and I spilled out. He jabbed his stun stick at a couple of desperates who were prepared to take a few bolts of crude electrotherapy just for the chance to stretch their legs and breathe something more closely approximating air for a few meagre seconds. He got them all penned up again, and bolted the door behind me.

He pointed his stick towards the stairs, then he pointed it back at me, to show me he was prepared to use it copiously, should the need arise, so I held my hands up to show him I was all meek and mild and full of love for all mankind, and headed in the direction he was wanting.

'What's this about?' I asked him.

'You'll see,' is all he said back. A man of infinite jest.

I asked him the time, and he told me.

Five forty a.m. seemed a strange time for a magistrate's court to be operating. Though, for all I knew, there were thousands of them all over the city working right round the clock. They'd probably have to be if they wanted to process even a small proportion of the bodies in these cells in any kind of humane time span.

Still, if this were a trip to the courtroom, I doubted they'd be carting us off one at a time. I figured maybe I was being taken away for a beating party, but, frankly, I didn't much care. A hail of blows from some professionally wielded rubber tubing would constitute welcome light relief after a night in those holding pens. It would be like a Caribbean holiday.

Something on my head was feeling strange. I put my hand to my hairline, and it came away gooey. My sleepover buddies had given my forehead a nice thick coat of their sleep spittle drool. Smashing. I'd have to remember to thank them for that, next time I could lay my hands on a heavy-duty cosh and enough room to swing it in.

We'd climbed up nine flights of stairs before my death wish kicked in big time, and I'd started to contemplate wrestling away the guard's truncheon, stripping out the safety and finding out what a diet of two hundred thousand volts could do for my peace of mind, when we took a left turn, instead of a right, and I was herded into an elevator.

Obviously, they were building downwards so fast, they hadn't had time to construct a lift shaft all the way to the bottom. Or maybe they couldn't build one that came so deep, for fear of giving the passengers the bends.

It was a slow elevator, and it had quite a trip to make. They should have provided us with some in-flight entertainment, or at least a seat, a magazine and some kind of inedible snack.

I tried to use the time to get myself centred. If this did turn out to be a trip to the courts, I'd need to be ready if an escape opportunity presented itself. I stood in the Wu Chi position and started some deep breathing. The guard ruined it all by turning his stun stick on full and zapping me in the arse with it, just for fun. Hysterical. This guy was a regular one-man comedy extravaganza. This guy was ready for his own TV show.

I was picking myself off the floor just as the lift arrived.

Zuccho was standing by the processing desk waiting for me.

'What are you doing down there, Pepper? Giving the guard a little head?'

Had it only been nine short hours since our last parting? How I'd missed the crazy bastard. I got to my feet and gave him my lovingest smile. 'Why, Captain Zuccho – I didn't know you were the jealous kind.'

Zuccho craned forward. 'Shit, what's that?' He peered at my head. 'Looks like he finished off all over your hair.'

The French cops all laughed, humouring the old dirt wad. Even though Zuccho technically had no jurisdiction here, the locals were clearly walking on eggshells around him.

I wasn't going to let them think I was scared of the loopy son of a basket case. 'Hey, Zuccho: next time I'm in Rome, I think I'll take you up on that offer to nail your wife. Know anywhere they sell industrial-strength Viagra? Can I book in advance, or do I have to join the end of a very long queue?'

The French cops laughed, but not too much.

Zuccho did his lip-biting thing. 'You're a funny man, Pepper. I'm going to enjoy seeing them lock you up and eat the keycard.'

There was an odd lack of conviction about the threat. I got the feeling something had changed, and changed in a way that Zuccho didn't much like.

'But that's not going to happen, is it Captain? Because I'm walking out of here, right?'

Zuccho turned away and grabbed the edges of the counter. His neck was glowing bright red, and I could see the veins in it bulging like mooring ropes. He was using all his best temper management strategies. He was counting backwards from a million in threes. He was thinking of all his favourite things and trying to imagine me amongst them. He was visualising himself in his happiest place. He was breathing in deep, holding it, and letting it go. He was doing a hundred things to bring down his blood temperature from way off the scale to just above boiling point.

It took a time, but it worked. When he finally turned back,

his face was hardly purple at all, and he only tore a couple of small, fist-sized chunks out of the countertop. 'Yeah. You're out of here. For now, you scum bucket.'

I walked up to the processing desk, trying to knock the gloat out of my step. Gloating is bad. Gloating never gets you anyplace you want to be. 'My ID finally checked out then?'

Zuccho shook his head. 'Fraid not, Pepperpot. You're in court Friday a.m. And I'm going to be there watching. Impersonating a fed? You can pull a ten-year stretch for that. By the time you get out, you'll have a sphincter that could accommodate the Orient Express. I'm going to spend the entire decade laughing.'

I didn't get it. 'Somebody bailed me?'

'Yeah, how about that? You've actually got an actual *friend.* I'm as surprised as you. It's probably your momma's pimp.'

The desk sergeant – a new shift – handed over the contents of my pockets, my belt and my watch. I slipped the watch on my wrist and started threading the belt through my trouser loops.

Somebody bailed me out? 'You got a name?'

'Yeah, I got a name. I got a name so I'd know who to hate. Lennox.'

Lennox?

'Terry Lennox. Ring any bells?'

I shook my head. The name sounded vaguely familiar. I thought an old-time boxer, maybe, or a footballer. 'What did he look like?'

'He was a she.'

A she? Thérèse Lennox? 'Young she or old she?'

'I didn't get to see the whore. She must like you plenty, though. She stumped up fifty thou to spring you. Money she could have spent having her gonorrhoea scabs removed.'

Fifty thousand euros? I don't know anyone who likes me fifty thousand worth. I don't know anyone who likes me fifty cents and a stick of gum. I had a secret admirer all right.

The desk sergeant handed over a pair of shoes. They were not my shoes.

'What are these?' I asked him.

'Going right out on a limb,' Zuccho answered for him, 'I'd say they were a pair of truly shitty shoes.'

I ignored Zuccho. 'These are not my shoes.'

The desk sergeant checked the label. 'This says they're your shoes.'

'Well, they're not my shoes. I had a pair of real leather shoes. Almost brand new.'

'Would you like me to check through the box for you?'

'I would be very, very grateful. Thank you.'

'Or maybe you'd prefer me to arrange a shoe identity parade with them all? You could maybe pick out your own pair from behind a one-way mirror at your leisure?'

'Listen, friend: I just want my own shoes back, is all.'

He leaned over the bar, real close to my face, and said, 'Fuck off.'

You've got to love those Paris cops. They could have their own vaudeville act. The Fabulous Flying Parisian Pigs. They could thrill audiences the world over.

I picked the filthy pair of parody shoes up and smelled them. I held them out to Zuccho. 'What do you think they're made of?'

He sniffed them. 'My guess? Pumpkin leather.'

I licked one of the toecaps. 'Good guess.' I nodded. 'Definitely a member of the squash family. I think maybe butternut.'

I slipped them on, trying not to think of that son of a bitch desk sergeant, who was, doubtless at this very moment, wearing my beautiful, beautiful shoes under the glittering mirror globe of the Lido ballroom, tripping the light fantastic like he was Fred A-fucking-staire.

I signed the docket. The desk sergeant gave me a piece of paper telling me not to leave the state, and which court I was to show up at. Nine o'clock, Friday morning. Right. Set your watches, people. I'll be there.

And just in case you're reading this and you're American, and you're having trouble wrapping your head around irony, I'll add the following:

Not.

With it now?

I thanked everyone for their kind hospitality, using only one finger, too, and turned to go.

Zuccho called after me. 'Hey, Pepperpot. Do me a favour. Don't show up Friday morning. I'd just love to come hunting you down like the dog you are so I can jam my Glock right up amongst your dingleberries and empty out the entire clip. That would make my life complete.'

I tipped him a grin. 'Can't wait, Zuccho. I'll keep a tub of Vaseline handy.' And I stepped out into the cool, free air.

TWENTY

I walked down the steps of police HQ and turned towards the hotel. It was just a little after six in the morning, but the roads were already starting to look jammed. Or maybe they were still getting unjammed from the night before, I couldn't tell.

I walked a few blocks, until I finally spotted Zuccho a little way behind, making a better job of tailing me than I'd have given him credit for.

I walked on a ways, until the inevitable happened, and Zuccho got himself involved in a violent confrontation with an innocent bystander who'd made the cardinal mistake of occupying a part of the boulevard at exactly the moment Zuccho wanted to walk on it.

I waited until Zuccho was fully distracted truncheoning the old lady to the ground with a sturdy cucumber he'd plucked from a convenient vegetable stand, then I slipped down a nearby alleyway and headed back in the opposite direction.

I couldn't go back to the Ambassadeur, of course. Even if Zuccho hadn't been watching it, someone would have been.

When I was confident no one was tailing me, I went up to my apartment. Like I said, it was pretty much four walls and a bed, but there was a tiny sink, and I did what I could to wash away the smells of my incarceration. I kept a spare set of clothes there, but that was all. Foolishly I hadn't thought to store a spare pair of shoes.

I picked up my IDs. I still had Cardew Vascular, Harry Tequila and, of course, Harry Salt. I didn't have a drop point in Vienna, so these would have to do me for the duration.

Vienna.

I'd be breaking the terms of my bail, and that would hit my secret benefactor in the pocket pretty hard, on top of which I'd be a federal fugitive, but all that was just too bad; I was going to make that date in Vienna, whatever the consequences.

Of course, if I'd known what the consequences were going to be, I would definitely have had second thoughts.

Vienna, then.

Question was: how was I going to get there? I couldn't risk using the airports. My likeness was probably posted all over the terminals as a flight risk. I didn't mind that too much; I'd had enough of air travel lately to last me a lifetime or twenty-four.

If I could get out of Paris, public transport strike and all, I might be able to pick up a train. But getting out of Paris, that would be a problem all in itself.

It seemed the best and only thing for it was to hire a car.

A car would be good. At least I'd be in charge, for a change. I wouldn't be throwing my fate into the lap of the gods. We hadn't been getting along too well of late, me and those fickle-lapped gods. Yes indeedy: the more I mulled it over, the more hiring a car started sounding like a damned fine idea. No pilots with vertigo to put up with. No ticket salesmen with attention deficit. No rabidly foaming passenger in the seat next door with halitosis, flaky eczema, a lethal new strain of Chinese influenza and an urgent need to share them all with me. Just me behind the wheel, the open road, and my own thoughts for company. With good luck and a following wind, I might even get where I was going by the time I actually wanted to be there.

I made a couple of phone calls. I placed my personal ads. I had only one set to place this time, of course. I thought, briefly, about setting up a meet with my remaining linkman, like Klingferm had done, but decided against it and just sent the usual AOK. Still, just in case, I dumped off my computer report on the Fabrizi thing and a few other bits and pieces onto a DVD. I slipped the disc into my old suit pocket and traded the suit in for a dry-cleaning ticket. I hacked into the French police central computer and obliterated my arrest photos. Nothing I could do about any that might already be out there in circulation, but at least I'd stem the tide. I took a little time out to dig up Zuccho's photo and put it in my arrest file. Just for fun.

I called the Ambassadeur, but Gina wasn't around, so I left her a message, saying I'd call again later and explain everything. But the truth was I didn't expect her to take my call, even if I managed to make it.

There's my life story, my friend. Boy doesn't quite meet girl, boy loses girl anyway, boy never gets girl back. Read it and weep.

I left the Paris apartment, walked around a while, back-tracking here and there, just to make sure I was still tail-free, then headed for the Rent-Ur-Car office I'd picked out of the Yellow Pages.

I hired a multifuel hatchback, a Fiat Affordable, which ran on a combination of batteries, steam and filtered cooking oil, along with a regular petrol tank, for emergencies. There were three good reasons for choosing the Affordable. First, with all those fuel options, there would be less risk of my running out of power along some deserted mountain track where cellphone signals dare not penetrate; second, it was a friendly little unpretentious model, that promised to 'get you where you're going'; and, third, as far as I could tell, it was the only motor vehicle actually available for hire in the entire state of France.

The rental clerk tried to run me through the controls, but, this being her first day on the job and me being her very first customer, it took her a good ten minutes to pinpoint the precise location of the steering wheel. I couldn't face the pain of watching her struggle through the next seven pages of the checklist, so I told a little white lie. I told her that I owned an

Affordable myself, and had done so for some considerable time, and I knew how to use it better than I knew how to use the lavatory. She was new, like I say, and reluctant to bend the rules and forgo the official procedure, but after much reassurance and oath-swearing on my part, she finally allowed me to sign the checklist, handed over the keycard and scurried off gratefully.

Now, starting a car, you'd think that ought to be an easy thing to do. You'd think that, in designing a car, a car designer would make starting the car a simple task that the average driver might accomplish without a lifetime of training. If a car can't be started, it's not a whole lot of use. A car that won't start is nothing more than an ugly lump of metal taking up valuable space on a shrinking planet. A car that won't start is only good for sitting in and/or kicking.

But, for the life of me, I couldn't work out how this particular car was supposed to start. I tried, foolishly, to start it up using my powers of logic. I had a keycard. The keycard must surely be involved somewhere in the ignition process. Ergo, there must doubtless be a slot of some description into which I might insert, or through which I might swipe the aforementioned keycard. QED, surely?

I studied the dashboard with the same fierce intensity a young boy might use to scrutinise a pack of erotic playing cards.

It appeared to be perfectly smooth.

Not a slot in sight.

I ran my fingers over every millimetre of its surface, and then again in the opposite direction. Nothing. Not even a glove compartment. I checked the steering column. No slots. I checked it a second time, even more thoroughly, in case there was a secret button concealed along its shaft that would magically reveal a hidden keycard slot in the dashboard. To no avail. I checked the doors. I tried inserting the card in the cup holders. I tried popping it into the air conditioning vents. I tried rubbing it comprehensively over every available surface, including the windscreen.

I pulled down the sun visors and tried rubbing the card there. I tried swiping it behind the vanity mirror.

I got out of the car and looked under the seats. I got in the back of the car and checked the back of the seats. I managed, by some unlikely miracle, to pop open the boot of the car. I had one brief but false eureka moment when I found a likely-looking device, but it turned out to be the multi-disk CD changer. I tried inserting the card in that, anyway.

It was slowly beginning to dawn on me exactly why this was the only available rental car in Paris.

It's a mark of quite how hopelessly desperate I was, that I turned to the manual.

Refreshingly, it seemed to be quite a good manual.

In fact, it was one of the best manuals I've ever encountered: clear, well written, in crisp, clean English, and with illustrations so ample and comprehensive that it would have enabled a monkey who'd just had the top of his head lopped off and his brains eaten with a spoon to have taken to the road with confidence. There was even a long, clear and laudably detailed section on starting the car.

All I had to do, apparently, was insert the keycard *(fig. 7)* into the keycard slot *(fig. 9)* and tap in my security code on the keypad *(fig. 31)*.

How much simpler could it have been?

Problem was: as far as I could tell, my particular model wasn't blessed with a keycard slot *(fig. 9)* or, indeed, a keypad *(fig. 31)*. In fact, after yet another exhaustive inspection, my particular model seemed to be missing everything from *fig. 8* all the way through to *fig. 97* entirely.

Somehow, I'd contrived to hire a car with eighty-nine missing *figs.*

The only tiny ray of light was in the 'Troubleshooting' section at the back of the book. It had nothing to say about the correct procedure to employ should you encounter a whole truckload of missing *figs* on your dashboard, but it did have some sage advice to offer: 'In the event of the car not starting,' it suggested, 'contact your vendor or authorised technician.'

Could I do that now?

Could I go back to the rental clerk and admit that I couldn't so much as turn the damned car on? After swearing to her on my mother's eyes and the sacred heart of the sweet baby Jesus that I had an identical vehicle of long standing nestling on my drive at home? A vehicle in which I had avowedly enjoyed many thousands of kilometres of trouble-free driving ecstasy? Could I seriously, after all that, slope back into her office after fully twenty minutes of futile struggle, and ask her where the keycard was actually supposed to go?

I checked over the car again. I checked everywhere. I checked the wheel hubs and the mudflaps. I checked under the mats. I checked the mirrors. I checked the headlamps and the indicator lights.

I gave up, steeled my stomach for a large portion of humble pie heavily crusted with crow, and was starting back towards the office, when a loud, officious voice shot me in the back.

'Hoi! Excuse me!'

I wheeled round. Salvation was addressing me in the shape of a mechanic in yellow overalls.

I did a double take, because he looked inexplicably familiar. He was standing hyper-erect, with his back slightly arched and his chest all pigeonned out. He was wearing a peaked yellow hat over a pair of mirrored shades, and his lower jaw was jutting out arrogantly, with a thick, defiantly petulant lower lip in charge of the whole face. Suddenly it clicked.

He was a dead ringer for Benito Mussolini.

Benito was standing by my risibly immobile Affordable wiping his hands with an oily rag. 'Is this your car?'

I started back towards him. 'Yes. I just hired it.'

'You can't park it here, Mister.'

'I'm not. Technically, it's not parked.'

'This space is for cars that are waiting to be hired, see.'

'I know. I'm just picking it up.'

'This car was checked out forty minutes ago.'

'Yeah. That's about right. But I'm having a problem.'

'Damn right you're having a problem. You're parking in a restricted zone.'

'Like I said: technically, it's not parked. It's never actually been in motion. For it to be parked, see, I'd've had to start it up, move it away, bring it back, and park it.'

'Well, you're going to have to move it.'

'Believe me, there is nothing I want more than to move that car. In a perfect world, I'd like to move it all the way to Austria, but, for now, I'm aiming low, and I just want to get in that car and move it out of your forecourt. And I was hoping you might help me in that endeavour.'

'It's a simple thing, Mister: you just start it up and drive it away.'

'Yes, I agree. That sounds simple. It really ought to be simple. Thing is: I can't get the damned thing to start.'

'Are you saying it won't start?'

'I'm not saying it won't start, I'm just saying I don't know how to make it start.'

'All our vehicles are thoroughly checked between rentals, Mister.'

'I'm sure they are.'

'Hundred-and-eighty-seven-point check.'

'That's very commendable.'

'There's no way this vehicle is in anything less than tip-top condition.'

'I don't doubt that for a second. But, here, what I'm saying is: I, personally, haven't got a clue how to switch on its engine.'

'Well, it can't stay here.'

'Will you help me start it up?'

'You just agreed with me there was nothing wrong with it.'

'There is nothing wrong, apart from the fact that I can't start it.'

'Well, I'd call that a problem.'

'Once again, we're in agreement. There is not a single point here on which we disagree. And yet, inexplicably, I feel we're not getting along.'

'You signed off on the checklist, didn't you?'

'Yes.'

'So the car must have started correctly when you ran through the checks.'

'Not exactly. Look, I'm sure we've both got more interesting things to do than stand around this forecourt talking about problems that really don't exist. We can end this whole thing here and now if you'll just give me the benefit of your unquestioned and much admired technical expertise, and show me how this car is supposed to start.'

He cocked his head and looked at me, to see if maybe I appeared saner sideways. He wiped his hands some more. 'Let me get this straight. You're saying the car *will* start, it's just that you don't know how to start it?'

'That's exactly what I'm saying.'

He looked at the car, then he looked at me again. 'Did you try turning it on?'

I could have gone the sarcasm route, but I didn't think that was the fastest way to Vienna. 'No.' I looked down at my pumpkin shoes. 'No, I didn't.'

'You haven't even tried to turn it on?'

'I don't know how to do that.'

'You don't know how to do that?'

'I'm really, really hoping you will show me.'

'D'you want me to get the rental clerk to run you through the checklist again?'

'No. No need, really. If you could just demonstrate the

turning on of the engine, you'll make me a very, very happy man.'

Cravenly, I'd given him power. And he knew it. He squeezed what he could out of it with a stupidly long pause, as if somewhere in the dark recesses of his undercrowded cranium he actually had a mind to make up. Finally, he elected to show mercy. 'You've got the keycard?' He held out his hand.

'Absolutely.' I handed the card to him.

He took the card, looked at it a while, tapped it on his fingernails, and strolled over to the driver's door. He leaned inside the car and studied the dashboard for a long, long time. But I didn't lose my patience: he was a small-minded man, and if he wanted to drag out his pathetically pinheaded moment of triumph, I wasn't going to hold it against him. If he did get the car going, I might take the opportunity to run him over with it and reverse up and down over his big fat head a couple of times, but until that moment, I was on best behaviour.

Finally, his head still in the vehicle, he spoke. And what he said wasn't good. What he said was: 'Where is it?'

I was hoping I'd misheard. 'Where is what?'

'Where is the slot for the keycard?'

'Are you saying it isn't where it should be?'

'I don't know.' He straightened out of the car and turned to face me. 'Where should it be?'

'That's my entire problem, see. That's why I can't get the motor car started.'

'Have you tried reading the manual?'

'Absolutely. Cover to cover. I even memorised large portions of it.'

'And it didn't mention where you put the keycard?'

'It said to put it in the keycard slot.'

'And where's the keycard slot?'

'I have no idea.'

His eyes drifted back to the car. 'You'd have thought it'd be on the dashboard someplace.'

'Wouldn't you just?' I smiled a comradely smile. The two of us: men against machines. We weren't about to let them win, were we?

Apparently, we were. The mechanic shrugged his jutting lower lip. 'Well . . .' He handed me back the keycard. 'You can't park it here, and that's a fact.' And he started to walk away.

'Wait!' I called after him. 'Are you saying you don't know how to start this car?'

He didn't look back. 'Not unless you can find a slot for that card.'

'But you're a mechanic, aren't you?'

'Yes, I am. I'm just not a very good mechanic. I don't work with these multifuel vehicles. They baffle me.'

I looked forlornly at the keycard in my hand, taunting me with its false promise of exotic travel. I sighed, and with all the enthusiasm of a feeble old gelding being led to the glue factory, I trudged back to the rental clerk's office.

TWENTY-ONE

Thankfully, the rental clerk was sweet about the whole thing. But then, why shouldn't she be? She was young and pretty and life hadn't yet taken time out to club her to the dirt and relentlessly kick the enthusiasm out of her. Once she'd identified the steering wheel again, and both the accelerator and brake pedals, she ran through the checklist with amazing speed. This is not so much a testimony to her efficiency, but more correctly attributable to the fact that, largely, none of it was actually there to check. No on-board computer, no multimedia entertainment system, no warning lights, no switches, no airbags. No *figs 8* through *97*.

And definitely no keycard insertion slot. Definitely no *fig. 9*.

It turned out that the entire fascia was removable, for security purposes, and somebody had removed it, for theft purposes.

Now, I don't want to get all cranky on you here, and start whining about what a state society is in, when criminals have sunk so low they go around actually stealing motor vehicle security features, but I can't deny I was thinking along those lines.

I mean, what is the point of stealing an anti-theft device? What earthly use could it be? What could you use it for, except to steal an identical model with a removable dashboard that had already been removed? But, if that was your intention, why not steal the whole car in the first place? Maybe there was a way to get the dashboard up and running at home. Maybe there was a big demand out there for multimedia entertainment systems equipped with utterly redundant indicator lights, a tachometer and twin airbags. Maybe no modern teenager's bedroom is complete without one.

Mercifully, there was a replacement fascia in the workshop, but because I'd signed off on the checklist, it was chargeable to me. Fine. What did I care? I had a car, and there was every good chance the car would now go. Lawks a mussy, it might even go where I wanted it to. Riches beyond dreaming. The fascia seemed to cost more than the entire car could possibly have been worth, but why should I care, right? It wasn't my money. In fact, it was probably your money. You don't mind, do you?

When I arrived back at the Affordable clutching my shiny new fascia in my pathetically eager mitts, I shouldn't have been surprised to find the car had been clamped. But I was.

The yellow-overalled mechanic was standing by it, wiping his hands on his oily rag again, torn between admiring his handiwork and enjoying my reaction.

I smiled at him. I hoped, for his sake, that he spotted it as a dangerous smile. 'I'm parked in a restricted zone, right?'

He smiled back at me, the petty-minded son of a bitch, and nodded.

'You told me I couldn't leave it there, didn't you?'

He nodded again. 'Several times, as I recall.'

Carefully, neatly, I stripped the bubble wrap off the fascia. 'And, refresh my memory: did I explain to you that I couldn't move it? That the car was, to all intents and purposes, an immovable object. Did you not, in fact, physically test that hypothesis personally? And as a result of said examination, did you not concur along with me that the vehicle was, indeed, enjoying a state of incurable stationariness?'

He shrugged with his Mussolini lip again. 'That's not the point here –'

I interrupted him, but quietly. 'Oh, I think it is the point here. I think it's precisely the point here. You see, I'm not quite sure how, in your amusingly original perception of reality, you thought I might accomplish the transportation of this woefully static, ironically named "automobile" from its state of acknowledged irreparable immobility to a more desirable state of elsewhereness.'

I was overcooking, now. English may be the legally enforced lingua franca of Europe, but the English use of irony has failed to travel beyond the shores of its birthplace. Il Duce just stared at me blankly, and wiped and wiped his hands.

I broadened my smile and tried again. 'How did you expect me to move it?'

'I didn't. That's why I went to get the clamp.'

I lowered my voice even further, and cranked up the smile one final notch. 'I see.' My teeth were so fiercely gritted by now, and my vocal volume so low, I was probably only audible to blue whales. I fought off a mental image of me using the mechanic's teeth as a xylophone and the fascia as a mallet to thrash out the 'Flight of the Bumblebee' in its entirety.

I leaned into the car and clicked the fascia onto the dashboard to buy some time to compose myself.

My investment failed, because when I straightened up to face him, I had a heart full of colourfully murderous plans, and a mind all ready to act them out.

'Okayyyyyy . . .' I wound the long tube of bubble wrap around my fists, making what I hoped were eyeball-popping sounds, 'all that remains is for you to remove that clamp, and I'll be on my way.'

I must have looked like I meant business, because Benito's face dropped, its colour drained, and he took a shaky and involuntary step back. 'I can't do that.'

'Of course you can,' I assured him, winding the bubble wrap tighter.

'No, really, I can't remove the clamp.' He sounded genuinely apologetic, which was beginning to worry me.

'I don't mind paying a fine.'

'You don't understand. I can't remove the clamp; I don't have the key.'

'You don't have the key?'

He shook his head. 'The clamping firm, it's a private company.'

'But you put the clamp on, did you not?'

'Yes. You don't need the key to put the clamp on.'

'So . . .' I kept my lips pursed in the 'O' formation for some considerable time. 'So. My threatening to strangle the life out of you, using this bubble wrap as a makeshift ligature, that's probably not going to get me anywhere in this particular instance?'

'No,' he agreed, again apologetically. 'Probably not.'

'Very well, then. Who do we call to get the clamp removed?'

'You can't do it over the phone. You have to go in person.'

'Why?' Pop, pop, pop. 'Why would that be?'

'I think they want to maximise the inconvenience. Illegal parking is a major problem in Paris. They're really cracking down on it.'

They? All of a sudden, this whole business was the fault of a faceless 'They'. The fascist mechanic no longer wanted to be my adversary; he wanted to be my friend. He wanted us to be just two innocent bystanders swept up in events beyond our control, instigated by nameless bureaucrats who spent their time making rules just to screw people like him and me over.

'Okayyyyyy . . .' I wound the bubble wrap tighter still. I was beginning to find it soothing. 'Soooooooo . . . where exactly is the clamping firm's Paris office?'

'In Toulouse.'

'Pardon me?'

'They closed down the Paris office. It was too busy.'

'Wait a minute.' Poppety, pippety, pip, pop, pop, pop. 'Are you saying they closed down the Paris office because it was too busy?'

'That's what I'm saying.' He shook his head ruefully and made some 'tch' sounds.

'So now I have to go to Toulouse to get my car unclamped in Paris?'

He just carried on shaking his head, wiping his hands and doing the 'tch, tch, tch' thing.

'And just bear with me, because I'm having a wee problem with this here: how the hell am I supposed to get to Toulouse, exactly?'

He gave me a helpless, wide-eyed shrug. 'Bus, I guess. Or train. Or . . .'

He had nowhere to go from here. We both knew what we both knew about the public transport strike. 'Or . . . ?'

'Or, you could always hire another car.'

'I could hire another car?'

'Just a suggestion.'

'Well, now. This is an interesting scenario. I lash out a fortune hiring yet *another* vehicle from you nice people at Rent-Ur-Car, and in the unlikely circumstance that this second vehicle actually *goes*, I then drive in it all the way to Toulouse, pay a fine, drive back to Paris, wait for the unclampers to show, then pick up the original hire car, and finally I can start to go where I actually wanted to go in the first place. Is *that* the new fucking master plan? Is *that* the genius scheme you're suggesting? Anyone spot a *flaw* in that proposal? No hurry. We appear to have all day.'

'Just trying to be helpful, Mister.'

'You knew this when you put that clamp on, didn't you?'

He looked at the clamp, then he looked back at me. 'I guess I wasn't thinking it through.'

He guessed he wasn't thinking it through.

'All right. All right. I'll do it. I'm not going to go to Toulouse, because that part is fucking madness. But I am prepared to hire another car. Can we do that? Can we do that very quickly, please, before I go into a psychopathic rage and kill everyone on the lot in a bubble wrap strangling frenzy?'

Of course, there were no more cars to be hired. I knew it, and he knew it, and he knew and I knew we both knew we knew it. He finished wiping his hands and put the rag in his pocket. He hiked his thumb towards the office block. 'Why don't I go and check with the rental girl?' he offered, all chirrupy and helpful, now. 'See if anything's come in?'

I let him go. I think that surprised him. I think he'd pictured spending the next few hours, which would be his last, dangling by a bubble wrap noose from the nearest lamp post. I watched him trying not to actually run away, but failing, then turned around and started looking around the lot.

The truth was, I wanted him out of the way now, so I could just jemmy off the clamp and be on my way. I found a rusted tyre iron, which would probably do the trick. If it didn't, a certain yellow-overalled mechanic would find himself wearing it for the rest of his life, like a fairy wears a Christmas tree.

I bent to the back wheel and prodded the clamp with the tyre iron. It split apart without any force being necessary. Il Duce hadn't been lying. He really was a truly bad mechanic.

I slid into the driver's seat and popped the keycard in its slot. The new dashboard lit up like a Las Vegas million-dollar slot machine – *fig. 8* all the way through to *fig. 97* all present and correct. I don't mind telling you, I sang a little samba myself. I tapped in the four-digit pin code and the engine purred into life.

As I cruised out of the lot, I spared a glance at the rental office window. The mechanic was peering out at me from behind the flimsy sanctuary of a grinning cardboard cutout of a fictionally helpful Rent-Ur-Car assistant. It was only when I gave an understated victory salute in his direction that I noticed the bubble wrap was still wound around my fist. Tightly, too. I could barely feel my fingers.

If ever I'm called upon to rewrite the classics, I'll have a whole new list of labours for Hercules. Bringing Cerberus the

Hellhound from the Kingdom of the Dead? That won't even make the top ten. That won't even be in the charts. Hiring a rental car from Paris? I'd like to see old Hercules try that.

I'd like to see him try.

TWENTY-TWO

I'd been driving for six hours, and Vienna by Wednesday was beginning to seem a trifle ambitious. I was thinking perhaps I should lower my sights a tad, and just aim to get out of the Champs-Elysées before my pension was due.

Cunningly, the city planners had chosen the day of an all-out public transport strike to introduce a super new one-way system to the city, and no matter which turn I took, I always seemed to be heading for the Arc de Triomphe. Today, all roads did not lead to Rome. Today all roads led to an Eiffel Tower souvenir stand with a red, white and blue striped awning. Well, it was certainly a radical new traffic concept, not without its merits. You force all the vehicles down exactly the same street, and free up the rest of the roads for pedestrians. It could catch on.

The entire city was going nowhere, slowly. As planning cock-ups go, this was an average affair: at least the traffic was actually moving. True, it was all moving in the same direction and down the same road, but even that was better than the total gridlocks we were getting used to. Three years ago, a new pilot road scheme had brought Madrid to a standstill for five days. Cars had to be airlifted out to Barcelona so they could start again from somewhere else.

There were workmen at every junction frantically adjusting the signs as you drove past. It must have been hard and challenging work for the poor, beleaguered devils, and it wasn't made any easier by the legions of frustrated motorists pelting them with various projectiles, assertions about the validity of their lineage and threats of lethal violence *en passant.* I felt sorry for them, really I did, but that didn't stop me buying some rotten fruit from a roadside vendor and hurling a few tomatoes their way.

I just stuck at it, stoically. They couldn't keep me driving down the Champs-Elysées for ever, could they?

But eventually, as night began to fall, I began to believe they could. I began to believe I would spend the rest of my life in a Fiat Affordable, driving slowly towards Napoleon's great arch, then circling slowly around and driving slowly towards it again. If I ever wanted a family, I'd have to raise them in the back seat, and send them to school in the trunk.

The weird thing was, there were hundreds of motorists who kept risking my life and theirs to *push in front of me.* What for? We were all going the same way round in a gigantic circle, for crying out loud. What was the point of hurrying to get one car closer to the Arc de Triomphe, so you could reach it for the twenty-fifth time in order to turn back and go round it again? Yet, for these crazy fruitcakes, it was a matter of life and death, and anyone who failed to let them pass the instant they blared their horns was subjected to a torrent of wild screams and threats and vividly sexual gesticulations. Really. Where's that bin bag full of faecal matter when you really need it?

Eventually, somebody somewhere worked something out, after a fashion. And, likewise eventually, the car's GPS system actually caught up with the new traffic arrangements and managed to guide me out of the city and onto the open road.

Just before the first stretch of motorway, I pulled into a service station and topped everything up: the batteries, the cooking oil, everything. I had planned to stop overnight in Germany, but I was so far behind schedule, I decided to opt for the motorway's automised lane. You pay a mileage fee, key your route into the central motorway computer and let it take over the driving for you. With a 56 kph upper speed limit, it wouldn't be the fastest way to travel, but at least I'd be moving while I slept. And after my single buttock's worth of human pyramid slobber slumber last night in the pens, I needed sleep badly. My right cheek was the only part of me that was fully rested.

I stocked up on what few edible comestibles the services had to offer, with the Affordable's detachable fascia under my armpit at all times, and one eye over my shoulder for abseiling clampers. I truly was half expecting to be arrested by a clamping firm SWAT team from Toulouse. Maybe driving up the same road in Paris for fourteen straight hours had left my nerves a trifle jangly. But here's a little tip from me: people who tell you you're paranoid? They're almost certainly in on the plot.

I slid the car into the auto lane and felt a gentle lurch as the system took over the controls. I searched out something light but offensive on the radio, and eased the driver's seat back as close to horizontal as it would go. I found a 'privacy' button on the dashboard control panel and pressed it. The windscreen and windows slowly filled with a translucent black liquid. Gradually, the tension began to seep out of my body. I shouldn't have let it. I should have hung onto that tension, because I was going to need it. Very soon.

I hate people who dream sensible narrative dreams. I hate them most because they tell you all about those dreams. They love nothing better than to pin you down and recount every millisecond of their dreams in infinitesimally small detail. Because the bizarre thing is: these so-called dreams they dream are mind-numbingly dull. They're exactly like reality, only *nothing interesting ever happens in them.* Nothing at all. They are beyond mundane. There are no hobgoblins chasing anybody, no gravity-defying flights over skyscrapers, no familiar faces that melt into demons. Nothing. Their dreams are entirely made up of boring, awful ordinariness. They must surely be, in fact, even more boring than the boring dreamer's real life. Otherwise they'd blow their own brains out without a moment's hesitation, rather than face another morning. I can't see why anyone would bother dreaming these kinds of dreams in the first place, let alone boasting about them the next day.

Me? My dreams are insane. They make no sense at all. One minute they're one thing, the next they're something else. I'll be in a strange room with a woman I've never met who seems to know me, then all of a sudden a band of rowdy itinerants will start climbing in through the window, and I realise I'm sitting on a toilet with no lock on the door and it's really an aeroplane and I'm running down the aisle. See what I mean? Unconnected nonsense. And that's just a small, nonsensical portion of just one of my insane dreams. But that's how dreams are supposed to be, isn't it? Melting clocks and burning giraffes? Isn't that where the word 'surreal' comes from in the first place? Can you imagine if Dali had dreamed those dull narratively sensible dreams? 'Oh, look – a painting of a horse in a field. And look: the horse is eating some hay. Salvador, you are one weird motherfucker.'

One day, I'm going to buttonhole some of those dull dreamers and force them to listen to a dream or two of mine. Maybe that will shut the boring suckers up.

The random dream I'd been having had been broken by the buzzing of the doorbell on my friend the orang-utan's penny-farthing bicycle. As I jerked back to reality, the doorbell was still buzzing. Instinctively, I tried to get up to answer it, only to be snapped back immediately by some kind of restraint. My sleep-addled mind began racing away before sanity could catch up with it. Clearly I'd been shanghaied and strapped to a bed by persons unknown. What were they after, these wicked sons of bitches? Rape? Murder? Torture? Torture and *then* murder? And why were the evil bastards piping easy-listening music into the room?

After these few small moments of dislocated panic, I managed to remember I was actually in a car.

I don't know how long I'd been sleeping. Long enough to render every single joint in my body stiffer than a teenager's bed sheets. I swear, even my ears had rigor mortis. I rolled my poor, thick head around. My neck cracked, and just kept on cracking. It sounded like an army marching on gravel.

I felt under the seat for the tilt control and raised myself back into the driving position. I massaged my eyes until I could focus on the dashboard readout. I'll be frank: if the display had indicated I was in Bratislava town centre, or heading pell-mell along the Sarajevo ring road, I would have been less than astonished. But no, as far as I could tell, I was pretty much where I ought to be, still heading in a Viennese direction, and making fine time, to boot.

The doorbell started buzzing again. A red light was flashing on the fascia. It was the low fuel warning. Incredibly, I'd been sleeping for more than eight hours.

I instructed the computer guidance system to pull into the next service station. I figured I could afford a short stopover for some breakfast and even a badly needed shower. There was a pretty ripe aroma in the car doing battle with the dangling car freshener that smelled like baby sick, and I had an awful suspicion the culprit might be me.

I flicked the car out of autodrive and pulled into the service station car park. I opened the door. There was a glorious aroma of fresh baking. I cracked my sleep-ravaged body out of the vehicle and upright. I stretched all the parts of me I could legally stretch in public. I sounded like a barrage of photographic flashbulbs at a Leicester Square movie premiere. I was in pain and more than a little dishevelled, but on the plus side, I was scant minutes away from some fresh carrot juice and good French coffee. I wish I'd relished the moment a little more. Pain or not, this was as good as I was going to feel for some considerable time.

I detached the fascia. I didn't want to take it with me, in case the shower facilities in the service station were, by some miraculous accident, actually usable. I decided to risk leaving it in the boot. I walked round to the back of the car and popped it open.

There was a man in the trunk.

I didn't remember leaving him there.

He looked fairly dead.

I closed the hatchback.

I glanced around the car park. It was busy, but no one was paying much attention to me, so I risked opening the boot again. Yes, he was still there. His eyes were open, but they weren't seeing much. I had to make sure, though. As nonchalantly as I could, I checked for a pulse. His wrist was colder than a woman's foot in a winter bed. He was more than fairly dead. He was quite exceptionally dead. I turned my head sideways to see if I recognised him. His face did seem familiar, somehow, but I couldn't quite place it.

There was nothing in the car I could use to cover the body, so I rested the fascia on top of him, then closed the boot again and locked it.

This was a problem. I decided against simply fuelling up and driving off. That wasn't going to make the problem go away. I needed to think this through. I went into the cafeteria, picked up a large jug of coffee and found a seat by a window I could watch the car from.

There was a dead man in my car.

I couldn't for the life of me work out how he'd got there.

I hadn't actually left the vehicle since I picked it up in Paris. Had someone, some time in the night, leapt on my travelling car with a corpse over his shoulder, opened the boot, dumped the body inside, then closed the boot and leapt off again without me or anybody else noticing? Surely that would require a perpetrator with the combined super powers of Spiderman and Captain Invisible.

Had the car been stopped, somewhere along the way, without my realising it?

Had there been some kind of vastly improbable accident, where the poor victim had been propelled through his windscreen into my inexplicably open boot, which had then slammed shut on him, sealing his fate? That would certainly explain the expression on his face.

Something significant registered itself on the periphery of my vision. I looked over at a TV screen in the corner of the room. A news report was playing. The lead item appeared to feature my uninvited hitchhiker.

I knocked the coffee jug over.

I mopped up most of the spillage and walked up to the screen, but the news had moved on. I had to wait till the end of the bulletin for the recap. Sure enough, his image appeared behind the newsreader's shoulder again. And my problem suddenly got a whole lot worse.

The corpse in my car belonged to the French Minister of the Interior.

TWENTY-THREE

The way I saw it, I had three choices. I could call the authorities, and explain to them that the French Minister of the Interior was not in fact missing, as they thought, but was currently occupying a considerable proportion of the cubic capacity of my boot space in a dead manner, and would they like to come and collect him, because I had a schedule to keep to?

That option seemed to require more in the way of explanations than I could reasonably come up with. Let's face it: they'd probably want to know how the French Minister of the Interior got himself into my boot, and, like as not, they'd want to know how he got himself all dead, too, and I had the distinct feeling that an affable shrug and 'Beats me' on both counts would not adequately satisfy their curiosities, so I put that one on the back boiler.

I could try and deposit him somewhere in the service station forecourt, but it was broad daylight, the car park was starting to pack out, and even if I managed to pull it off without anyone noticing, there were video security cameras all over the place, and I'd be unlikely to avoid a starring role in the *News at Noon*, or I'd achieve my fifteen minutes of fame later in the year on the TV show *Europe's Dumbest Criminals*. No thank you.

No, the best plan seemed to be to fill up and drive away, then find somewhere en route to drop off my stowaway that was a little more discreet. Like a bustling shopping mall. I bought a couple of car rugs, a picnic blanket and some heavy-duty bin liners and headed back for the car. I opened the boot as if there were absolutely no dead politicians in there at all, took out the fascia and arranged my purchases over the corpse.

I felt I was handling a difficult situation with admirable composure. I even smiled at a couple of pretty girls passing by, while the boot with the body in it was still gawping wide open. I congratulated myself that I was thinking pretty damned clearly. I was not.

It wasn't until I was back in the autodrive lane that the shock began to wear off, and I got round to asking myself the vital question: how likely was it that the corpse of the French Minister of the Interior had found its way into my car accidentally? That out of all the vehicles that could have been used to accommodate a dead politician, all the hatchbacks and trucks and station wagons that might have happily lodged a deceased French Interior Minister, my little Fiat Affordable had been chosen at random? It was unlikely, was it not? Was it not, in fact, much *more* likely that somebody had planted him there, at the very least to cause me some discomfiture, if not to out and out frame me for the crime? And were there not, furthermore, some alarming ramifications to be extrapolated from that fact?

The only possible someone who might have even a slightly credible motive to do such a thing would be Johnny Appleseed himself.

Which meant that Klingferm's killer definitely knew more or less who and what I was. And what's more, he knew where I was going to be, and when.

On top of which, the bastard was clearly toying with me. He could have put a bomb in the car, or hooked the exhaust pipe up to poison me with carbon monoxide fumes while I slept in the autodrive lane. He could, presumably, have done to me whatever he'd done to the French Minister of the Interior, and left my staring corpse as a neat little gift in the boot of some other poor swine's Fiat Affordable, with that wide-eyed expression of understandable surprise contorting my features from now until the Day of Judgement.

So, clearly, my cover was blown. I'd made the transition from hunter to hunted in the space of one excruciatingly uncomfortable catnap.

There is a theoretically inviolable procedure for such a circumstance. Basically, I'm supposed to contact my link-man, and find a way to leave a trail for him to follow in the extremely likely event my warranty gets voided. But somewhere at the back of my head, my little voice was telling me not to do that. After all, that's what Klingferm had done, and look where it had gotten him. Look where it had gotten *me.* I had to face the possibility that my tormentor *wanted* me to call in back-up. Why else would he have given me the opportunity? He could wipe out the entire network that way. He could pick us all off, one at a time like clay pipes at a fairground, without breaking sweat.

So I decided to violate the inviolable procedure. The chances were that would be my best shot at short-term survival. And I had to start being unpredictable.

The first thing I had to do was to get out of the autodrive lane. Much as I needed to think, I couldn't afford to leave the car under the control of the motorway computer system. One malicious phone call and I'd be pulled over onto the hard shoulder, immobilised and locked in.

The autodrive system didn't want to let me go, of course. It kept asking me if I was sure, and though, yes, I told it, I was sure, it felt perhaps I really wasn't sure I was sure, and I was only saying I was sure because I was, perhaps, confused, so under the circumstances it felt obliged to make sure I was definitely sure, so it asked me again if I was sure, and when I assured it I was really pretty damned sure I was sure, it forced me to run through a humungous checklist to prepare me for the gritty horrors that awaited the unwary innocent who was foolhardy enough to take control of his vehicle into his own hands. The entire procedure was designed to minimise refunds, I think. And in other circumstances, it would probably have worn me down enough to surrender. In fact, when it came to question fifty-seven: 'Are you awake?' I damn near did give up.

But I persevered. I persevered through a hundred and twenty-one checks and questions. I persevered through a protracted negotiation over the precise amount and method of refund. I didn't even scream when it asked me one final, final time if I was absolutely sure that I was sure I wanted to go ahead and do this crazy thing.

And my perseverance was rewarded.

A countdown reluctantly appeared on the screen, announcing that I had 'THIRTY SECONDS TO SELF DRIVE' with all the calm understatement you'd expect from a nuclear alert.

I felt like a schoolboy at the end of summer term final assembly. If I'd had a cap, I'd have thrown it in the air. I followed all the onscreen instructions like a dog follows pheromones. Even though I was pretty certain the computer couldn't possibly check if I was complying, I wasn't about to risk failure this close to victory. Like the nice computer said, I checked the rear-view mirror. Most of it was obscured by the legend: 'Objects appearing in this mirror are closer than they seem.' Obediently, I likewise checked the wing mirror, which was almost as useless thanks to the marvellously helpful inscription: 'Objects appearing in this mirror are actually behind you.'

Ten seconds to release. I identified a suitable gap in the traffic and flicked on the appropriate indicator. I placed my hands on the steering wheel in the ten to two position. I placed my right foot gently on the accelerator.

The countdown reached zero, the car filled with an impressive array of ominous warning sirens and whoops and the words 'SELF DRIVE' flashed in violent red on the screen. The door locks released themselves. I flicked one final check over my left shoulder and gently eased the wheel clockwise.

You know, I am *such* a cock-eyed optimist, I actually

expected the car to respond. I really did. What a lunk. What a palooka. What a putz.

The car, it goes without saying, did *not* respond. Of course it didn't. The car just carried on pootling along in the autodrive lane as if the last twenty minutes hadn't happened at all.

I tried pressing my foot down on the accelerator. I tried stamping hard on the brake. I tried wrenching the steering wheel left and right with demented enthusiasm. I might as well have been in a Noddy car on a toddler's merry-go-round. I had no more control over my trajectory than a limbless skydiver without a parachute.

I tapped away at the computer screen, for all the good that was going to do me. Naturally, the system couldn't release me from autodrive, because it already had done so. 'SELF DRIVE' was still flashing its mocking crimson on the display, was it not?

I kept my hands on the wheel, still harbouring some kind of vague, unlikely hope that the computer would eventually tire of baiting me and suddenly relinquish control, but the computer showed no such inclination. Gradually, I released my grip.

I had no idea how far away the next services were, but I tapped out instructions for the computer to pull into them anyway. The computer had a problem with that, of course, since I was theoretically driving the car myself.

It wasn't hard to see where this was going. The car would carry on pootling until its fuel ran out, leaving me stranded in full public glare, no doubt blocking traffic in an immobile vehicle, with the mortal remains of a stiff kidnapped politician in my boot.

There's a heart-warming school of positive thought that urges us to perceive problems not as obstacles, but as opportunities. When you find yourself bang up against an insurmountable obstacle, and you recall that particular gem of wisdom, you may feel a strong compulsion to seek out the progenitors of that theory, grab them by their throats and bang the backs of their heads against your obstacle until their brains start squirting out of their ears like a raspberry and banana smoothie fountain. That was certainly the uppermost fantasy in my mind at this particular juncture.

But as I ran through my list of options – which seemed, as far as I could tell to consist only of a) stay in the vehicle until it stops then make a doomed attempt to bolt for freedom, and b) there is no b – it occurred to me that I might turn the situation to my advantage, after all.

Since the car was under the illusion it was being driven by a real human being, I was now clearly surplus to its requirements. Theoretically, the car shouldn't mind if I left it to its own devices.

Hopefully it wouldn't even notice.

If I could somehow contrive to depart its vicinity, there was no reason to believe it wouldn't carry on pootling along with its stiff ministerial cargo until its fuel ran out.

The plan had a couple of downsides, in that it involved my vacating a moving vehicle, and in the middle of nowhere, to boot, and you know how I feel about the whole falling thing. Still, it seemed marginally more appealing than trying to convince a couple of black helicopters full of trigger-happy Europol anti-terrorist armed response units of the absolute totality of my innocence in the entire affair.

I hit the privacy button and punched up the speedometer. A steady 56 kph. Is that a respectable speed at which to pitch yourself out of a racing automobile? I couldn't be sure, but my guess was that it was probably a smidgen on the overly rapid side of safe.

I started to ease myself onto the passenger seat. This action provoked a warning sound from the dashboard. A computer voice counselled me that it was a serious breech of traffic regulations to attempt to drive a vehicle from anywhere but the driver's seat, and unless I repositioned myself immediately, the appropriate authorities would be alerted. Well, I couldn't have that, now, could I? So I complied.

So, the car would rat me up if the driving seat were vacated. Well, as luck would have it, I just happened to have a spare driver in my boot. He didn't have to do anything except sit behind the steering wheel, and even a dead interior minister can pull that off.

It was a complicated manoeuvre. I had to jack the driver's seat back as far as it would go, then pull the backs of the rear seats forward in order to get at the boot, and every time my centre of gravity left its optimum driving position, the siren went off and the stool pigeon of a computer threatened to grass me up. Then there was the considerable problem of extracting the extremely heavy and extraordinarily stiff stiff from the boot and dragging him up to the front.

It was painful, sweaty and intimately unpleasant work, and by the time the extremely ex French Minister of the Interior was safely ensconced behind the wheel, the very last thing I felt like doing was hurling myself out of a hurtling vehicle.

I had to pick the right moment to do it: somewhere poorly lit and between security cameras, when traffic was reasonably light, and on a bend as the car was slowing down.

I held open the passenger door, watching the road and the speedo, and trying to ignore the computer's incessant and wholly unnecessary observation that the passenger door was open, for a good twenty minutes.

I began to despair.

I appeared to have decided to make my move at the start of the longest stretch of perfectly straight road in the whole history of human construction. There was probably a plaque somewhere along here proudly testifying to that very fact.

Finally, I saw a bend approaching. Under normal circumstances, I would have classified it more as a slight kink, but it would have to do. Otherwise I might find myself travelling all the way to Vienna with my backside dangling out of the passenger door. At least I'd have a tiny window of cover from the car behind.

I watched the speedometer. It slowed from a potentially lethal 56 kph to a stately 52 kph. Marvellous.

I jumped.

TWENTY-FOUR

I jumped. As I did so, I tried to swing the passenger door shut and simultaneously brace myself for the impact. I am living testimony to the fact that you cannot achieve both of those goals at fifty-two kilometres per hour.

I managed to get the door shut.

I expected the impact to hurt, and let me tell you I was not disappointed. I did, however, expect it to stop hurting at some point, but it didn't. I bowled along the aptly named hard shoulder for some considerable distance like a giant tumbleweed, only with nerves for hurting and blood for bleeding and skin for bruising, without appearing to decelerate in any appreciable way, each point of impact finding a brand new part of me to inflict with pain.

I finally came to rest in a shallow ditch just off the highway.

I lay there a while. I would like to think I wasn't whimpering like a lovesick schoolgirl, but I find that unlikely. I analysed the feedback from my body, hoping some small part of me would report in undamaged, but none did. I felt no particular urge to move again, ever. The ditch seemed as fine a place as any to settle on as my grave. If someone had come up and offered to shovel me over with dirt, I'd probably have thanked them. I'd probably have offered them money.

But I didn't have time for such luxuries as losing my desire to go on existing. The Fiat might carry on undiscovered for hours, but there was no guarantee of that. It might just as well pull over at the next services, leaving the dead French politician with more explaining to do than he could likely handle. I had to be out of here and as far away as I could get, as quickly as I could humanly get there.

I rolled over onto my front. My ribs didn't like that, but screw them, right? I placed my palms on the ground either side of my shoulders, and they complained too, but frankly they could just shut the hell up and get in line. With an effort of will I would class as way beyond superhuman, I hoisted myself to my knees. None of me liked that. My arms were complaining, my shoulders were whining, my knees were seriously considering industrial action and my back was threatening to take me to court and sue me for every penny I'd ever even thought of. I told them all to take a ticket and get in the God-damned queue.

I hauled myself to my feet, and swayed until I was as close to upright as I was ever likely to get. I felt like Tony Montana just before the final gunshot from behind.

What now? I had to make ground, and lots of it. Not to escape the authorities. That was pretty much a done deal already. They'd find my fingerprints all over the car, of course, and all over the body as well, but then they'd discover those fingerprints were registered to fourteen different dead servicemen in various jurisdictions around Europe.

Of course, they'd trace the vehicle back to the Rent-Ur-Car hire place in Paris, and they might even get around to eliciting a description from Mussolini the mechanic, and even the rental clerk, but I wasn't too worried about that. I've been identikitted once before, and even I didn't recognise me. Only about one in fifteen witnesses is any use at all at remembering faces, and even if the police artists were geniuses, they'd be working with a composite from two people's memories. On top of which, I probably looked considerably different now. I probably looked like one of the more radically decomposed zombies from *Return of the Living Dead.*

Even if they did somehow come up with an accurate description, it's easy enough to change your face these days.

A hypodermic full of bee venom here, a jab of Botox there, and you'd need a map just to shave your own beard. Worst-case scenario, I could track down Dr Rutter and get him to swap my face with my arse. True, I'd probably wind up looking a lot like Captain Zuccho's handsomer twin, but like I say, we are talking worst case.

I'd rented the car as Harry Tequila and I'd have to abandon that particular identity, which was a shame, not only because I had a peculiar schizophrenic fondness for old Harry Tequila, but also I was rapidly running out of people to be.

Truth be told, I was dropping like flies.

What I did have to worry about was Johnny Appleseed. Was I right to be thinking of him as a single perp? There could, I suppose, have been several Johnnies. He certainly seemed to be all over the place. But I had to make certain assumptions or die, and to me, the whole set-up had the efficient feel of a lone-wolf operation. I also chose to assume that it was a man. Probabilities.

There was no way of knowing for certain precisely when he'd picked up my trail, or exactly how intimate he was with the progress of my investigations, but it was safest to take the position he had been on to me from the start and knew everything. Which meant I'd be very foolish indeed to try and keep Klingferm's appointment in Vienna.

This much was certain: my cover had been blown wide open. I was officially what we in the business call 'dirty'. Which meant I couldn't risk contacting any of my associates or agencies that might help me, for fear of tainting them. I was too dirty even to turn myself back over to Home. I was, in short, utterly alone. Which left me two alternatives: lie down in a lime pit, die and disappear, or head back to my London base to regroup and try and steal a march on the bastard. I wasn't used to being quarry, and I didn't much like it.

But I was a long, long way from London.

Still, like the Zen man said, even a journey of a thousand miles begins with a single step. I looked around. There could have been a nice gentle grassy slope for me to amble down, but there wasn't, naturally. Naturally, there was a vindictively steep and gallingly high escarpment for me to climb, complete with stiff thickets of vicious gorse, stinging nettles and impenetrable undergrowth, doubtless concealing countless layers of putrefying wild animal crap.

What larks.

I sighed the sigh of an entire beleaguered nation and started to climb.

I didn't plan to walk for long.

I never plan to walk for long.

Walking is primitive. Let's face it: walking was invented by monkeys, and even they don't like doing too much of it. They break it up every once in a while by swinging through some trees, to speed things up a little. Walking is a stupid way of getting from A to B, or any other capital letter for that matter. It's slow, it's ponderous, it's dull and it requires an uncommon amount of effort for scant reward. That's how I feel about walking even when I haven't just thrown myself out of a speeding vehicle at fifty-two kilometres per hour, cracking every single one of my ribs and scraping so much skin off my knees they wouldn't have looked out of place in a butcher's window next to the calf's liver.

So walking was not only boring, it was downright painful, and I had an urgent lust for alternative transport. I had it in mind to reach a town of sufficient size to warrant a bus service, if not, heaven forbid, an actual train station, in reasonably short order. Failing that, I hoped I would sooner or later wander across a road of sufficient sophistication to bear some kind of traffic that might be flagged down. Failing all the above, I surely had a reasonable chance, at least, of encountering another human being who might be persuaded to give me a piggyback for lots of money.

But no.

Of all the places I could have picked, I had chosen to leap out of the car in the absolute dead centre of the Land That Time Forgot. I swear to you: it's probably marked exactly that on the map. You'll find it right at the end of the Infinitely Long Straight Road. I walked for over an hour and a half without finding so much as a roughly trodden path. Cavemen hadn't even wandered here. It would not have caused me a moment's surprise if a giant pterodactyl had swooped down and swept me off in its jaws as a titbit for its nest of cawing young.

I stopped off in the absolute middle of the middle of nowhere and buried Harry Tequila in an abandoned badger's sett. I filled it up with stones and bracken, to discourage any sabre-toothed tigers or giant woolly mammoths that might come snuffling around, and carried on walking.

The thick underbrush was hacking at the dismal remnants of my pathetic butternut squash shoes and shredded ankles, and there wasn't a millimetre of my entire body that wasn't racked with pain. I don't want to undermine my tough guy image with you, but I was feeling very, very sorry for myself. I wanted to cry. I wanted my momma. But I wanted those things in a very tough guy kind of way.

Finally, after doing the monkey thing for close on four hours, I came across a cultivated field. Where there's a cultivated field, there's a civilized human not far away. Or a farmer, at least.

For a few moments of mad enthusiasm, I actually broke into a lively, grinning hobble, but the neatly furrowed fields just seemed to carry on endlessly to the horizon, and I quickly fell back into my broken, wretched stagger. I had traversed enough fields to last me this and the next dozen lifetimes before I finally saw the smoke rising from a distant farmhouse chimney.

It was a large farm, but wholly underpopulated. The farmyard was occupied by a handful of the usual suspects: chickens, a few pigs, the odd cow, but they all seemed terribly lacklustre, as if beset by a strange animal ennui. The chickens could barely muster a disgruntled squawk and a couple of desultory wing flaps at my appearance. There was a sorry-looking tractor sitting sadly in its shed. All in all, the word 'thriving' did not come to mind.

I spotted a brimming rain barrel by one of the outbuildings, and it suddenly struck me I was uncommonly thirsty. All I'd had to drink in the past twenty-four hours was the coffee in the service station, and most of that had wound up on the cafeteria table.

I walked over to the barrel and scooped up some icy water in my hands. My hands were so caked in unnameable filth and dried blood, the water came up dark purple, but I drank it anyway. I sucked it down by the filthy gallon. When my thirst was finally sated, it occurred to me that my appearance might benefit from a little tidying up before I encountered any humans or farmers, so, crisp as the air was, I stripped down to my vest and set about soaplessly scrubbing myself in the Houdini cold rainwater. It wasn't going to get me anywhere close to what an unfastidious blind man would pass as 'clean', but it might stop small children from running away screaming at the sight of me.

As I came up for air, I spotted a face watching me through a broken window pane in a surely derelict shed across the yard.

It was an old face, weathered and worn. From the proximity of the chin to the nose, I surmised it was probably toothless, too. I would not have been able to guess at its sex were it not garnished with a masculine, old, flat cap. Although it appeared to be looking in my direction, it didn't much seem interested in what I was doing. It didn't much seem interested in anything. I kept him in my field of vision, though, just in case. I shook myself as dry as possible and dabbed at my face with my vest. And then I heard that sound again.

The terrible sound of a shotgun being cocked behind me.

TWENTY-FIVE

This time, I didn't feel any fear; I guess I'd plumb run out. All I felt was a dull kind of resigned exasperation. I exhaled long and deep and raised my hands dutifully, because that's what people with shotguns trained on my person always seem to expect of me, and waited for either instructions or an explosive death, not much caring which.

An old ratchet of a voice with a thick country accent advised me to turn. Obviously, I turned.

I surmised it was a woman behind the shotgun, because she was wearing an extremely voluminous black skirt, and sporting a black headscarf rather than a flat cap. In every other respect, she looked identical to the sad old man in the shed. Her face was set in a grim, defiant gurn, so that her chin actually kept touching her nose. I swear, she could have had both those features fitted with metal segs and made a living performing some kind of facial tap-dance.

I wasn't too happy having her point the gun at me. She was truly ancient, and I really couldn't vouch for the reliability of her muscle control. I needed to diffuse the situation as quickly as possible. I thought about flashing a good old detective badge at her, but that little voice inside me warned that might not be the best idea. I never got the chance to thank the little voice, but, looking back, it probably saved my life. Instead, I dug out and slapped on my most affable, harmless grin and asked her, all polite and nice manners, if she wouldn't mind at least lowering her weapon.

She wasn't inclined to do that.

She just stood there clacking her chin against her nose, looking me up and down with a mixture of loathing and distrust, like the Pope might look at Satan if the Prince of Darkness turned up uninvited to a Vatican whist drive. Then she turned her head to one side, spat out an unlikely volume of brown sputum, then turned back to me and said something strange. Now, she was speaking some kind of French, only in an obscure, ancient dialect, and brogued with an unfamiliar accent, so I'm translating for you as best I can how it came to me.

What I think she said was: 'You fellers sure an' have an appetite for buckshot.'

Well, I have absolutely no appetite whatsoever for buckshot, and I certainly don't belong to any group of fellers that do, but before I could avail the termagant of that knowledge, the voice from the woodshed shouted out: 'Him besn't one o' them 'mission fellers.'

The old woman winced at the voice and spat back at it: 'You besn't even here, so I never heard that.'

I couldn't work out what kind of madness I'd wandered into here. Had I heard right? The crazy old witch was saying the old man didn't exist? If so, he seemed remarkably underperturbed. 'Mebbe I bes here or mebbe I besn't,' he said. 'Don't alter the fact that him besn't one of them 'mission bassards, either ways.'

The woman steadied her aim at my chestal region. 'You pay him no mind.' She flicked her head dismissively in the direction of the shed. 'Him besn't here, and you besn't seen him, neither. You follow?'

I nodded. 'He's definitely not here,' I agreed, 'and I certainly haven't seen him.' This seemed to mollify the old trout, so I chanced my arm and added: 'But he's right.'

She cocked her head at me and chinned her nose, mulling it over. 'You besn't one of them 'mission fellers, then?'

'No.' I shook my head slowly and broadened my winning smile. 'I definitely besn't.'

The voice from the shed chipped in petulantly: 'Told yers.'

This was too much for the woman. 'You never told

nobody nothing!' she shrieked. 'Being as you besn't here, you stubborn old pig shagger.' She was screaming with her face towards the woodshed and waving the shotgun around agitatedly in my vague general direction. I was trying to sway along in sort of counterpoint to it so it was only aimed directly at me about fifty per cent of the time. Not ideal, not cool, not elegant, but it doubled my chances of survival, I reckoned.

The shrew turned back to me. 'You stand still, Mister.' Reluctantly, I complied. 'Mebbe you besn't 'mission. But mebbe you's from the 'surance, though.'

The old man shouted again. 'Him besn't from no 'surance, neither.'

I really wished he'd stop helping me.

The woman jumped up and down in fury. 'How many times!? You besn't here! Can't you get it through your fat daft skull, you senile old farty?'

The old man shouted something back at her, something about him besn't having a skull at all, daft or otherwise, if him besn't there, most of which was unfortunately lost on me, because it was around about that point the old biddy fired the gun.

Her exasperation finally caused her twitching finger to tighten on the trigger involuntarily, and I was slightly distracted from the course of the dialogue by the puff of smoke and the lethal projectile that issued from the barrel of the shotgun, in the vague direction of my head at pretty close to the speed of sound.

TWENTY-SIX

I never actually heard the blast, but there must have been one.

They say you never hear the one that kills you, and – let's face it – there can't be a whole lot of eyewitness evidence to support that particular proposition, but I can confidently confirm this from savage personal experience: you *definitely* don't hear the one that sails so close to your head it scorches your eardrum and melts the wax protecting it.

The shot blew a basketball-sized hole in the outbuilding behind me, burrowed clean through a large pig and sailed right through the wall at the rear and, as far as I know, it's travelling still. She missed splashing my brains all over the farmyard cobbles like so much animal mulch by the width of a woodworm's hard-on. I didn't even have time to flinch.

The old harridan looked even more startled than I did, which was saying something, because I was the colour of Marcel Marceau. She dropped the gun and bustled over to me, waving her hands and shouting things. God knows what things she was shouting: apologies to me, curses on herself, and blame on the sad old git who didn't exist, in all probability. I couldn't be sure, because all I could hear was a dull, sonorous kind of echoing ringing, interlaced with a long, low, howling wind.

Bluntly, I'd had enough of country life by now, and I really just wanted to be on my way and walking on a city street just as soon as life could whisk me to one, but the hag kept harrying me across the yard and up the steps to the farmhouse kitchen, all the while yattering away inaudibly to me, and examining my head. I don't know why she was examining my head. Making sure it was all still there, I guess.

She sat me in front of the stove and threw an ancient blanket that smelled of old people around my shoulders. I didn't protest. I just let it happen. I actually felt strangely high and detached, what with my Quasimodo hearing and the near-death-experience-induced endorphins racing round my system, working their wily wonders on my jangled nerves.

She ladled out a ceramic mug of soup from a cauldron on the stove, and I laced my fingers around it gratefully. For the first time in as long as I could remember, someone was offering me succour, and I appreciated it. I'd have preferred not to have gone through the whole accidentally-almost-shooting-my-head-off episode in order to get it, but I wasn't in a mood to be pernickety.

My hearing was beginning to return. I could vaguely make out a distant, incessant yakking noise that seemed to be coming from the direction of the old woman as she busied about the kitchen, doing old womanly things with bits of laundry and buckets.

I sipped at the soup. It was tongue-blistering hot, but, I kid ye not, it truly was the greatest food I've ever tasted, and I've tasted plenty. It was some kind of meat and vegetable country broth. I couldn't make out what the meat was: sort of halfway between rabbit and chicken. I didn't much care. It could have been cholera-infested warthog and bubonic sewer rat for all I cared. I sucked it down greedily.

A good home-made soup is the world's finest medicine. I was already feeling better before the elixir even had time to hit my stomach. I felt like I was glowing. My hearing returned. Even the old hag was beginning to seem less dreadful. She bustled over to me carrying a steaming rag in a pair of wooden tongs. She seemed intent on applying it to my person, for some reason. I caught a whiff of its steam. It stank. Truly, it stank. It smelled like lonely death. I tried to wave her away, but she wouldn't take no for an answer.

She wrapped the malodorous hot poultice around the poor skinned knuckles of my right hand. It stung at first, and she laughed when I winced, showing off a single ochre tooth in the middle of her gaping maw, and stroked my head, making mock soothing noises, as if I were a baby, and a pretty cowardly baby at that.

She biddled on back to her steaming slop bucket and fished out another stinking rag with her tongs. She told me to take off my clothes. I hesitated, naturally, and she laughed again, and mimed mock virginal coyness. Kindly as her intentions were, I really wasn't enjoying watching that laugh, so I made a resolution to obey all her future instructions without question, rather than risk provoking more of that demonic cackling. Besides, I did not feel my honour was under major threat, so I removed my trousers.

Pretty soon, I was swathed from head to toe in steaming, stinking bandages. I remembered a food photographer had once shown me one of his tricks of the trade. To keep the food looking hot during the shoot, he soaked a feminine hygiene product in boiling water and secreted it on the plate. That's what I must have looked like: a giant hot tampon steaming by the stove.

While we waited for the poultices to do their stuff, we talked.

I asked her what I should call her, and she said as long as she could remember everybody had always called her Mamma. I didn't feel our relationship was ready for such Oedipal intimacies, so I let it go. She asked me how I'd come to this pretty pass, and I made up some yarn about a gang of thugs yanking me out of my car and bundling me into some ditch. She asked me if they'd been young tearaways, and since that's what she seemed to want to hear, I told her yes, they'd been teenage thugs. She nodded sagely and clucked something despairing about young people and respect.

I glanced over at the kitchen window. The old geezer had dared to venture from his shed, and was looking hungrily in the direction of the steaming cooking pot on the stove, his face pressed up against the pane. The old woman caught my gaze and got herself all worked up again, grabbing up a broom and shaking it at the window, yelling all kinds of imprecations and threats. The old fellow just looked at her forlornly, then turned and slouched away sullenly, back towards the lonely comfort of his derelict shed.

The woman stared after him, hands on her hips, shaking her head. 'What's a body to do with him? Him just won't have it him's dead.'

I looked up slowly and stared at her through the steam from my mug. 'He's dead?'

She nodded. 'I been a widder now for more'n a year, and him still won't have it.'

Clearly, I was on dangerous ground here, but really I felt someone had to speak out for the old chap. 'Well, he's got a bit of a point, don't you think?'

'Don't *you* start. It's bad enough *him* not wanting to be dead anymore, without you stirring things up. Lookee this.' She thrust an official document in my face. 'There's him's death certificate. It's all signed, official and everything.'

The death certificate certainly looked authentic enough. 'How did you get this?'

'In the post. Signed by the county coroner, see? You can't get deader than that.'

'Well, you can. I mean your husband does seem to be enjoying more . . . robust health than a lot of dead people I could think of.'

'That's what him says! Lookee . . .' She span a kitchen chair round so the back was facing me, straddled it like Marlene Dietrich in *The Blue Angel* and sat. She was incredibly limber for a hundred-and-forty-year-old. And she went into her tale. It was one of those yarns where all you can do is listen and smile and nod in what you hope are the right places.

'I used to feel the same, at first. It all started when us got this letter, see, from the social security. It was all nice and sympathetic saying sorry Pappa was dead, like, and offering us condolences and that, for the loss of us husband. Well, that upset him and us both, naturally, him not even being slightly dead. So us bain down the social office in a right strop and told 'em, like, that him warn't dead at all, and this was him, here, standing there in front of 'em, all alive and hale and hearty, and thems'd probably made a mistake and got him all confused with somebody else. Well, them wouldn't have it at first, of course. Said it was us'd made the mistake and him probably wasn't my husband, and us was just a bit confused. Well, that done it. That really done it. Him made quite a scene, I tell you. Quite a scene.' She chuckled fondly at the memory. 'Him wasn't one to take no nonsense, wasn't Pappa. Not when him was alive, God rest his soul.' She crossed herself. I just kept on smiling, non-committally, and wishing I was on that city street again.

'Anyways, them came over all apologetic, and sorry, like, and them was going to put things to rights and not to worry and blah-de-blah-de-blah. And us thought that's be an end to it. But no. A week later, us gets another letter of condolence from the social, only this time it's got his death certificate in it, and a big cheque an' all. Very big cheque, it was. A widder's payment, it said. Lump sum. Start of a regular widder's pension, and all. Well, that got us thinking. Mebbe us should stay quiet about it, and keep the money. Him groaned and grumbled, of course. Him was a very proud man, my husband. Not one for taking handouts. Him was all for going back and shoving that cheque up them's mossy ends. Only, the next day, us get another letter. The 'surance company sends *its* condolences, too, and inside that, there's another big cheque. Well, even *him* starts to see the logic then. See, us'd lost the farm a couple of years earlier. Them 'mission fellers, them had been paying us not to grow nothing. Us hadn't been growing nothing for two seasons, and getting good money for it and all. But my old fool of a husband, him got bored just sitting around not growing nothing, pay or not, so him started planting. Just for something to do of a day, see? Us weren't going to sell it, or nothing. It were like an hobby for him, is all it were. Well, them 'mission fellers come up at harvest time, and them didn't see it like that at all. Them said us was in breach, and this and that, and the upshot was us lost the farm. So us was stuck. Us still couldn't grow nothing, only now us weren't even getting paid for it.

'So this money, this 'surance money and widder's pension, that were a godsend. So us agreed it were best if us didn't argue, and just accepted that him was dead.

'Him moved out to the woodshed, and kept out of the way whenever the social comed round, or them 'mission bassards or the 'surance fellers turned up.

'It worked out nice. The widder's pension kept on coming, us had a fortune in the bank: everyone happy.

'But that besn't good enough for him. Oh no. Him gets bored of it, don't him? Like it's too much bother for him: sitting in him's woodshed dawn to dusk, being dead. So him starts knocking on the door, saying him's bored with being dead now, and can him move back in the house? Move back in the house! I asks you! Well, I tells him straight. "Being dead," I says, "besn't sommat you gets tired of. You has to stick at it, being dead, or us'd wind up in prison, like as not." Him says him could be just as dead in the house as in the woodshed. In the house! "And how's that supposed to look?" I says. "Us, a widder woman sleeping with the corpse of us dead husband? That'd get tongues wagging, and no mistake. Them'd have us in a straitjacket and cart us off to the nutty farm, quick as buckshot."

'Well, him didn't want that, us whisked off to some padded cell Lord knows where. Him's lonely enough already, what with being dead and stuck in the woodshed morning, noon and night. So him gives it up for a while. Then him gets all restless again and starts follering us round the yard when I'm about us chores. All that time, sitting there wi' nothing to do but be dead, him's got nothing better to do than thinking and scheming.

'Now, him says him's got this big plan for us to go off somewheres with all the money and live a life of leisure. Somewhere far away. Like Nice, him's saying, or Monte Carlo. Because it just won't sink in, him's dead. Him can't go nowhere. Him's got no passport, no social number, no identity card. Soon as him shows him's face in public, then them 'mission fellers'd be the least of it. Us'd have the social after us, the police and the 'surance fellers, too. And them 'surance fellers is worst of all. Them'd lock us up and swallow the key.'

She creaked off her chair and biddied towards me. 'But, of course, him won't let it lie. Him's always worrying away at one barmy crackpot scheme or another. So now, I do us best to ignore him.' She peeled back the poultice from my right hand and peeked underneath. 'It's not easy, mind. Him's always finding sommat to try and shag things up. Him's even taken to ploughing the fields in him's tractor, the barmy old bat. If that's not going to bring them 'mission fellers looking, I don't know what is.' She seemed satisfied with the work the poultice had done. 'That's all better, I reckons,' she clucked, and unwrapped the rag.

I looked down at my hand. Where the knuckles had been skinned raw, there weren't even scabs, just fresh, pink skin. I flexed it. I made a fist. No pain. Now, I've been around a lot of places, and I've seen some pretty strange stuff, but I've never witnessed anything quite as close to miraculous as the healing mojo Mamma had used on me. I looked up into her rheumy old eyes. I was trying to think of an adequate way to say thanks, but it wasn't necessary. She shushed me with her eyes. My expression was enough gratitude for her.

She unpeeled me and I was all pink and pain-free, all over. Even my ribs felt good. I pulled on my dry, warm clothes gratefully. I was renewed. I looked up to see her holding my tattered old butternut shoes like they were a pair of rats she'd found on her breakfast plate. 'Thim's aren't no good for walking in,' she said.

I laughed. 'Thim's aren't no good for making pumpkin and paper planes out of.'

'Pumpkin shoes?' She shook her head. 'I bets that's another of them 'mission fellers' brilliant ideas.'

'Yeah. They are full of them, aren't they?'

'They're full of sommat.'

Without any kind of warning or further consultation of any kind, she hooked open the door of the stove and threw my shoes into the flames.

Well, marvellous. It had been hard enough getting around in the bloody awful cardboard and squash shoes. Now I'd have to walk back to civilisation in a pair of socks that were so shredded, I was almost barefoot. Not good.

But she stooped to a cupboard in the corner of the room and tugged out a pair of very sturdy, proudly polished boots. 'I reckons thims'll be your size, more or less.'

'But . . . aren't they your husband's?'

'No good to him, is they? Thim's him's Sunday shoes.' She genuflected. 'May him rest in peace.'

She held the boots out and, reluctantly, I took them. I had to admit, they were a pretty good match for my size, and after my extended experience with vegetable footwear, they qualified as way beyond comfortable, let me tell you. It was like slipping my feet into warm honey. I laced them up tight and stood. I really was feeling ready for anything now. I'm not saying I looked like a style guru: I wasn't about to be invited to grace a catwalk or headline at a Paris fashion show, but I was fully kitted and ready to go. And I needed to be. This whole interlude had taken up far too much time. I was in good shape physically now, but I was still a key suspect in the abduction and assassination of a major politician, I still had an incredibly wily and accomplished killer dogging my every move, and I was still a dirty agent, stranded outside the loop of what I laughingly call my community. I wasn't exactly in a position to relax.

The old biddy was looking me up and down with a sense of proud accomplishment, like she'd raised me from a suckling babe and now I was all growed up and ready to take on the world. I felt bad about taking the old man's shoes, but not bad enough to give them up. I smiled at her. I thanked her. God help me, I actually did call her Mamma.

I walked down the kitchen steps onto the cobbled farmyard. I was trying to think of some way to repay the kindness I'd been shown, so I didn't notice the proud sound my footwear made on the cobbles. The old corpse in the shed looked over. He spotted the shoes and his forehead unfurrowed so rapidly his cap almost shot off his head. He looked over at Mamma in disbelief, then back at the boots, shook his head despondently and returned to his long, lonely brown study.

Mamma called from the kitchen doorway: 'You'll be wanting a ride into town, won't you?'

Well, I didn't want to impose any more than I already had, so I was about to turn the offer down. Then I saw the hole in the outbuilding that could have been my head, and I decided it probably wouldn't be too much of an imposition after all. 'Thank you kindly,' I said.

She threw over a bunch of keys. 'You'm can take the tractor.'

The old guy winced. So did I.

I looked down at the keys, then over at the woodshed. The old man looked away. 'I can't take your tractor,' I protested.

'Sure you can,' Mamma said gleefully. 'Stop certain folks who besn't here from using it and getting us all in bother.'

I looked down at the keys again, then back at the woodshed. The old guy just kept staring ahead, stoically. He wasn't about to give her the satisfaction.

I was in a pickle here. I didn't want to deprive the old

fogey of his pride and joy, but I was in big-time trouble, and I had to make some distance, fast.

I settled on a compromise. I tossed the keys a few centimetres in the air and caught them. 'Tell you what,' I said aloud, aiming at no one in particular. 'I'm going to sit here on the tractor, on the passenger seat, and put the keys in the lock.' I strolled over to the tractor shed and hoisted myself into the cab. 'And I'll just sit here and see if anything supernatural happens. Such as, maybe, the spirit of your departed husband takes over the controls.'

The old guy looked over at me, then looked away.

I waited.

He looked over at me again. Then he looked away again.

I was losing patience. 'What do I have to do here? Hold a seance?'

He stood up and stretched, then wandered over in my vague direction unhurriedly. He stopped by the tractor's front wheel and kicked at it offhandedly. 'I'll give you a lift to the station,' he said, 'if you admit I besn't dead.' He looked over at Mamma defiantly. Mamma looked over at me. I couldn't please them both. Really, Harry Salt's number one inviolable tip for peace, happiness and long-term survival: never take sides in a marital dispute.

I looked up at the heavens. 'I sense a ghostly presence,' I said. 'I hear a voice from the Other Side. I really don't want to take this tractor, departed spirit. Give me a sign that I don't have to.'

The old man shook his head and evacuated a long thick plume of brown sputum onto the hay-strewn cobbles. 'You'm as stubborn as her,' he said, 'you bassard.' And he climbed in the cab.

TWENTY-SEVEN

Travelling in a tractor, well, it's not a massive improvement on walking. It's almost as slow, and easily as boring. It's also unbelievably noisy and smoky. On top of which, the magnificently engineered suspension has the same therapeutic effect as applying a pneumatic drill on full throttle to the base of your spine. It picks up every judder of the engine, every nuance of the road, every obstacle, rock and stone the wheels pass over, amplifies them a thousandfold and delivers the combined shock direct to your backbone.

The old guy didn't say anything for quite a while, or at least I didn't hear him say anything. He just drove on, staring morosely through the windscreen. It struck me that this was the second time today I'd been a passenger with a dead man at the wheel.

Finally, he did pipe up: 'Thim's my Sunday shoes, besn't thim?'

I looked down at the boots. They were so damned comfortable, I'd forgotten they were there. I heaved a reluctant sigh. 'D'you want them back?'

'What for? I besn't no need of Sunday shoes. Don't allow corpses at morning mass.'

'I don't mind paying you for them.'

'What would I do with the money, young feller? Casn't spend it. Casn't do nothing, when you've passed away.'

And he fell back into his glum silence.

After five minutes or so, he chirped up again: 'Comfy though, those bassards, isn't thim?'

I rolled my eyes back in their sockets. He wasn't going to let it go, was he? 'They're very comfy, yes. They are comfy boots. They are *the* most comfortable boots my feet have ever laid their little tootsies in. All that notwithstanding, I am fully prepared to return these boots to you and make the rest of my incredibly long journey totally unshod, in nothing more than my poor and bleeding shredded socked feet, if that is what you desire. So tell me, Pappa, once and for all, finally and irrevocably: would you like me to restore the boots to your possession?'

Pappa shrugged. 'I already said you'm could keep the bassards.'

'One last time, just to make sure we're completely on the same wavelength. Are you absolutely sure you don't want me to take these boots off my feet and give you them back?'

He waved me away with his hand. 'Let the living benefit, I says.'

We phutted along a while further.

After another five minutes or so, he cocked his head and looked at me sideways. 'You'm a lucky young bassard, you know.'

If this was about the bloody boots again, I was fully prepared to remove them both and force them down his gullet, laces and all. Lucky for both of us, it wasn't about the bloody boots again.

'Lucky?' I said, surreptitiously reaching down for the laces.

He said: 'There were a 'mission feller last week. Him weren't so lucky.'

I suddenly remembered Mamma's reference to fellers with an appetite for buckshot.

'Him come round wanting to chuck her out of the farmhouse. Chuck her out of the farmhouse been in her family this two hundred year gone? Daft bassard. Sending one feller to chuck out Mamma? You'm'd need eighteen battalions of the Foreign Legion, minimum. Toughest bassards them could lay them's hands on. And even then, them'd better bring cannons.'

'What are you saying, Pappa? Are you saying she shot him?

She shot an investigator from the European Farming Commission?'

'I besn't saying nothing, young feller.' He grinned so wide his chin ground against his nose. 'Besn't possible I were there to see nothing, I being dead.'

The rest of the journey passed without conversation, for which I was grateful.

Eventually, we came to a bend in the road, and Pappa pulled the tractor over.

'Railway station's just down the road a step.' He nodded in that direction. 'Casn't take you no closer, on account of me being all dead and causing a fuss and all, corpse showing up on the platform.'

I'd made my decision. I turned to face him. 'Look, Pappa, you and Mamma have been very kind to me . . .'

'Part from near blowing your noggin off your shoulders.'

'Apart from that, yes. Apart from the near decapitation, you've been kindness itself. So I want you to have this.' I handed him a wallet.

He took it from me. 'I don't understand. What's this?'

'It's a life.'

'A life? How d'you mean, young feller, a life?' He flipped it open.

'It's another identity. All the papers you'll need to bring you back to the land of the living.'

He flicked through the contents. 'Birth certificate, driver's licence, identity card, passport, credit card . . . ?'

I reached over and removed the credit card. I wasn't feeling that generous. 'You'll have to get the photographs changed.' I scribbled down a phone number. 'Here's a man who'll do that for you, in Paris. He'll charge you, but there's enough money in there to cover it.'

'Well, you've gasted my flabber, young feller. Have I got this right? Are you saying . . . I can be you?'

'That's sort of what I'm saying, yes.'

'I don't have to be me no more?'

'Absolutely.'

'But . . . what about you? Who'll you be?'

'Don't worry.' I smiled. 'I've got someone else I can be.'

'And I won't have to be dead no more?'

'You won't have to be dead another second. But listen: I'd move away from the farm, if I were you. Mamma's right: those 'surance fellers are the worst. You stay at the farm, they'll smell an ID swap scam all the way from Brussels. And if she really did shoot that 'mission feller . . .' I tailed off. I really didn't want to think about that.

'Cardew Vascular . . .' he read. 'Cardew Vascular?' He mulled over his new name. 'I don't much like that name. Sounds a bit like a snotty old sod. I don't know how Mamma'll feel about hanging around with a feller name of Cardew Vascular.'

'It's the best I can do.'

'Cardew Vascular. Fancy that. Mamma walking out with a hoity-toity like Cardew bloody Vascular. And us barely a year in us grave. Bloody hussy.' He laughed, the same familial monodental cackle I'd grown to loathe slightly less.

I climbed down from the cab.

'And us can go anywheres us wants? Cardew and Mamma?'

'The world is your oyster.'

'Us could go as far as Nice or Monaco, even?'

I had to smile. Both Nice and Monaco were probably less than three hours' drive away, if you travelled by anything faster than tractor. To Pappa, they were lands of fable. They might as well have been just around the corner from Alpha Centauri or three doors down from the dog-star. Frankly, I really couldn't see the two of them fitting in with the Nice set. Mamma would probably want to take her shotgun to the harlots sunbathing naked on the beaches. I couldn't easily picture them swanking around casinos either. Still, they'd find somewhere to belong.

'You can go where your fancy takes you. Don't forget to change the photos.'

'I won't, young feller. Besn't you worry.'

I started off down the road. Just before I rounded the bend, Pappa Cardew called out: 'Young feller?'

I turned.

'Tried the soup, did you?'

I nodded. 'That I did.'

'Tasty, ain't she?'

'Very tasty.'

'You know what Mamma calls that? She call it 'mission man broth she do.' Laughing, he slipped the tractor into reverse.

I just stood there and watched him go.

'Mission man broth?

Tasty indeed.

So the bassards aren't completely useless, after all.

TWENTY-EIGHT

Now, country folk have a lot of different perceptions from city folk. What they consider to be edible, for instance – and I'm not just talking about 'mission man broth – what passes for acceptable entertainment of an evening, or what constitutes a satisfactory size for a gene pool. But nowhere is the difference more profound, in my humblest of opinions, than when it comes to distances.

If country folk offer to take you on 'a brisk walk', don't do it. Don't even think about it. A brisk walk is likely to involve what any sane person would consider intercontinental exploration, and will certainly include a touch of mountaineering, and possibly a spot of wading through white-water rapids, and it will definitely include a lot of scrambling over enormous stone precipices that were specifically designed to keep civilised people safely out of reach of barbarians – and what were barbarians, anyway, except country folk? It is not an activity that is 'good for the constitution', nor is it a desirable means of 'working up an appetite'. It is a cruel and deliberate torture, and it is likely you will never make it back home to your loved ones again.

To a city dweller like myself, the phrase 'just down the road a step' means somewhere very close. Somewhere within extremely comfortable walking distance. Somewhere you could probably reach with the tip of your head if you simply relaxed your knees and fell forward. It would certainly require your destination to be visible from your starting point, and with the naked eye, rather than the Hubble Space Telescope. So imagine my dismay when I rounded the little bend where Pappa had dropped me to find no evidence of train stations or timetables or waiting rooms or even railway tracks within the perceivable environs.

Still, there was, at least, a road of sorts, albeit of a crude, probably Bronze Age sort, and I was superbly equipped with footwear more than equal to the challenge, so I set off walking.

Walking.

After a quarter of an hour that felt like a season of Turginev plays, I made out what looked like a straight line on the horizon that might well have been a railroad. A step down the road indeed. What, to Pappa, would constitute a marathon? Signing on for one of Magellan's lengthier expeditions? Throwing a thermos and a ploughman's lunch into a backpack and following the Voyager probe out of the solar system?

I don't want to start backtracking on the whole hatred of walking thing, but it did seem to help me get my thoughts in order. It struck me that old Johnny Appleseed had contrived to be ahead of me at every turn I made. What I had to start doing was being unpredictable. Going back to London might not qualify in that category. On the other hand, I was operating with extremely diminished resources. Giving away Cardew, I'd lost yet another identity, my third in as many days. I was down to my core ID now. Like it or not, I had to stick to being Harry Salt. On balance, though, I figured my best course of action would be to keep Klingferm's appointment with Twinkle. Anything else would have been going backwards.

The train station was surprisingly modern. It was also surprisingly large. It seemed shockingly out of place and unlikely, nestled in the middle of this primordially rural outback where electricity feared to penetrate and political correctness dared not tread.

There was a vast, paved concourse at the front of the building, with an elaborate fountain of golden mermaids gushing water from their shells as its centrepiece. To the left, a multi-storey car park that might have housed thousands of vehicles twisted up into the sky. It looked more like a station that would serve a major European port than a backwater farming community comprising eighteen cows, four tractors and seven men who tilled the land and dated sheep.

There was a huge bank of timetables ranked along the walls by the entrance, which seemed to promise that the station was well served by trains. I studied them for some considerable time, trying to find a service that might actually take me closer to civilisation, as opposed to deeper into this pastoral purgatory. Finally, I identified a train that promised to deliver me to Vienna.

Vienna was good. Vienna was where I wanted to be.

Of course, I'd have needed several years of legal training to work out what time the Vienna train ran, or from which platform, because every single service was marked with a bewildering array of caveats and exceptions. The 12.27 service, for instance, didn't run on Sundays or Saturdays or Tuesdays, bank holidays or leap years, unless it had a buffet car that didn't serve hot snacks, in which case it only ran on Wednesdays, though not in August, or on alternate weekdays during officially designated engineering maintenance work periods. Provided, naturally, you didn't want a first class carriage, which was a whole nother ball game. This is par for the course in modern railway services. It serves to minimise successful complaints by making it impossible for customers to prove any particular train arrived unreasonably late, or, indeed, was actually ever meant to arrive at all.

Unfazed, I wandered into the station entrance. My new boots clicked satisfyingly on the marble floor.

There was a large, well lit, pristine-looking cafeteria on the left, next to a coffee and croissant stall, a generous news-stand and a small but elegant bistro. Naturally, they were all closed.

I clicked over to the windowed counter on the right which claimed to provide tickets and information. I needed both.

The ticket office was protected by a reinforced window that appeared to be capable of repelling tank shells, which I thought seemed overkill in this unthreatening rural setting. But then, I hadn't met the station manager yet. Behind the quadruple-thick glass there was a small office, housing an elaborate ticket-printing machine and a computer screen set on a desk. The office was distressingly deserted, but by the screen a coffee mug was steaming promisingly.

There was a bell on the counter, mounted above a sign which read: 'Please Do Not Ring This Bell'.

Oh fucking dear.

I peered in through the glass. There was a door at the back of the office, which was open. I strained to listen, and I could definitely make out the sounds of someone engaged in some kind of business back there. There was some paper rustling, and what sounded like the occasional scrape of a chair.

I waited a while.

I waited a while longer.

I waited long enough for the ticket clerk to have gone to the loo, washed and brushed up, made a couple of phone calls, read the morning newspaper and filled in the crossword.

I had waited sufficiently, I thought, to earn me the right to use the English coughing technique to attract attention.

I coughed. I thought it unlikely that, given the otherwise utter customerlessness of the place, the person who'd left the coffee mug steaming hadn't heard me arrive, but I coughed anyway.

I waited. Then I coughed again, only louder.

I coughed again, this time directly into the circular grille cut into the window. And again. I must have sounded like I was in the terminal stages of tuberculosis.

When I was satisfied the coughing wasn't going to get me anywhere, I decided to employ the crass American system of actually asking for assistance.

‘Hey?’ I called. Then again, more forcefully: ‘Hello there?’ Then: ‘Anybody there?’ and again: ‘Hello?’

From behind the open door, I heard a weary sigh.

I waited.

Still, I waited.

I tried again, only slightly angrier this time. ‘Hello? Is there anybody manning this ticket office?’

I heard another weary, resigned sigh, a kind of mumbling barked expletive, and the rustling of paper.

The ticket clerk emerged from his den. He was a short man, always worrying in these circumstances, with thick wiry black hair and matching eyebrows that made him appear in a constant state of surprise. He had a newspaper folded under his arm. It was folded neatly. Too neatly. That newspaper spelled trouble to me. A man would have had to use a set square and a steam iron to achieve newspaper-folding precision like that.

He didn’t acknowledge me. He didn’t even glance over at the window. He strolled slowly over to the desk, opened a drawer and placed the newspaper inside it. When he was completely satisfied, adjusting the newspaper so its edge was absolutely flush with the side of the drawer, he closed the drawer gently. Then he opened a second drawer, removed a clipboard and set it on his desk. He crouched over it like a snooker player, making tiny adjustments to its position until he was certain it lay precisely at right angles to the leather trim of the desk. He closed the second drawer and opened a third. From this he selected a pencil. He held the pencil up to the light, to check the lead was a hundred-per-cent sharpened.

I could see where this was going.

‘Excuse me,’ I said. ‘Could you tell me when the next train to Vienna is due?’

He closed his eyes and winced at the sound of my voice, but that was his only reaction. He took out a pencil sharpener and pulled a wastebasket from under his desk. He checked the pencil again, narrowed his eyes at the tip, trying to decide if it truly needed honing, and, if so, precisely how much honing it truly needed. He mulled it over with the same level of intensity as a stunt rider might contemplate a leap of death on a 125cc motorcycle over an erupting volcano, and finally decided the pencil would, in fact, benefit from a little bit of a sharpening.

Slowly, very slowly, as if he were a microsurgeon threading a fibre-optic probe through the most delicate part of a beloved friend's brain, he inserted the pencil into the sharpener.

I tried again. 'Listen: I just want to know the time of the Vienna train, that's all.'

He bit his lip. I could have sworn I saw a tear of frustration welling in his eye. He shook off my intrusion, found his concentration again and gently twisted the sharpener. A thin curl of wood edged out between the blades. His tongue edged out of the corner of his mouth.

'The Vienna train?'

A bead of sweat started to drool down his forehead. He carried on twisting.

'What am I? The invisible fucking man?'

There was an abrupt snapping sound. He stopped twisting and slowly removed the pencil from the sharpener. The tip was gone. He looked at me with Mafia-quality hatred. He held up the pencil for me to see what I'd made him do. Then he bared his teeth, held the pencil between his hands and snapped it in two. He threw the ends into the wastebasket and started rifling through the drawer for a second pencil.

Well, he'd baited me. He'd asked for it. And now he was going to get it.

I rang the bell.

He froze over the drawer.

In for a cent, in for a euro. I rang the bell again.

His body remained immobile, but his head twisted towards me, exorcist-like. There was horror on his face, mingled with disbelief. Had I actually, truly gone and rung the bell?

We stared at each other. I stared long enough for him to start believing maybe he'd been hearing things, and maybe I hadn't rung the bell, after all.

Then I rang the bell again.

And I rang it again. And again. I rang out the allegro climax of 'The Ride Of The Valkyries' on the bell.

When the final ring had finished echoing round the marble hall, the ticket clerk straightened and spoke, for the first time. His voice was low and calm. 'Did you ring that bell?' he said.

'I rang the bell,' I said.

Gently, he asked: 'What is the matter with you?' He took a tentative step towards the window. 'Can you not read?' And another step. 'Is there not a sign beneath that bell?'

I leaned back and pretended to focus on the sign. I pointed at it. 'You mean this sign?'

'I mean precisely that sign. That's exactly the sign I mean.' He reached the window. 'And does that sign not say "Please Do *Not* Ring This Bell"?'

I leaned back again, pretending to focus, and concurred. 'That's pretty much what it says, yes.'

'No. That is not *pretty much* what the sign says. That is *exactly* what the sign says.' He still hadn't raised his voice. All his anger, and he clearly had plenty of anger, was internalised. His entire stomach was probably one giant ulcer. But his voice was calm and controlled.

Once again, I leaned back slowly. 'You're right. That's exactly what it says.'

'"Please Do *Not* Ring This Bell".'

I nodded, and repeated: '"Please Do *Not* Ring This Bell".' Just to show him I wasn't the argumentative kind.

'Good. Because, for a minute there, I thought I was somehow mistaken about what the sign says.'

'No.'

'So the sign doesn't say: "Please *Do* Ring This Bell"?'

I shook my head. 'Nope.'

'And it doesn't say: "Please Do *Not* Ring This Bell, *Unless You Feel Like It*"?'

'Not as far as I can see, no.'

'And yet, even though that sign was there, even though you read and understood it, despite all that, what you did was: you went ahead and you *actually rang the bell*?'

I showed him my palms and grinned. 'Guilty.'

'Please don't grin,' he asked politely.

'I wasn't grinning.'

'That sign is there for a reason. Didn't you think that sign was there for a reason?'

'I'll be frank with you: I couldn't work out why there would be a bell here that nobody was supposed to ring.'

'You couldn't?'

'It didn't make a whole lot of sense to me.'

'Would you like me to tell you the reason?'

'Actually, for my money, we can forget all about bells and signs now. All I want to know is the time of the next train to Vienna.'

And in exactly the same tone of voice, with exactly the same inflection and at exactly the same, measured volume, he said: 'Would you like me to tell you the reason?'

Clearly, I was dealing with a man on the edge. I wasn't going to get anywhere without humouring him. Flatly, and definitely without grinning, I said: 'Yes.'

And again, as if I hadn't replied at all: 'Would you like me to *tell* you the reason?'

I began to feel grateful for the bullet-proof shield between us. I nodded. 'I really would like you to tell me the reason.'

He stared at me for a long time, his face unmoving, his lips pursed. 'Well, I'm not going to tell you the reason. It isn't for you to know the reason. You know why? Because you're a customer. You don't work here. You're not even an employee of Railouest, are you?'

'No.'

'You're not by any chance the managing director of Railouest South? You wouldn't be, perhaps, the chief executive officer of Railouest Intercontinental, Lord of the Railways?'

'No. I'm just a poor traveller, trying to travel, that's all.'

'Do you expect us to train every single customer in every single aspect of Railouest procedure? Do you? Have you any idea how long that would take? To talk every single passenger through every element of every single procedure? Explain every single reason why every single thing is done the way it's done here? Nobody would ever catch a train, my friend. Nobody would even reach the platform.' He grabbed a very thick red book from under his counter and slapped it down. Then he carefully aligned it with the edges of the brass counter tray. 'That volume is the Railouest training manual. Would you like me to run through it with you?'

'No.'

'It wouldn't be a problem. So long as you have six weeks to spare, plus another three months for on-the-job training. If you've got a four-and-a-half-month window in your schedule, I'd be glad to take you through it.'

I closed my eyes. 'I just want to get from here to Vienna. That's all I want.'

'I mean, you could see I was busy, couldn't you? When you rang the bell you shouldn't ring? You could see I was occupied with vital Railouest administrative business?'

'You were sharpening a pencil.'

'I was sharpening a pencil?'

'You were sharpening a pencil. Slowly.'

'Is that what it looked like to you? Is that all it looked like I was doing? Sharpening a pencil?'

'It looked to me like you were sharpening a pencil. It looked to me like you were sharpening a pencil slowly. Very slowly.'

The ticket clerk flung his hand towards the clipboard on

the desk. 'I was about to fill out a *safety* report, my friend. A *network* safety report. Can you even begin to imagine what might happen if I filled out a Railouest network *safety* report with a blunt pencil? If, because the pencil was blunt, just one letter of that report turned out illegible? Say, an "F" turned out like a "C" or an "M" or even, God help us, a "J"? It may not seem important to you, Mister. It may seem a trivial thing. But that's because you haven't worked your way through this baby!' He slapped the training manual, hard. 'That one small error, that "J" instead of an "F", that could result in the death of thousands. It could send a train heading for "Jontainebleau" instead of Fontainebleau. It could derail the entire network and cause carnage beyond imagining. And what would I say in my defence? What excuse would I give to those poor families whose loved ones would never return? "I'm sorry, I didn't bother to sharpen my *pencil* properly"? "I'm sorry little Johnnie's head got ripped off his shoulders in the worst rail disaster of all time, but I simply couldn't be arsed to sharpen my pencil"? Could little Johnnie's parents live with that? Could I? Could you?'

'There's no such place as Jontainebleau.'

'Which is why sending a train there could be so potentially lethal.'

'Can I see the station manager, please?'

'You want to see the station manager?'

'You do have a station manager, don't you? A station this size?'

'Yes, we have a station manager.'

'Then I would like to see the station manager, yes.'

'Why do you want to see the station manager?'

'Well, I think that's between me and the station manager, don't you?'

'I have to know why you want to see the station manager.'

'Why do you have to know?'

'Because I have to know if you have a problem that needs dealing with at station manager level.'

'That's in your book, is it?'

'Page five five seven, my friend.' He started leafing through the pages. 'Paragraph thirty-nine b.'

He found the page and twisted the book round for me to see.

I wasn't about to read it. 'All right. I'll be blunt with you. I want to see the station manager because I'm not happy with the service I'm getting here, at the ticket and information desk.'

'You're not happy with the service?'

'No. I'm getting plenty of information. Unfortunately, none of it is the information I want. And I'm certainly not getting any ticket.'

He reached into a cubbyhole out of my sight and started flicking through some forms. 'Well, sir, if you have a legitimate complaint about the service, there are official channels for dealing with –'

'I want to see the station manager, and I want to see him now.'

'Believe me, it won't help you.'

'I want to see him, slash her, anyway.'

He shook his head. 'Like I said, it's not going to help you.' He reached under his counter and pulled out a peaked hat. He turned away, tugged on the cap, straightened it, and took a breath. Without warning, he span back round to face me, his eyes wide and his teeth bared in a grin of mad triumph. 'Because I *am* the motherfucking station manager.' And for punctuation, he slammed his stationmaster whistle on the Railouest manual.

I let him enjoy his moment. He stretched his chin to crack his neck, and smiled politely. 'Good afternoon, sir, how can I help you? Please be brief, I'm a very busy man. I have a station to manage here.'

I'd had enough. I really had. I wasn't dealing with a common or garden jobsworth or petty dictator type here. This man was at least clinically neurotic, if not an out and out psycho. There was only one way to deal with him. I leaned close to the glass and whispered dangerously: 'I want to know the time of the next train to Vienna, I want a ticket for that train, and I want to know which platform the Vienna train leaves from. If I am not holding that ticket in my hand within thirty seconds, I'm going to come around the back of your little domain there, slap you to the ground, pull off your pecker and your love sacs with my bare hands and whip you senseless with them while I make you my donkey bitch through the bloody new hole in your groin.'

The stationmaster didn't move. He just stood there, frozen, staring at me, with his cheeks sucked in. A small but telling fart forced its way through his ultra clenched buttocks. I stared right back at him with a fiercely calm smile that confirmed I was utterly capable of making good on my lurid threat. Finally, he made a kind of inverted whistling sound, decided that the balance of power had irrevocably shifted, and, for urgent health reasons, it would be better for him to stop being an utter dickwit and start playing along with the nice psychopath. 'The next train to Vienna, eh?'

'The next train to Vienna.'

He glanced over at his wall clock. 'The next train for Vienna comes through here at twelve twenty-seven.' The wall clock showed 12.17. He started punching the keys on the ticket machine. 'First class, second class, Eurotraveller or cargo?'

'First.'

'I'm sorry, there is no first class on the twelve twenty-seven.'

'I see.' My eyes flitted towards his back door.

He picked up my point. 'I'm sorry, but I have to offer it you, anyway.'

'Company policy, right?'

'Tell me about it. Second class to gay Vienna . . . ninety-five euros, fifty-seven cents.'

I slipped two fifty bills under the counter window.

He looked down at the notes, dismayed. He looked up and pursed his lips again. 'I'm sorry, I'm afraid we can't accept cash.' Reluctantly, and with Oliver Hardy gingerness, he pushed the notes back through the slot.

Cash is almost useless nowadays in the US of E. If you don't have plastic, you don't exist. Cash is only good for putting in a bank or buying something illegal.

Well, I didn't want to use my credit card, see? I had no intention of leaving a plastic trail for anyone to follow Harry Salt. On top of which, the clock was a tick, tick, tocking, and the Vienna train would be rumbling down the track in a matter of minutes. I pushed the notes back through the slot. 'You do today.'

He looked down at the notes again, and made the right decision. 'You're absolutely right,' he said. 'Today, cash will be splendid.' He picked up the notes and stared at them. The wall clock was showing 12.19. His eyes flicked right, then left, then right again, then back down at the notes.

'I do have a train to catch.'

'We don't have any change.'

'You can keep the change.'

'There's a company policy on employees accepting . . .' I looked towards his door again. He got the message. 'I'll keep the change.'

He slipped the notes into a drawer and printed out the ticket. He checked the ticket and slipped it under the window like he was passing a scalpel to Hannibal Lecter. 'Platform Five.' He smiled, winningly.

'Thank you so very much.' I smiled back, and turned to go. A thought struck me. I turned back and hit the bell again. His eyes and his smile stayed in situ, but the rest of his face winced.

TWENTY-NINE

I walked through the doors out onto the vast platform. The station clock showed 12.22. I was on Platform 1. Platform 5 was, of course, the furthest platform from me. Achieving it would involve a journey up over the metal passenger bridge far away to my left at the end of Platform 1. The bridge, naturally, traversed Platforms 2 through 4. The voyage, I estimated, would take an Olympic sprinter at the peak of his training a good six minutes. I had less than five.

There was nothing for it. I leapt off the platform and onto the track. I could feel the stationmaster's eyes burrowing into my back. I was probably violating pages 419 through 587 in the big red book. I crossed the lines and clambered gruntingly up the maintenance steps onto Platform 2.

As I jumped down from Platform 3 I felt a rumble underfoot. A train was coming. I glanced up at the clock. 12.25. Platform 4 was about twenty metres away. Two thoughts struck me simultaneously. If the Vienna train were on schedule, it would obviously arrive at the station *before* 12.27. And what if the monkey in the ticket office had got the platform number wrong? You wouldn't put that past the bastard, would you? What if the Vienna train were at this very moment hurtling pell-mell towards me along the very track I was about to traverse?

Right on cue, I heard the electronic blaring of the engine's horn. I decided to make the dash. On balance, I preferred the risk of getting splatted by a train to the more urgent, nightmarish danger of having to stay one single second longer in this bucolic limbo.

I didn't run. Tripping over a rail or a sleeper was not top

of my list of desirable objectives right now. But I did hurry. The vibrations from the train were juddering up my leg now, and I could hear the chackety-chack of the wheels getting louder. And louder.

The up–down cadence of the blaring horn again, shockingly loud now. I looked to my left. The nose of the train was in view. It seemed to be moving very fast and in my direction. I was halfway between the lines for Platform 3 and Platform 4. It was impossible to tell which line the train would take. No point in going back now. I scrambled over the lines and made it to the track at the foot of Platform 4.

I looked around for the maintenance steps.

There were no maintenance steps.

The horn again.

I glanced left. The train was close now. I could see the driver.

I grabbed the rim of the platform and tried to hoist myself up.

I failed.

There was a time I could have pulled off such a manoeuvre without raising my heart rate. Not so long ago, too.

I looked again for the maintenance steps.

There had to be some maintenance steps.

There were no fucking maintenance steps.

And again, the horn. Loud enough now to make me wince. I looked over at the train. It still hadn't made up its mind whether or not it was going to squidge the messy life out of me. I could read the promise of Vienna on its destination board. I could clearly see the driver and his co-driver now. They were deep in amiable conversation. They didn't seem to have noticed there was a large man on the tracks in front of them. I could see their lunch boxes on whatever passes for a train's dashboard. I tried waving my arms and shouting, but it was hopeless above the engine's roar.

I had one chance. The big man's chance. Momentum.

I took five steps backwards, took a deep breath, then ran forward and launched myself at the platform.

My palms slapped down on the platform edge. I straightened my elbows. Pain shot through my wrists like twin bolts from Thor's hammer. I swung my right leg onto the platform and tried to swing the left after it in a continuous motion.

But the left leg didn't make it.

Its shin caught the rim of the platform painfully, and the rest of the leg decided to go all dead on me.

Almost three quarters of me was on the platform now. I was that close to staying alive, but my left leg was dangling useless, its dead weight dragging the rest of me down, and my right foot couldn't find any purchase. The boot scraped desperately at the slimy wet surface of the concrete, but it was losing the fight. I needed something extra. Anything. A foothold. A dry patch of platform. Just the tiniest thing to stop me slipping.

I tilted my head back and looked at the train, upside down. It had reached the tip of the platform. It had made up its mind.

It was coming my way.

Now I could see the driver needed a shave. I could see a swimwear calendar tacked to the back of the cab. I could even read the bloody month. My only choice now was: would I prefer the train to slice me neatly in half, from top to toe, or would I be better off dropping onto the line and taking one neat hit face-on?

There was a crackle of static, and the stationmaster's voice boomed over the PA system: 'The twelve twenty-seven for Vienna will now be arriving at Platform Four. That's a platform change. Railouest would like to apologise for any inconvenience caused.'

I found the something extra.

The inspiration of pure, primal hate.

I had to live. I had to survive in order to kill the stationmaster.

My fingernails dug into the platform like eagle talons into a rabbit, and with my bare hands I hauled the bulk of my body weight onto the platform. The rest of me followed.

I was actually upright and dusting myself down by the time the engine reached me. The driver and his mate were looking down at me, open-mouthed. I smiled and tossed them a nonchalant wave.

The engine thundered past.

So did the first carriage.

So did the second.

I began to wonder when the train was going to start stopping.

As the fourth carriage rumbled by, I suddenly realised what was happening.

The train was not going to start stopping at all.

The Vienna train never had any intention of stopping at this station.

Because no trains ever stopped at this station.

They probably never had.

THIRTY

The entire station was just one big mistake, with its deserted shopping plaza, and its customerless restaurants and its newspaper-free news-stands and its multi-storey car park where no tyre had ever left its tread.

It was doubtless some local council planning blunder, probably funded by some ineptly apportioned lottery grant. Maybe someone, somewhere had filled out a station requisition form with an overly blunt pencil.

And the stationmaster had been sent here to take proud charge of this magnificently equipped, state-of-the-art flagship station, to find the only thing missing was passengers. That's why he'd been so neurotically keen to demonstrate that what he did was important. He came into work every day and supervised a station where nothing ever happened, and spent his time filling out safety forms that nobody ever read.

I caught a glimpse of him in the gap between the sixth and the seventh carriages. He was hastily mounting a bicycle. And I was thinking, well, he'd better hastily mount a bicycle. He'd better know how to pedal it faster than the yellow jersey in the mountain section of the Tour de France, too, if I missed this train.

But I still hadn't given up on the 12.27 to Vienna. I'd been through a lot to get me a ticket and get to the right platform. I wasn't in the mood to let it thunder out of my life without a fight.

The train was not travelling at its full speed – they have to slow down when they pass through stations, even stations as meaningless and ineffectual as this one. I don't know why;

they're still travelling fast enough to squash any passengers who might inadvertently find themselves stranded on the tracks, or who decide, as they seem to do with bewildering frequency, that throwing themselves in front of a train seems like a fun way to commit suicide.

But I had acquired a certain degree of expertise in the field of alighting from moving vehicles, and that was surely more dangerous than trying to board one.

Fortunately, the Vienna train was a long one, and I had plenty of platform to work with. I took a deep breath and centred myself, then kicked off running in the direction the train was heading. In a perfect world, I would exactly match the velocity of the train, and hop on board without so much as scuffing a toecap. Of course, that would mean achieving a running speed way beyond the reach of the swiftest jungle cat. I would just have to improvise.

I got up a pretty good lick for a big guy who hates walking, but I wasn't going to be able to sustain it for long. I kept glancing at the carriages to my right for some sort of handhold, some protuberance, some jutting feature of any kind. But there was nothing. No running-boards, no hand-rails, no door handles. Just polished, sleek, featureless smoothness.

Passengers were looking down at my progress with various degrees of amusement, as if the big guy running alongside the train were some kind of sideshow laid on by the railroad to break up the monotony of their journey. I tried signalling them to pull the emergency cord, but the ones who noticed just mimicked my tugging action and made 'choo-choo' shapes with their mouths. Funny people. I resolved, if ever I made the train, to find their carriage and beat the living breath out of every single one of them with a rolled-up copy of *Paris Match*.

I glanced back over my shoulder and ran smack into a stanchion holding up the platform canopy, flinging me violently backwards. Even as my rump hit the floor, I was back up again and running. I was dazed and hurt. My ear hurt, my head hurt, one of my buttocks hurt, but I didn't have time for pain.

When I'd got up to speed again, and my vision had cleared, I checked for oncoming bastard stanchions, then risked another glance over my shoulder.

The last carriage was coming up.

It was a different colour and a different design from all the others. I was hoping it might be the goods truck, that it might be equipped with large doors through which large things might be loaded, with big, robust and grabbable handles, or steps of some kind, or even a cargo winch. Alas, no. The last carriage was just as polished, just as sleek, and, if anything, even more featureless than any of the other carriages. It didn't even have windows.

It did have one thing going for it, though: because it was a different design, it didn't quite attach to the rest of the train in the same neat way as all the other carriages. That was the choice then: stay here in the back of beyond and certainly miss Klingferm's appointment in Vienna, or attempt a leap into the gap between the last two carriages, and pray there was something to hold on to.

If I'd had more opportunity to think, I wouldn't have tried it. There were so many things that could have gone wrong. I could have timed it badly and slipped between the final carriage and the platform edge, and been spread along both like a peanut and jam sandwich filling. I could have timed it perfectly and found myself between the trucks with nothing to hang on to, my desperate fingers clawing at a featureless façade, as I slid with slow inevitability straight through the gap to be trammelled to death under the relentless chackety-chack of the wheels. I could have got wedged in the gap, unable to move with a significant part of me protruding, ripe for removal by the next convenient tunnel.

But I didn't think of these things; I was probably still

dazed from my collision. I didn't think of anything at all except getting aboard that train.

I got up my speed as close as I could to a sprint, all the while dividing my attention between glancing back over my shoulder and glancing forward again for looming stanchions and other violently static platform menaces with cruel intentions.

It was a one-shot-only deal, with zero margin for error.

The gap was now parallel with my shoulder.

I made my judgement.

And I leapt.

THIRTY-ONE

My judgement was perfect, but that's the only good thing I can say about the entire enterprise.

I hit the gap between the speeding carriages, but, of course, the carriages were speeding faster than I was speeding, and they had urgent, Newtonian plans to make up for that.

The front of the rearmost truck hit me like . . . well, like a speeding train, sending the wind out of my body and hurling me hard forwards into the back of the penultimate truck, which then returned the favour.

My head was being batted back and forth like a demented woodpecker on a lethal binge. All the while the carriages were playing their little game of badminton with my brain as the shuttlecock, my hands were clawing blindly for something to grasp, and my feet were scrabbling away to find some kind of foothold.

I finally got control of my neck back and settled into the train's ragged motion. When my lungs remembered how to perform the whole in and out breathing thing again and my brain had stopped hurling itself around my skull like a kamikaze hamster flinging itself against its cage, I found myself standing sideways to the two carriages, my arms outstretched between them, as if holding them apart, like Samson between the temple pillars, and my feet precariously straddling the madly juddering buffers.

I can't say I was comfortable.

The carriages were mismatched. They lurched sadistically, and never in the same direction, threatening alternately to crush me, then dump me mercilessly on to the track. I was probably developing exactly the right muscles to enable me to play the complete works of Mozart on an industrial-strength concertina without a break.

I thought I caught a glimpse of the stationmaster standing by his bicycle on the top of a passing hill, straining to scan the tracks by the platform for gristly evidence of my splattered remains, but I was being vibrated so vigorously, and the cruel turbulence was whipping my hair into my eyes with such relentless ferocity, that I couldn't be certain.

I couldn't go on like this. There was no knowing when the train might reach the next station. For all I knew it might carry on all the way to Vienna without stopping at all. I had to get inside.

There were doors in the ends of both carriages, less than a metre behind me. The doors, in an astonishing coup of design innovation, actually had handles. I just had to work out a way to get to them, that's all. The problem was, it was taking just about everything I had simply to stay where I was.

I managed to work out a kind of backwards shimmy with my hands, in rhythm with the lurching carriages, while my feet did their best to keep their grip on the buffers. It was slow progress, it was uncommonly dangerous, and it hurt, but after about a quarter of an hour, I was within reaching distance of both doors. Slowly, I slid my right hand down behind me towards the handle of the foremost carriage. I felt the glorious kiss of cold metal. I braced myself and twisted it.

It didn't move.

Obviously, I hadn't got a good enough grip on it. I spent another few minutes shimmying to get into a better position. I slid my hand down towards the handle and grabbed it again. I grabbed it good this time. I gave it a firm twist, but it refused to budge. Surely it can't have been locked? What would be the point of that? Just who would they be trying to keep out of there? Did somebody truly feel it was necessary to protect the passengers from the kind of lunatics who would leap onto a charging locomotive and wedge themselves between the wagons? Surely that would be taking safety precautions too far. I mean, how often did that kind of thing come up? Was this train constantly beset by invasion attempts from deranged potential boarders who leapt between the carriages with scant regard for their own personal safety? I doubted it. I doubted that kind of incursion happened very frequently at all. The handle was probably just stuck, that's all.

I twisted at it again.

I jiggled it, in case it *was* just stuck, and all it needed was a light jiggle in the right direction to free it up. I jiggled it a lot. I jiggled and I twisted it. I tugged and pulled and rattled it. I jerked and yanked and wrenched it. Finally, I just out and out tried to rip the damned thing off.

There was no getting away from it. The door was locked.

I spent the next few minutes shimmying my right hand back to shoulder height. I got back to the Samson-between-the-temple-pillars position again, and hung there, trying to catch my breath.

I was going to have to try the other door. The more I thought about it, the more it made sense they might keep the passenger carriage door locked to stop the scant number of customers they actually allowed on the train from accidentally wandering through and falling onto the track. Fair enough. But the guard's van? There was no earthly way that door would be locked, too, was there? Why have a guard in a van who couldn't access the rest of the train? What would be the point of that?

I shimmied my left hand down the rear carriage door. Again, I hit cold metal. I took a deep breath, and slowly applied the twisting movement. The handle didn't seem to give. Perhaps that's because I was trying with my weaker hand. I steeled myself, and with a barbarian roar twisted the handle with everything I'd got.

I don't know why I bothered.

So both the doors were locked, then.

I shimmied back to base camp.

Surely there were people in those carriages? Surely some of those people must have noticed the door handle rattling? Was there not a single one who thought that might be an odd thing? That someone rattling the doorknob from outside a moving train was just a little bit strange? Was not one of them inquisitive enough to get off his useless backside, stroll down the carpeted carriage and take a little peek?

I had to try and attract their attention. After some painful contortions and a couple of near-death experiences, I managed to work out a way of crabbing backwards with my hands above my head, and slowly, agonizingly, I edged my head back towards the windows. It was a stretch, let me tell you. My internal organs must have been pulled into shapes that resembled amusing balloon animals. But I made it. I was bent backwards almost double, I was in considerable pain, and I had no idea if it was even possible to move back upright out of this position, but I made it.

I stretched myself just a little bit further and peeked into the window of the penultimate carriage, sideways. I did it as slowly as I dared. I didn't want people to be shocked by the sudden appearance of a horizontal head at their window.

The carriage appeared to be empty.

I watched for a while, in case there were someone at one of the window seats further down the carriage, out of my line of sight. But there was no sign of life. There was nothing.

Well, what did you expect? What did you expect from a train service that *doesn't actually stop at stations?* Did you expect the cars to be *heaving* with passengers? Did you expect them to be *jammed to capacity?* Did you expect passengers to be so tightly packed in there, they'd actually be climbing over each other to get to the window for some air? How could they be? Passengers couldn't even get *on* the train, if the train never stopped to pick them up. What a brilliant concept. Passenger-free transport. Hats off to Railouest! In a single master stroke, they'd eradicated all of the problems associated with running a rail network, by the simple expedient of eliminating the passenger from the system.

They'd obviously worked out the plan to its minutest detail. They'd even arranged for the access doors to be locked, just in case some mad reckless bastard tried to board the train, and thereby become a dreaded *passenger*, while the train was hurtling through a station at speeds in excess of one million kph. Superb.

I twisted my head over to the guard's carriage. The blind was pulled down over the window. Why? Who were they worried was going to spy on them from this angle? Certainly not the passengers in the adjoining carriage, because there were no passengers in the adjoining carriage, because, and I think we've already covered this, no one could get on the fucking train.

But then: a drawn blind?

Didn't that suggest occupancy?

Didn't that suggest that someone might be in the carriage?

Could Lady Luck finally be smiling on me?

If there were someone inside – and if not, why the drawn blind? – I had to work out some way of attracting their attention.

I had to find some way of banging on the window.

And the only bit of me that was spare for banging was my head.

And that was going to be a problem.

The problem being: my head hurt.

It hurt a lot.

All over.

I had a bruise on the back of my skull the size, topography and rigidity of a Mr Universe contestant's left arse cheek. On the forehead above my right eye I had a mottled lump I could have painted white and used as a golf ball. My brain had, in the course of a few short seconds, taken the kind of chronic, brutal pummelling a very poor bare-fist boxer might experience over the entire span of his punishing and unsuccessful career. When I thought it over, it seemed most unlikely that I wasn't already suffering from some kind of concussion. If that were the case, I might faint dead away any minute and slip down onto the murderous tracks.

I rubbed my forehead against the window pane, trying to feel out the spot of least pain.

I selected an area just above my left eyebrow and tried a tentative knock.

The area just above my left eyebrow didn't hurt, but the rest of my head thought it was being used as a clanger in one of Notre Dame's larger bells.

I sucked in a big one, and banged my head hard against the window. And I waited.

I waited till the buzzing in my brain stopped, and banged my head against the window again. Harder, this time.

I had just about summoned up the inner strength to bang again, when I spotted a movement. The corner of the blind definitely trembled.

There *was* someone in the carriage. I was almost certain now.

Steeled by this faint glimmer of hope, I banged my poor head on the window again. I banged out SOS in Morse code. That's nine bangs, people. Nine. I think I must have lost consciousness, if only for an instant, because I was suddenly aware that my hands were sliding out of position. I barely managed to pull myself back in time.

The blind moved aside slightly and a guard in a peaked cap peered out. He saw my horizontal head and froze.

He stared at me for an uncommonly long time. I don't suppose you could blame him. I wouldn't rank as one of the more commonplace apparitions a railway guard might expect to find at his window.

I yelled at him to let me in. He probably couldn't hear me – *I* couldn't hear me – but you wouldn't have to be a gifted lip-reader to work out what I wanted.

He yelled something back at me, but I had no idea what he was saying. I tried to mime that I couldn't hear him, but that's hard to pull off when you've only got your head to work with. He yelled again, presumably louder, but it didn't help. I shook my head, and tried to convey incomprehension.

He let the blind fall back.

I assumed he was going to open the door.

I was wrong.

After a short wait that could only just be classified as a geographical era, he lifted the blind again and held up a piece of paper to the window. I craned back to read it.

In scrawly biro, the guard had written: 'You shouldn't be there.'

Well. Thank God. At last, I was working with a bona fide genius. A mastermind of such raw wit and naked acumen, he instantly and instinctively *knew* it was wrong to find a man wedged between two carriages of a speeding express train, and, what's more, he wasn't afraid to put his neck on the line, and come right out and say so.

When he was finally satisfied I'd read and fully digested his startlingly frank opus, he took down the paper and looked at me, waiting for my response.

I had no idea what he wanted me to do, or why he thought the situation warranted a protracted and intricate conversation. I nodded my head, to acknowledge the unassailable wisdom of his observation, and once again tried yelling for him to let me in.

He looked puzzled, then cupped his hand to his ear.

He really was a fucking Einstein when it came to non-verbal communication. I yelled again that I wanted to be let in, and added a violent nodding of my head in the direction of his carriage.

He let the blind fall again.

I was wilting badly. The prospect of relaxing my arms and slipping down to the tracks began to seem strangely beguiling.

After another short wait during which a small puddle of single-celled pond life might have evolved into a sentient species and designed its own space shuttle, he lifted the blind again, and pressed another sheet of paper to the window.

I craned my aching neck back and read it.

It said: 'What do you want me to do?'

Well, now. What did he think I wanted him to do? Did he think I wanted him to dig up whatever costumes and props he could find in the guard's van and mount a one-man amateur production of *Annie Get Your Gun* for my delectation?

I mimed, with hyper-exaggerated lip and jaw movements, 'Ooopeeeennn theeeeee duh-oooorroooorrrr.' Then smiled and nodded like an idiot, as if that would help.

He blinked and cupped his hand to his ear again. He really was an intellectual giant.

I tried again: the long and exaggerated idiot version of 'Open the door,' only I think I might have inadvertently inserted twenty seconds of the word 'fuuuuuuuuckkkkk-kiiiiiiiiiinnnnnnnnnnng' somewhere around the middle of it.

He let the blind drop again.

And then someone spat on my face.

Well, what a marvellous turn of events.

I'm wedged, perilously, battered and bruised, between the two rearmost carriages of a cross-country intercity express, and some gentle soul decides that's not torment enough for dear old Harry Salt; they have to raise the ante just a little on his suffering by hacking a big green one straight into his defenceless face.

I was confused as to where the spit might have come from. Not from either of the carriages – they were sealed tighter than a homophobe's buttocks at a gay pride parade. Not, as far as I could see, from the roofs of the carriages, either.

Had I enjoyed the gross misfortune to be hit at random by a haphazard sputal glob serendipitously hurled by some mischievous train-spotter?

Then another one hit me.
Right on the kisser.
Yum, yum.
Not spit at all, you see. Much, much worse than spit.
It was starting to rain.

THIRTY-TWO

The blind lifted again, and another work of astonishing astuteness was pressed against the pane. It was a piece, in my opinion, vastly superior in its scope, innovation and basic understanding of the human condition than even Sigmund Freud's acknowledged masterwork *The Interpretation of Dreams.* It showed a more clear-headed grasp of the fundamental nature of the universe and reality than Hawking's *A Brief History of Time.* For sheer intellectual accomplishment, it easily outgunned the entire combined lifetime output of Marcel Proust, Karl Marx and Richard Dawkins.

What it said, quite simply, was: 'Do you want me to open door'.

Breathtaking.

Awesome.

Did I want him to open door?

See? He'd even *saved time* by omitting the definite article.

Not for this literary leviathan the predictable pedestrian prose of a lesser author. Not for him slavish obedience to the unforgiving master Grammar. He'd even managed to slash the writing time still further by entirely missing off the question mark.

Genius.

Did I want him to open door?

You bet I did. You bet I wanted him to open door.

I nodded. I smiled my idiot smile and nodded my idiot nod.

Obviously, I couldn't hope to communicate at his elevated

level of sophistication, but I think he understood me. I think he did.

He dropped the blind again.

Even though it forced me into a painfully unnatural pose, and even though it allowed the thick globules of mucal rain that were gobbing down with increasing frequency to glop straight into my eyes, I strained my head back so I could see the door handle. It was surely going to twist soon, that stubborn old hunk of metal. Surely.

I was probably grinning like a kid who's been given a bicycle-shaped parcel. For all I know I was panting and slobbering like a St Bernard at walkies time.

Surely that handle would tremble soon, and turn.

Surely.

The rain was beginning to get quite annoying now. It was really starting to annoy me.

The handle didn't turn.

But the blind did get lifted up again. And another sheet of paper was thrust against it.

He was offering me yet another composition. How could he have known that was exactly what I needed right then? I didn't even know myself. I thought that all I wanted right then was for him to open the door and let me in, thereby saving my life. But no, that trifling sequence of events was as nothing compared to the lofty and enviable privilege of enjoying this, the third in a trilogy of lofty masterpieces.

I read it eagerly. I drank it in. It did not disappoint.

I reproduce it here in its glorious entirety:

'I open door if you give me you boot's.'

I admit, at first it baffled me. He open door if I give him my boot's what?

But when I grappled with his concepts further, I began to see the light. In a startling leap of creative imagination, he was toying with the whole notion of the apostrophe, in a kind of post-postmodern return to the jejune, using it not as an indicator of the possessive case, but rather as a redundant method of flagging the plural.

He coveted my boots.

In short, he was extorting me.

What choice did I have? My beloved boots, or certain death?

Believe me, I thought about it. I thought about it as long and as hard as I dared. Much longer and harder, under the circumstances, than any sane man would.

In the end, I capitulated.

I signed his Faustian pact with my trademark enthusiastic idiot nod grin.

He smiled, gave me a thumbs-up sign, and dropped the blind again.

Now, you may be thinking I was a fool to give up the boots so easily, but you would be wrong.

Because I had a plan.

I can't say it was the world's most cunning plan, but then a simple, straightforward plan is often the best, don't you find?

My plan was to dupe him into thinking I was going to go ahead and let him have my boots without even making a fuss. Thus lulled, the unsuspecting fool would open the door and admit me to the guard's van. Once safely there ensconced – and this is the beauty part of the plan; this is the glorious ironic twist to it – once I was safe inside, I would immediately set about kicking the bastard to death . . . *with the very boots he craved*!

I must have been feeling extremely light-headed by now, because I think I actually threw back my head and laughed like a caricature villain. I know. I know. It doesn't sound like a thing I'd normally do, but I'm pretty sure I did it.

The rain was coming down quite thickly now. I could actually hear it battering the top of my head. My fingers were beginning to slip, and it was getting more and more difficult to slide them back into position.

I watched the door handle.

I saw it move.

It moved only slightly. But it definitely moved.

The door remained closed.

The handle moved again. It rattled this time. It rattled quite long and hard, but the rattle never managed to blossom into a fully grown twist, which was, let's face it, what the situation urgently required.

Then the handle fell still.

My hands were slipping a lot now. They were slipping pretty much all the time. The rain was imbuing the surface they were supposed to be gripping with a greasy, almost soapy sheen. I had minutes left, if that.

The blind was raised again. There was yet another note.

Glory be. Just what the doctor ordered.

Though the driving rain was now slashing at my eyes and the window pane was dotted with its thick globules, I strained to read the latest instalment of *Thoughts From A Mental Train Guard.*

It was to be his final piece. At least as far as I was concerned. Incredibly, it not only maintained the quality of its forebears, I would say it actually surpassed them.

There were only three words, but what words! And so gloriously arranged.

I'm going to give you them one at a time, that's how good they are.

Door

is

locked

'Door is locked.'

And one more time:

'Door is locked.'

So.

The door was *locked*!

It was locked *all the time.*

Gee, Huckleberry, maybe that's why I couldn't open the door myself in the fucking first place!

He took away the page, offered me a friendly, but fatally final shrug and let down the blind, once and for all.

My fingers slipped, and, this time, they wouldn't stop slipping.

I scrabbled at the carriage surfaces, but they just plain refused to offer any kind of purchase.

I slipped and slipped, I scrabbled and slipped.

There was nothing to grab on to. Nothing at all. I had no way of stopping my slide before I slipped below the bottom of the carriages.

Then something punched me hard in my back, and I did stop.

I was lying flat out, now. My boots were jiggling about on one set of buffers, my shoulders were being badly buffeted by the other.

I was uncomfortable, don't get me wrong: I was prone and helpless in the gap between two coaches of a speeding express with monsoonal rain hammering down on my defenceless body, on top of which I felt like an excessively heavy-handed sushi chef was practising his chopping skills on my shoulder blades; but at least I thought I was reasonably stable. I thought I could probably have held that position for some considerable time, barring mishaps.

But I couldn't bar mishaps, could I?

Exactly at that moment, as if cued by the great Stage Manager in the sky, the train decided to perform some kind of violent manoeuvre.

I was thrown, I don't mind telling you. I had it in mind that trains, by their very nature, were incapable of attempting violent manoeuvres. I had it in mind that, in fact, that was the very point of rail travel: trains are supposed to go along in as straight a line as humanly possible, for as long as humanly possible, thereby avoiding the whole concept of violent manoeuvres altogether.

Well, this particular train had different ideas.

It began with a howling screech of tortured metal, which translated itself into a rapid series of vicious, sudden jolts.

I was tossed about helplessly. I grabbed on to the buffers with my hands as best I could, but the jolts kept tearing them free. Miraculously, I managed to hang on. The screeching stopped. The jolts subsided.

Somehow, I'd contrived to get myself turned completely over, so my forehead was now enjoying the metallic chopping delights of the buffeting buffers, and I was staring down at the tracks below.

Then the screeching started up again.

And the jolting.

This time, I didn't hang on.

This time, my feet were jogged up clear of the buffers, and came down short.

As the toecaps of my boots hit the track, they caught a sleeper and yanked the rest of me after them.

The buffers carved two neat scars down my forehead as they dragged themselves clear.

My hands were flailing madly over my head as I disappeared under the carriage.

THIRTY-THREE

I did grab on to something. That metallic hook and eye contraption that links two carriages together, I think. I couldn't be sure. I had other things on my mind.

I was kind of concentrating on being dragged along backwards at full stretch underneath a speeding train.

My heels were juddering over each and every sleeper, threatening to snag one and drag me under. And there were a lot of sleepers.

I tried kicking off with my heels and flailing at the undercarriage with my legs, in case there was anything there I could hook my feet onto. If there was, my feet couldn't find it.

The question was: what would happen if I were to let go?

Would I land on the track flush between the train's grinding wheels, so the carriage would pass over me, leaving me relatively unscathed, or at least on the right side of alive? Was that possible? Were the rail lines far enough apart to accommodate my bulk? Was the gap between the train and the track deep enough? Or was there some cruel, sharp machinery under the carriage that would split me down the middle like a Burns Night haggis?

I really couldn't afford to take a chance.

I didn't have much slack for manoeuvring. I let my arms go to full stretch, which didn't feel like an enormously safe thing to do, and tried to crank my neck forward to look down the length of the undercarriage. It was dark down there, and my face was jiggling like the blubber around a road driller's buttock cleavage, so it was pretty hard to make anything out.

I tried craning my neck back, to see if I could get a better view underneath the carriage behind me, but I'm admitting to you now, I was slightly nervous the train might jolt again and the top of my skull might catch on a sleeper, removing it neatly, leaving me with a head like an egg cup so that anyone who took a fancy could dip a hot, toasty soldier into the middle of my sloppy, living brain. I know that doesn't count as positive thinking, but the image really put a crimp on my enjoyment of the situation.

As far as I could tell, the undercarriage was clear except for a large lump of cruel, sharp machinery jutting down from the centre, serving God knows what purpose. What could it possibly be *for*? Why attach such a vicious and unnecessary device to the *underside* of a train, where it might cause lethal harm to an innocent person who, through no fault of his own, just happened to find himself wedged on the line beneath a speeding train? It beggared comprehension.

If I survived this, if I lived through this day, I was going to write a very long, very stiff letter of criticism to the company that designed these trains.

The howling started up again. The deafening screech of tons of protesting metal all around me. Sparks from the grinding wheels cascaded over my body.

What the hell was this train trying to do? A fucking wheelie? Was it gearing up for some kind of stunt jump over a row of motorcycles?

There was a new, violent force tugging at my arms. They really wanted to let go, but I had to override them.

The screeching went on and on, amplified demoniacally by the confines in which I found myself. The sparks kept on showering me, the sleepers grabbing at my feet.

I couldn't do it. I couldn't hold on.

No matter how I tried, my fingers started straightening themselves. I was shouting 'No! No!' like my fingers were going to listen to that kind of pathetic begging.

I was going to let go. Like it or not, I was going to let go.

I tried to find some kind of hope. Maybe that cruel chunk of inexplicable machinery was unique to the previous carriage. Or maybe the guard's carriage was a completely different design altogether, a vastly superior model that managed to fulfil all its functions without requiring any lethal undercarriage additions whatsoever.

Then the screeching stopped and the train lurched forward, and somehow I managed to tighten my grip.

In this small moment of relative quiet, I did have a chance to think. There might still be a way to live through this. There might just be a way. It would require perfect timing and more than a little luck, but we all know I've got plenty of both. Those, I have in spades, my friend.

All I had to do was let go and roll quickly over to my right before the under-train slicing machine got to me, timing it so I hit the gap between the wheels perfectly.

I'll admit, there were a lot of things that could go wrong with the plan. There were far too many unknowable variables, to start with. I had no idea what speed we were going, for instance, or how long a span of time I would have between the moment my body hit the track and the moment the obstruction obliterated me. I had no idea how many wheels a train carriage might have, or how far apart they might be. Nor did I have the slightest inkling if there would be sufficient space between the line and the undercarriage for me to fit my body through when I tried to roll out clear. I would have liked to know all of these things, and if I'd had the time and the facilities I would have investigated them in full. I would have assimilated all the variables, double-checked all the measurements, performed all the calculations, and possibly even built a working scale model before I even thought about attempting such a blatantly stupid stunt. Perhaps even two or three working scale models. I would have also liked a short break before I tried it; possibly even a nap and a shower. If I were really pushing the boat out, I would have plumped for a fortnight's vacation in the

Maldives, followed by a six-month intensive course in under-train diving and railway-line rolling, held by the world's leading experts in the field, until I could safely accomplish the manoeuvre in my sleep.

But I didn't. I didn't have those luxuries. All I had was this short interlude between now and whenever the next howling, screeching, spark-showering incident occurred to come up with the plan, and the plan would have to do.

I braced myself. I was trying to decide whether it was better to try and hold on for as long as I possibly could, or to let myself go immediately before my brain had time to mull the whole thing over and see sense, when the matter was taken out of my hands. Literally.

The trained lurched, the metal shrieked, the sparks flew and my fingers were wrenched clear of their grip. I scudded on my backside along the track in the bedlam din of the yowling wheels and the hellfire glare of the strobing sparks. I was still travelling in the same direction as the train, hats off to good old Isaac again, but I was slowing down thanks to massive arse friction, likewise courtesy of the good Doctor. I would have been better off if I'd been facing the other way, in that I'd actually have been able to see things like wheels and deadly protruding machines before they reached and passed me, but I didn't have time to visit the complaints department.

I saw a set of wheels flit past my head, and I rolled to the right.

The roll was good. I timed it well. I can't say there was a whole lot of skill involved, I just closed my eyes and went.

I hit the gap between the wheels perfectly.

And I wedged myself quite firmly between the train and the track.

THIRTY-FOUR

Well, that wasn't in the plan. Getting wedged twixt train and line. That wasn't what I wanted to happen.

The train was dragging me along the line face down with me straining my neck back to stop the savage metal from planing away my nose and the rest of my facial features.

I had a sneaking feeling I wasn't going to be able to travel like this all the way to Vienna.

In front of me, it was November the fifth, the fourth of July and the Venice Carnivale all at the same time. The screaming wheels were shedding great plumes of sparks like a barrage of firecrackers had landed in an ammunition dump.

I had no choice but to watch the sparks as they launched themselves at my face with considerable ferocity.

And then I realised the sparking wheels were getting further away from me.

Or to put it more accurately, I was getting further away from the sparking wheels.

I was being slowly dragged backwards.

And behind me, there would be another set of wheels.

Sooner or later those wheels would catch up with me.

Sooner or later those wheels would buzz-saw me in half like a Damien Hirst exhibit.

And the first I'd know of it was when the wheel hit my scrotum.

Well, that wasn't what I had planned for my future, Ma. Never did it figure in any of my career plans to be slowly sliced in two from the bollocks up by the wheels of a train. I'm pretty sure I never ticked the box of that particular option.

I tried not to think about it.

I tried to focus on getting from under the train. But this powerful image kept slamming into my mind's eye and breaking my concentration, and I just couldn't shake it. I couldn't help thinking of the moment just after the wheels had passed through me: of me lying there for a couple of seconds with an extremely pained and shocked expression on my face, then each half of me plopping either side of the line like two gigantic portions of lobster thermidor.

I had to find a way of rolling free.

I wrenched my body, I kicked at the air, I wriggled, I squirmed, but I wasn't getting anywhere. I needed something to give me leverage, something to kick off. I didn't dare risk kicking at the ground in case my foot got caught in a sleeper and I was dragged back all the faster, delivering my juicy, unprotected sweetmeats to the cruel blade of the wheel at the speed of a rocket-fuelled dragster.

I raised my left arm, the arm that was outside the train, and slammed my palm against the side of the carriage.

And still I didn't budge.

I slammed it again, harder this time.

And this time I did budge.

It was only a fraction, and it didn't completely dislodge me, but it was sufficient to send me scudding back towards the very wheel I'd been trying to avoid.

I heard it howling behind me. I'm pretty sure I felt its sparks cascading onto my legs.

I kicked inwards with my left leg – it was an involuntary thing, my body instinctively trying to protect the family jewels, I expect – but my foot actually made contact with the side of the wheel, and I just kind of plopped free and rolled out.

And I made it.

I made it out over the track and from under the train.

I really did. I made it. I mean, don't try this at home, kids, but it is possible to roll out from under a speeding train. I know, because I've done it.

I hit something that stopped my roll. Something very hard and unyielding. It knocked out what little wind I had left in my body, and sent me rolling back in the other direction.

Of course, the other direction was the direction I'd just come from. The other direction was back under the train.

Well, excuse me; I didn't want to go back under the train. I'd just expended a not inconsiderable amount of energy with the precise objective of not being wedged under a train.

But I was helpless. Helpless. I kicked and thrashed, but I couldn't stop rolling.

I felt the track roll under my back.

I waited for the *coup de grâce.*

But it never came.

The train had passed me.

The train had gone.

I lay there for a couple of seconds, grateful now for the rain on my face. Now it felt like angel kisses.

And then I realised something. The track wasn't vibrating. The track wasn't vibrating, and I could no longer hear the train. I wondered why.

I hauled myself to my feet and turned.

The train was standing at rest not fifty metres away from me.

The train had stopped.

The obstacle I'd bounced off was, in fact, the tail-end of a station platform. If I'd held on for maybe thirty seconds longer, the whole death-defying rolling manoeuvre would have been utterly unnecessary.

I walked along the track to the maintenance steps and dragged myself up.

My first instinct was to wrench the guard's van door off its hinges and make good on my plan to Jean-Claude Van Damme the bastard to death, but I wasn't up to it. I was feeling pretty weak, as a matter of fact. A geriatric bedridden incontinent could have probably beaten the living crap out of me with a half-filled colostomy bag, truth be told.

People were gawping at me.

And no wonder.

My suit was in tatters. My hair was matted and wild. My face was streaked with grime and grease – they don't clean the underside of those carriages, you know. I fully intentioned to mention that oversight in my stiff letter to Railouest. I must have looked like a comedy professor staggering out of an amusing lab explosion. I had bumps, I had bruises, I had blisters. I had a broad band of friction burn from the railway line straight down the middle of my body. I could probably have applied for a job as head freak in a circus sideshow. I'd have been the star attraction. The crowned heads of Europe would probably have flocked in droves to see The Incredibly Battered Man.

I noticed I was limping. I looked down at my feet. The soles of my beautiful boots were hanging off, flapping freely with every step. The toecaps were missing, too. My beautiful boots. I don't think I cried, but I wanted to.

I mustered together what I thought was a pretty good facsimile of dignity, and flapped down the platform like I was wading shin-deep through glue to find myself a nice, comfortable compartment to die in.

It turned out the train did have a first class carriage, after all. There was a guy in waiter's livery standing by the steps that led to it. He didn't help me on board though. I didn't blame him. He probably couldn't believe I was happening. I climbed the steps, found a seat and fell into it.

Or, to cut a long story short: I caught the 12.27 to Vienna.

THIRTY-FIVE

I tried to catch some shut-eye. I wasn't particularly tired, I just wanted to close down for a wee while and let my body do some auto repair work. But the truth is you can't get any kind of useful sleep on a train. There's a well honed system specifically designed to prevent it. It's very clever.

The seats, for instance. The seats are made just a little bit too uncomfortable. Even if they've got a recline control, they only tilt back by a maximum angle of seven degrees. There is no discernible difference between a seat that is fully upright, and a seat that is fully reclined. Really. You'd need a very good protractor and a lot of patience to detect the difference. Many times, I've sat in one of those seats and pressed the tilt button, only to find it's already completely reclined.

And the seat cover material is hand-picked to be just a little too rough for comfort; not quite out and out hessian, but not far off. Just rough enough to leave an indelible sackcloth impression on your face if you're foolish enough to try resting on it for thirty seconds.

And the headrests. What are they? They aren't what they claim to be. They aren't rests for the head. Not unless you've got a metre-long neck. And they put those crazy little pillows on them. Tiny little Barbie pillows, set just that little bit too high to reach with any useful part of your head.

And the armrests. They're not armrests – they hurt. They're hard metal poles loosely covered in hessian. Have you ever tried to use the middle armrest with someone sitting next to you? You can't both use it, that's for sure.

Who designs those seats? Do they ever try sitting anybody

in them? Do the designers ever try sitting in them themselves? Is there a correct position to sit in a train seat? Is there a specific shape you're supposed to be so your arm can relax on the armrest and your head can loll back on the headrest, simultaneously? If so, it's not a human shape. Why are they designing seats to accommodate alien species? Aliens with incredibly long, thin arms and giraffe necks and a little bump high at the back of their skulls, who get vertigo if they lean back more than seven degrees from upright. They'd love train seats, those aliens. I don't know why they don't use the railways more.

And even if you do manage to override the manifold discomforts of the seats, and against all odds you somehow manage to drop off, there's the announcements system to jerk you back awake.

The staff constantly make redundant announcements, in dull monotonous voices, on speakers that are deliberately set just a little too loud, timed with clinical perfection to wake you up the absolute instant you fall into alpha-rhythm sleep.

Why bother telling you what the next station is thirty minutes before you get there? Who is that information supposed to be for? Even if it's your stop, you're not going to stand up, gather your luggage and wait patiently by the door for the next half-hour. You know damned well they'll announce it again ten minutes before you actually arrive. Maybe it's to warn errant passengers who are accidentally riding the line in the wrong direction. Even so, what are they supposed to do about it? They're not going to leap from the speeding train and start running back where they came from. Not unless they're me, they're not. No. All the announcement's going to do is make them spend an extra half-hour panicking pointlessly. And they announce *all* the stations the train's going to call at. Every single stop on the line. Who needs to know that eleven stations from now, we're going to be calling at Grenoble? What am I supposed to do with that information? Start counting down? Ooh, after this stop there's only nine stations until Grenoble. I can hardly wait. But I don't need to do that, do I? Because the announcer's going to give me a vital upcoming-stations update as soon as I try to close my eyes.

And I *know* the buffet car's open. I know it's open because they told me it was open *exactly fifteen minutes ago.* And the fifteen minutes before that, too. And I *know* it serves a selection of hot and cold snacks and beverages, savouries, cakes and confectionery and a range of wines, beers and spirits, because that's *exactly what it was serving* the last time they told me, and the time before that, *and* the time before that. It would make some kind of sense if they were to suddenly announce that the buffet car had started serving erotic lingerie, or a range of flat-pack build-it-yourself greenhouses. That would be a surprising and interesting announcement to make. If it suddenly started selling toasters or motor cars, or assault rifles and ammunition, yes, I would like to know that information. But other than that, leave me in peace.

Incredibly, despite Railouest's cunning attempts to thwart me, I did manage to get some sleep. I don't know how much, but not a lot, I can assure you. Nobody ever got more than twenty minutes' shut-eye on a train, unless they were dead drunk, or just plain dead.

My head must have been lolling in the aisle, having given up on the whole headrest business, because I was slapped back to the land of the living by a hefty blow on the back of my defenceless cranium. I sat up immediately because, and I don't know why, my first instinct was to pretend I hadn't been sleeping at all. Putting a hand to the back of my head was only my second instinct, which was curious, I thought. I'd have to have a word with my instincts about reprioritising things.

A waiter was leering over me. He was sporting one of those fashionable topiary Afro cuts, trimmed in the shape of the Roadrunner. He apologised for accidentally almost clubbing me to death, and asked if I intended to dine. I reached over for the menu he was offering me, and found myself eye-to-eye with his enormous erection.

It was a whopper, let me tell you. His trousers were bulging like a marquee at a Boy Scout jamboree. Really. It looked like a rolling pin jabbed through a parachute. It looked like a sausage dog with rigor mortis wrapped too tightly in a shroud.

I grabbed the menu and turned away as quickly as I could to study it in intense detail, but not quickly enough: the image was burnt into my brain, and it would remain there for all time.

He stayed there while I scoured the menu. He seemed bizarrely unembarrassed by his tumescence and stood with his hands behind his back in time-honoured waiterly pose, waving the bloody thing only centimetres from my face. It was not an appetite enhancer.

I had no idea what had caused it, his monstrous tumefaction. I was praying it wasn't my doing. It's hard to imagine that a bruised and battered man snoring and drooling could arouse such a powerful expression of desire, but it takes all sorts.

Then a terrible and almost unrepeatable thought struck me: was that what had woken me up? Had I been roused from sleep by a blow to the head from his gigantic didgeridoo?

I wanted him to go away as quickly as possible. I really was no longer hungry, but I figured it would be quicker to order than to try sending him away and risk him hanging around trying to talk me into ordering. I picked a couple of dishes at random and handed back the menu. I held it high, very high, to make absolutely certain I didn't accidentally brush it against his straining love pole and encourage him in any way.

He thanked me, bowed slightly, took the menu and turned to head back up the aisle. In doing so, he clouted me across the ear with his sex truncheon.

I tried not to let on, but he'd felt it, obviously he'd felt it, and he turned back again to apologise. I waved away the apology with a benign, tight grin and an even tighter nod. He moved away again, and I couldn't help ducking, but he'd sensibly decided to back away this time. He went first, and his erection followed behind.

Halfway along the aisle he backed into the ticket inspector. I don't know how railway staff rank in relation to one another, but I imagined the ticket inspector would be the waiter's superior. I imagined he would spot the erection – how could he not? – and fire the horny bastard on the spot. But no, that isn't even close to what happened.

They had some high jinks trying to pass each other in the narrow aisle, as you might imagine, but it was all conducted in an amicable, even jokey way. Leaning in and out of seats; after you, no, after you. Clearly, the inspector was not only aware of the erection, he even remarked on it. He made jokes about it. He pointed at it and made fun of it. Baffling.

Eventually, they negotiated the passage, and the ticket inspector inspected my ticket and asked me for the upgrade fee. I supplied it, cash again, naturally. While he was filling out the receipt, I plucked up the courage to mention the waiter.

'That waiter . . .' I nodded down the aisle.

'You mean Lupo?'

'Is that his name? The one with the, erm . . .'

'The Roadrunner haircut?'

'That's the guy! The Roadrunner haircut.'

'That's Lupo.'

'Lupo. Yeah. He seems . . . He's a very happy person, isn't he?'

'Lupo? Yeah. He's funny. He's a funny guy.'

'What I'm trying to say: he seems . . . excited.'

'Excited?'

'Overly excited. Downstairs.' I flicked my eyes towards my flies, briefly. 'In the trouser department.'

'Oh, I see what you mean. Yes, sir. He is very excited downstairs in the trouser department. Very.'

'Yeah. I mean, he's carrying a very fully charged love pump down there. It looks like it might go off any second.'

'He's priapic.'

'I'll say.'

'No, I mean he's got priapism.'

'Priapism. Right.'

'His penis is permanently erect.'

'I know what priapism is.'

'Apparently, it can be pretty painful.'

'It certainly can. Especially when it coshes you on the head.'

The inspector laughed, tore off the receipt and handed it to me. 'Next time, remember to duck.'

'I will. Believe me, I will.'

The inspector moved off down the train. I suddenly realised that ordering food had been a big mistake. Because, now, Lupo would be coming back to serve me.

Now, I don't want you thinking old Harry's going all homophobic on you, here. I really have no problem with what consenting adults choose to do with their willies in private. I just have a problem if they're going to start slapping me round the ears with them while they're serving me bread rolls.

One good thing: my desire for sleep had gone completely. I got up and flapped down the aisle towards the washroom. Two points to this plan: I could clean up before dinner, and I didn't run the risk of any sexually over-primed serving staff sneaking up on me unawares.

The first class washroom was pretty swanky, as train facilities go. By which I mean the toilet wasn't jammed to overflowing with caramel-streaked paper or brimming over with various breeds of faeces. I don't know what kind of people take a dump in a blatantly blocked lavatory on top of other people's floaters, but they do. People do.

I freshened up as best I could in a microscopic metal sink that was designed for aliens with tiny, tiny hands, and presumably only existed in two dimensions so they could actually turn to the towel once they'd finished and dry their tiny, tiny hands in the space provided. Still, it was better than nothing. And at least there was soap. It wasn't nice soap. It smelled of cheap institutions. It was asylum-scented soap. But it was soap. It got me clean.

I had to crush myself against the sink and bend backwards over the lavatory to open the door, but even then, it only opened halfway and I had to squidge round painfully before I popped clear.

I could see there was a cloth on my table now, and cutlery laid out. Good. I'd managed to avoid at least one, if not two of Lupo's visits. I spotted a rack of computer tablets for hire just by the washrooms; a nice first class touch. You plug them into a socket by your table, and bingo, you're online. You can web-surf, play games, download movies. You can also pick up the latest news reports. I could have used one pretty badly. It had been, what, five hours or more since I left the French Minister of the Interior at the wheel of my car. Almost certainly, he'd been found by now. It would have been nice to know if I was in the top five of the Europol Most Wanted list or not, but it meant I'd have to swipe a credit card, and I didn't want to leave a plastic trail to Harry Salt, in case anyone was interested in following it.

Then I remembered I had Cardew's card. I was pretty sure Pappa wouldn't mind my taking his name in vain.

I ran the card through the slot. It only took about a hundred and five attempts for the suspicious machine to recognise it as a legitimate credit card and not, say, a pickled herring or a bowl of exotic fruit some chancer was cunningly trying to pass off as a legitimate credit card, and the bolt holding the computer finally slid back, releasing the device into my temporary care.

I glanced back up the aisle and saw Lupo approaching my

table again, carrying a steaming soup bowl. I pretended to study the tablet intensely, back and front, finding something fascinating to examine with every twist and turn. But when I looked up again, Lupo was still there, still with the soup in his hands, waiting patiently for me to return to my table, so there was nothing for it but to meet the challenge.

I flapped back up the aisle. Lupo was standing just a little too close to my seat – not most of him, just that one significant bit of him – so rather than squeeze past, I sat on the seat opposite mine, and I did it in a way that, I think, suggested I'd intended to do so all the time.

Lupo looked a little puzzled, but he didn't let it throw him. He took a couple of steps forward and placed the bowl down on the table in front of me, then he turned to collect the cutlery he'd set out to accommodate my original position, and, in turning, swept the salt and pepper pots to the floor with his German soldier.

I tried not to have noticed. I fiddled about with the computer, making it look tricky to plug the thing into the wall socket, while Lupo bent to his knees, not an easy manoeuvre in his condition, and replaced the cruet set on the table.

He collected my cutlery. In order to place it correctly, he had to lean over me, but the train rocked quite violently and his Mini Me couldn't help but nudge my soup bowl. Some of the steaming liquid splashed over the rim and landed on his proboscis. It was hot soup. Stupidly hot. It had probably been blasted in a microwave. Lupo screamed and leapt back, catching the lip of the bowl with his injured wang, and sending it spinning into the air. Fortunately for me, he'd flipped the bowl in the opposite direction, so I avoided a scalding soup bath, but a lot of it hit Lupo, and the table was a hell of a mess.

He fell to the floor, drew up his knees to the foetal position, and started moaning softly, cradling his favourite friend.

I got up and crouched by him. I offered to help him up, but he waved me away. I wanted to help him, but what could I do? Offer to inspect the damage? Loosen the zip? That could do more harm than good. Rub some burn cream on his injury for him? Give it mouth-to-mouth? I decided, on reflection, it would be best if I went to look for help.

When I came back with the ticket inspector, Lupo had gone. I don't know where. I doubt he could have manouevred himself into that cramped lavatory. And if he had, there was no way on earth he'd ever get out again. Not without a hacksaw.

I sat me down at a clean table and left the whole Lupo problem to the inspector. I plugged in the computer tablet and logged on to Euronews.

They'd found my car all right. And they'd found the French Minister of the Interior, too. But it wasn't the headline I was expecting. The headline I was expecting ran something along these lines: 'Minister Found Dead Behind Wheel Of Mystery Man's Car'. Or: 'Assassin Plants Minister's Body In Moving Vehicle'. Or even just plain: 'Harry Salt Sought For Murder', with a nice, accurate identikit photo of me splashed all over the lead page.

No. The actual headline was: 'Mad Minister Dies In Police Shootout'. And it was accompanied by a photo of the French Interior Minister, presumably taken when he was alive, together with a dramatic picture of the Fiat Affordable with the minister's body hanging out, the both of them riddled with bullet holes. There goes my no-claims bonus.

Well, when I left the minister, he was in very poor condition to take part in any kind of gun battle with the police, or even a mild argument, and as far as I recall, he had no discernible holes in him, from bullets or anything else. I was about to click on the video report, when I spotted Lupo coming down the aisle towards me. He was carrying a clean tablecloth and some fresh cutlery. He'd changed his jacket, but there were still soup stains on the front of his shirt. He had patches of pink ointment on his face, but he was still wearing his professional smile.

Far from being discouraged by its experience, his bulge appeared to have actually grown in bulk. It took me a couple of seconds to realise it must have been bandaged. I don't know who did the bandaging. Lupo apologised for the incident. I told him not to worry about it, and lifted the computer from the table while he laid the cloth. He set down the cutlery, but I told him to forget about the soup. He looked crestfallen, but I really didn't want to take the risk. He apologised again and backed away.

I clicked on the video link.

THIRTY-SIX

EURONEWS LOGO
Exciting, urgent music. Animated graphics with spinning globes and everything.

ANNOUNCER'S VOICE:
(OVER) Euronews! Europe's number-one round-the-clock news channel, bringing you the happening news . . . while it happens. Twenty-four seven, three sixty-five. Or six.

CUT TO:
NEWS STUDIO, NEWSREADER AT DESK
CAPTION BEHIND HER EMBLAZONED OVER A PHOTO OF THE FRENCH MINISTER: MINISTER MADNESS

NEWSREADER:
The missing French politician, Sidney Plumier, was finally tracked down early this afternoon by German police, in a dangerous motorway chase that ended in tragedy.

CUT TO:
HELICOPTER SHOT
The Fiat Affordable trundling along the autobahn, with police cars in pursuit. The police vehicles keep trying to draw level with the Fiat to coax it off the road, then giving up and dropping back.

NEWSREADER'S VOICE:
(OVER) Despite repeated requests by police officers, Plumier

refused to pull over the stolen Fiat, or slow down in any way. After a thrilling motorway chase, broadcast live and exclusively by Euronews, one police officer claimed he saw Plumier produce an automatic weapon and wave it out of the window.

CUT TO:
INTERVIEWER WITH POLICEMAN
CAPTION: POLICE OFFICER WILLI KOHL
Kohl seems very excited. Wide-eyed, he is grinning inappropriately and seems to find it hard to keep still.

KOHL:
The guy had definitely lost it, man. Definitely. He kept shouting 'F**beep**k the police!' and 'Death to German pigs!' I mean, he was loco. No question. Dangerous. He was ready to kill, man.

INTERVIEWER:
You claim that a number of shots were fired from the vehicle.

KOHL:
Claim nothing. He was shooting all over the place. Bam! Bam! 'F**beep**k the police!' Bam! Bam! He thought he was Wild Bill Hickock. He thought he was Dirty f**beeeep**g Harry, man. He was wiiiild.

INTERVIEWER:
And how do you respond to statements that no other eyewitnesses saw or heard any shooting from the Fiat, at any time?

KOHL:
A lot of cops saw the shooting, man. They all saw it. Ask them.

INTERVIEWER:
And there was no evidence of gunfire from the Fiat on the news helicopter video footage.

KOHL:
Ask the other cops. They saw plenty of shots.

INTERVIEWER:
And that's when you decided to return fire?

KOHL:
The dude wasn't giving me any choice, man. He was wiiiild. Those bullets could've hit innocent children or sleeping babies, man, or something.

INTERVIEWER:
But the autobahn had been cleared.

KOHL:
I mean, I know the road had been cleared, but who knows who those bullets could've hit? Tiny little innocent babies, or something.

CUT TO:
HELICOPTER SHOT
The Fiat Affordable still trundling along the autobahn, with police cars in pursuit. A police vehicle, presumably Kohl's, draws level with the Fiat and we see a puff of smoke from the police car's passenger window, and hear the crack of a gunshot.
A reporter in the helicopter is providing live commentary.

REPORTER:
(OVER) And the police car now seems to – Oh my God! What was that? Was that a gunshot? That was a gunshot! I think we have gunfire. Oh my Lord – the police are shooting! The police are shooting ... *with guns*! Bullets are quite

literally being shot! Get the hell out of here, Sergio. I'm a God-damned sports reporter! Those crazy mothers're firing down there. It's a *war* zone! Get the God-damned chopper out of here!

There are five more puffs of smoke from Kohl's vehicle, followed by five more cracks, then it drops back. Two other police vehicles accelerate and draw level either side of the Fiat.

The police open fire with machine-guns, in a double broadside attack. Sustained bursts.

The helicopter reporter's voice gains an octave.

REPORTER:
(OVER) Now they're shooting with automatic weapons! The police are firing with tommy-guns! The police are quite literally unleashing a hail of what I can only describe as 'deadly bullets', and for some mysterious f**beep**ing reason, *we're still flying over them like sitting ducks*! Get us out of here! I'm a sports reporter for Christ's sake! I'm supposed to be covering the Bayer–Münchengladbach game! Those crazy f**beep**ers could kill us all!

CUT TO:
POLICE CAR VIDEO CAMERA
Filming through the windscreen of one of the pursuing vehicles. The Fiat is seriously holed. At least two of the tyres are burst and the wheels are wobbling erratically. The driver's airbag is inflated. Smoke is billowing out of the bonnet.

NEWSREADER'S VOICE:
(OVER) Though almost certainly riddled with dozens of bullets, Plumier, the former French Minister of the Interior, managed to carry on manoeuvring his vehicle away from the police pursuit.

CUT TO:
INTERVIEWER WITH SENIOR POLICE OFFICER
CAPTION: SUPERINTENDENT GÜNTHER GROSSE

GROSSE:
Yes, it was my decision to deploy the rocket launcher. We had to stop him before somebody got hurt.

INTERVIEWER:
Yet there was no suggestion that, at that time, Plumier was capable of returning fire.

GROSSE:
Is that a question?

INTERVIEWER:
Plumier's car had been comprehensively strafed by dozens of rounds of machine-gun fire, and the minister himself was almost certainly mortally wounded, if not already dead. Did you still consider him a threat?

GROSSE:
Is that a question?

INTERVIEWER:
Yes.

GROSSE:
We already had reports that the man had fired shots at police officers expediting their duty. We couldn't afford to take chances with public safety.

INTERVIEWER:
And you don't think firing a heat-seeking missile on the main motorway to Munich was in any way compromising public safety?

GROSSE:
(PAUSE) Is that a question?

INTERVIEWER:
(PAUSE) Yes.

GROSSE:
No.

INTERVIEWER:
So, it isn't true, as some commentators have suggested, you deployed the missile simply because it had reached its legal use-by date, and you were worried that for budgetary reasons, that if you didn't use it, it wouldn't be replaced?

GROSSE:
I don't concern myself with budgetary issues. I made the judgement call to deploy the rocket. And, indeed, my judgement was thoroughly vindicated when, subsequently, a number of very dangerous weapons were recovered from the vehicle.

INTERVIEWER:
And you deny those weapons were planted by police officers?

GROSSE:
Of course I deny that.

INTERVIEWER:
Yet we do have news footage suggesting that those weapons were not in the car prior to the police inspection of the vehicle.

GROSSE:
(LONG PAUSE) Says you.

CUT TO:

POLICE CAR VIDEO CAMERA

Speeding behind the badly wounded Fiat.
Over the radio, we hear:

GROSSE'S VOICE:
(DISTORTED) Pursuing vehicles, drop back. All pursuing vehicles drop back. We are about to deploy surface-to-surface weapons. All vehicles drop back to safe positions.

The car retreats. Rapidly. As it does, an armoured vehicle comes into the camera's field of vision. A special forces officer is standing in the vehicle's turret with a tubular weapon hoisted on his shoulder, drawing a bead on the Fiat.

NEWSREADER'S VOICE:
(OVER) The German police's decision to deploy the missile later came under heavy criticism from many MEPs ...
The officer gives the thumbs up sign, presumably to indicate he has locked on to the Affordable. He fires the weapon. A large projectile screeches out of the barrel and screams at astonishing speed towards the Fiat, leaving a thick vapour trail behind it.

NEWSREADER'S VOICE:
(OVER) ... especially since the missile missed its intended target ...

Just before the missile reaches the Fiat, it veers away. It loops high, almost out of camera shot, then plunges rapidly down, disappearing behind the tree line. There is a short, trembling pause, followed by a rapidly rising cloud of smoke and then a large, muffled explosion, which causes the camera in the police car to judder violently. Debris is lofted high in the air. Some of it actually reaches the road and rains down on the police vehicles. The debris appears to include at least one set of udders and a cow's head.

NEWSREADER'S VOICE:
(OVER) . . . and instead obliterated a small tanning factory, killing several cows.

CUT TO:
INTERVIEWER WITH SUPERINTENDENT GROSSE

GROSSE:
The cattle were all scheduled for slaughter, anyway.

INTERVIEWER:
So that's all right then, is it?

GROSSE:
What?

INTERVIEWER:
They were all going to be slaughtered anyway, so it's all right for the police to blow them to chunks of stewing meat with a heat-seeking missile?

GROSSE:
(LONG PAUSE) Yes.

CUT TO:
ON-THE-SPOT NEWS CAMERA
The Fiat has now given up the ghost and stopped. Heavily armoured police marksmen are encircling the stricken, smoking vehicle. One of them tries to push the camera away.

NEWSREADER'S VOICE:
(OVER) Finally, the stolen vehicle was rendered inoperable by superior police manoeuvring, and officers restrained and arrested Plumier without further violence.

One officer kicks open the car door and fires an entire clip into the motionless driver, then swiftly moves aside. Plumier's body slumps out of the car. He is pocked with bullet holes.

NEWSREADER:
(OVER) The minister was rushed to hospital, but unfortunately, he was declared dead in the ambulance.

CUT TO:
INTERVIEWER WITH SUPERINTENDENT GROSSE

INTERVIEWER:
How do you explain the fact that there was almost no blood in Plumier's car, on his body, or indeed, *in* his body?

GROSSE:
Our forensic experts are looking into that now. It could well be that he suffered from a medical condition, which we don't yet know the name of, which causes blood to coagulate more quickly than normal. Or he could have been on drugs.

INTERVIEWER:
What kind of drugs?

GROSSE:
I don't know. The kind of drugs that make you steal cars and shoot at police officers. What are you, stupid?

INTERVIEWER:
What do you say to allegations that Plumier was already dead? That he was, in fact, dead long before the shooting began?

GROSSE:
That's a pile of s*beep*t.

INTERVIEWER:
I'm sorry?

GROSSE:
That's a pile of stinking s*beep*t. What is wrong with you? Why can't you ask nice questions, eh?

INTERVIEWER:
Nice questions?

GROSSE:
Now, if you'll excuse me, I have to speak to Carole Villbanger from CNN. *There's* a girl who knows how to interview a guy *professionally.*

CUT TO:
NEWS STUDIO, NEWSREADER AT DESK

NEWSREADER:
Friends and colleagues of Sidney Plumier have disputed the German police's account of the incident. The French First Minister himself released the following statement.

CUT TO:
PHOTOGRAPH OF FRENCH FIRST MINISTER
In the top right corner of the screen.
His speech scrolls up the left-hand side:

FIRST MINISTER:
Sidney Plumier was a trusted and valued member of my cabinet. He abhorred violence, and always threw his weight behind anti-gun laws. It is unthinkable that he would have committed the acts the German authorities have attributed to him. I have ordered an inquiry into the incident at the highest level. Sidney was a bright and dedicated politician, and not only the people of France, but the whole of Europe is poorer for his passing. Unless, of course, he *was* taking drugs, in which case, let's face it: the degenerate bastard got what was coming to him.

THIRTY-SEVEN

The report went on, charting Plumier's illustrious career, and hinting strongly that he had been planning to stand for the European Parliament. He was known as an outspoken supporter of the Russian application for entry into Europe. This was a very controversial issue: a lot of Europeans still had a lot to hate the Russians for, but the addition of Russia to the Union would add some serious heft to the USE's international bargaining power. Me? I thought it was inevitable and we should just get on with it. But then, I didn't have any relatives who were minced in the Cold War.

Then I got my fifteen seconds of fame. They were focusing on the Fiat. They showed a cop from the forensics team actually numbering the bullet holes made by the machine-guns. He'd got up to number 135. I don't know if he was trying to number them in the order they were fired or not. Either way, his work would clearly be of immense help to the investigation. They'd traced the car back to Paris, and back to a man named Harry Tequila. They threw up a police identikit picture, but, as I'd expected, it didn't look much like me. It didn't look much like a human. It looked like Dr Zeus out of *Planet of the Apes*, if you want my opinion.

And I was missing, presumed dead. A victim, no doubt, of Plumier's insane rampage.

Well, that was no bad thing. It could have panned out a lot worse for me. Being dead gave me a lot of operating leeway. It was hard to see how even the German police could sustain their lunatic spin on the story indefinitely, and I hoped, for Plumier's sake, that the truth would eventually work its way through the system, but it left me in the clear for now, which was where I needed to be.

Well, I wasn't completely in the clear, of course, I was still a bail-jumping fugitive, which was, in itself, a federal rap. But at least I wouldn't have to change my face, and I was thankful for that. It's painful stuff, that bee venom, and when you jab it into your forehead and jaw, your face swells up in a none too handsome way. However you start out, you always wind up looking like . . .

Oh God.

You always wind up looking like Benito Mussolini.

Just like the Parisian garage mechanic.

That's when Plumier had found his way into the trunk. The whole fascia thing, the whole clamping business, that had been a distraction, first to get me away from the vehicle, and then to stop me inspecting it too hard before I drove away.

I'd been face-to-face with Johnny Appleseed. Twice. I'd had long conversations with him. I'd been within bubble wrap throttling distance of the son of a bitch, and I hadn't even known it.

But there was something even more important. Johnny had disguised himself. Painfully, too. And he'd added the hat and the mirror shades to make extra sure I didn't recognise him.

Which almost certainly meant that Johnny Appleseed was someone I knew.

THIRTY-EIGHT

The train pulled into Vienna. At least there was that. I'd envisioned having to take a cab from Salzburg, or Minsk, or maybe being forced to jump an alpine cable car from some distant ski resort, high above where Julie Andrews used to sing, which would have really screwed up my schedule, but no, the train arrived where it was supposed to arrive, and what's more it arrived on time. It didn't even plough through the buffers at the end of the track and deposit us all in the main station news store. It stopped where it was supposed to stop, and I got out.

I freshened myself up in the station superloo. The family of Kurdistani refugees camped in there didn't bother me, and I didn't bother them.

I even had some time to kill before the Plaything Club was open, so I found an old-time shoe repairer and asked him if he could fix my poor boots. He shook his head sadly, and told me they were way beyond resuscitation. I left them with him anyway, and asked him to do what he could. Maybe, at least, they'd get a decent Christian burial.

That aside, things were starting to look up for good old Harry Salt, though. I actually found a menswear shop that stocked my size, and I picked up some clean threads that truly fitted me. I left my old suit, and therefore a lot of my DNA material, in the changing rooms.

I couldn't track down any leather shoes, of course, but I did manage to hunt out a comfy pair in melon hide, which seemed sturdier than the vegetable crap I'd been getting used to.

I even had time to put in a call to the Ambassadeur, but

Gina was with a guest and I didn't want to interrupt her while she was wearing someone else's shirt. I left another message.

By the time the Plaything was up and swinging, I was ready for anything. I checked myself in a shop window and kidded myself I looked pretty good. True, I had so many lumps on my head they probably spelled out the first line of the twenty-third Psalm in large print Braille, but most of the damage was hidden under the hairline, and I could live with that.

The Plaything Club was hard to get into. Harder than it should have been, given that I passed all the entrance requirements with flying colours: I was male, I was dressed and I was prepared to spend stupid amounts of money in a ridiculously frivolous way.

Trying to establish the impeccability of these credentials with the overzealous blind bouncer was another thing. He was, I have to say, built for the job: big, that is. Ugly, too. His face was tramlined with those nasty bar brawl beer mug and glass ashtray scars you try not to stare at, but can't help yourself. Unfortunately, he seemed to think that his job entailed preventing customers of any description from entering the establishment.

It was the first time I'd ever been subjected to a body search that included my face. What was the crazy mother looking for? Exploding spectacles? Edged weapons concealed up my nasal passage? Some kind of tiny ear pistol? Or maybe the bumps on my head really did spell out 'The Lord is my shepherd' and the bouncer was deriving spiritual succour from reading it. Who knows?

I took the mauling for ten minutes, then slipped past him. He was still interrogating thin air while I paid my entrance fee and checked my coat.

The main room was dark, but individual spotlights picked out pockets of table dancers going about their business. A nice bunny girl with breasts that could have dominated the

Macy's Christmas parade showed me to a table by the stage. She recommended the house champagne. Since I don't have 'sap' tattooed on my forehead, I ordered a beer, and tried not to wither under the contempt of her smile. She spun round and wiggled her white fluffy derrière over to the bar.

My eyes adjusted to the light. I wished they hadn't. Lap dancing establishments don't bring out the finest qualities in the male of the species. Lust looks great on a woman, but men just can't wear it. Their eyes bulge. Their palms sweat. They salivate. Their tongues dangle out. They look like village idiots catching flies. They look like someone's stuck a straw in their ear and started sucking out their brains. Tell me now: do women find that dribbling gawping look attractive, or do they just put up with it?

It certainly makes me feel uncomfortable, so I didn't want to look at the customers, and I didn't want to watch the dancers, in case I went all frogified and brain-dead-looking myself, so I read the tapas menu on the table a couple of hundred times while I waited for my beer.

The bunny's breasts arrived at my table and the rest of her sashayed over just a couple of minutes later. She set down a glass of beer-coloured sarsaparilla, and a bill which was presumably intended to send the sarsaparilla through college and put down a deposit on its first home. She asked me if I'd like her to be my bunny for the evening. Reluctantly, I declined, and asked her if there was a bunny around called Twinkle or Twonkle.

She pulled a pretty stunned expression. It looked like her eyebrows swapped places acrobatically. 'Twinkle?' she agogged. 'You're sure you'd prefer *Twinkle* to me?'

I assured her I would. She swapped her eyebrows back and shook her head. Her bosom left the table and pretty soon her shoulders turned round and followed it.

I wondered what kind of roadkill Twinkle would turn out to be.

I didn't have to wait too long.

I heard a cough behind me. A pretty phlegmy cough, too, like it had some serious tobacco abuse behind it. I twisted my head, and I was looking at Twinkle.

Twinkle was not your average bunny. For a start, your average bunny is not bald. Your average bunny is usually under eighty. Your average bunny tends to be a girl. Twinkle must have been a hundred and seven years old if he was a day. His little white gloves and starched cuffs covered up most of the liver spots, but the skin on his arms looked like someone had draped the Dead Sea Scrolls over a broom handle. I swear, it flapped when he moved his hands. I'd never seen a loose bunny suit before, and I'd rather not see one again. The fluffy tail dangled limply between his bony legs. The bodice hung baggy over his concave, ribby chest. The fishnet tights bunched up around his knees and bagged over the map lines of varicose veins that networked his calves. Hell, even the bunny ears were limp.

His lips parted in his best bunny smile, but his denture fixative wasn't up to its job, so the teeth stayed nestled on the bottom while his upper gums did all the work. He closed his mouth and did some repair work with his tongue, looking for all the world like a decrepit mongoose struggling to swallow an oversized and lively snake. Finally, the dentures clicked into place. He smiled again, better this time, said his name was Twinkle and asked if I'd like him to dance for me. I gathered, from his accent, that Twinkle was from England, originally. From the north country.

Well, I didn't want him to lap dance for me. I didn't even want to think about him lap dancing for me. I turned him down politely, patted the seat beside me and asked if he'd like to join me for a drink.

He seemed relieved. He thanked me, put his gloved hands on the table and lowered himself creakily onto the red leather sofa with a low, drawn-out moan of chronic rheumatic pain. After a minute or two, he recovered from the effort of sitting down, got himself more or less straight in the chair and flashed me another bunny smile. 'Hang on a minute,' he said, and with two hands lifted his left leg over his right, presumably to comply with regulations on how the bunnies were supposed to sit when entertaining a customer. It took more than a minute. It also took a lot of creaking and groaning and more than a few smothered expletives. When the legs were finally crossed, he flashed his smile again, though his exertions had wiped some of the sheen off it, and asked if I'd buy us a bottle of champagne.

Now, I would never order 'champagne' in a joint like this. Not unless I had a spare piece of beachfront property in Monte Carlo I didn't mind remortgaging. 'Wouldn't you rather have a beer?' I offered, as charmingly as I could.

'Aye.' He nodded wistfully. 'Frankly, I'd rather have a glass of stout and a pickled egg. Only, we've got to order champagne. House rules, see.' He nodded at a bunny colleague, who sashayed over to the bar. 'Course,' Twinkle plucked at his fishnets, 'pickled eggs are illegal now. I don't suppose you remember 'em.'

I did remember pickled eggs, vaguely. A hazy childhood memory. I once spotted them lurking dangerously in a greasy recess of some antiquated seaside fish and chip shop. As I recall, they looked fossilised – green-tinged ovoids submerged in a huge jar of murky vinegar. I never tried one, but that won't come high on my list of regrets. Still, I affected lamentation at their passing for Twinkle's sake.

He warmed to his theme, and started listing some of life's deceased great pleasures. Beer in pints. Pubs that didn't serve food. Pubs – and this was stretching even Twinkle's memory – with men-only snug bars for swearing in. Some kind of beer called mild. Pubs with sawdust on the floor, supposedly to facilitate cleaning up spilt beer and blood. Cars without seat belts. Riding motorbikes without helmets. Roads without speed limits. Police without breathalysers.

Twinkle was *old*.

His colleague returned with a bottle in an ice bucket, two

glasses and a bill that was surely intended to cover the national debt of Nicaragua rather than the fizzy slop in the bottle that couldn't have passed as champagne to an eight-year-old schoolgirl enjoying her first drink. Damn. Now I'd have to settle with a credit card. I certainly wasn't carrying that kind of cash. Let's face it: Credit Suisse didn't carry that kind of cash.

Twinkle said, 'Champion,' and upped his glass. He swallowed, paused, let out a belch like Krakatoa – which, in actual fact, is *west* of Java – and begged my pardon. 'It's the champagne.' He belched again. 'Filthy stuff. I've got a gas ball in my gut like the planet Jupiter. Any road,' he took out his lipstick and a small hand mirror, 'enough about me. Let's talk about you, big boy. Are you here on business, or . . .' Suddenly, his entire frame was racked with a coughing fit that came alarmingly close to putting him in his grave. He carried on coughing at more or less full intensity through three entire songs. I fully expected him to bring up an entire lung, possibly along with some other vital organs and a good length of intestine as garnish. In the end, all he produced was a ball of phlegm the size and texture of a Portuguese man-of-war, which he thoughtfully ejected into the champagne bucket. He recovered his composure almost instantly, shot me another patent bunny smile and finished: '. . . pleasure?'

I watched in fascinated disbelief as he attempted to outline his mouth in bright red lip gloss with a hand that was less steady than an amphetamine addict's ECG.

I asked him what had drawn him to erotic dancing. He smacked his lips together. 'Dunno, really.' He decided he was satisfied with the effect and put the mirror away. 'The glamour, I s'pose. The missus used to lap dance till she were well into her nineties. Till the cow ran away with that Japanese porno star. I took it up for summat to do, really.'

I figured I'd made enough small talk and paid a fat enough bill to warrant talking business, so I asked Twinkle if he knew a guy called Klingferm.

That got his attention. 'Dick? You know him?'

'Yeah, I know him.' I didn't use the past tense, in case Klingferm had been a friend of his. No point in upsetting Twinkle unnecessarily. 'He leave any messages for anyone?'

'You're Harry Salt?'

'That's what it says on the office door.'

'You'll have a card, then?'

I fished out the card I'd picked up at Klingferm's dry cleaners and handed it over. Twinkle studied it, and sighed. 'This mean he's dead, then?'

'I'm afraid so.'

Twinkle handed me the card back and sighed again. 'Aye, he gave me a message for you. Dunno what it means, mind.'

'Maybe I'll know.'

'He said I was to tell you "locker one nine nine".'

'Locker one nine nine?'

'Or nine nine one.'

'Locker nine nine one?'

'One of the two.'

'That's it?'

'I'm pretty sure it was one nine nine.'

'No mention where the locker might be?'

'Or three nine nine.'

'But that's it? Just a locker and a number?'

'Or nine nine three.'

Marvellous. I had a locker number and a key. Actually, I had four locker numbers and a key. Surely Klingferm would have left a hint where the locker might be. I tried pumping Twinkle a little further. 'He didn't give you a place to tell me?'

'It might have been nine nine nine, but I'm pretty sure it wasn't.'

Great. I was getting less information the more I pumped. 'Are there any lockers here, at the Plaything?'

'Not that I know of.'

'And when did Klingferm give you this message?'

'Yesterday.'

'*Yesterday?*'

'No. The day before.'

'Tuesday?'

'Or Monday, possibly.'

'Definitely this week, though?'

'Oh, yes. Definitely. Definitely this week.'

Well, that was good, at least. I was getting closer to Klingferm's trail. I was getting warmer.

A loud electronic fanfare boomed. Twinkle looked up. 'Oh bugger,' he shifted his teeth around with his tongue, 'it's Horny Hour.' He grabbed his knees again and started to uncross his legs, accompanied by the usual gurning grimaces, grunts and grinding of worn-out cartilages. I looked around. All the bunnies were getting ready to dance.

Twinkle was going to dance, too. Twinkle was going to dance for me. I really didn't want that image pressed in my book of memories. I had to stop him.

'No,' I said, 'I didn't come here for the lap dancing.'

''S all right,' he grunted. 'It's Horny Hour. This one's on the house.'

He creaked himself almost upright, then his knees suddenly gave way, and he crumpled towards the table. I shot up and caught him just in time to stop him cracking his head open.

There was a loud whistle.

I asked Twinkle if he was all right.

Breathlessly, he wheezed, 'You'll have to let go of me.'

'Let go of you? Why?'

'You're not allowed . . .' He tried to catch his breath. There was another whistle, closer now, and the sound of feet running towards us in a big bad hurry. 'You're not allowed to touch the bunnies.'

I heard the whistle again, just behind me, now. I half turned, but I caught a vicious jab to the back of my head, just exactly where I really needed a vicious jab right now, and went down.

I hit the floor and rolled over immediately, in case whoever was handing out free vicious jabs was offering a two-for-the-price-of-one Thursday night special. I sent the champagne bucket scuttering across the floor. It was an expensive fall.

I looked up. The blind bouncer was swinging away at thin air with his telescopic white stick, which doubled as a pretty effective, pretty nasty cosh. Somebody shouted out that I was on the floor. I didn't blame them: the bouncer could have hit anyone with one of those wild swings. He started kicking out, but I'd managed to roll out of range of his flailing feet.

A group of German businessmen at a neighbouring table started laughing and calling out directions, so the bouncer could home in on me, like it was the *Golden Shot* or something. I was turning into a sport.

I scrabbled to my feet and headed straight for the table that was grassing me up, shouting taunts at the sightless lunk so he knew exactly where to head.

The bouncer waded into the Germans' table, swinging his cosh with merry abandon. Bottles and glasses started flying all over the dance floor, along with blood and teeth and German mucus.

Nobody else seemed eager to finger me, so I backed away, straightened myself up and left them all to enjoy the floor show.

I didn't settle the bill.

Quite frankly, I was disappointed with the service.

THIRTY-NINE

It was 2 a.m. when I left the Plaything Club. The street was bright. The bars, nightclubs and cafés were all in full swing. Vienna was jumping. There were plenty of late-night revellers happily milling along the pavement.

I put my hand to the back of my head and winced. Another lump. Any more of this and I'd wind up looking like the bloody Mekon. I'd have to shave my head and paint it, so I could pretend I was permanently wearing a motorcycle helmet.

I'd had no idea where the Twinkle lead might point me, so I hadn't bothered booking a hotel. I still had no idea where the lead pointed. Klingferm wouldn't have left me a clue I couldn't make sense of. But what did it mean?

I wasn't bothered too much that Twinkle couldn't remember the precise locker number; he'd given me a narrow enough range, and once I'd tracked down the lockers, the lock would match the serial number on the key. On the other hand, it would have been nice to know whether I was looking for a place with two hundred lockers or a thousand.

Somehow, Klingferm would have given me enough to work out where the lockers would be. There was a part of my brain somewhere that already knew it.

I thought I'd find an all-night café and worry at the problem over a coffee and some strudel.

I walked along the street, only ten per cent aware of what was around me. The rest of me was turning the locker conundrum over and over in my mind. That's how the male brain works, well, my male brain, anyway: it obsesses. That's how it invents things. That's how it creates. That's how it solves problems.

That's also how it overlooks small details. Small details that sometimes turn into lethal problems.

That's how I failed to spot a threat lurking in a doorway shielded by burst garbage bags until it was far too late.

I felt something very stiff jab into the small of my back. It didn't feel like a knife, but it didn't feel like a roll of liver wurst, either. A mouth hissed close to my ear, bringing with it a pungent wave of stale breath. 'This isn't a hard-on pressing on your spine, buddy.'

'No?' I rolled my eyes sideways and caught a glimpse of an unfriendly smile through a rack of teeth that looked like a wooden glockenspiel someone had thrown on a fire, then ill-advisedly rescued. 'What is it then, buddy?'

Dumb question. The smell, the teeth; I didn't figure him for a professional. I figured him for some street trash junkie with a rolled-up copy of the Viennese *Big Issue*, an urgent appetite for some kind of white powder and a whole lot of bluff. I was wrong. A bolt of electricity of sufficient voltage to illuminate the whole of New Orleans throughout the entire period of the Mardi Gras shot up my backbone, deep-frying my brain, scorching my lungs and singeing my pubic hair.

'It's a police stun stick,' my tormentor told me, unnecessarily. 'With the safety stripped off,' he added. Like I hadn't worked that out already.

I didn't go down. I just stayed there, swaying, waiting to find out, with a detached kind of interest, if my lungs would ever recover sufficiently to accommodate air again. My cheeks and my eyes must have been bulging like a toad that's had an air hose jammed up its rectum. I suspected my hair was standing on end. I hoped I wouldn't die like this, because whoever had to identify my corpse would certainly collapse in a fit of uncontrollable laughter.

After a couple of failed attempts, I finally did manage to

suck in some oxygen, and with it the raw beginnings of some kind of dignity, and my panic subsided.

'So, let's move it, Lard-arse.' Glockenspiel Teeth jabbed me again. 'Unless you'd like another dose.'

That really got my goat. Lard-arse? I don't think so. I'm not the world's trimmest guy, but in no one's imagination could I be called fat. You think a fat man could have caught that 12.27 to Vienna? On top of which, I have a beautiful arse. A truly beautiful arse. I have a really tight, pert little number back there. My arse could have its own modelling career. It could earn enough to keep the rest of me in the lap of luxury if it put its mind to it. Lard-arse? I think not, my friend. I wasn't going to let him get away with that. 'If you ever even think of using that thing on me again –' I began.

I never finished.

I swung back to cruel consciousness in the back of a moving car full of unpleasant aromas, some of them mine.

For a terrible instant, I was afraid I might have voided my bowels in the white pain of that second shock, but I was mercifully spared that particular indignity. Clearly, though, somebody *had* recently lost their lunch through their underpants in the back of this vehicle, and although the physical evidence had been cleared away, the memory lingered. On top of that, there were the overpowering smells of burnt hair and singed flesh. My own humble contribution, I was guessing. Last and certainly not least there were the foul exhalation's from the dentist's dream lounging beside me.

The driver was shielded from us by some sturdy-looking smoked glass. I felt a very strong urge to vomit, and instinctively reached over to the passenger window button. The steel cattle prod cracked down hard on my knuckles by way of admonition. I gave myself the satisfaction of not yelling in pain.

'You don't learn too quick, now do you, you roly-poly jerk?' He leaned back in his seat. 'I like that.'

I fought the instinct to nurse my reddening knuckles, and

tried to put some steel in my voice. 'Hey, here's the bottom line, Mr Colgate: I'm going to throw up. Would you rather have it inside the car, or outside?'

'Puke away, Fatso. Wouldn't be the first time.'

I hauled myself higher up my seat, partly to reclaim a little dignity, and partly to fight the contractions in my stomach. I wasn't going to give him the satisfaction. 'Hey, friend,' I grinned big, to show him what colour teeth really could be if you applied a little paste once in a while, 'I have two words that could change your life: car freshener.'

He grinned right back. 'Me? I like the smell in here. The sweat, the cak, the hurl . . . Reminds me how good I am at my job.' He took out a very long, very thin stiletto blade and started picking away at his fingernails.

That was an interesting point: he *was* good at his job, assuming his job was sneaking up behind innocent strollers, griddling their livers and bundling them into kidnap vehicles without making a fuss. He'd shanghaied me in a brightly lit and crowded main street, in full public view of a couple of hundred schnitzel eaters, subdued me and loaded me into a car without raising his pulse or causing a commotion. He was good, all right. Which meant but one thing: he didn't work for any legitimate operation.

Which fact almost certainly carried negative implications for my immediate future.

The knife was a professional choice, too. You can forget about those twelve-inch Rambo blades with their serrated edges and cruel curves. Sure, they look nasty enough, with that channel carved down the middle for blood to run freely, and they'd cause plenty of damage, no question, in a brutal, ungainly way. But a thin blade with a very, very sharp point will puncture a body deep and quick, with a minimum of effort. Less surface resistance, see? Elegant, almost, if you're a connoisseur of these things.

I watched him use this fine weapon to work out some fingernail filth that had probably been around since the dawn of civilisation. He had long hair, lank and thin, that looked like it only encountered shampoo on the twenty-ninth of February, and not regularly, even then. The fringe hung down filthily over the right side of his face, so you only saw one of his eyes. The teeth encompassed a small colour palette, ranging from light ochre to woody brown. Some of them were so pointed, they looked like they'd been sharpened on purpose.

Maybe they had.

He was wearing a suit that had been expensive at some point in its career, but debris from dozens of ineptly consumed meals had irrevocably merged with the fabric, from the lapels to the trousers, somewhat undermining the splendid work of Italian tailors. Now, you'd think that this blatant disinterest in personal hygiene would indicate a certain lack of self-respect in an individual, but no. Timmy Taser here was bedecked with gold jewellery. Adorned with it, he was. Expensive stuff, too. On his wrists and on his fingers, in his ears, and through his nose. He probably wore a foreskin stud.

I prayed I would never find out.

Not wanting to aggravate him, but not wishing to sit in silence like a good little puppy, neither, I asked him, polite enough, if he'd like to tell me what this was all about.

He shrugged. 'Someone wants to see you, pally.'

Someone wanted to see me. That was good, assuming that the someone wanted to see me alive.

We drove on a while. My stinky companion didn't go in for conversation in any big way. I closed my eyes and tried to get a little sleep, just to show old sewer breath I wasn't worried about him, or his mean little arsenal.

I pulled it off, too. This was my third night, now, without bedrest, which helped, I guess. When I opened my eyes, the car was stopped, but the engine was still running. We were up in some hills, and dawn was busting out all pretty and pink over the top of them. It was one of those picture-book dawns that make you wish you'd brought your camera, then realise you're glad you didn't, because those picturesque dawn photos really suck.

We were in a traffic queue, waiting to cross some kind of bridge over a quaint mountain stream. It was a narrow bridge: only wide enough for one car to pass over at a time. It was a surprisingly busy thoroughfare. The queues were pretty long in both directions for this time in the morning. Clearly, there was some kind of unwritten etiquette to the system: one car goes through, then the next one waits for the one in the opposite queue to pass, and like that.

Only our driver wasn't hot on etiquette. Our driver was the impatient kind. He slipped through out of turn, there was a small bump, and we were wedged in, fender to fender, with a shiny new steam-powered saloon.

The most civil of arguments ensued. The guy in the expensive steam car smiled all nice and made a polite gesture to our driver, implying our vehicle should be the one to back out. I saw the back of our driver's head shaking a negative, and a small hand movement to indicate his own, personal theory, that the steam car, in fact, should be the vehicle which did the backing out.

There were a couple more head shakes, a couple more gestures, with the smiles growing thinner and more strained, and then the steam car driver made a big mistake. A very big mistake.

He tooted his horn.

Sewage Breath next to me swore and cracked open his door. He smiled at me, to let me know he was going to enjoy this and he hoped I did too, slipped his cattle prod up his sleeve and stepped out of the car.

He put on a smile that covered up the worst of his oral problems and walked unhurriedly towards the steam car driver's window.

I looked at the door he'd left open.

Of course I thought about running. It would have been

stupid not to think about running, even though I don't much like it as a pastime.

But I had the feeling the door had been left open to tempt me into trying exactly that. Could I outrun Stinko? I doubted it. He was lean and mean, and he could probably give me a ninety-metre start in a hundred-metre race.

Besides which, I had a pretty good idea who'd invited me on this little trip, and frankly I wanted to meet him.

So, no. I didn't run. I didn't even get out and stretch my legs. I just sat back and watched the unsuspecting steam car driver wind down his window, still thinking with almost beautiful innocence that the argument was going to remain civilised and verbal, only to find himself electrically immobilised with the polite smile still frozen on his face. He was still smiling, albeit involuntarily, as he was dragged out of his vehicle, thrown to the ground and subjected to a sustained, businesslike kicking administered in an almost desultory way by a true professional.

I tried to feel sorry for the guy, but he was wearing a blazer. You can never feel truly sympathetic towards any man who chooses to relax in a jacket with gold buttons, no matter what ills befall him.

When it became clear even to Darren Dentistry that the gentleman was unlikely to be capable of coherent speech for the rest of the day, much less rise up and give chase, he slipped into the steam car, and started it up. He got out again, twisted the steering wheel and pressed down on the accelerator pedal with his hand. The car shot forwards through the bridge rails and tumbled down to the stream below. Both lines of traffic remained completely static. Nobody tooted. Glockenspiel watched the steam car go, ran his fingers through his lank mop, and gently rolled the still-grinning blazered bundle over to one side with his toe so we didn't run him over, which I thought was a caring touch. Then he looked directly at the driver now at the head of the queue in front, who looked away immediately and forgot our number plate. I looked behind. Everyone in that queue suddenly found something terribly important to examine beneath their dashboards. When the local law eventually wormed its way to the scene, there would be no valuable witness evidence to be garnered here.

Stinko slid into the seat beside me and grinned. 'You didn't feel like taking a stroll, dough boy? That disappoints me.' He nodded to the driver and we moved off. I noticed some fresh stains on his trousers, and re-evaluated my earlier interpretation of the blemishes on his suit.

They weren't food stains at all.

They were blood, mucus and dried human gristle.

Nice.

FORTY

I don't know how long we'd been driving – seven hours maybe – when I finally worked out where we were going.

We were on a winding mountain road, a civilised four-lane blacktop, when we rounded a bend and I caught a glimpse of a fairy-tale castle. A real fairy-tale castle, mind. Sleeping Beauty's abode, as I understand it. Or Cinderella's. One of those two dames.

We were going to Disneyland, Austria.

Disneyland, Austria was a massive project that had been aborted a decade or so ago, just before it was due to open, at a cost of hundreds of millions of dollars. It was the casualty of some unpleasant trade dispute between Europe and America, something about tit-for-tat export quotas, and it caused a lot of bad feeling at the time. I think the Disney corporation tried to sue the European government for compensation. Yeah, right. Good luck, Mr Mouse. Me, I'd forgotten all about the place till I saw those magical spires.

We drove through the massive parking lot, designed to accommodate many thousands of vehicles. The tarmac was all cracked and mossed over now, though, with long grass growing through it. We parked up by the entrance gates.

Stinko stretched and cracked his knuckles, called me a few nasty names and told me I should get out of the car. The journey hadn't improved his manners any.

He prodded me through the gates and we walked through the deserted streets of old New York, past the abandoned trolley cars and the faded hot-dog stands. The driver stayed in the car.

Stinko stayed behind me, but close, with his thumb on the stun stick switch. Ever the professional.

We had the place to ourselves, all right. We had the VIP ticket. No queues for me and Stinko. All I needed was a roast turkey drumstick and a lemon-flavoured snow cone to make the day perfect. We strolled past the enchanted castle, took a right by Geppetto's workshop, and climbed a bridge over Hook's pirate ship. Finally, we came to a cable car at the base of Mystic Mountain.

I deduced, from the sharp jabs between my shoulder blades, that I was supposed to get in the car. Great, we were working on our relationship, me and Stinko. We were improving our communication skills.

Stinko followed me in, turned to shut the door, I killed him, then the cable car jerked into action and started its climb.

Whatever was waiting for me at the top of Mystic Mountain – and I had a good idea what that might be – I felt I'd be able to deal with it more efficiently if Captain Cattleprod weren't around to share the experience with me. I stripped away his stun stick and slipped the stiletto down my sock. I patted him down, and found a small gun in his sock. A little derringer thing. Quaint. Not much use unless you were actually pressing the barrel to somebody's eye when you pulled the trigger, which is probably how old Stinko used to use it, but I thought it might come in handy and trousered it anyway.

I turned the corpse over, just to double-check it *was* a corpse, and wasn't going to show up again in a bad movie kind of way, so I'd have to kill him twice, or even three times. His hair fell away from his face. He had no right eye. He hadn't lost it, there was just no place for a right eye to go. I rolled him back over. Even dead, he had bad-breath issues.

I looked up. The cable car was almost halfway up the face of Mystic Mountain by now. I had a decision to make: stay in the car and meet what was waiting for me, or try to leap onto the sister cable car that was making its way down the mountain towards me on a parallel set of cables.

I looked at the oncoming car. I looked up. I looked down.

No contest, really. I was pretty much done with leaping in general, and leaping onto moving things in particular. I wasn't about to start Clint Eastwooding onto a cable car three hundred metres above the magic kingdom at this stage in the game, and I really wasn't in the mood for getting my brains dashed out on the spire of Aladdin's hamburger palace below. Not my kind of death, thank you very much.

Besides, where would I go, even if I made it? I'd spent a lot of effort looking for Johnny Appleseed, and now it was time to meet him.

I let the car go by.

And I waited.

The cable car lurched into an opening at the top and came to a halt in a docking bay.

The lights were very dim. Emergency maintenance lights, probably. Though why the place had any power running to it at all was a mystery to me. I stepped out of the car and onto a wide walkway. There was only one way to go, so I went there.

There was a giant arch at the end of the walkway, fashioned as though you'd be stepping through the gaping mouth of some cartoon villain or other.

As I passed through, the cartoon villain laughed an evil laugh and welcomed me to Mystic Mountain.

Ho ho ho.

I stepped into the light.

The room was a vast cavern hewn out of the mountain's peak. It was stuffed with glittering Disneyesque treasures: hundreds of caskets overflowing with paste jewellery and gold-painted chains. Gold statues, golden vases. It was big on gold. There was a panoramic window carved out of the rock, looking out on a truly spectacular view of the Alps and the derelict Disney horror show below.

And standing against the window, looking pretty small against the breathtaking vista, was Johnny Appleseed himself.

He smiled and said hello.

I said, 'Hello, Klingferm.'

FORTY-ONE

It had been a while – the best part of a decade, in fact – but it was Klingferm, all right.

His face was still swollen from the bee sting crap he'd injected himself with, but the features were unmistakable.

He smiled. He had a winning smile, old Klingferm. 'Good to see you, Salty, old boy.'

He even sounded like he meant it. I wanted to puke. I really did. I would have killed him there and then, only he was holding a very powerful handgun. He wasn't brandishing it, or pointing it in my direction or anything so crass. He was just letting it dangle in his hand, his arms crossed, casually leaning against the panoramic window. Just letting me know the gun was on hand if I found myself getting a little too cheeky. He nodded his head to let me know I should start walking towards the far end of the chamber. Me? When someone is holding a good gun in their hand and they know how to use it, I always give special attention to their requests. I started walking.

Klingferm shouldered himself off the window and started to follow. 'I take it Wolfie won't be joining us?'

'Wolfie? He the guy with breath as fresh as a mountain stream?'

'That's Wolfie.'

'No, Wolfie won't be joining us, Dick. He had a dental appointment or seventy-nine.'

Klingferm fell quiet for a few steps. I didn't know whether he was lamenting Wolfie's passing or not. I'd have found that hard to believe; even Wolfie's mother would probably be doing the cancan when she got the telegram. Or maybe he'd figured out I now had some of Wolfie's dirty little arsenal. Whatever he was thinking, clearly I'd surprised him. For once, it seemed, he'd underestimated me. I'd done something unpredictable. Good. I decided to break his train of thought. 'Where are we going?'

Klingferm shrugged. 'Do you care?'

'I'm guessing you've got something extra neat lined up for me.'

'Nothing but the best.' He grinned. 'You wouldn't expect anything less, now, would you, good buddy?'

'And how many other people die this time? How many bystanders? How many innocents in my elevator car?'

He shrugged again. 'It's just a job to me, Harry. Que sera, sera and all.'

'How many people have you killed, as a matter of interest?'

'You think I count 'em, Harry? You think I carve notches on my bedpost, or something like that? You think I'm a monster? How many have you killed? I mean, not counting Wolfie back there in the cable car? You're not above playing a little God yourself, when it suits you. So why don't we let slip the whole moral indignation thing altogether, OK?'

'So, the Fabrizi dinner party thing. Mind if I ask?'

'Ask away.'

'Who was the target there?'

'The dinner party?' Another shrug. 'It didn't really matter, much. Any or all of them. A couple of the politicos, I was hoping. But there was a lot of talent at that party. A lot of shakers and movers. Quite a result, to bag them all. I wasn't particularly going for that soap opera guy, but I'm glad I nailed him. He really was an awful actor.'

'I'm still not getting it: what was the point of it all? I mean, what was the why of it?'

'Oh, come on. You must have worked it out for yourself. Smart guy like you. Must have seen I had me a theme going there.'

'I know you're American undercover. That much I know.'

'Well, bully for you, Harry. Then you should be able to guess the rest. Just being a good patriot. Running a little interference. Doing my bit.'

'Are you official CIA or deeper?'

'Deeper, Harry. This isn't official policy I'm pursuing, here. Not yet, anyway. I'm just deep enough so people in the agency who appear on the regular balance sheets and draw a salary all nice and legal can have credible deniability of me and mine. Not as deep as your organisation, Harry, but deep enough.'

'You were trying to undermine the European Union? Is that what you were doing?'

'In my small way, Harry. Every little bit helps. Every little setback. Every good politician who bites the dirt. Every piece of promising material I can do away with. It all stacks up.'

'Because a united Europe, that's a frightening thing to America.'

'A united Europe that's got its act together, sure. Scares me. Scares the hell out of me. And it scares a lot of people like me, too. Europe's huge. It's huge geographically, and it's huge economically. Suddenly the dollar's starting to look not quite so al-God-damned-mighty. Suddenly, there's another big guy on the block, and you know where that's heading.'

'Are you kidding me? You're worried Europe gets too big for its boots, and suddenly America starts looking like a juicy target? A war between Europe and America, is that where you think it's leading? That's insane. Democracies don't fight each other.'

'Think about it, Harry. Most of Europe hates America. I mean, *really* hates us. I don't know why, but they do. They hate our economic imperialism. They hate our McDonald's. They hate our Coca-God-damn-Cola. They drink it, but they hate us for it. Go figure. What happens if Europe really does get its show on the road? It gets the economic clout, and suddenly it has the means to express that loathing? I'm not saying they're going to come right out and start rolling the tanks down Sunset Boulevard, or firebomb New York a week on Tuesday. They'll have power, and they'll use it against us. Trade. Foreign interests. It'll be us against you, Harry. Somewhere down the line, one way or another. Us against you. So what I do, what people like me do, we do just enough to keep you off balance. Keep you from meshing. That's all.'

'Right. Well, when you put it like that, Dick, you're actually doing us all a favour. You're stopping us from going head-to-head in a terrible conflagration. I should be thanking you.'

Klingferm smiled. Like I said, he had a fetching smile. 'I knew you'd see sense, my man. I just *knew* you'd see it my way. I'm the fucking caped crusader, that's all. I'm a God-damned peacenik when it comes right down to it. I should be blessed.'

'And Plumier? The French politician? You wasted him because he was pro-Russia?'

'Don't even talk about that. I mean, you'll give me a cardiac. Can you imagine Russia joining the European Union? I get the sweats just thinking about it. Russia *part* of Europe? No, thank you, my fine friend. Russia on its own had us all tied up and jumpy for half a God-damned century. Russia standing side by side with Germany? And Britain? And France? And Italy? To name but five. Turkey? Greece? Jesus. It would be the biggest, nastiest alliance in the history of fucking anything. Can you see those good ol' boys climbing over each other to buy Chevrolets? I don't think so. How long are they going to sit down for American military outposts in their backyards? Long-range missile bases? Early warning stations? American nukes under their feet? If we're going to stay a world power – *the* world power – we can't give up those things. And what then? We're going to lock horns, is what then.'

'Have you taken a look around you here? Seriously? I mean, we're hopeless. I'm wearing shoes made of melon. We imprison greengrocers for selling carrots that aren't the right shade of orange. We churn out a hundred new laws and regulations every day, so fast we can't keep up, and turn the entire population into unwitting criminals. We're crap. We don't even like each other. OK, we're nominally united, but the Greeks hate the Turks, the Italians hate the French, the French hate the Germans, and the Germans hate everyone ... We're like a gigantic dysfunctional family on a self-destruct mission. We can't agree on anything important. We're wallowing in a stinking cesspool of historic national hatreds that date back centuries.'

'*Now*, you are. But for how long? Twenty years down the line, it'll be different. Thirty, forty years on? A century? How long did it take Texas to feel part of the United States? There's still a good bunch of Texicans who'd polish up their muskets, put on their old grey Johnny Reb uniforms and happily march into Washington whistling 'Dixie' if they got half a chance. One day, Europe will click. It'll see sense. It'll see the power in unification. It *will* happen. It's inevitable.'

'Unless you can stop it? Is that what you're saying?'

'Like I said: I'm just running interference, Harry. Doing what I can to keep you off balance. I can do no more.'

'Rip Van Winkle. That was good. The American sleeper. Ha ha ha. You liked to leave me little clues, didn't you, Dick? You enjoyed screwing with my head. Johnny Appleseed. Spreading your Yankee poison all over the land. Harry Lime, faking his own death.'

'Terry Lennox, too. *The Long Goodbye*. You missed that one, didn't you?'

'It goes back a long way, doesn't it? Right back to the start in fact. You had this planned even before you met me.'

'You were always going to be the biggest threat to my operation, Harry. I knew it would come, sooner or later. You started thinking about sniffing around the Fabrizi thing, remember? I had to get you first. The truth is: you were a little slow about the whole business. You were supposed to bring the others along. I could have chewed up the whole network one man at a time. That was the whole point of it all. But you didn't follow procedure, Harry. Did you think you were ever in control of the situation? You must have known you'd been made. I could have rolled you over at any time and pissed in your ear, boy. But you didn't call in the cavalry, like you were supposed to. That was a personal disappointment to me, Harry. I thought I trained you better. You always were a stickler for procedure. What changed?'

'Part of me guessed that's what you wanted. Not you, I mean, I didn't know you were you at that point. But I thought that's what Johnny Appleseed was after.'

'Well, I'm still after it, Harry. It's still what I want. And I'm going to get it.'

We'd reached the end of the chamber. We walked through another gawping mouth and got another evil laugh.

Ho ho ho.

We stepped onto another walkway. There was a rank of carriages on a track, some kind of ride.

I turned to face Klingferm. 'We're going on a trip?'

He grinned. 'A little pleasure trip, sure. Firstly, though, I think you've got Wolfie's gun and his blade.'

'It's not much of a gun.'

'No, but it's a lot of a knife. I think we'd all have a more comfortable ride if we left them behind, don't you?'

I shrugged. Did he really not know about the stun stick? I fished out the little pistol, holding its barrel between my thumb and forefinger, with my pinkie out, too, and set it on the ground. While I was down there, I drew the stiletto out of my sock and laid it down beside the gun. I backed away from them and climbed into the fun wagon.

'In the front, Harry. You'll get a better view.'

I climbed over the seats to the front of the car. Did he really, really not know about the stun stick? He'd never allow himself to get close enough to pat me down. He knew what I could do from that range.

Klingferm started towards me. 'You disappointed us, you know, your little country. We always had it in mind you'd jump into our boat.'

'Are you kidding? Become the fifty-third state?'

'Why not? There were backroom talks about it. Serious talks.'

'Britain become an American state? That was never going to happen, my friend. That's somebody's crazy pipe dream.'

He stooped, picked up the gun and the knife and climbed elegantly into the back of the car. He was a metre and a half, maybe two, behind me. 'Why's that? Because you guys never shall be slaves? Is that it? Get real: you're a nation of serial slavery. The sad historical fact is that your little burg has been invaded and dominated with whimsical regularity by just about anybody who had a mind to try it and didn't have anything better to do that particular wet Monday. There isn't a nation in Europe hasn't left some strand of its helix in the British gene pool.'

'We've kept a pretty clean sheet for the past millennium or so, wouldn't you say? And where d'you think Americans came from? You think they jes growed? Americans are made up of the trash that Europe rejected, if you're going to start getting personal.'

'Well, lookee here. Old Harry Salt got hisself all riled up and patriotic on me. Aren't you just full of surprises?'

I hoped I was. I hoped I still had one big nasty surprise left up my sleeve. I didn't want him thinking about it. I wanted to keep him off balance.

'You know why you're not well-liked around the globe? Because you're an island race. You think the world ends just east of Ellis Island. Only one in ten of you even *owns* a passport, much less uses it. You have national sports that no one else on the planet even plays, then have the barefaced gall to declare yourselves world champions. You have, what: five, six per cent of the world's population? You consume more than two thirds of its narcotics and put out more than half of its pollution. And you don't care. You couldn't give a hootenanny. You don't *engage* with the rest of the world, Dick. That's America for you. The Great Masturbator.'

'Well, here's me all telled off an' put in my place: sitting in Europe's trash can, beating my meat and slurping away at a triple-thick milkshake. Thanks for that, Harry. I'm suitably humbled.'

There was a jolt and the car moved off.

I started worrying about the stun stick. Did it still have enough charge left in it? Old Wolfie had used it pretty liberally, and it put out a lot of power. Was there still enough left to work with?

We chugged slowly out to the lip of the mountain, made a turn and trundled along, looking down at the derelict dream.

'See, Harry: this place is a case in point. Y'all got cold feet about American investment in Europe and pulled the plug here. Look what you done. What a waste. Seriously cold-cocked *my* plans, I can tell you. I had the Screaming Thunder ride rigged, all set to screw up on opening day. The inaugural ride, there were going to be a whole bunch of European bigwigs, and a bunch of American politicians, too. Pro-Europe dudes, of course. There was a fault in the track. Their carriage was going to shoot off of the end and come down to land somewhere in that mountain range yonder. Double whammy. Hell, it would have been a hoot. Some Austrian engineers take the rap – hey, everyone's a winner.'

'Seriously, Dick, just out of interest: how many people *have* you killed over the last decade? I'm not moralising or anything, it's just you may deserve a place in some record books, I reckon. Old Ted Bundy better start looking out.'

'I don't just kill, Harry. I have lots of tricks up my sleeve.'

Up his sleeve? Was that an oblique reference to my stun stick? Was he going to let me think I had a jump on him right up to the last moment, then whisk it cruelly away? That was certainly his style. 'What kind of tricks?'

'I don't know. Like, say some lawyer someplace starts

making convincing noises about repealing Article thirteen one nine nine. Now, I *like* thirteen one nine nine; it makes my work a whole bunch easier. So I hack into his personal life, send some kiddie porn to his computer, where he doesn't even know he's got it. Subscribe him to some nasty paedophile service with his own credit card number and tip off the appropriates. Wham! He's finito Benito. Whether the charges stick or not, his credibility's out the window. Nobody hurt, really. Just one less asshole out there singing the wrong song.'

'Neat.' I spat.

'I got a million of 'em.'

The carriage trundled along some more. It wasn't the world's most thrilling roller coaster, but it had plenty of view. We took time out to enjoy it, me and Dick. Sometimes, you have to smell the roses to remind you life doesn't stink all the time.

We were coming to another entrance in the rock face. The end of the line, I was thinking.

Klingferm said: 'How did you kill Wolfie?'

I didn't want him thinking too hard about Wolfie, or Wolfie's legacy to me. 'How? You mean how was a chump like me capable, or what method did I use?'

'No, I knew you were capable, Harry. You're a dangerous man. I didn't expect it, though. That's not the way you've been playing things. Why didn't you whack that cop, for instance? That awful captain from Rome? You knew he had a hard-on for you. You knew he was tailing you. You should've whacked him. Standard Proc. I thought you'd gotten soft. I never figured you'd ice Wolfie.'

'I did it quick, if that's what you're wondering. I didn't make a big thing of it. He didn't see it coming.'

Klingferm nodded. His swollen face was all contorted. What had Wolfie been to him? His lover? Jesus. I had to get him off the subject. 'What was Twinkle all about? The key? The locker numbers?'

His smile came back. 'Twinkle? Oh, that was nothing. I knew I'd lose track of you somewhere along the line, and I just needed to know you'd be in Vienna by midnight on Thursday. I needed to know where you'd be at a particular time, is all.'

'And the locker numbers?'

'That was just so you had something on your mind. Something distracting you, so Wolfie could pick you up.'

His eyes went all maudlin. We were back to Wolfie again. Shit.

The cart trundled into the mountain and stopped behind a line of carts in a dimly lit tunnel. You had to climb up out of the cart to get onto the platform. I was thinking that this might be the moment, that Klingferm would be indisposed just for a fraction of a second climbing out of the cart, and that might be the best and only time to make my move. But Klingferm was too good for that.

'What I'd like you to do now, Harry,' he said, 'is to climb up out of the truck and lie down on the floor, facing away from me. D'you think you could do that for me, good buddy?'

I clambered out, and lay on the floor like the man said.

Klingferm said '*Muchos gracias*' and jumped up onto the platform nimbly. 'OK, we can walk a ways now.'

I hauled myself to my feet and started walking.

The tunnel let out into an airy hall, lined with shops and restaurants. Klingferm nodded I should keep walking forwards. I wondered where we were going. Then I saw it. We were headed towards a ride. The Screaming Thunder ride.

FORTY-TWO

There was a long list of people who shouldn't use the Screaming Thunder ride: pregnant women, children, the elderly, people with cardiac problems, people with epilepsy, people with vertigo, claustrophobics, haemophiliacs, people recovering from head injuries or surgery, people on drugs. Anyone, in fact, who wasn't a fully fit Olympic athlete with a string of gold medals was advised to avoid the ride.

Klingferm steered me through the barrier and into a dark chamber. The only illumination was from some glowing red bulbs set into the walls, and none too many of them, neither. It took a while for my eyes to adjust.

There were some metal mesh steps leading up to a metal mesh platform. The platform went on for maybe two hundred metres. At the end of the walkway, I could see a large, cigar-tube-shaped capsule set on a monorail. The capsule had seats, I reckoned, for forty or so passengers. Its lid was open.

I stepped up to the platform and started walking along it. Klingferm followed me.

We stopped at the capsule.

I asked him: 'You want me to get in the capsule?'

He nodded. 'Anywhere you like, this time, Harry. I won't be joining you on this trip. You're going to be flying solo.'

Good. I'd be off the metal walkway, and Klingferm would be on it. I climbed in. I didn't know how well the mesh would conduct the charge, or even if there'd be enough of a charge to conduct, but this was my shot. This was my shot.

'I'm not going to bullshit you, Harry. I'm not going to insult your intelligence. I can't let you live, we both know that. But I am going to need the name of your linkman, and the magazines you talk to him through. That's all. It's not a big thing. It's not like you'll be pulling the trigger.'

'You know that's not going to happen, Dick. You know I'd never give that up.' My arm below the lip of the capsule, I let the stun stick slip down my sleeve.

'Ah, but you haven't heard the deal yet, Harry. You haven't heard my sales pitch. Here's my offer, my special, once-in-a-lifetime bargain offer you can't refuse: you give me those things I want, and in return I don't waste Ms Pallister in the crudest, most vicious way conceivable. How's that sound, old buddy? How d'you like *them* apples?'

Gina? How the hell did he know about Gina?

'You're thinking it over, I can see that, Harry. I told you you were going soft. You gone and got yourself a *girlfriend*, girlfriend! I don't blame you. I'm not pointing fingers. We all of us get lonely. We all get tempted. That's OK, Harry, we're none of us perfect. You give me the names, you give me the good stuff and I'll leave Gina alone. I swear I won't ever touch her. I swear I won't rape her slowly with a white-hot poker, then use it to break every single bone in her beautiful body, one at a time. Scout's honour, I won't do that. I promise I won't remove her face slowly with a scalpel and get Dr Rutter to sew it onto some beggar's ass, while she's still alive. Can I be fairer than that? Is that the Deal Of The Century, or what?'

'That is a heck of an offer, Dick. That certainly does sound like one hell of a bargain I should just snap right up. Thing is, you being an amoral, evil son of a bitch, and my just having driven your boyfriend's nose bone through his brain, how do I know I can trust you?'

'I'm giving you my word, Harry. I'm giving you my word as an English gentleman.'

'Well, in that case, Dick . . .'

I pressed the tip of the stick to the mesh and thumbed the trigger.

It still had charge all right.

It still had plenty of charge.

The first jolt hurled Klingferm against the walls of the cage, which wasn't the best place to be. The fingers of his right hand curled involuntarily around the mesh and locked him there while the voltage just kept on coming, just kept on travelling through his body. He was juddering badly. He was shaking and quaking, his eyes wide open and staring at me, his teeth set grim, trying to fight the pain, but it wouldn't stop, it just wouldn't stop. Just kept on coming. His flesh started smoking. I could smell it. I could smell his hair burning. A dark stain suddenly blossomed around his crotch, and where his urine hit the mesh out of the bottom of his trouser leg, it sizzled, hissed and boiled and steamed clean away.

His left arm was rising, quivering, shivering, but rising slowly all the time. Rising to point at me. The arm with the gun on the end of it.

It was a hell of a struggle for poor old Klingferm. I know, because I've been on the other end of that voltage, and I don't understand how he was keeping upright, much less finding the strength of will, finding the reserves to keep raising that arm.

But he did it. He got it raised. And when he was almost there, when the gun was almost aimed directly at my face and ready to blow my head out of this realm and into the next, I let my thumb off the button.

He jerked wildly. His arm flung itself out and hurled the gun into the air. It clattered on the edge of the platform and tumbled into the capsule, maybe ten rows behind me.

Klingferm prised the melted flesh of his right hand open and crumbled to his knees. An unworldly hiss escaped through his gritted teeth.

'Shit, Harry,' he croaked through his charred throat in a voice that was hardly human any more. 'Wolfie *swore* to me he'd gotten rid of that damned thing. *Swore* to me. I told him that damned thing was fucking *dangerous*.'

I turned my head and looked back along the capsule's seats. I had a choice now. I could get out onto the platform and take Klingferm on, hand-to-hand, or I could race down the capsule and try and recover the gun.

Klingferm was hurting, certainly there was that, but there was no telling how well he was hurting, and he was still armed with that popgun and that wicked blade, at the very least. I had the stun stick, but there couldn't be much more left in it. There couldn't be much left in it at all. I could try it again, but to try it and fail was to die.

Klingferm was still on his knees, nursing the smouldering remains of his right hand, but I could see in his eyes he was doing the same arithmetic as me.

I started scrabbling over the seat, back towards the gun, all the while looking back to see what Tricky Dicky was up to. I saw him haul himself to his feet. I kept on scrabbling. I'd expected Klingferm to start running towards me, but he didn't. He staggered backwards and crashed against the mesh.

What the hell was he trying to do? Had I really fried his brain?

I got back to where I thought the gun had fallen, and started looking for it, but it was dark and I was hurrying and I had to keep on checking what Klingferm was up to, in case I lost track of him and wound up with a derringer pressed to my eyeball.

He was feeling around the wall back there. He was looking for something, but I didn't know what.

I decided I'd got the wrong row, and climbed over the seat back to the next one.

As I hit the seat, there was a loud click, and an electronic sort of whining sound. The carriage juddered.

Klingferm had started up the ride.

The lid of the capsule was coming down. Whoopy sirens

started up. A recorded voice told everybody to remain in their seats with their arms inside the capsule. I was about to leap clear and take whatever small chances I might have, unarmed on the platform against a very armed and very pissed-off Klingferm, when the carriage lurched forward and the gun clattered out from under the seat.

I scooped it up and flicked off the safety. The capsule had started moving now, and the lid was coming down, coming down. I looked out, but I couldn't see Klingferm. He wasn't where he'd just been. Over the whine of the motors, and the whoop-whoop of the sirens, I heard footsteps on metal, coming from behind. Klingferm had run right past me while I'd been scrabbling under the seat. Run pretty fast, too. I was surprised he still had it in him.

I aimed the gun at his disappearing back. The lid was coming down and the capsule was speeding up, and I reckoned I had one chance of a shot, and I took it.

Klingferm staggered, then kept on running.

The lid came down, and the capsule accelerated out of the tunnel.

I was pretty sure I'd hit him, though.

I was pretty sure I'd hit him in the head.

FORTY-THREE

Screaming Thunder, as I recall, was supposed to have been the park's headline ride. The biggest, scariest, most vertigo-inducing ride in the history of roller coasting. The big draw ride. The one that was supposed to make the trip from Timbuktu worth the air fare.

Of course, that had been ten years ago, and Screaming Thunder was probably a wussy now, compared to, say, the Molten Mambo in Disneyworld, Brasilia.

It looked pretty hot to me, though.

The track looped up and away and coiled over itself time and time again, winding all over the park before disappearing into Mystic Mountain once more, presumably emerging on the other side.

Of course, at some point there was a fault on the track. At some point, probably at the very peak of its acceleration, the capsule would leave the track behind and launch itself towards the distant mountain range.

I didn't want that death. It was a cartoon death, somehow. It was something that might happen to Wile E. Coyote. It lacked dignity. Not for me, that death. No, thank you.

The first thing I ought to do, I decided, was to look for the emergency stop button. There had to be one, somewhere. I figured it would be at the front.

I started climbing over the seats towards the nose. I should have been watching the track more closely, but there's only so much a man can do at one time. I was halfway between seats, with both hands on a safety rail, when the capsule went into a giant nosedive, and I flipped over backwards like a monkey on a stick, winded myself neatly on the headrest behind, then slid helplessly forwards to crack my nose on the headrest in front. Headrests, eh? Who needs 'em?

My body crumbled forward and started trying to suffocate me on the back of the soft sucking vinyl seat.

I tried to push myself back, because I was in a mood to breathe, but I'm a big guy and there was a lot of body fighting against me, and as the capsule accelerated into its dive, my body weight was double or even triple what it was at normal gravity.

Just when I thought I'd breathed my last, the pod hit the bottom of its dive and arced upwards. I pushed myself clear then, all right. I pushed myself clear and went scuddering backwards over the seat tops, catching each one with my unprotected testicles, until I hit a safety bar at the back of the capsule's tail with the absolute dead centre of my coccyx. As we carried on arcing up I glanced at the track. As far as I could tell, this was the first in a sequence of four or five giant loops, each one bigger than the last.

To be honest with you, I didn't feel like repeating the whole business even once again, let alone four more times, and with increasing severity to boot, so I struggled into a seating position, fastened the seat belt and clamped the safety bar around me.

I felt more than a little stupid, belting myself in for a death ride, but I didn't see what else I could do.

I tried to pretend I wasn't burning up valuable time by scoping out the back for the emergency stop, but I didn't even convince myself.

I glanced out at the track again, trying to work out where the pod was headed, so I could anticipate a slightly more stable opportunity to make my way to the front.

As we came out of the final loop, it seemed there would be a suitable window. A good length of level track.

I was ready for it when it came. My stomach was lodged somewhere near my Adam's apple and I felt like ejecting my last nineteen meals all over the pod, but I was ready.

I unclasped the seat belt, threw back the safety rail and scampered over the seat tops to the front row.

And there it was. A beautiful big, red, safety button, right in the centre of the nose, just out of reach of anyone belted in, and shielded by a glass case so it couldn't be hit accidentally. It was even helpfully marked 'emergency stop', and there was a big sign beside it explaining for people who found 'emergency stop' a difficult and challenging concept, that it was only to be operated in the event of an *emergency*, and that there was a fine of €500 for improper use.

Well, this qualified as an emergency, in my opinion.

In my opinion, preventing the capsule from launching itself at speed into the side of an Alp would constitute thoroughly proper usage of the emergency stop button. And if they were going to fine me for it, well, that was a risk I was just going to have to take.

I reached down to smash the glass with my fist, and the capsule went into a sudden, unannounced, ninety-degree vertical climb.

I crashed back into the chair.

I had a wonderful view of what was coming.

The track just kept on going up and up, like the Tower of Babel. Up and ever upwards.

At the end of the climb, at the very top there, high in the clouds, the track levelled off for a few short metres, then plummeted down at a parallel angle.

I had to assume this was the Big One. I had to assume the capsule would arc up out of that dive at maximum acceleration towards the mountains, and leave the track.

I had to hit that button before the capsule hit the top.

At least we were going slowly. At least I had that in my favour. It would take the pod a good three minutes to reach the top of the climb.

I tried reaching out from my seated position, but that was never going to happen. I scrambled around, put my feet on the chair back and pushed myself upright.

I stretched my arm above my head and came up a good ten centimetres short of the button. I found if I stood on tippy-toe I could just about touch the glass with my fingertips. I jabbed at it a couple of times, but I couldn't get enough of a backswing to break the glass.

Then I remembered the stun stick.

Now, where had I put it?

Ah, yes. I'd put it down when I picked up the gun. That's where I'd put it. I'd needed two hands on the gun to get my shot off, see?

The stun stick was now rolling around somewhere at the back of the carriage.

But I still had the gun. I had the gun tucked into my belt.

I tugged it clear, flicked on the safety and hammered the handle into the glass. But the glass didn't break. I was at an awkward angle, and it was hard to get any heft into the blow, but that glass should have broken. I was beginning to wonder at what point in the ride the designers thought a normal human might be able to actually *get* at the emergency button. What was the point of fitting an emergency button in the first place, if a normal human couldn't ever actually use it while the capsule was in motion? Were you only supposed to use the emergency button when the capsule was stationary? What would be the point of that? I mean, Superman could have hit that button. Superman could have flown up there, punched the glass with his super strength and hit that button, easy. But then Superman wouldn't have needed the emergency stop button, would he? He could have flown outside, lifted the pod off the track and lowered it gently to the ground. So why have an emergency stop button no normal mortal could ever use?

I hefted the gun again. And still the glass held.

We were almost at the top of the climb, now.

I hammered the gun as hard as I could, and the glass finally shattered. It exploded into tiny fragments that blasted into my face with all the destructive force of an antipersonnel grenade. Now, that's what I call a good safety feature. That's what I call a well thought through design: a safety feature that's actually more dangerous than the danger it's supposed to be saving you from.

I managed to shield my eyes from the worst of it, but I had about two million tiny little painful cuts on my arm and my forehead.

There was a jolt, and the capsule started levelling off.

I fell forwards off the seat and onto the capsule floor. I put out my hands instinctively to cushion the fall, pressing my palms quite heavily and at speed into a few thousand shards of sharp glass that had tumbled from my face and my arm with the express purpose of wounding me twice. I wiped the blood from my eyes, cutting myself even worse, and hit the emergency stop.

But we didn't stop.

We kept on trundling towards the Big One.

Even though it hurt to hit the emergency stop button, because it pressed splinters of glass even deeper into cuts that were already quite painful enough, thank you so very much, and even though I knew it was almost certainly futile, I hit the button again.

And we kept on trundling.

Well, of course the emergency stop button didn't work. Klingferm was hardly going to leave me with a working emergency stop button, now was he?

I had to start thinking a little more clearly than that.

The problem was, I'd run out of time.

The pod went into its dive.

I was flung face first into the nose of the capsule, along with all the glass that hadn't yet managed to embed itself in my body.

Wow, it was exhilarating.

The ground rushing towards you at breakneck speed, with your face pressed smack up against the window, with tiny slivers of glass working their way deep into your cheeks and lips, pulling maybe five or six Gs.

I can certainly recommend it for thrill power.

It only lasted a few short seconds, because, as I say, we were coming down very, very fast. Then we hit the bottom of the dive and the capsule swung over sideways, hurling me and my little glass buddies against the window, and whipped round a wicked bend.

Wahoo.

Well, at least it wasn't the Big One. At least we weren't hurtling off into deep space. At least we were still on the track.

I had to come up with another plan. It seemed to me that my best shot was to somehow work out a way to prise open the capsule cover. The ride was bound to slow again at some point, and I could at least climb out and jump onto the track. How I'd get down once I was out there was a whole nother ball game. But first things first, right?

I hadn't encountered anything that looked like an emergency release lever on my travels, and I wasn't about to waste any more time looking for one.

I took out the gun and, shielding my eyes with my left arm, drew it back and smashed it against the window. I smashed it against the window quite a few times. Hard, too. I gave that window one hell of a hammering. When I looked to inspect the damage, I couldn't even find a scratch.

The gun handle was cracked, but the window was unscathed.

Fine.

If that's the way the window wanted to play it, that was fine with me.

The pod lurched upright again, and slid inside the mountain.

I picked myself up, dropped into my shooting stance, aimed for the far window at the tail of the pod, and fired.

The window did not shatter.

The window didn't even crack.

The bullet just bounced off it.

Well, now. If I'd had the time, I would have been thinking how sensible that was, to encase the capsule in bullet-proof glass, and how handy that would be should the pod ever come under a hail of gunfire, which probably happened all the time at Disneyland; it was probably an everyday event, just before the big noontime parade, but I didn't have the time to think anything at all, as it turned out, because somebody shot me in the ear.

Well, actually, *I* shot me in the ear.

The bullet ricocheted around the capsule and took my ear lobe clean off. I didn't feel any pain, I just heard something rip and felt a hot, wet splash on my cheek.

I should have ducked, because the bullet probably hadn't finished ricocheting – my little ear lobe was hardly likely to slow it down too much – but I didn't. I put my bloody hand to my ear and it came away bloodier still.

Well, I was fresh out of options. But that didn't really matter much now, because as the pod burst out of the mountainside, I could see the big drop, the really big drop, looming up.

And this time, it really was the Big One.

Right at the bottom there, I could clearly see where the track was broken.

It curved up at the bottom of the dive and just ended.

And there, in the distance, I could see the snowcapped peak I was about to be launched towards.

Take-off, I reckoned, in two minutes, and counting.

FORTY-FOUR

I was about to be launched in a glass and metal coffin into a mountain range.

And I didn't have a plan.

I really didn't.

Of course, I didn't just sit there playing cat's cradle while the capsule went into its final, deadly climb. I hurled myself against the window. I beat at the window with my fists, but it was more out of rage and frustration than the product of a coherent plan of action.

I took out the gun again and beat the window mercilessly until the handle shattered and the gun split in two.

That helped.

That really helped a lot.

I decided to head for the pod's tail, like, I don't know, I'd be safer there, or some such nonsense. Like the pod would crash into an Alp at a zillion miles an hour and the people at the back would somehow be spared the worst of the impact.

Yeah, right, Harry. Good plan.

Only, I didn't want a front-seat view, that was for sure.

It was painful, clambering over the seats to the back, because the pod was perfectly vertical. So I clambered and crashed and tumbled my way to the tail.

Hell, it was something to do. It took my mind off worrying about other things for a couple of seconds.

I hit the back seat roughly and found, to my delight, that all the glass fragments that hadn't yet found their way into my blood supply had all gathered back there. Yummy. It was a tiny glass case that had housed the emergency stop button, but somehow they'd managed in a feat of engineering genius to cram more glass into it than there was in Harrods' entire shopfront.

I glanced to my right and found, to my utter astonishment, that there was an emergency release lever.

There was a white metal handle with 'emergency release lever' printed in red on it. Sure, there was a sign saying it was only to be used in an emergency, in case anyone mistakenly thought it was an everyday release-just-about-any-time-you-feel-like-it lever, and once again there was a hefty penalty for improper use, but I felt I could justify pulling that lever. I felt like the circumstances warranted it.

I slid over and grabbed the handle. There was even a helpful little red arrow painted over it, telling me which direction to pull the lever. It was pointing upwards.

So I pulled the lever upwards.

My slimy, bloody hands just slipped right off it.

I tried again, but the same thing happened. I just couldn't get any grip.

I took off my jacket and wrapped it around the lever.

I tugged.

I tugged hard.

But the lever didn't budge.

The lever wasn't for budging.

I lay on my back and put both my feet against the lever, and strained with all my strength.

I bent the lever. I actually managed to bend it. But I couldn't make it move one millimetre out of its original, locked position.

Just in case, just in case some idiot had painted the little red arrow in the wrong direction – and that wasn't outside the realms of possibility, now, was it? – I tried pulling the lever downwards. I tried pushing the lever inwards, and then pulling the lever outwards.

That lever wasn't going to move.

I thought about shooting the lever. Not so much because I thought that might encourage it to budge, but more to punish the lever for being such a bastard. But, of course, the gun was at the front of the capsule, on top of which it was broken.

The pod lurched again and came down level.

I had maybe thirty metres of straight track to come up with a plan and execute it successfully.

But I was fresh out of plans. I was fresh out of everything.

The pod trundled along.

I looked out at the mountain range I was about to become a more or less permanent part of. I'd appear in picture postcards of the Austrian Alps. You see that big red splat there? That's Harry Salt, my friends. That's what's left of good old Harry Salt. See? If you look real closely, you can just about make out what's left of his delectable derrière sticking out of the rock face.

The capsule trundled right to the brink.

And it stopped.

The electric whine of the engine wound down, and the lights blinked out.

The capsule had broken down right on the very brink of the Big One.

And I had the strange feeling that if I moved just one millimetre forwards, I'd send it scooting over the edge.

FORTY-FIVE

Well, three cheers for piss-poor workmanship, eh? Three hearty cheers and a rousing chorus of 'For He's a Jolly Crap Workman'.

Only, now what?

I was trapped in an airtight, rocket-proof capsule, teetering on the brink of the pinnacle of the world's highest man-made drop, and if I so much as sneezed, I might go careering over the edge into a death dive. On top of which, I was right in the middle of a deserted theme park that not even the buzzards visited any more.

Well, I'd just have to make the best of it. I'd just have to live out the rest of my life on the back seat here. How bad could that be? I had a great view. Of course, I had no supplies, so I'd have to start eating myself eventually, but if I started with the left arm, and then worked my way through both my legs, I could probably last three or four weeks without suffering too many hunger pains.

I heard a sound behind me. The whirr of an electric motor, straining very hard. I risked a look back. There was some kind of truck coming towards me along the track. A maintenance wagon.

Well, naturally there would be a maintenance wagon for just this kind of contingency. Should a capsule ever get jammed on the track, they were hardly going to airlift the passengers clear in air-sea rescue helicopters, now, were they? What would that do for the company profile?

The question was: who was driving the maintenance wagon?

Surely not Klingferm?

Surely my head shot had put paid to that son of a bitch.

Then it occurred to me that the capsule maybe hadn't broken down at all. It occurred to me that maybe Klingferm had cut the power to the capsule from below. And now he was trundling towards me with a big hole in his head and a whole lot of bad feeling to try and get those names out of me before I took the dive.

And my gun was all broken. Even if it hadn't been, it was up at the front of the carriage, where I couldn't possibly reach it.

But the stun stick. The stun stick was still lying somewhere around here. It was lying between the seats, maybe three or four rows in front of me.

Did I dare risk going forward to look for it?

Did I dare not?

The wagon was straining up the vertical climb.

I had about three minutes, I reckoned.

I didn't rush things, though. I moved as gently as I could over the seats in front.

The capsule didn't mind that. It didn't lurch at all.

I climbed over the next row; again, all slow and genteel.

Still, the capsule remained stable.

I put my leg over the next row, and the capsule tilted forward, then lurched back again.

The stun stick rolled out from under the seat I had my leg cocked over. I waited as long as I dared, then tried moving forward very, very gently. I got my right leg onto the seat. I started to bring my left over, and the capsule lurched again, so I brought it back immediately.

I waited for the capsule to right itself again.

I couldn't see the maintenance truck from here, but I could hear it whining. It was getting closer. I had to make my move, or I'd be a sitting duck, perched over the top of the seat here like a broncobuster.

I swung my left leg onto the seat and immediately threw all the body weight I could muster backwards.

The capsule tilted again, then swung back level.

I bent my knees and reached for the stun stick.

The capsule lurched again, and the stick rolled out of my grasp.

Again I transferred my weight backwards and waited.

The capsule lolled back horizontal, and the stick rolled back into range. I grabbed it. I grabbed it good.

I grabbed it just as the maintenance truck reached the capsule's tail.

I climbed back onto the seat behind, and crouched on the floor below it.

There was a jolt as the truck made contact with the capsule. I thought for one terrible second that it was going to nudge me over the edge, that that had been the entire purpose of the trip, but no. The maintenance truck was just docking with the capsule.

That was good, because its extra weight would make the capsule more stable. What it also meant, though, was that there was almost certainly a way of gaining access to the capsule from the truck.

There would be some kind of concealed door built into the pod's tail for transferring passengers from the capsule to the truck.

I heard it whirring away, and I saw a metre-wide circular opening magically appear at the back of the pod, and start sliding to one side.

I ducked down.

I thought this might be a good time to test the stun stick. I didn't want to be rushing at an angry psychopath I'd recently holed in the head brandishing just an empty hollow tube to prod him with. That was only going to make him angrier still. I thumbed the trigger. There was a tiny little 'zizz' sound and nothing else at all.

The stick was dead.

And so, in all probability, was I.

The emergency door stopped whirring, and I heard someone step through.

There was a small silence that lasted just less than a giant sea turtle's lifetime, and then there was a voice.

It wasn't the voice I was expecting.

It wasn't a voice I thought I'd ever want to hear again.

But, right now, it sounded like angel music.

The voice said: 'Pepperpot, you son of a fricking bitch. Did you really think you could get away from me, you shit stain on a harlot's tampon?'

Zuccho? How the hell had the anger management madman got here? And what did he want? Was he rescuing me or arresting me?

Well, whatever plans he had in mind for my long-term future, it had to be better than becoming an integral part of the Alpine scenery. I stood up and grinned. 'Why, Captain Zuccho. I can't tell you what a pleasure it is to see you again.'

His eyes bulged with mad delight. 'The pleasure's all mine, you filthy piece of dog puke.'

And then the bastard shot me.

FORTY-SIX

I blacked out. I had no choice in the matter. The bullet hit my body, my body registered the pain with my brain, and my brain just said, 'Lights out.'

When I came to, I was in the maintenance truck, heading back down to Mystic Mountain with Zuccho bending over my leg tightening a makeshift tourniquet around it.

'Zuccho?' I said. My mouth was very dry.

He looked up at me. 'Listen. I'm going to apologise to you for that little fracas back there.'

The little fracas, presumably, in which he almost blew my leg off. 'Yeah, right.' I nodded. 'I know. You got a little overly frisky.'

'That I did. I didn't mean to be shooting you, it just sort of boiled up out of me.'

'Zuccho, have you ever considered trying Prozac?'

'I'm *on* Prozac, Pepperpot. I eat Prozac like it's jelly beans. You should've seen me before I was medicated. I was a fricking nightmare to live with.'

'Not that I'm not grateful and all, hole in the leg notwithstanding, but what the hell are you doing here?'

'I tailed you. I tailed you from the Plaything Club in Vienna.'

'How did you know I was going to be there?'

'I may have rummaged through your belongings while you were down in the holding cells in Paris. I found the card. I was waiting in there when you showed up. While you were off chit-chatting with that disgustingly decrepit bunny boy – which whole interlude, I have to say, I found revolting – I popped a tracking bug in your overcoat lapel, just in case you gave me the slip again. I was about to pounce when I got into a little . . . well, let's call it an altercation. Next time I looked, that zap-happy greaseball was nailing you instead.'

'And you tailed me here.'

''Sright.' He tugged on the tourniquet, just a little too tight.

'What did you hear?'

'I heard plenty. Not everything, but I heard enough. That Yankee doodle dandy guy was really out there.'

'You said it.'

'Tell me, Pepperpot, just who the hell are you? I mean, really.'

'I'm nobody, Zuccho. Like the federal man said: I'm the original guy who wasn't there.'

'You're something. I don't know what you are, and I probably don't want to know.'

'Probably not,' I agreed. 'You probably don't.'

The maintenance truck docked at the platform, and Zuccho helped me out.

'What about Klingferm?' I asked him.

'The whacko Yank? He ran off. But wait, you're going to love this.'

He led me along the platform and shone a torch on the wall. There was a big smear of blood along it.

'I got him?'

'You got him, all right.' Zuccho nodded. 'You got him big time.' He panned the torch to the mesh floor. There was a wet-looking blob of something fairly gristly lying there. 'You shot out a big chunk of his brain.'

'His *brain*? I shot out a chunk of his *brain*? And he kept running?'

Zuccho nodded again. 'I've seen it before. They say we only use about two per cent of our brains. Yankee boy better pray that's true, 'cause two per cent is about all he's got left.'

'You'd better watch out, Zuccho. Those kind of credentials, he'll be after your job.'

Using Zuccho as a crutch, I hobbled out of the mountain entrance into the startling snow-bounced sunlight, and we climbed into the cable car. Wolfie's body was gone. There was a big streak of gore and mucus where Klingferm had dragged it out. Must have been a tricky job for a guy missing a hippocampus and all points west.

I saw Zuccho looking at the stain, too, doing the same arithmetic as me. 'D'you suppose he could live?' I asked him. 'You think anyone could survive a shot like that, long term?'

'Survive? It's possible, he gets himself to a world-class neurosurgeon within the hour. That's assuming he can remember the word "neurosurgeon". Either way, let's face it: he's got a hole in his head you could fly a biplane through. He's not going to be making too many Blofeld-type plans for world domination in the near future.'

Zuccho said the words and he sounded like he meant them, but I couldn't help noticing he kept his right hand within very easy reach of his shoulder holster for the rest of our walk out of the park.

There were splashes of drying blood scattered in an unpredictable pattern on the paving all along the way, suggesting Klingferm had staggered an elaborately erratic route. It must have taken an effort far beyond superhuman for him to hoist Wolfie's body all that way with the wind whistling through his half-empty skull. I kept on expecting to turn a corner and find the pair of them lying there, corpsing up the cobbles of old New York, but it didn't happen.

The splatters diminished in frequency as we approached the exit, and disappeared altogether in the car park.

There was a sticky puddle of coagulate where Klingferm must have spent a wee while struggling to get Wolfie's body into his car, which suggested, bizarrely, that he was working alone and unaided. Could he possibly have driven away on his own, the condition he was in?

Maybe. But not for long. He wouldn't get far.

Zuccho had reached the same conclusion. 'You think we

should chase after the Yankee freak with half a fricking head? I could put out an APB. He wouldn't exactly be hard to spot: just look for the guy with only one profile.'

I thought about it, then shook my head. 'He's lost, what, four pints of blood here? Plus, like you said, Zuccho: the man's not about to become world chess champion anytime soon. Even if he makes it, it'll take his entire remaining intellect and years of retraining for him to work out which orifice he's supposed to poop through.'

It was sound enough logic, but the truth was: despite everything Klingferm had done, in spite of what he'd put me through, I had no desire to see first-hand the damage my bullet had inflicted on him. Especially if he did miraculously manage to survive it on any kind of long-term basis. That was one nightmare I could live without, thank you so very kindly.

Zuccho nodded. 'Besides, you lost a lot of blood of your own back there. You should probably be thinking about getting your extremely ugly self to a bullet doctor, double-quick time.'

He helped me over to his hire car and propped me against the wing while he opened the passenger door. For the first time in quite a while, I started realising I had a future, and I was beginning to wonder what that might be. 'What's the deal here, Zuccho?' I said. 'You wouldn't be thinking of arresting me, now, would you?' I'm not saying I'd exactly grown fond of the deranged detective, but I was in no mood to be inflicting any kind of unnecessary hurt on him, neither.

'Arresting you, Pepperpot? What are you talking about? I never even saw you. I'm here on fricking vacation, is all. This is me, relaxing. What happens next, I drop you off at a bullet-hole repair man, then I'm on the next flight home. And hopefully you make a lifestyle decision to avoid Rome and its immediate environs for the next couple of millennia or so. That's the deal, if it's jake with you.'

'It's jake with me all right. Just one small detail: I do the driving.'

'You? Drive? Get serious. You're pumping blood like a bad matador with haemophilia.'

'Better that than travelling six hours along slender winding Alpine roads with Italy's anger management champion for the last eleven consecutive years at the wheel.'

Zuccho thought about it. He thought about getting mad about it, too, but he mastered the urge. 'OK'. He nodded. 'You've got yourself a point. I nearly killed myself a dozen times along the way here. Fricking cyclists.'

FORTY-SEVEN

The pilot almost landed at the right airport, but missed the runway more or less entirely, so we had to leave the plane by way of the emergency chute and I lost my shoes again.

I wasn't too bothered this time; the damned things were made of melon anyway. What did bother me was that the self-inflating dinghies failed utterly to live up to their name, and we had to swim to the terminal building.

I was fairly tuckered out by the time I'd limped through Customs and Security, dripping wet and in my stockinged feet, lodged the usual useless lost luggage claims form with a narcoleptic baggage complaints clerk who fell asleep seventeen times during our conversation, and sloshed my way to the taxi rank to find the queue stretched back almost as far as the nation state I'd originally flown in from.

But I waited patiently. I wasn't in too much of a hurry.

Now my cover was blown beyond repair, thanks to the redoubtable Captain Zuccho, I had nothing much to go back to. Technically, I should have killed Zuccho, of course – Klingferm had been right about that – but what for now? So I could go back to a job I'd learned to hate, and a life that wasn't worth living?

I didn't want any part of it anymore. I didn't know what I was going to do, except start living again. Maybe I'd start up a private detective agency and spend my time chasing faithless wives and cheating husbands, if I could bear the tawdriness of it all.

But I'd think about that tomorrow.

And tonight?

Tonight I had a date with a copper-topped dame that was so hot, you could use it to cut through bank vaults.

I would like to thank all the team at Orion for their saintly patience while we all waited for this book to show up, especially my editor, Simon Spanton. I would also like to thank my agent, Jonny Geller – without him, this book might not have happened at all. Thanks, also, to the crew at The Victoria Stakes, who helped me through the dark days of this novel with kindness, succour, and even more importantly, lots of beer.